12DAYS: STOCKING FILLERS COMPILED AND EDITED BY MATTHEW CASH

12 Days copyright Matthew Cash Burdizzo Books 2016
Cover design copyright David Phee, SM:ART design.
Edited by Matthew Cash, Burdizzo Books.
All rights reserved. No part of this book may be reproduced in any form or by any means, except by inclusion of brief quotations in a review, without permission in writing from the publisher.
Each author retains copyright of their own individual story. This book is a work of fiction. The characters and situations in this book are imaginary. No resemblance is intended between these characters and any persons, living, dead, or undead.
This book is sold subject to the condition that it shall not, by way of trade or otherwise, be lent, resold, hired out or otherwise circulated without the publisher's prior consent in any form or binding or cover other than that in which it is published and without similar condition including this condition being imposed on the subsequent purchaser
Published in Great Britain in 2016 by Matthew Cash, Burdizzo Books Walsall, UK

CONTENTS

Matty-Bob's Foreword	4
Keir's Story - Paula Thompson	6
Foreword - Graham Masterton	8
Dedication	10
Anti-Claus - Graham Masterton	12
A Grim Fairytale Of New York - Bekki Pate	44
Don't Let The Bells End - Edward Breen	58
Avenging Angel - Helen Claire Gould	76
Christmas Shoes - Delphine Quinn	96
Last Christmas I Gave You My Heart - Duncan P. Bradshaw	108
Gifts From A Star - Jonathan Butcher	118
Here We Come A-wassailing - Em Dehaney	122
I Saw Mummy Kissing Santa Claus - Betty Breen	132
I'll Be Home For Christmas - Michael Noe	146
O Christmas Tree, O Christmas Tree - Dani Brown	172
Pigs In Blankets - Craig Saunders	186
Driving Home For Christmas - James Josiah	196
The Food Chain - Andrew Bell	200
Silent Night - Fiona Dodwell	218
Sleigh Of Bones - Holly Ice	234
The Christmas Story - Matthew Cash	244
The Merry Gentleman - Christopher Law	252

Last Christmas - Theresa Derwin	276
Wood For The Fire - Michael R. Brush	282
Yet To Come - Lex H. Jones	286
You Better Not Pout - Kayleigh Marie Edwards	302
If We Make It Through December - Amanda M. Lyons	312
Slay Belles - Ash Hartwell	318
A Bauble And Twelve Drops - J.G. Clay	330
From Whence Alas Came The Flesh - Kitty Kane	340
Sweet Silver Bells - Tamara Fey Turner	356
All I Want For Christmas Is Ewe - Matthew Cash	360

Matty-Bob's Foreword

I FIRST HAD THE IDEA for an anthology based around each line of The Twelve Days of Christmas last year. I had in mind various different types of story for each of the 'gifts', from gross-out horror to, maybe, gritty police dramas. Every one of the lines inspired me to create something, and as usual these would have fallen in the weird or horror categories. But rather than do it myself and just have twelve stories all in my style, I thought it would be a better idea to offer it up to selected authors to get a variety.

And that is what I did, and 12Days was created. But then it started to pulsate and cause my muse to peel back a eyelid, yawn, stretch and suggest an expansion. I decided to make my little project bigger. The twelve different stories would countdown to something- a great big gluttonous, gore-fest of a Christmas anthology.

All proceeds from this book, any Kindle releases related to it, are going to Cystic Fibrosis UK.

Last year I found out that my little niece, Victoria, had been diagnosed with this condition. It wasn't the first time I've come into contact with cystic fibrosis, (there was a girl I knew once, a funny, vibrant soul.) Although I live several hundred miles from my brother and his family I wanted to try and give something back to the charity that helps her.

The world is a lot smaller than I expected. When I approached fellow writer, Adam Baxter, for a contribution to 12Days he mentioned a family friend who has CF and their success story. I thought it would be great for you to read about this, and hopefully a small insight to where your money is going.

Keir's Story - Paula Thompson

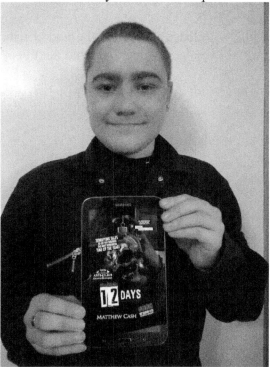

MY SON KEIR IS a teenager with CF who has worked hard to spread the work of the trust and despite being very ill never gave up. He had a transplant in early 2016 and is doing well although he realises he still has a fight ahead of him.

Keir was becoming more poorly, the CF Trust gave him an opportunity to be involved in publicity for the CF BREATHE video, and also for transplant and donation publicity.

It meant the world to us because we didn't know if Keir would get his lungs. It gave us a precious memory - thankfully Keir's is living a full life post transplant. The work with the CF Trust is very important because without their fundraising, fantastic work and commitment, Keir may not have received lungs at all.

As a family, we feel very grateful for the amazing work the CF Trust do in helping to See off CF and for all CF sufferers to look towards living a life unlimited by CF.

It's my plan to release a different themed charity anthology every year, and I've already decided what next year's is going to be.

I hope you are not disappointed.

Foreword - Graham Masterton

FEW PEOPLE REALISE that the writers and readers of horror fiction are among the most understanding and tolerant people you could ever hope to meet. They understand pain, they understand fear, and they understand helplessness.

No horror anthology could be more appropriate for the sufferers from cystic fibrosis than 12 Days. Christmas is a time when families gather and give thanks for the year that has just passed, and for cystic fibrosis sufferers every year is a year to celebrate.

But for them, there is the added poignancy that they are a danger to each other, and so there are no cystic fibrosis groups where they can gather together, even at Christmas, and share the constant struggle that they have to endure.

The stories in this collection are stories of people facing very different struggles, but each story has been contributed in the hope that it will bring relief to those who have to wake up every day, even on Christmas morning, and face the demons of their own genetic destiny.

12 DAYS: STOCKING FILLERS   MATTHEW CASH

Dedication

THANK YOU TO JAMES Jobling for being a good buddy, believing in me, and sorting out the cover. Stay away from the lightsabers Carol-Ann.

To everyone featured in this book I thank immensely, I am privileged to have you in this and you all have that something special to make me do that evil cackle whilst reading your work.

I'm giving a special thanks to the legendary Graham Masterton, who kindly offered up a story to an already growing anthology, and was kind enough to write a small piece that I've decided to include as a foreword.

Thank you also to Scott Carter of Southcart Books Walsall for helping to make Graham's foreword piece happen. You need to go check out his shop, and admire the wares and especially the amazing posters. But under no circumstances ask him if he sells cake paraphernalia.

So for my niece Victoria, the girl I once knew- Belinda Moloney I think her name was, Keir and his family and to everyone who has Cystic Fibrosis, this is for you.

Anti-Claus - Graham Masterton

IT WAS THE BITTEREST October for eleven years. An ice-storm swept down from Canada across northern Minnesota and didn't let up for nine days and nine nights, which meant that Jerry and me had no choice but to book a couple of rooms at the Sturgeon Motel in Roseau, population 12, 574, and wait until the weather cleared.

We spent most of the time in the North Star Bar, talking to the locals and listening to country songs about miserable trappers and women who wouldn't stay faithful. Outside the world was being blasted with ice, so that power lines snapped and trucks got stranded because their fuel had turned into wax and people went temporarily blind because their eyeballs froze over.

Jerry was as placid as a fireside dog and didn't seem to care if he spent the rest of his life in the North Star Bar, but I started to get cabin fever after only two days. I just wanted to get on with the job and get back to my family in St Paul. I called Jenny twice a day, and talked to the kids, too, Tracey and Mikey, but their voices sounded so tiny and far away that it only made the isolation seem sharper.

Most of the time we talked to the barmaid, Alma Lindenmuth. She had piled-up bleached-blonde hair with the roots showing and a thick, cigarette-smoke voice. She wore a studded denim shirt which showed a lot of cleavage and she smelled of Tommy Girl and something else, sex I guess, like burying your face in the sheets the morning after.

"You guys shouldn't of come up here in the fall, you should of come in August when it's real warm and beautiful and you can fish and everything."

"Well, we didn't come to enjoy ourselves. We're doing a survey for the Minnesota Forestry Department."

"Can't you enjoy yourselves just a little bit?"

"Oh, *I* can," said Jerry, with one eye closed against his dangling cigarette. "But Jack here, he's married, with two young kids. Enjoyment *verboten*."

Alma leaned forward on the bar, provocatively squashing her mole-spattered breasts together. "Do you know how to merengue?" she asked Jerry.

"Sure, I can cook anything."

We also talked to an old guy who sat at the far end of the bar knocking back Jack Daniel's one shot glass after the other, one shot every ten minutes, give or take. He wore a wild high-combed grey hairpiece which looked older than he was, and a skinny, emaciated face with white prickles of stubble where he couldn't shave into the creases. He was dressed entirely in black, and his eyes were black, too, like excavations to the center of the earth.

"So you've come up here to do what?" he wanted to know, without even looking at us.

"A survey, that's all. The Forestry Department wants to cut down a few thousand acres of jack pine and pitch pine and replace them with white pine and Austrian pine."

"Why do they want to do that for?"

"Because white pine and Austrian pine are much more commercially profitable."

"Ah, money. Might have guessed it. And so where are you doing this survey of yours, precisely?"

"Up in the Lost River Forest, mainly, between here and the border."

"Up near Saint Nicholas?"

"That's right. Saint Nicholas and Pineroad."

The old man gave a dry sniff and pushed his shot glass forward for a refill. "Know why they called it Saint Nicholas?"

"I don't have any idea."

"They called it Saint Nicholas because that's where Santa Claus originally originated from."

"Oh, really? I thought Santa Claus came from Lapland or someplace like that."

"North Pole, isn't it?" put in Jerry, and gave his distinctive little whoop.

The old man turned to me and there was something in his expression that was deeply unsettling. I had only seen that look once before in my life, when a farmer drove up to me in his Jeep when I was carrying out a survey in Lac Qui Parle, and came toward me with a pump-action shotgun like he really intended to use it. He said, hoarsely, "There's Santa Claus the story and then there's the real Santa Claus. The real Santa Claus lived on his own in a cabin on the Sad Dog River."

"Oh, sure," said Jerry. "So how come he turns up every year at Dayton's department store?"

The old man knocked back his refill and pushed over his shot glass for another. "You want to learn something or don't you?"

"Go on, then," I encouraged him, and gave Jerry a quick shake of my head to indicate that he should keep his smart remarks to himself.

The old man said, "This was just before the turn of the century when there was only five or six hundred people living in Roseau. Life was pretty much touch-and-go in those days, and in 1898 the spring wheat harvest failed and some of the farm families were pretty close to starvation. But this guy turned up one day, just like out of nowhere, and said that he could change their fortunes if they agreed to give him ten percent off the top.

"Of course they didn't believe him but he went out into the fields and he performed this kind of ritual on every farm, with bones and smoke and circles drawn in the dirt. He did this every week for the whole season, until the farmers came to accept him like they would the veterinary surgeon or the milk-collection man.

"He set up home in a shack, deep in the tangly woods by the Sad Dog oxbow, and he painted that shack as black as night, and nobody knew what tricks he got up to, when he was alone, but some people say they heard screaming and shouting and roaring coming from out of that shack like all the demons in hell. The local preacher said that he was an emissary of Satan, and that no good would come of all of his rituals, and behind his back that was what the people of Roseau started to call him, Satan, even though they carried on allowing him visit their farms with his bones and his smoke because they was superstitious as well as religious and if he really could make their wheat grow, then they wasn't going to act prejudicial toward him.

"Well, the upshot was that the winter harvest was the very best ever, and they brought in more than forty thousand bushels of hard red wheat. They rang the church bell and they gave their thanks to the Lord. But that was when Satan came around asking for his ten per cent off the top.

"Of course none of the farmers would give him nothing. They said that bones and smoke and patterns in the dirt was jiggery-pokery, that was all, and that God had provided, God and good fortune, and a long warm summer. So Satan said okay, if you won't give me my due, then I'll take it. I can't walk off with four thousand bushels of wheat, so I'll help myself to whatever takes my fancy."

Alma Lindenmuth came up and filled the old man's glass again. "This one's on me," I told her.

"John Shooks, you're not spinning that old Santa story, is he? He tells it to everybody who's too polite to shut him up."

"Hey, it's a very entertaining story," said Jerry.

"I could entertain you better than that."

"I'll bet you could. But we're not pressed for time, are we?"

"That's what the people of Roseau thought," the old man remarked. "But they had no time left at all."

"So what did he do, this Satan?" I asked him.

"On the night of December 10, 1898, he went from one farm to the next, five farms in all, and he was riding on a black sledge drawn by eight black dogs and he was carrying a sack. Several people saw him but nobody guessed what he was up to. All but one of the farms had locked their doors and windows, which was pretty much unheard of in those days, but mostly everybody in Roseau had taken Satan's threat to heart and they wanted to make sure that he didn't lay hands on any of their hard-earned property.

"But it wasn't property he was looking for, and he didn't take no notice of their locks. He climbed onto their rooftops and he broke a hole through the shingles and he climbed down into their children's bedrooms. Remember they had big families in those days, and in one house alone there was seven kids. He cut their heads off with a sickle, all of them, regardless of age, and he stowed the heads in his sack and off he went to his next destination.

"Nobody knows how he managed to break into those houses without anybody hearing him, or how he killed so many kids without waking up the others. But he murdered twenty-seven in all, and took all of their heads. Worst of all, he was never caught. Of course they sent out a sheriff's posse to hunt him down, and for a few miles they could follow his tracks in the snow. But right on the edge of the woods the tracks petered out, and the dogs lost his scent, and the sheriff had to admit that Satan had gotten clean away. The posse went to his shack and they ransacked it and then they burned it down to the ground, but that was all they could do. Satan was never seen again and neither was the children's heads."

"You won't read about that night in any of the local history books, and you can understand why. But when it's Christmas time, parents in Roseau still tell their children that they'd better be good, and that they'd better pay up what they owe, whether it's money or favors, because Satan will come through the ceiling with his sickle looking for his ten percent off the top."

"Well, that's some yarn," I admitted.

"You think it's a yarn and you don't believe it, but Santa is only Satan spelled wrong, and two Decembers back we had some professor up here from Washington, DC, because the FBI was investigating nine children who had their heads whopped off in Iowa someplace and she said that the mode-ass operandy was exactly the same as the Sad Dog Satan."

"That *is* interesting."

"Sure it's interesting, but I'll tell you what the clincher is. This professor said the same mode-ass operandy has been used for hundreds of years even further back than Saint Nicholas himself, which is why I say that the Sad Dog Satan is the real Santa and not your bearded fat guy with the reindeers and the bright red suit, although you can see why the story got changed so that kids wouldn't be scared shitless. The real Santa comes at night and he climbs through your roof and takes your kids' heads off and carries them away in his sack, and that's not mythology, that's the truth."

Jerry lifted his empty glass to show Alma Lindenmuth that he was ready for another. Alma Lindenmuth said, "Same old story, over and over."

"It's a great story. And that never occurred to me before, you know, Santa being a palindrome of Satan."

"It's an anagram," I corrected him, "not a palindrome. A palindrome is the same backward as it is forward."

Jerry winked at Alma Lindenmuth and said, "You're forward, Alma. How about doing it backward?"

On the tenth night the storm cleared and by morning the sun was shining on the ice and there was even a drip on the nose of Roseau's founder, Martin Braaten, standing in the town square with one of those pioneering looks on his face.

Jerry and I said goodbye to Alma Lindenmuth and John Shooks and we drove northward on 310 into the Lost River Forest. It was a brilliant sparkling day and we had two flasks of hot coffee and fresh-baked donuts and everything seemed pretty good with the world. Jerry seemed particularly pleased with himself and I guessed that Alma Lindenmuth had paid him a farewell visit last night at the Sturgeon Hotel.

Saint Nicholas wasn't much of a place, only five houses and a gas station, but it did have an airfield. We had rented a helicopter from Lost River Air Services so that we could take a look at the forests from the air, and make some outline recommendations to the Forestry Department about the prime sites for felling and replanting. Mostly we were looking for sheltered southern slopes where the young saplings would be protected from the north-west winds, giving us quicker growth and a quicker return on the state's investment.

The blue-and-white helicopter was waiting for us with its rotors idly turning. Jerry parked the Cherokee and we walked across the airfield with our eyes watering and our noses running and the dry snow whipping around our ankles.

The pilot was a morose old veteran with a wrinkly leather jacket and a wrinkly leather face. "You can call me Bub," he announced.

"That's great," said Jerry. "I'm Bob and this is my pal Bib."

The pilot eyed him narrowly. "You pulling my chain, son?"

"No sir Bub."

We climbed into the helicopter and buckled up and Bub took us up almost immediately, while Jerry unfolded the maps. "We want to fly west-north-west to the Roseau River and then south-south-west to Pierce's Peak."

We triangulated the Lost River Forest for over three-and-a-half hours, taking photographs and videos and shading in our maps with thick green crayons. At last I said, "That's it, Bub. I think we're just about done for today. Are you okay for tomorrow, though, just in case we need to double-check anything?"

"So long as the weather holds off."

We were heading back toward Saint Nicholas when Jerry suddenly touched me on the shoulder and pointed downward off our starboard side. "See that? The Sad Dog River oxbow. That's where Satan had his shack."

I turned to Bub and shouted, "Can you take us down lower?"

"You're paying."

The land was flat and scrubby here, and the Sad Dog River squiggled its way across the plain before dividing itself into an oxbow. In the middle of the oxbow, I could make out the ruins of an old shack, with only its stone chimney left standing. The river ran on either side of it, shining in the two o'clock sunlight like two streams of molten metal.

"Let's take a look!" I yelled.

"You want to land?"

"Sure, just for a couple of minutes."

"Bib's thinking of buying this place for a summer home," put in Jerry.

Bub angled the helicopter around the trees and landed only fifty feet away from the shack. Jerry and I climbed out and approached the shack with our coat-collars turned up. It had been burned right down to the floorboards, so it was impossible to tell if it had ever been painted black, but because most of the timbers had been reduced to charcoal they hadn't rotted. The roof had fallen in, and there was nothing left of the door but a corroded metal catch, but there was still a wheelback chair beside the fireplace, burned but intact, as if it were still waiting for its owner to return home.

"What are you actually looking for?" asked Jerry, clapping himself with his arms to keep himself warm.

"I don't know…I just wanted to see the place, that's all. I mean, if the stable where Jesus was born was still standing, you'd want to take a look at that, too, wouldn't you?"

"This place gives me the creeps."

I looked around and I had to admit that the Sad Dog River oxbow was a pretty desolate location. Bub had shut off the helicopter's engine and the quietness was overwhelming.

The Sad Dog River itself was so shallow that it barely gurgled, and there were no birds singing in the trees. All I could hear was the fluffing of the wind in my ears. A crow fluttered down and perched on the back of the wheelback chair, staring at us with its head on one side, but it didn't croak, and after a while it flapped off again.

I had the unsettling feeling that somebody had walked up behind me, and was standing very close to me, staring at me.

"Come on," said Jerry. "I'm in serious need of a drink."

We were walking back to the helicopter when Jerry stumbled. "You got it wrong again," I told him. "It's drink first, *then* fall over."

"Goddamned tripped on something."

He went back and kicked at the tufty grass. Then suddenly he hunkered down, and took out his clasp-knife, and started to dig.

"What have you got there?"

"Some kind of a handle."

He kept on digging out chunks of turf and at last he exposed a rectangular metal box with a rusted metal handle. He tugged it, and tugged it again, and at last he managed to wrench it free.

"The lost treasure of the Sad Dog River Satan," he announced.

"Okay…let's see what it is."

The box was locked, and the lock was thickly rusted, but Bub found a long screwdriver and after considerable cursing and grunting we managed to pry the lid open. Inside was a soft grey cloth, in which a collection of bones were carefully wrapped; and seven glass jars containing some kind of powder; and five blackened sleigh-bells. Jerry lifted up one of the glass jars and peered at the hand-written label. "Human Dust."

Bub said, "What is it, magic-making stuff?"

"It looks like it. Did you ever hear of the Satan of Sad Dog River?"

Bub shook his head. "Wasn't brung up in these parts. Came from Sweet Home, Oregon, me."

"He was supposed to have lived in that shack. Killed twenty-seven children by cutting their heads off."

"No shit."

Jerry closed the box and said, "Let's go find that drink. I reckon this could be worth something. You know, maybe the Roseau town museum might be interested in buying it."

"You think so? They don't even want to *talk* about what happened that night, let alone commemorate it."

We took the rusty old box back to Roseau and showed it to John Shooks.

"There," he said, picking over its contents with undisguised triumph. "Told you it wasn't mythology."

Alma Lindenmuth puckered up her nose in disgust. "It all looks horrible. What are you going to do with it?"

"Sell it, most likely," said Jerry.

"Not in Roseau you won't," said John Shooks. "That'd be like trying to sell bits of airplane wreck to the people in New York."

"I think maybe we should find out exactly what all of this is," I suggested. "I mean, if the Sad Dog River Satan used it to make the wheat crop grow, how did it work?"

Jerry said, "He was lucky with the weather, that's all. You don't seriously think that Human Dust and old bones can give you a bumper cereal crop?"

"I'd just be interested to know what kind of a ritual he was carrying out. And don't be so dismissive. I saw a TV documentary about a Modoc wonder-worker once, and *he* used bones and powders and circles in the dirt. He brought on a rainstorm in under an hour, and it went on raining for three weeks solid."

"Oh, please. What was that, the Discovery Channel?"

"Okay, but I still think we ought to look into it. Suppose it can help us to make pines grow quicker?"

"Good soil, good light, regular rainfall, that's what makes pines grow quicker." Jerry lifted out the jars of powder one by one. "Not Crushed Mirror, Rowan Ash, Medlar Flower, Houndstongue, Sulfur Salt and Dry Frog Blood."

"Well, sure, you're probably right," I told him. But I still couldn't shake off the feeling that had crept over me by that burned-out shack on the Sad Dog River, like somebody coming up close behind me and breathing on my neck.

We were called back to St Paul the following afternoon. Since there seemed to be no prospect of making any ready cash out of Satan's box, Jerry let me have it. I wrapped it up in a copy of the *Roseau Times-Region* and packed it in my suitcase along with my cable-knit sweaters.

Even in the city it was minus 5 and when I drove back out to Maplewood my neighbors were clearing a fresh fall of snow from their driveways. We lived in a small development close to Maplewood golf course, just six houses in a private loop. I parked outside and Jenny opened the door wearing jeans and a red reindeer sweater, her blonde hair shining in the winter sun. Tracey and Mikey came running out after her, and it was just like one of those family reunions you used to see on the cover of *The Saturday Evening Post*.

My neighbor Ben Kellerman raised his woolly hat to me to reveal his bald dome and called out, "Go back to your woods, Jack!" It was joke between us, based on some Robbie Robertson song about a hick trying to make it big in the city.

There was chicken pot-pie that night, and candied yams, and the house was warm and cozy. I took Tracey and Mikey upstairs at seven o'clock and sat on the end of Mikey's bed and read them a story about Santa Claus. Not the Santa Claus that John Shooks had told me about, but the jolly fat guy with the big white beard.

"When it's Christmas, I'm going to stay awake all night so that I can see Santa coming down the chimney," said Mikey. He was seven-and-a-half, with sticky-out ears, He was a whirlwind of energy during the day, but he could never keep his eyes open later than a quarter of nine.

"*I'm* going to bake him a Christmas cake," said Tracey, sedately. She was such a pretty thing, skinny and small like her mother, with big grey eyes and wrists so thin that you could close your hand around them.

When the kids were tucked up in bed, Jenny and I sat in front of the fire with a bottle of red wine and talked. I told her all about Satan from Sad Dog River, and she shuddered. "That's a *terrible* story."

"Yes, but there must be some truth in it. After all, we found Satan's box of tricks, so even if he wasn't responsible for making the crops grow, he existed, at least."

"I don't know why you brought the box back with you. It's *ghoulish*."

"It's only a musty old collection of different powders, and bones."

"What kind of bones?"

"How should I know? Dog's, probably."

"Well, I don't want it in the house."

"All right, I'll put it in the garage."

"I don't know why you don't just throw it in the trash."

"I want to find out more about it. I want to know what this Satan was actually trying to do."

"Well, I don't. I think it's horrible."

I put the box on my workbench at the back of the garage. I stood looking at it for a while before I switched off the light. It's difficult to explain, but it definitely had a *tension* about it, like the wheelback chair, as if it were waiting for its owner to come back and open it.

I locked the garage door and went up to bed. Jenny was waiting for me and she looked so fresh and she smelled so good. There's nothing to compare to a homecoming when you've been away for two weeks looking at trees and more trees.

When she fell asleep I lay awake next to her. A hazy moon was shining, and just after one o'clock in the morning it started to snow. I turned over and tried to sleep, but for some reason I couldn't, as tired as I was, as contented as I was.

Just after two o'clock I heard a rattling noise, somewhere downstairs. I sat up and listened, with my ears straining. Another rattle, and then another, and then silence. It sounded like somebody shaking dice.

I must have fallen asleep around three, but I dreamed that I could hear the rattling again, and so I climbed out of bed and made my way downstairs. The rattling was coming from the garage, no question about it. I pressed my ear against the door, listening and listening. I was just about to turn the key when the door was flung wide open, and a white-faced man was standing in the doorway, screaming at me.

I sat up in bed, sweating. The moon had passed the window and it had stopped snowing. I drank half a glass of water, and then I dragged the covers over me and tried to get back to sleep again. There was no more rattling, no more screaming, but I felt as if the house had been visited that night, although I couldn't understand by whom, or by *what*.

The next morning Jenny took the kids shopping at Marshall Field's, which gave me a chance to go into my study in my blue-striped robe and my rundown slippers and do some research on the internet. I sipped hot black coffee while my PC looked for Santa and Satan and fertility rituals and crop circles.

I was surprised to find out how recently our modern idea of "Santa Claus" was developed. Up until Clement Clark Moore published his poem *The Night Before Christmas*, Santa was almost always portrayed as a haggard old Father Time figure, with an hourglass and a scythe – deeply threatening, rather than merry – the pallbearer of the dying year. But Moore described him "chubby and plump, a right jolly old elf", and in the 1870s the illustrator Thomas Nast drew him as a white-bearded figure in a red suit with white fur trim. In the 1930s and 1940s, Haddon H. Sundblom, an advertising illustrator for Coca-Cola, painted dozens of pictures of the grandfatherly Santa as we think of him today, with his red cap and his heavy belt and boots and his round, rosy cheeks. The gaunt, doomy Father Christmas -- the *real* Father Christmas -- was forgotten.

Much more cheerful, I guess, to tell your kids that Christmas is the time for lots of toys and candies and singing, rather than remind them that they're one year nearer their graves.

After I had checked out Santa, I went searching for any rituals involving Human Dust and Crushed Mirrors. It took me over an hour, but at last I turned up details of a ceremony that dated way back to the days of Nectanebo I, the last native ruler of Ancient Egypt, in 380 BC. Apparently, good king Nectanebo had an entourage of black magicians, who were employed to do deals with the gods. They were said to have derived their powers of sorcery from a god called Set, a dark and sinister being who is historically associated with Satan. It was Set who murdered the fertility god, Osiris, in order to steal his powers, and Set who blinded Horus, the Egyptian war god, which led to the invasion of Egypt by Assyria and Persia and other foreign invaders.

In the *Les Véritables Clavicules de Satan,* a 14th-century book of demonology which was banned by Pope Innocent VI, I found an account which said, "Satan walks abroad, offering his assistance to those in the direst need. When cattle give no milk, he will work his magic to restore their flow. When crops die, he will ensure that they flourish. He will appear to be a savior and a friend to all, but woe betide any who do not pay him what he demands, for he will surely take more than they can bear to give him."

The ritual for reviving crops was recounted in detail. It involved lighting five fires, and sprinkling seven spoonfuls of powder into each of them, and inscribing a five-pointed star in the soil. The sorcerer would then tap five bones together and repeat the words of the Satanic invocation five times. *"I summon thee, O Prince of Darkness, O Spirit of the Pit – "* and so on.

I made a few notes and then I sat back and had a long think. This sounded like total mumbo-jumbo, but if it didn't work at all, why had it survived for more than twenty-three centuries? And what had *really* happened in Roseau, when the wheat harvest had failed?

While Jenny and the kids were out, I decided to try an experiment. I pulled on my boots and my thick plaid coat and I took Satan's box out into the snow-covered yard. I lit five fires out of kindling, and drew a five-pointed star with a sharp stick, and then I walked around each of the fires in turn, spooning in powder from Satan's screw top jars. To finish up, I unwrapped the bones, and held them between my fingers, and rattled them together while I read out the Satanic invocation.

"I adjure thee to grant my will and my pleasure. I adjure thee to make my crop grow tall and strong. Venite O Satan, amen."

It was then that Ben Kellerman looked over the fence with his duck-hunting cap on. "Christ, Jack, what the hell are you doing out here? Cooking a chicken with the feathers still on it?"

"Sorry, Ben. Just trying something out."

"Well next time you want to try something out, make sure the wind's blowing in the opposite direction."

I had to admit that Ben was right. As the powders crackled in the fires, they gave off swirls of thick, pungent smoke, and the smoke smelled of incinerated flesh, and hair, and scorched wool. It was what witches must have smelled like, when they were burned at the stake.

After I had finished the invocation, I packed the bones and the powders back into the box and went back inside. I watched the fires for a while, in the gathering gloom of a winter's afternoon, but eventually the wind began to rise, and scatter the yard with sparks and ashes.

I had to go to Portland, Oregon, that weekend, to attend a convention of wood pulpers. As you can imagine, wood pulpers are not the most scintillating people you'll ever meet. They're very rich, most of them, I'll grant you that. They're deeply concerned about the environment, too – mainly because of the eye-watering fines they're likely to incur if they don't replant the acres of forest that they've turned into cardboard boxes. But when I wasn't discussing the comparative profitability of different species of fir, or the joys of corrugated packaging, I retreated to my hotel room with the latest James Patterson novel and a large glass of Canadian Club.

On the third evening, when I returned to my room, the red light on the phone was blinking. It was Jenny, and she had left me a voice message. "Something so weird has happened…it's in the back yard. There's *grass* growing, right up through the snow."

And so there was. By the time I got home, mid-morning on Monday, there were hundreds of thin green spears of grass rising at least three inches clear of the snow, all over the yard, and a few weeds, too. I knelt down and brushed the palm of my hand across them.

"Grass doesn't usually grow in November, does it?" asked Jenny. "Not like this."

"No, not usually."

"There isn't any grass growing in anybody else's yard, only ours."

I stood up. "I know. I know there isn't."

So it worked. The ritual performed by the Sad Dog River Satan actually worked. He *had* revived their wheat crop. He *had* been responsible for giving them a bumper harvest, and saving them all from starvation. Of course there was no rational scientific explanation for it. None of the powders had been sprinkled on the ground in sufficient quantity to act as a growth accelerant, even if any of them had been components of any recognized fertilizer, which they weren't. You can't make your cabbages grow bigger by showering them with smashed mirrors and frogs' blood.

I went back into the house, but I couldn't resist looking out of the window from time to time, and each time I looked it seemed as if the grass was even taller, and even thicker.

If this ritual worked, then I was going to be rich. No two ways about it. I could sell my services to every farm and forestry department in the country. Think of it. They would never risk losing a crop to drought or storms or diseases. They wouldn't need nitrogen, phosphorous and potassium any more, only me. I would save them billions of dollars, and I could charge them millions.

"You're very quiet," said Jenny, over our spaghetti supper.

I smiled at her, and nodded. "I was thinking about Christmas, that's all. I think it might have come early this year."

During November the grass in our yard continued to grow thick and lush, and I had to cut it with a sickle every weekend. I took two weeks off work, and I sat down with my accountant George Nevis and mapped out a business plan, although I didn't tell George exactly what my product was. "Just take a look out of the window, George. It's the middle of winter, in St Paul, and I can make the grass grow. This is my very first test, but I believe I can do the same thing for every cash crop in the world."

George blinked at me through his thick-lensed eyeglasses. "Jack, you're talking very serious profit here. But not just profit. This has huge political implications, too. Like, *huge*. Even the President can't make the grass grow in the middle of winter."

I patted him on the back. "It's a new era, George, and it belongs to me."

Two days before Christmas Jenny came into my study and said, "There's somebody to see you. He wouldn't give his name."

I was having a headache working out a franchise scheme for Miracle Crop Services. Obviously it was going to be impossible for me to visit every potential customer in person, so I would have to employ people to tour the country and perform the ritual for me. The principal problem was that – once I had told them how it was done, and given them the wherewithal to do it -- they could go out and do it on their own and tell me to stick my franchise where you don't need Ray-Bans.

"Sorry – whoever it is, tell him I'm busy."

But Jenny came back a few moments later and said, "He says he really has to see you. It's about the grass."

"Okay, okay." I left my desk and went to the front door. A tall, thin man was standing in the porch, one side of his face illuminated scarlet by the sunshine that came through the stained-glass window; the other side yellow. He wore a black wide-brimmed hat and a long black coat and his hair was almost shoulder-length, dry and grey.

He had a large nose, but otherwise his face was strangely unmemorable, as if he had moved his head while his photograph was being taken.

"Hallo, Jack," he said, but he didn't extend his hand.

"Yes? I'm very busy, I'm afraid."

"Well, I've come to relieve you of all of that."

"Excuse me?"

"I believe that you have something that belongs to me. In fact, I only had to look over into your backyard to *know* that you have something that belongs to me."

"I don't know what you're talking about. I think you'd better get off my property before I call the cops."

"My box, Jack. My trusty old box, with all of my powders and my bones and my -- " and here he held up his finger and thumb and made a little shaking gesture " *– jingle, jingle*, sleigh-bells."

"I don't have anything that belongs to you. I don't even know who the hell you are."

The man gave the faintest of smiles. "I think you know exactly who I am, Jack. I'm the kind of man who can wait a very long time to get what he wants. I'm the kind of man who can follow you right to the ends of the earth. You have my trusty old box, Jack. I went back for it and it wasn't there and it sure took some sniffing around to find out what had happened to it."

"It was abandoned. It was lying in the dirt. Who's to say it's yours?"

"It's mine because it's mine, Jack, and I want it back."

"Well, forget it. Okay? You understand English? That box is mine now and you don't have any way of proving different."

"So what are you going to do with it, Jack? Apart from making your backyard look like Kentucky?"

"I don't have to tell you what I'm going to do with it."

The man smiled even more widely, his eyes glittering in his red-and-yellow harlequin face. "I know. You think you're going to make your fortune, don't you? You think you're going to be rich beyond the dreams of men. But it doesn't work that way, Jack. Never has. The ritual works once and only once. It gives you a helping hand when you're lower than low and you don't know what else to do. And it always carries its price, and one way or another, you have to pay that price, in full."

"Okay, you've had your say. Now I'm calling the cops."

"You still don't get it, do you? The ritual isn't an act of kindness. I'm not in the charity business, Jack, never have been. The ritual is temptation. The ritual is what you turn to when the Lord thy God appears to have abandoned you. Why do you think I come at Christmas-time? Is there anything more satisfying than having somebody deny their faith on the very eve of the Virgin Birth?"

"You're crazy. Get out of here."

"I want my trusty old box, Jack, I'm warning you, and if I don't get my trusty old box, you're going to have to pay me recompense."

I slammed the door in his face. He waited outside for a while: I could see his face through the hammered-glass porthole. Then he turned and went away, closing the screen door very carefully so that it didn't make a sound.

Tracey and Mikey came scuttling down the stairs and Mikey said, "Daddy banged the door!"

"The wind caught it," I told him, tousling his hair.

Jenny came out of the kitchen looking worried. "Who was that man? What did he want?"

"Nothing. Just a bum, looking for a handout."

"You were angry with him. I heard you."

"I told you, it's nothing."

I tried to go back into my study but Jenny caught my arm. "There's something wrong, isn't there? Ever since you came home from Roseau, you've been acting so strange."

"There's nothing wrong. In fact everything's one hundred and ninety percent right. This year we're going to have a Christmas we'll remember for the rest of our lives."

It snowed on Christmas Eve and carol-singers came around from house to house, carrying lanterns. Tracey and Mikey knelt up on the window-seat looking out at the street and their faces were lit up by the Christmas lights. Jenny squeezed my hand and said, "Mikey's so excited I think he's going to be sick."

We had supper together, and then the children put out Tracey's Christmas cake and a glass of Canadian Club for Santa. The cake was lopsided but I assured Tracey that Santa wouldn't mind, in fact Lopsided Cake was his favorite. I hugged them both before they went to bed and believe me there is no smell like the smell of your own children at Christmas. You don't need spices or mulled wine.

As we sat together that evening, Jenny said, "I wish you'd tell me what's really going on."

"Nothing at all. I'm planning to go into crop management, that's all. I've had enough years of experience, growing things."

"But that man. He wasn't just a bum, was he? He said he wanted to talk to you about the grass."

"He was being nosey, that's all."

She frowned at me. "It isn't just a freak of nature, is it, that grass?"

"What else could it be?"

"You tell me. There's some sort of connection, isn't there, between the grass growing like that and you wanting start up a new business? Why can't you tell me what it is?"

"You wouldn't understand it even if I told you. It's too technical."

She suddenly sat up straight. "You used the things in that box, didn't you, like that man in Roseau?" God, women and their intuition. "You did the same ritual, and it worked."

"Jenny – don't be ridiculous. You can't make grass grow by burning fires and sprinkling powder on it."

"There were ashes on the snow, I saw them. You did it, didn't you, and it worked?"

I took a deep breath. "All right, yes. I did it and it worked. And if it works for the grass and it works for wheat it's going to work for corn and broccoli and potatoes and rutabaga. God knows, it may even work for sheep and cows. That's why this is going to be the best Christmas ever. This is the Christmas when we start getting very, very rich."

"So what did that man want?"

"I told you. He was sticking his nose in where it wasn't wanted. He saw the grass and wondered how I'd managed to grow it."

"And you slammed the door on him?"

"Jenny -- "

"Jack, I have a very bad feeling about this. I mean it. Using the things in that box – that's like making a deal with the devil."

"It's folk magic, that's all. It's perfectly harmless."

At that moment the phone rang. Jenny answered it but it was Jerry, wanting to talk to me.

"Listen, Jack, I don't want to spoil your Christmas Eve, but something's happened."

"What is it? You sound terrible. Do you have a cold?"

"I called Alma. You remember Alma from the North Star Bar?"

"Of course I remember Alma. What about her?"

"I called her. I was going to invite her down to St Paul for New Year's."

"So? Is she coming?"

"She's dead, Jack. They found her this morning. She and John Shooks, both. It seems like a guy came into the bar two nights ago asking about a tin box. He talked to Alma and he talked to John Shooks and it seems like they wouldn't tell him nothing, and there was some kind of an argument.

"It was Alma's day off yesterday, but when she didn't show up this morning the manager went to look for her. He broke into her room and there she was in bed with her head cut off. Tortured, too, all of her fingernails and toenails pulled out. The cops went round to John Shooks' place and the same thing had happened to him. Jesus -- they haven't even found their heads yet."

I talked to Jerry a while longer, just to calm him down, but then I had to put the phone down, because I was starting to shake. That was how the man in the black hat had discovered where I lived. And if he could do that to Alma Lindenmuth and John Shooks just to find me, what was he going to do to *me*?

"If I don't get my trusty old box, you're going to have to pay me recompense."

We went to bed late that night, well after midnight. All I told Jenny about Jerry was that two of his friends had been killed in an accident. I didn't want *her* to start worrying, too. We tippy-toed into the children's room and filled the pillowcases they had left out for Santa – a Bratz doll and a hairbrush set for Tracey and a collection of Harry Potter figures for Mikey, as well as candies and oranges and nuts.

I left their doorway a couple of inches ajar and then I followed Jenny to the bedroom. "You're so *tense*," she said. "What's the matter?"

"Nothing, really."

"Jack – what I said about making a deal with the devil – I didn't really mean it."

"Well, maybe it was a pretty stupid thing for me to do."

"If you think it's really going to make us rich -- "

I took hold of her hands and kissed her on the forehead. "I don't know. Sometimes you can stop and take a look at yourself and it hits you -- my God, is this really *me*, behaving like this?"

"You're a good man, Jack."

"I used to think so. Now I'm not so sure."

We went to bed but this was another night when I couldn't sleep. The hours ticked by and the clock in the hallway chimed each hour. At three o'clock, after the chimes had died away, I was sure that I could hear a faint jingling. Just an echo, probably. I had a brief fight with my pillow and tried to get comfortable, but the covers were all twisted and I didn't want to pull them too hard in case I woke Jenny.

As I settled down, I heard the jingling again. It was slightly louder this time, and closer. I lay in the darkness, waiting and listening. Then I heard a hollow knocking sound, right outside our bedroom window, as if something had struck the fascia boards around the guttering. I eased myself out of bed and looked outside.

It was steadily snowing, and the street was glistening white. There, in our driveway, was a long black sleigh, with eight shaggy black dogs harnessed in it, panting patiently. The sleigh was empty, except for a heap of black sacks. I suddenly realized what the knocking sound had been – a long ladder, placed against the house.

"Jenny!" I shouted at her, shaking her shoulder. "Jenny, wake up! Call the police!

She sat up and stared at me blurrily.

"Call 911! Do it now!"

But right above us, I heard footsteps crossing the roof, and then the creak of shingles being torn out. The children, for God's sake. He was trying to get to the children.

I hurtled along the landing to the children's room, but as I reached the door it slammed shut, and I heard the key turn. I pummeled against the paneling with my fists, and I threw my shoulder against it, but it wouldn't budge.

"Tracey! Mikey! Wake up! Open the door! Open the door and get out of there, quick!"

I heard more creaks as nails were dragged out of the roof. I hammered on the door again and shouted, "Tracey! Mikey! Wake up! You have to get out of there!"

Now I heard Mikey crying, and Tracey calling, "What is it? What is it? The ceiling's breaking!"

"The door's locked! Turn the key and get out of there, quick as you can!"

Jenny came hurrying along the landing, her hair wild. "The police are coming right now. Five minutes, they said. What's happening?"

"Open the door Tracey goddamnit! Open the door!"

"I can't!" wailed Tracey. "The key won't turn!"

"What's happening?" Jenny screamed at me. "What's happening? Why can't you open the door?"

"It's him," I told her. "It's the man who came this afternoon. It's Satan."

"What? What have you done? Get my children out of there! Get my children out of there!"

I held onto the banister and kicked at the door with my bare feet, but it was too solid to budge. Inside, Tracey and Mikey were shrieking hysterically.

"Daddy! Somebody's coming through the ceiling! Daddy, open the door! It's a man and he's coming through the ceiling!"

Oh shit, I thought. Oh shit oh shit. Jenny was totally panicking now and beating at the door so hard that she was breaking all her nails and spattering the paintwork with blood.

God there was only one thing to do and I hoped it wasn't too late. I ran along the landing and down the stairs, three at a time. Jenny called after me, "Where are you going? Jack! We have to open the door!"

"Mommy! Mommy! I can see his legs! Open the door, mommy!"

I careered through the kitchen and opened the door that led to the garage. I seized the metal box from my workbench and went running back upstairs with it.

"What good will that do?" Jenny screamed at me. "You could have brought your ax!"

But I went up close to the door and shouted out, "Listen to me! I have it! Your box! If you let my children alone and open the door you can have it back right now!"

I heard a crack-*thump* as the man broke through the last of the plaster and dropped down onto the floor. Tracey moaned and Mikey gave that little yelp that he always gives when he's really, seriously scared.

"Can you hear me?" I asked him. "I have it right here in my hand. You can have it back, no questions asked, no charges brought, nothing. Just open the door and take the box and we'll let you leave."

There was a long, long silence. I could still hear Mikey mewling so the man couldn't have hurt them yet.

"Please," I said. "Those are our children."

Jenny stood close beside me, clenching and unclenching her bloodied fists. Then she suddenly screeched out, *"Open the door you bastard! Open the door!"*

Another silence, and then the key was turned. The door swung open by itself.

Tracey and Mikey were cowering down behind Mikey's bed. The man was standing in the middle of their bedroom, his black clothes covered in plaster-dust. He had torn a hole in the ceiling three feet across and snow was whirling into the bedroom, and melting as it touched the carpet. He was holding a large curved sickle, with a black handle and an oily blade.

I stepped forward, lifting the box in my left hand. "Here," I said. "Everything's in there, except for the powder I used on the grass."

He smiled at me, and hooked his sickle into his belt, and took the box in both hands.

"I'm sorry I took it," I told him. "I didn't realize that it was yours…that you were still alive after all those years."

Jenny skirted around behind me, took hold of Tracey and Mikey, and hurried them out of the bedroom. The man raised one eyebrow and said, "Beautiful children. You were wise."

"No…I was just what you said I was. Greedy. Wanting something for nothing. And I almost lost my family because of it."

"Oh, I shouldn't be too hard on yourself, Jack. We all make mistakes."

His mistake was to put the box down on the floor and open it up, just to make sure that everything was there. He should have trusted me. While he was bent over it, I swung myself around like a baseball pitcher and lifted the sickle that I was holding in my right hand. He sensed my movement and began to raise his eyes but it was then that I hit him across the back of the neck and the sickle chopped right through his dry grey hair and right through his vertebrae and halfway through his throat. His head dropped forward onto his chest as if it were attached by a hinge, and blood jumped out of his neck and into the box. He looked at me – he actually looked at me, upside-down, from under his arm, and that look would give me nightmares for countless Christmases to come. Then he fell sideways onto the carpet.

I didn't want to do it, but somehow I knew that I had to. I turned him over and hacked at his neck twice more, until his head was completely severed. After that I didn't have the strength to do anything else, but kneel beside him with gloves made of gradually-drying blood, while the snow fell onto my shoulders, and a police siren warbled closer and closer.

It was Christmas Day, and Santa had been.

12 DAYS: STOCKING FILLERS   MATTHEW CASH

A Grim Fairytale Of New York - Bekki Pate

"LET ME OUTTA HERE yer feckin' pricks!" Owen balled his fists up tightly against the cell door and continued to bang them on the cold metal. It didn't budge.

Nobody came to his aid, no one paid any attention to him at all.

"I didn't feckin' do nothin'!" he screamed, alcohol slurring his words, the blood from his hands staining the door as it dried. In his drunken stupor he noticed the marks his hands had made, and looked at them for the first time properly since the incident.

"Oh, oh my God!" he whimpered, trying to wipe off the blood against his trousers. "Oh dear God get me out of here please."

His mind spun with what had happened that evening, how only a few hours ago it had all seemed so wonderful; he was on top of the world. Him and Mary. *Mary.* His beautiful girl.

Tears pooled in his sore, bloodshot eyes, and for a second or two he was calm again. His head bowed, dipping against his chest, but then he smelt the strong, metallic smell of blood on his shirt, and anger once again took over.

"It's feckin' Christmas Eve! You *have* to let me see her! She's hurt!" he banged and kicked and punched the door, until loud, heavy footsteps pounded the corridor and a loud American voice as shouted through the door.

"Goddamit will you shut the hell up!"

"I need to see her!" Owen yelled back. "Please, just let me see Mary."

"Your crackwhore? She's dead! How do you like that? You killed her, you fucking son of a bitch!"

"John!" another voice shouted in a forced whisper. "What in the hell are you doing? We need to wait for his lawyer..."

"Fuck the lawyer, this paddy dick is dead anyway." John's heavy boots moved away from the door, and Owen was stunned into silence.

She can't be dead; he's lying. No, he's not; all the blood. The head injuries. The drugs. If she makes it out alive, who's to say she'd even be the same old Mary?

Why did I even come to America?

Owen slid down the side of the wall, his heart pounding, alcohol still clouding his thoughts. His hands shook as he undid his trouser belt and pulled it off clumsily. He tied it around his neck and buckled it tight, and then looked around for something to attach it at the other end. Something that might take his weight. Something that wouldn't snap.

The only thing that would be remotely feasible was the bar at the end of the bed. He strapped it around, but he had to sit on the floor, and pull forwards to get any effect. He closed his eyes and felt his temples start to throb as the blood flow was cut, and he swallowed nervously as breathing became difficult. He leaned forwards more, suddenly feeling light-headed as his eyes started to beat in time with his thrumming heart. *Come on. Just get it over with already.* How long did people usually take to suffocate? He might be here for another ten minutes with no results, in this agony, his own life in his hands. Was he actually going to finish the job, or was he being dramatic because he was drunk and emotional? He wasn't sure.

A noise brought him out of his thoughts. Someone was singing. It was an old folk song, one he recognised from childhood.

> *Thiddle I ay di diddle dum thiddle I ay di diddle dum, thiddle I ay di diddle dum rum a dum dey*
>
> *Thiddle I ay di diddle dum thiddle I ay di diddle dum, thiddle I ay di diddle dum rum a dum dey*

He opened his eyes, and through the haze of alcohol and blood rushing to his head, he almost screamed when he saw a figure. A man. Old. Crouched in front of him, his nose almost touching Owen's. Owen leapt back in fright, and the man smiled, his mouth almost devoid of teeth. His eyes were dark, empty looking, and Owen wasn't sure whether he was a threat or not.

"Where the fuck did you come from?" he rasped, his voice sore.

"Undo that stupid thing, yer fecking eejit," the man said, pointing to the belt Owen was still wearing around his neck. Owen loosened it but did not remove it, still dumbfounded.

"Did they put you in here with me?" he asked.

"Nah. I made me own way in." The old man smiled again, his dark eyes dancing.

"Why?"

"To talk."

"Talk?"

"Aye."

"About?"

"About what happened. To Mary."

Mary. Her name caused him physical pain. He looked away from the man.

"I didn't do nothin' to Mary," Owen answered, wiping his nose with a bloodied sleeve.

"Tell me about the evening," the old man said. "Where did it start?"

"Where did what start?"

"Jesus, boy. Do yer answer every question with a question? Where did yer meet? Talk me through it."

"Alright," Owen said, still afraid of this old man with the empty eyes who had suddenly appeared in his cell. "Wait a minute, you're not my lawyer, are yer?"

The man looked at Owen, blinked and then threw his head back. His laugh was like a dry bark, like a dog with a cough.

"No I ain't your fecking lawyer, boy. Now get talkin."

Owen – still confused – decided to humour the old man, and turned to the window as he thought back to that wonderful night with the Irish girl he'd met in a bar in New York.

Owen had spotted Mary's beautiful red hair, her green eyes and blue swing dress from across the other side of the bar. The place stank of yanks and cheap beer, yet suddenly it was just him and her, alone in the room, moving slowly towards one another.

She smiled, shyly, yet her lips twitched playfully.

"Can I buy yer a drink?" Owen offered.

"Well of course you can, thank you." She blushed. "I'm Mary."

"Owen."

They shook hands rather formally, and they found a quiet corner of the room. Mary lit a cigarette, and took a deep drag. She offered one from her pack to Owen, who took it.

"So where yer from?" Owen asked.

"Here and there," Mary answered. "Originally from Derry. But I've been in America a long time now. You?"

"Cork, *originally.*" Owen mimicked Mary's mysterious tone, and they both laughed. "Well, cheers, Mary." He held his pint up to her glass of wine. "Merry Christmas. I have no idea why a beautiful woman like yourself would be out here on Christmas Eve, on your own, in a bar full of yanks, but here we are."

Mary smiled. "Merry Christmas."

They sipped their drinks in silence for a few moments, and then Mary began to talk.

"So, what brings you to New York?" she asked.

Owen scoffed bitterly before taking a swig of his drink and swallowing it down. "The American Dream," he answered. "How about you?"

"Culture," she smiled. "And history."

They both chuckled into their drinks, and it wasn't long before they'd finished their glasses and ordered more.

They left the American bar with a swing in their step and headed for one of the Irish-style pubs. Inside, people were smoking, laughing, talking, music was playing on the jukebox, and the various Irish accents of New York City all rose into the air and made Owen smile.

"What'll ya have?" Mary asked him. "I'm buying."

"I'll have whatever you want to give me, darlin'," Owen replied, alcohol making him brave. She just smiled at him before turning to the bar. Two pints of Guinness soon landed next to them, and they clinked glasses before drinking the whole pints down in one.

Owen watched a middle-aged lady – still slim and pretty – place a few coins in the jukebox. She selected a few songs and then skipped back off to her husband who was waiting for her at the side of the room.

Frank Sinatra's 'Strangers in the Night' flooded Owen's senses and the pub grew a little quieter. That lady and her husband stood in their own little space by the jukebox and started to dance. Owen looked back at Mary and felt something he'd never felt before. His heart leapt as he held his hand out to her.

"Let's dance," he said, nerves causing his tongue to fall over his words.

"I'd love to," Mary replied.

The heat from her hand sent a shiver through him, and she pressed herself against his chest as they swayed to the song. A few others joined in, and the pub had suddenly turned into a ballroom.

Owen pulled her close.

"We don't even know each other," he said to her breathlessly.

She looked at him, her eyes glistening.

"I think we do," she replied.

They kissed long, and slow, and gently. Owen had never kissed or had been kissed in such a way before; it was as though they'd done it a thousand times, and a thousand times later it was still as magical as the first. They broke apart as 'New York, New York' came on and joined in the laughing and dancing and singing.

Owen pulled Mary through the crowd and out into the night, where they kissed again and ran like children, through the streets.

Mary pulled Owen into another bar and ordered a bottle of wine. Excitement from being with this beautiful young girl stirred Owen's need to keep himself on a high. He kissed Mary on the cheek before visiting the bathroom. He then checked each cubicle before entering the end one and locking the door. He'd been saving the last few dregs of coke for Christmas day, but since he was already in a good mood, there was no sense in saving it. He lined up what he needed on the back of his hand and snorted it down. The effect was sudden, like electricity coursing up his spine, and he closed his eyes. *Mary. Beautiful Mary. My Mary.* Could it be that he'd fallen in love with her already? He wondered if she would be up for trying some of the coke he still had left, or whether she would turn away in disgust.

He washed his hands and face and then returned to the bar, where Mary was sat at a table with the bottle of wine still unopened, and two empty glasses.

She was talking and laughing with a tall, dark-skinned man, and Owen suddenly felt sick with jealousy. *Who is this prick?*

He stalked over to the table, and had to dig his fingernails into the palms of his hands whilst he watched the dark-skinned man kiss Mary lightly on the cheek. She smiled up at the man before he then turned away into the crowd.

Mary's smile remained as she looked around, her eyes landing on Owen's.

"Hey, I was getting worried about you," she said, smiling.

"I saw you found someone to keep you company," Owen said, his eyes stinging with rage.

"Oh, Matt? He's just a friend. Come. Sit down."

Owen sat at the table and Mary leaned in to kiss him. She smelt of something light and fresh, like lemons and washing powder. Owen breathed her in, forgetting his anger.

The bottle of wine was gone within the hour, and another was put in its place. Owen's head began to spin, and after he'd gone to the bathroom to take more coke, he opened the cubicle door to find Mary standing there, her arms folded over her breasts.

"You're not going to share that, then?" she asked, and smiled.

Owen paused only for a second, before then standing to the side and letting Mary inside the cubicle.

"My apologies," Owen replied. As he locked the cubicle back up and prepared a row for Mary, blood began to rush to his groin at the thought of him and Mary in such a tight, private space. He watched, his balls aching, as she took his hand and licked up the line of coke, her tongue lingering on his skin a little longer than necessary. Unable to control himself any more, he pulled her close, and kissed her forcefully, fumbling at different buttons and zips on her dress, pulling down her tights and underwear. She kissed him back, pulling him free from his jeans and massaging him.

He was almost light-headed from the need to be inside her, and when he finally pushed his way in, she grasped him around the neck and bit into his shoulder as they fucked.

It was over within seconds, but it was the best fuck Owen had ever experienced in his life. He watched her pale, green eyes as she looked back at him, her lips red and full.

"I love you, Mary," Owen said, breathless. Owen's heart dropped at the sight of her face hardening, and she threw her head back and laughed.

"Oh, Owen, don't be silly now," she replied. "Come on, let's enjoy the evening."

"But..."

"Come on." Mary suddenly stood before him, fully dressed. Somehow she'd managed to put her clothes back on as he'd been stumbling over his emotions.

He pulled his jeans back up and followed Mary out of the men's toilets, suddenly feeling sick from all the alcohol. As they exited, a small middle-aged man ventured over and slapped him on the back.

"A night with Mary, eh buddy?" he laughed. "You look after her now."

Owen gazed at the man, confused, when he noticed that another man had begun talking to Mary, handing her a drink, which she gladly took.

Owen's blood boiled in his veins. *What the fuck is going on?*

Before he knew what he'd done, the man who'd bought Mary's drink was already on the floor, cradling his nose.

"You fucking crazy son of a bitch!" he yelled from the floor. "What was that for?"

"You stay away from my girl!" Owen yelled.

The man stared at Owen for a second before suddenly bursting into a loud, pointed chuckle.

"*Your* girl, buddy? *Your* girl? Only as long as she keeps the meter running, kid."

"Fuck you," Owen said through gritted teeth, before turning to Mary, who for some reason, looked annoyed. With hands on hips, her eyes burned hard into him.

"Come outside," she said to him. "Now."
Owen followed her out, wondering what the hell had just happened. As soon as they'd turned a corner and were behind the back of the pub, she whirled around.

"What the *fuck* do you think you're doing?" she spat.

"You're having every man and his dog buying you drinks now, eh?" Owen seethed. "Well I won't have it."

"Who are you to tell me what I can and cannot do, boy? You're just another punter, wanting to get his leg over before going home to wifey."

"Mary, what's happening? I thought we were having a good time."

"Well for the right amount of money, you can have anything you like," she said. "But *don't* interfere with my other customers."

"What?" Owen's head spun from the coke and alcohol, confusion making him dizzy.

"Your mate in the bar where I met you. He gave me this." She lifted out an envelope from her handbag. "There's $2000 here. He said it's mine if I show you a good time."

"What are you talking about? What *mate?*"

"Don't act stupid, Owen."

"But Mary, I love you..."

Mary laughed at him once again.

"You love me? You've known me five minutes."

"*Don't* laugh at me."

"Or what?"

Owen's confusion had given way to seething hatred as he realised what she was. He was only her latest customer out of God knows how many that week. He'd been fooled, someone had set him up, and he'd fallen for it.

He grabbed Mary by the throat with one hand and punched her with the other. She tried to scream but he punched her again, wild with rage. If she couldn't be his, she couldn't be anyone's. He'd make sure of that. She reached up to try and claw at him but he punched her again, blood spurting out from her bust lip and spraying his hands and shirt.

He barely realised when dozens of arms pulled him away, and he was dragged into the back of a police car, leaving Mary a bloody mess on the ground.

"So, when you say you didn't do nothin', you mean that you actually beat this poor woman to death?" the old man said.

"She...she mislead me. She made me think..."

"She did exactly what she was told. Exactly what I asked of her."

Owen's heart began to race.

"*You* gave her that money?" Owen replied. "Why? Why would you do such a thing?"

"Mary was a whore, wasn't she? Just like in the bible. It wasn't right, she needed to be punished."

"What?"

"And you were a womanising drug addict. I thought, two birds with one stone and all that."

"You're a feckin' lunatic,"Owen seethed. "Get away from me."

"I'm many things, but I can assure you I'm very sane."

"So what are you doing here then, with me?"

The old man leaned into Owen, just like he had when Owen first opened his eyes.

"I'm here to make sure you never leave this room."

Owen scoffed at this puny little old man in front of him, but fear grew in his heart. Whoever this man was, he was dangerous, and Owen should be careful. He thought about calling to to the cops outside in the halls.

"Wouldn't do any good," the old man said, smiling. Owen's blood ran cold.

Suddenly he was aware of the sunlight filtering into the room. In the distance he heard singing, like a choir or a band, and he smiled.

"It's Christmas," Owen whispered. "Christmas day. I think I recognise that song."

"The day of the birth of our Lord, Jesus Christ," the old man said. "What a beautiful day."

"So it is."

"You won't see another one," the old man replied.

Owen turned just in time for the belt to tighten once again around his neck, and it was held in place by an unseen force.

The old man smiled gleefully as Owen struggled to breathe. As he gasped for air, the old man started to sing once more.

All the grasses grow,

and the waters flow,

in a free and easy way.

But give me enough of the the rare old stuff,

that's made near Galway Bay.

As the life finally left Owen and he slumped forwards, the old man disappeared from the room, the song lingering for a few moments afterwards, before also dying away.

Don't Let The Bells End - Edward Breen

THE SURGEON HAD SAID he would never walk again. Six months later he took his first painful step, six months after that he was sent home from the private rehabilitation hospital the bus company had paid for, six months after that and his knee still hurt like a bastard. It annoyed Fionn that it was taking so long but at least he was walking. His friends tried to cheer him up, but they didn't know what it was like. To have to hobble like an old man.

The steep hill from the bus stop to the house was killing him. Well, mansion would be more appropriate. The place was massive, almost as big as his grandfather's old colonial palace. It had a tall tower above the front door, a bell tower it looked like. Then the rest of the building sprawled to the left and right across three stories. He approached the enormous wooden doors and pulled the chain for the bell, noticing the car in the yard as he did so. Even though it was a modest hatchback he got a pang of jealousy. I was nothing compared to his beloved 911 that was totalled in the crash, but it was still a car.

By the time he looked back at the door it had been opened. Stepping inside, he saw, who must have been, the owner of the hatchback in the yard. Her dress matched the blue of the car and she had an indigo hat and coat on over it. She had obviously just arrived.

'Oh, hello. Are you one of the organisers?' she said.

'No. You must be here for the murder mystery even as well,' Fionn said. He extended a hand to shake.

'Violet Blue, pleased to meet you,' she said, treating him to a watery handshake.

'Fionn McWitty. Any idea what we're supposed to do?'

'Not really, I haven't got any farther than here so far, nobody came to the ringing of the doorbell. I just walked in when the door opened.'

As she said it the door closed behind them of its own volition causing Fionn to jump. Then he noticed a little white square of paper on the inner door. It said:

Come in and welcome dearest guest,
Go through a pour yourself some of the best.
The night is young and you've come far
Though it may not have been in a car.

Underneath it had a little map showing the location of the drawing room. Fionn got a little chill at the words on the note. How did they know he didn't come in a car? Then he realised that it was a cheap trick. The chances were that one person at least wouldn't come by car and that it would be more unsettling due to its prophetic undertones. His shrink would be proud of his amateur psychology.

The hallway beyond the inner door was cathedral like in its magnificence with matching mosaic on the floor and ceiling. It was all decorated with Victorian style decorations. There was even an enormous tree with candles on it.

'I think it's in here,' Mrs Blue said, snapping Fionn's attention away from the splendour of their surroundings.

'Do you know, I think you're right,' he said, spotting the words "Drawing Room" inscribed above the Romanesque doorway.

Fionn followed her in and she was already pouring him a drink.

'Brandy, I think' she said as she handed it to him.

'Thanks,' Fionn said.

There was an envelope on a little table in the centre of the room. On the front was written simply: 'Guests' and on the back Fionn could see it was sealed with wax and written across the seams was the instruction not to open it until everyone arrived.

By now Mrs Blue—for that was how he thought of her; she being so much older than he was—was looking over his shoulder sipping a glasses of her own Brandy.

'Ooh,' she said. 'Isn't that exciting?'

'I th

'I'm sorry,' Mrs Blue said. 'It's just…I've been so excited about this night and it's not something I could usually afford. But the ticket was bought for me and I want to do it right. Please, forgive me. I just want this night to be perfect.'

Fionn's shock melted into sympathy. This woman had obviously had a rough time of it and he had no wish to make it any worse for her. He simply smiled and apologised for being silly.

They heard the front door open and both turned as if surprised by the sound, then look at each other and smiled. Of course, the other guests.

In the hallway was a tall woman with broad shoulders and narrow hips. In fact the only reason Fionn thought she was a woman was the cut of her green trouser suit, and her shockingly pretty face.

'Am I in the right place?' the woman asked. She had a minute quiver in her voice that Fionn couldn't quite place as nervousness.

'I hope so,' Fionn said. 'Otherwise we're all in the wrong place. You here for the Murder Mystery?'

'Indeed I am,' the woman in green said. 'Jade Verdant, nice to meet you.'

Fionn and Violet introduced themselves and showed her into the drawing room where he poured her a brandy—there didn't seem to be any other option. It was brandy or nothing.

'How lucky were we to get tickets to this?' Mrs Verdant said.

'I mean,' Mrs Verdant went on without waiting for an answer, 'the Christmas eve night is the most sought after of the whole year, although it seems difficult to get any tickets these days.'

Pretty lucky all right, Fionn thought, even better if you don't have to pay for it. He had heard that this night went for about a grand a head. Fantastic then that he had won it in a competition that he didn't even remember entering. He didn't want to let them know that, though, so he just nodded and took a swig of his increasingly tasty brandy.

An awkward silence fell on them after Mrs Verdant's emetic question and answer session with herself. They were saved by the sound of companionable voices emerging from the hallway and making their way to the drawing room.

The relativity of the people that enter the room amused Fionn even though he knows it shouldn't. The woman was graceful, tall and strong; ageless in her red dress and shoes. The man short and squat and dressed in a mustard coloured tweed suit that looked uncomfortable and itchy. His ruddy countenance is the only thing that gives them something in common, matching her dress perfectly. He supposes it's this oddness that causes the inhabitants of the drawing room to gawk and the newcomers' conversation to stop dead.

Then he recognises the woman in the dress. Is that why everyone has gone silent. Does she recognise the people in the room for the same reason that he knows her? Is she their therapist too?

Stilted introductions reveal that, of course, her name is Rose Rudd and his turns out to be Blaine Bowie; both doctors. Fionn introduced himself as everyone else had: as if he didn't know her. He no more needed these strangers to know he was getting therapy than he needed for them to know he was getting a free ride.

'We're all here, shall we open our next clue?' Mrs Blue said.

She tore it open and read the clue out to the rest of the guests, who by now had all been poured a drink and were finished with their introductions. The antique clock on the mantel piece said it was ten to nine. They had been there twenty minutes.

> *By now you've all had a chance to meet*
> *Please cross the hall so you may eat*
> *The night goes on tout suite tout suite*
> *Soon one of you will be dead meat*

'That was a bit darker than I expected,' Fionn said into the silence.

A gentle giggle from the collected melted the mood and they made their way back into the ornate hallway. Right in front of them was another deep set door with the words "Dining Room" above it, carved into the stone.

On the long table, which dominated the centre of the room, was an opulent spread of cold meat, fish, cheese and salads. Fionn supposed it was done that way to increase the mystery, not to mention to reduce costs. They wouldn't have to hire actors to serve during the evening. The meal would have been brought out just before hand and the staff gotten out of the way before the guests got there.

'Look,' Dr Rudd said. 'They've given us place markers. How quaint.' She sounded bored and contemptuous.

'Oh that's lovely. I guess we should sit and eat,' Mrs Blue said, seemingly oblivious of Dr Rudd's tone.

Eating, however was the last thing on Fionn's mind. Ever since he had left the drawing room he had been getting twinges in his stomach. They were getting lower and lower down and by now he felt like if didn't get to a toilet soon he would end up with a brown stain on the seat of his white suit trousers.

'I'm sorry, did anyone notice a toilet on the way in?' he said to the assembly.

Mostly blank looks greeted him until Dr Rudd spoke up.

'Yes, by the door. Let me take you. I hate having brandy without a cigarette. Anyone else need a smoke?'

Everyone politely refused and Fionn went with Dr Rudd out of the dining room. They didn't speak on the way, he thought that she was about to say something but he got to the door with the little picture of the chamber pot on the outside, thanked her and went in, in silence.

He was just glad to have got there in time. His bowels felt like they were about to explode. It was a close run thing but he made it to the bowl just in time. For the first time he noticed and was glad of the thick stone walls in the building. Otherwise he was sure to have been overheard back in the dining room. He thought he would have to warn anyone against going in there after him. The feeling of emptiness and incompleteness accompanied the cessation of the onslaught, but he thought it would be safe enough to go back in there. He paused to sort himself out and took a step to the sink to wash his hands.

There was a faint click and the feeling that the floor had moved ever so slightly. The lights went off. On the mirror in front of him was some green glowing writing that he hadn't noticed before,

Too fast to stop

is what it said. His mind went to the accident. The accident that destroyed his leg, that left him banned from driving, that killed that poor man. Then with a suddenness that mimicked that accident the mirror exploded toward him. The last thing he saw was his own face and that message, but his brain never had time to register it.

The scream reached Jade Verdant's ears just as she had read the letter that was in front of her at the table. It was swiftly followed by the deafening sound of the bells in the tower outside the dining room ringing out nine times.

She heard the message on the note repeated in her head, but nothing else as those bells swept the rest of the sound from the world.

Beware each time the bell doth toll
One of you must lose their soul

Of course, she thought, one of the guests was a plant. The one who is going to die. The shock of the scream and the bells had shaken her, though.

'Oh dear you look so pale,' Mrs Blue said to her. 'Here have some water.'

She passed her a tumbler of water.

'Nonsense,' Dr Bowie said. 'It's brandy you want. Great for the nerves.'

'You're right, of course,' Mrs Verdant said. She took a sip of the brandy that she had left just beside her knife.

They decided together to go to investigate the scream.

Out in the hallway Mrs Rudd was yanking at the handle of the toilet door. She was hysterical when the others reached her and Dr Bowie took her aside and sat her on a step. He and Mrs Blue then went to work on the door and eventually managed to break the lock.

What they found inside made Mrs Verdant feel faint all over again. If this was part of the act then they had really gone to town. There was a headless body slumped on the floor wearing Mr McWitty's suit. The white was stained with a lot of blood and some lumps of grey and white. Above this was what must have been the mirror above the sink. It had been projected out from its position with a long piston with enough force to smash the glass and pulverise his head against the stone wall. At least that was the effect it gave. Amazing, thought Jade Verdant, amazing what they can do with makeup these days.

'What do you think Dr Bowie?' Dr Rudd said. She was on her feet again and looking into the little room with the rest of them. 'This is your field of expertise isn't it?'

'Well, yes, but this is an act, surely. But if it's clues we're looking for then I suppose I might be best placed to look for them.'

Dr Bowie confirmed everything Jade had thought. Everything except for one thing. The body was a human body, and he was pretty certain it was Fionn McWitty's.

'What do you mean?' Mrs Blue asked.

'I mean this isn't a part of some pretend mystery. This man is dead.' Dr Bowie pronounced.

Jade almost fainted again. This was so unlike her. She was usually a sturdy person. She used to be a bus driver before she had to give it up. Even then it wasn't her fault that she had to stop. She had nothing to do with the accident.

'I don't feel well,' she said. She took another swig of her drink and the warming alcohol helped, a little.

'We have to phone the police,' Mrs Blue said.

'Has anyone got a phone?' Dr Bowie asked.

'No,' Dr Rudd said. 'We were asked to leave them behind, remember. It was a condition of our being here. To help with the atmosphere they said.'

Dr Rudd seemed to be recovering from her shock well enough, Jade thought. Then Dr Bowie spoke and she thought no more about it.

'Surely there will be a phone in one of these rooms.'

But there was none. There wasn't even a plug in the wall where a phone had been. After a quick search of downstairs Mrs Blue had the idea of trying the front door. Jade felt silly not having thought of it, but her mind was cloudy. She couldn't really think of anything much now that the adrenaline was wearing off.

She was glad to see the rest of them looked a little sheepish too, even the ever-radiant Dr Rudd. She hoped, that the woman wouldn't say anything to her, Jade didn't want everyone knowing that she was seeing a psychiatrist.

The door was locked, they all had a go at opening it, but it was shut fast. This injected a new sort of panic into proceedings. Jade saw this panic, but didn't feel it. Couldn't feel it. She didn't know why, but she was getting more and more numb as the minutes squeezed past. She wasn't even thinking about poor Fionn anymore. Poor Fionn and his smashed up face. That last thought made her guffaw with such suddenness that the rest stopped what they were doing with the door to gape at her.

'I'm sorry,' she said. 'I need to get a chair.'

'I think we should all retreat to the dining room and regroup anyway,' Mrs Blue said.

'I'm going to try some of the windows,' Dr Bowie said.

'I'll come with you,' said Dr Rudd.

Mrs Blue said nothing. Jade thought she could feel tension, so she piped up, 'I'll be okay. I'll just sit down and maybe try to eat something. It's just all the excitement.'

Mrs Blue nodded and went with the others while Jade went back to the dining room.

'Be careful now, won't you dear?' Mrs Rudd said. 'You don't look at all well. We don't want anything to happen to you.'

Jade didn't notice the tone. In fact, she barely heard what the woman had said. It felt as though her head was stuffed with expanding foam and if she wasn't careful it was going to come squirting out of her ears.

She sat down heavily and the clock said it was quarter to ten. When she opened her eyes again it was almost at the hour. She watched as the minute hand clunked into position, exactly vertical. Something in her told her she should run and hide, something in her told her she was going to die; it wasn't a knowing, just a feeling. At the first peal of those deafening bells she tried to get off her chair, she couldn't. The second was accompanied by the room suddenly plunging into darkness. From where she was a message appeared, glowing green in the sudden black light.

You should have been more careful

In the second that passed between the third peal and the fourth she remembered everything about that day. She had been driving her green double decker along the number three route. The white sports car overtaking her at speed made her remember she had to do something. Her foot mashed the accelerator and the bus lurched forward. The oncoming car, a hatchback, hit the bus and white car almost simultaneously. The speed of the white car, though, caused the hatchback to spin into her bus. The driver never had a chance.

The fourth bell arrived with the most excruciating pain that assaulted every inch of her body at the same time. After the accident, there had been a stench of burning flesh; she wondered if she could actually smell it again or if it was just her memory.

Dr. Bowie was stalling, suggesting checking the windows to get some time to think. He knew what the cause of death was: extreme blunt force trauma to the head causing complete implosion of the skull. The mirror had been reinforced with concrete and a servo attached to a powerful motor had driven it forward. He had found the pressure plate under the sink which he stood on, presumably triggering the block. This happened as the bells struck, because otherwise they would have heard the block smashing into the wall, via Fionn's head.

The coincidence made him suspicious. How was it that he was in the toilet at the exact time the bells rang? There was no obvious way Dr Rudd could have triggered it and everyone else was in the dining room with him.

In his puzzlement, he almost didn't even register the bells, or rather he didn't think what significance they had. Until he remembered.

'Where's Mrs Verdant?' he asked.

The moon like eyes of the two women was identical. The three of them hurried to the dining room where they knew she had gone and that is where they found her.

The blackened corpse was sitting in the chair Mrs Verdant had occupied when they were at dinner. A thin wreath of smoke surrounded it. Dr Bowie had seen a body like this before. Twice, actually. The first time had been a young man that had been contemplating suicide. He sneaked onto the railway and was obviously just getting ready for the train when he lay down on a live rail. The driver saw him from quite a way away and stopped. His face had been contorted in agony, a grotesque mask of pain. The other had been an electrician, of all people, who had seemingly forgotten to turn off the trip switch before rewiring a light fitting. The fire his smouldering corpse started burned the whole house down with a single mother and two young kids inside. He would always remember that one because it turned out that she had turned the trip switch back on.

Mrs Verdant was worse, by far, than the other two. Her face was also contorted into a death scream; he could see from across the room that her jaw had dislocated. Her eyes had popped and they were now just lifeless sacks on her cheeks, the liquid inside having been boiled off. There were clamps on her hands so she would have been unable to get away. And her skin had been dried and then burned to a black veneer tight against her skeleton.

The smell of burned meat was gag inducing, or would have been had he not had the iron stomach of a seasoned coroner. He was just thinking that the others were doing well not to have thrown up yet when he saw Mrs Blue approaching the corpse, hand extended, in a kind of trance.

'Stop,' Dr Bowie shouted.

Mrs Blue seemed to snap to her senses and quickly retrieved her hand.

'Don't touch her, she might still be live. Wait…do you hear that buzzing? It most certainly means that she is.'

The lights went off again and on the wall behind the corpse was written, in foot high glowing green lettering:

> *Two dead now, time's running out.*
> *To get through this you must be stout*
> *She sat on a wire which was live*
> *Find the killer if you want to survive*

The lights flickered back on and the buzzing stopped. Dr Bowie saw that Mrs Blue had fainted. She was on the floor near the chair. He ran to help her.

'Dr Rudd, could you bring me some water please, and maybe a pillow from the Drawing…'

Turning around he saw that she was gone. Mrs Blue's pulse was fine and she was breathing. He started moving her onto her side when she woke up.

'How are you feeling?' Dr Bowie asked, handing her a glass of water from the table.

Mrs Blue drank deeply and then took the brandy he offered after. 'I'm fine, thank you. It's just all too much. The people dead and the cruel, silly rhymes. I mean I knew this was a Murder Mystery evening. But I never dreamed it would be real.'

Dr Bowie place a conciliatory hand on her shoulder and said nothing. There was nothing to say and he wasn't about to tell her that Dr Rudd was missing. There was no point in compounding her misery, at least until she recovered.

They sat there staring at the section of wall that had the writing on it. There was nothing there now, but he could still see the words, burned into his consciousness. Especially the last line: *find the* right *killer*... It didn't fit with the rhythm of the other lines. He couldn't help but think it might be about him.

In thirty years as a police coroner he had been respected because of his accuracy and impartiality. Then there was the case. The crash where it seemed someone was at fault, more than that; where someone had planned the whole thing. The driver of the blue hatchback had died from a combination of the initial impact with the white car and the shear force involved with the secondary collision with the bus. At first it seemed like bad luck, then came the court case: the two drivers, who were kept apart to keep their testimonies separate, suffered from amnesia, not even remembering anything about that day until after the crash. He was interviewed on the witness stand and was adamant that it was accidental. There was no way, from the evidence he had gleaned, it could have been fabricated. He never told anyone, though, that he couldn't remember doing the examinations. He had his notes, written up in his hand, but he had no memory of the events. Not that he could tell anyone this. It would mean his career.

'Where's Dr Rudd?' Mrs Blue finally asked him.

'Gone,' he said.

'Gone where?'

'I don't know where, but I think I know why.'

He explained why he thought Dr Rudd was the killer. She was intelligent and driven. He could tell from the silence at the beginning of the evening that they all knew her. Him professionally, and he assumed the others as her patients. He knew that she would have the money and tenacity to carry out an elaborate scheme like this, and that she had done studies on serial killers that had divided the scientific community in the past: going, for some, too deeply into the diseased minds she was studying.

After listening attentively to what he had to say, Mrs Blue asked the most pertinent question: 'what do we do now?'

'I think we should find her before she finds us,' Dr Bowie said.

'Together?' Mrs Blue said.

'I think that would be best. We don't know what she has planned next or if this figures into her plans. We must be on our guard,' Dr Bowie said. 'So how do you know her?'

Mrs Blue looked shocked at his words, but then calmly told him her story: 'Tonight was supposed to be my first break. I've been a widow for just over a year and my husband left me with very little apart from massive debt. I sold my house, my car and most of my clothes. He was a powerful man and we were pretty well off, or so I thought. But it was all a lie, a charade.

'After a few months of turmoil, I began to see Dr Rudd for therapy. She was kind and wonderful and she helped me a lot. But the more I saw of her, the closer we got. She became obsessed and we had a…relationship of sorts. Not the kind a doctor is supposed to have with her patient, put it that way. In the end, I had to put an end to it. That was six months ago, and I didn't see her again, until tonight.'

They searched the ground floor in silence. Finding most of the doors locked. It was approaching eleven by the time they got to the last unlocked room, the kitchen pantry. It was dark and cold, clearly a later extension to the original house. The naked light bulb caused the appliances to throw rough and unusual shadows across the room. The clock on the cooker flashed 10:58.

'What was that?' Mrs Blue said, suddenly.

'What?'

'That sound, I could have sworn I heard something fall. It came from the drawing room.'

'I didn't hear it, are you sure?' said Dr Bowie, knowing full well his hearing wasn't what it used to be.

'I'm sure. Will you come?'

He followed her through to the hallway and through the heavy door of the drawing room. She turned to him and looked white pointing at an item on the floor. An antique letter opener, he could have sworn it wasn't there earlier.

'The curtain, it just moved,' she whispered.

The urgency in her voice and the flush in her cheeks prodded him to go and check. He laid a restraining hand on her shoulder and walked past her to the heavy curtains. Behind him there was the whirring of the bells' mechanism.

He picked up a heavy crystal decanter on his way past it as the first bell tolled. Why would Dr Rudd, a celebrated therapist, do this? He had heard of people breaking and committing crimes of passion before, but he didn't think her capable. At the fifth bell, he is sure he sees the curtain twitch himself. And the gruesomeness of the killings, the cruelty, why? The bells were nearing their end now. She was going to fail this time. He would not be caught unawares. He had her. The eleventh and final bell rang out and he turned in triumph at Mrs Blue before he yanked the curtain across.

The pain from the antique letter opener going through his left eye is astounding. But not as bad as when it comes out. He sees the offending organ on the tip of the blade, sliding down its length, but it still feels like it's in his head. In his shock, he drops the decanter and it shatters. The sight in his right eye is enough for him to see Mrs Blue stabbing at his belly with frenzied passion. Plunging the blunt brass instrument through his skin again and again. The pain is gone now, all that remains is the slowing thud of his pulse in his empty eye socket and the tearing and popping of metal tearing through clothes and skin. His right eye's last sight is the world upending and a crazed Mrs Blue jabbing the knife into his face again and again.

Dr Rudd knew he was dead. That bitch had fooled him and no mistake. What she didn't know was how Violet Blue found out about what had happened.

Hiding in a dark corner of the pantry, squeezed behind a chest freezer, Dr Rudd ruminated on this. They had been close enough to smell her until Violet had obviously realised that it was nearly time for someone else to die. She had hedged her bets and Dr Bowie fell for her trick. Of course, she reasoned, it could be Violet that was dead and not Dr Bowie. Not likely, though. Dr Rudd knew that woman's mind. It was not the kind of mind to be thwarted by a fossil like Blaine Bowie.

She should have known from the moment she got there that something was wrong. Although, by the time she was inside it was probably too late. Of course, none of the other patients would admit to having a shrink. Especially one like her who specialises in sexual problems and murderers.

She heard the click clack of high heels coming across the tiled floor of the hallway. Dr Bowie was dead.

'Rose dear, come out, I saw you hiding behind the chest freezer. We need to talk.'

Violet was standing at the door of the pantry. Her party dress was covered in large dark patches and even from the other side of the room Rose could smell the viscera.

'Where is Dr Bowie, Violet?' Rose asked. At least she could try to throw her off balance a bit.

'He met with an accident,' Violet said. 'Won't you join me?' She left the pantry, letter opener in hand.

They sat down in their assigned seats. More out of convention than conscious decision, Rose thought. The charred corpse of Mrs Verdant was still smoking slightly, the smell was terrible and familiar, too much like bacon burned on the pan.

'Why, Violet?' Rose said.

'You know very well why?' Violet shouted, slamming the hilt of the letter opener on the table.

'I don't know what you mean.'

Violet looked at her from underneath sardonic eyelids, her lips pursed.

'Well, let's start with Mr McWitty, that little toe rag. Really, he was the one that made me suspect you. I saw him coming out of your office one day, after my second last session. He was still banged up after the "accident". It made me suspicious but I couldn't believe you could be involved so when I saw your picture in the paper, you know the one where you are standing behind Jade Verdant, I was shocked. You were the one that got her off on mental instability. So, I did some digging and lo and behold you were medically trained alongside Dr Blaine Bowie. Was he one of your patients too?'

'Violet, you know I can't—'

'Oh cut the bullshit Rose. After all we've been through. I almost left my husband for you, you know?'

'I know,' Rose said.

'What, do you deny it? Are you saying you didn't kill my husband?'

'We were having a session when he died, you know that Violet.'

'The perfect alibi. Go on, I want you to say it, I want you to deny you weren't responsible.'

'It doesn't matter what I deny. What matters is how you feel about it, Violet. You are fixated on an outcome and determined to see it through.'

'I don't hear a denial and time's running out.'

'You're saying if I do so before twelve you won't kill me?'

'I didn't say that. But at least you will die with a clear conscience.'

'If I were you, Violet, I would be more worried about your own conscience. You've killed three people and you plan on killing four. How are you going to live with that? How will you go on?'

'I loved you Rose,' Violet screamed. 'Don't you know that? I loved you and you betrayed me. Why did you do it? Why did you kill my husband?'

'I've already told you I didn't kill—'

Violet lunged at her across the table and Rose grabbed her forearms. She held them, pinned to the table and glared into Violet's crazy eyes.

'He's dead because I knew you wouldn't leave him. If anyone is to blame it's you, Violet. I had been worrying actually,' Rose went on. 'Worrying they would remember something. I spent months hypnotising them so it wasn't likely, but it never hurts to make sure. Ideally McWitty and Verdant would have died in the crash. But you've tidied that up for me. Only you remain alive to tell. I will have to do something about that.'

She dragged Violet across the table and turned her, pushing her knee into her spine and wrapping an arm around her neck. With the other arm, she pushed Violet's head forward, suffocating her. Rose let go just as Violet lost consciousness and hoisted her up onto the chair she herself had been assigned. She picked up her own name plate and switched Violet's to where the woman was sitting now.

There was a buzzing coming again from the chair Mrs Verdant was sitting on. Rose knew exactly what she was going to do. First she retraced her steps from when she entered the house looking for any stray hairs and wiping anything she touched. Then she went through Violet's pockets and found the key to the front door and unlocked it, on the way making sure some candles were still lit on the Christmas tree in the foyer.

Finally, she went to the kitchen and opened all the knobs on the gas cooker. When she was happy they were flowing freely she went back to the adjoining dining room and prised the door open. The final touch was to take a fire poker and put it in Violet's hand. Then let it fall onto Mrs Verdant's lap. The smoke began to rise immediately from the sleeping Violet.

She had gotten a lift there that night from Dr Bowie, straight from work. So, her car was safely parked at home. Nobody else knew she was there. As far as her neighbours knew, she was home alone all evening; where she usually was Christmas Eve. All that remained was for her to walk the ten or so miles back to her house. A small price to pay for such a neatly wrapped gift.

12 DAYS: STOCKING FILLERS   MATTHEW CASH

Avenging Angel - Helen Claire Gould

LORCAN WILLIAMS SURVEYED THE road ahead of him. The glare of streetlamps flew out of the darkness at him every few seconds as the car sped northwards. *I could have done without that hold-up at the junction.* The accident had blocked the motorway interchange slip road. Lorcan's sister had been expecting them hours ago. "Can you just text Aunty Alice, Meryth? Let her know we're nearly there?"

No answer.

Lorcan's eyes flitted to the rear-view mirror. Both girls were as fast asleep in their seat-belts as his wife Sylvie was on the seat beside him. He heard a voice at the back of his mind say, *Well, you have to let her know, so go on, why don't you? There aren't any police about at this time of night...*

He disentangled the mobile from the drinks holder between him and Sylvie and touched the text icon, scrolled down to A and selected the number, not far down the list.

The contact opened. He touched 'Message' and glanced ahead of him. The road was empty. *The turning must be soon.* He spotted the sign for it.

The text box appeared. He got into the correct lane and crossed the white line into the slip road. It led onto a dark A-road. He had to look up. Trees obscured some of the streetlamps, and it wasn't particularly well-lit. *Probably the council cuts,* he reasoned. He knew he should pull over but there was nowhere to stop on this highway.

He typed, "B there in..." He still had thirty miles to drive. "30 mins."

And then his car crossed the white dotted centre line. He never saw the approaching vehicle. On the tiny screen he typed, "Lorcan xx."

The impact smashed the windscreen as the bonnet concertinaed.

He looked up. Glass cubes sprayed him. A piece impacted with his cheek.

My girls! Sylvie!

The car spun across the road and flipped onto its roof. Lorcan felt his ribs crack as the steering wheel thudded against his chest. He could barely breathe for the pain.

The airbags didn't deploy. The Focus skidded along upturned for a few feet before the next impact. He shut his eyes by instinct. When the car had stopped moving, he opened one eye, then the other. A leafless branch poked through the smashed windscreen.

What have I done? What have I done?

He thought he heard mocking laughter, but it could have been his imagination.

Meryth was aware of her surroundings for a while before she truly woke. Every part of her felt fuzzy and distant. Someone called her name several times; that sounded blurred as well.

When she opened her eyes, she had the distinct impression of someone saying, "We have optical nerve input," but that faded into the general miasma around her. A fog totally enclosed her: one of those fogs that carry smells amidst the moisture. She smelt blood first, then a vile mixture of shit and sulphur, the saltiness of ejaculate, the acridity of urine. "Where am I?" she mumbled.

"Youuu…are in Hell." The voice was at once a caress and a hiss. It combined the promise of threats with a stench of filth, worse than mere halitosis. "And I am…you may address me as Lucifer."

She went to sit up.

"You won't be able to move yet," the demon said.

"We have neural cord input," came the faint voice she'd heard first of all.

"Why am I in Hell?"

"You're dead – a ghost. You have a mission." The mist parted to show her the face of a man, with beautiful features that were marred by his eyes. That surprised her; they were a baleful yellow, the pupils mere vertical slits; and his tongue, she saw as he spoke, was that of a serpent. The curled horns of a goat adorned his temples, and as he loomed over her she realised that those horns were the source of the vile smell.

"Fully functional in this realm," the background voice said.

"And on Earth?"

"As you'd expect for a ghost."

"What is my mission?"

"Your father caused your death. You will return to Earth and take your revenge on him. Otherwise you – and your family – end up here."

The mist stirred around her and parted. Meryth saw children carved into little pieces that were still animated, chimeras with features of many different animals committing male and female rape, murders that were re-enacted over and over. And the ground was on fire. She shut her eyes and the mist eddied back into place.

"Go now," said the demon, and the mist whipped around her and carried her away from the place he'd described as Hell.

Verity was in Debenhams when she saw her sister the first time. She looked up from browsing the makeup counter in her lunch hour, and saw her not ten feet away. There was the blonde bob, hanging straight to her shoulders; the petite form with the promise of curves to come; and the blue t-shirt she'd been wearing when the accident happened – scored and stained with blood.

But she gave no sign that she was aware of her appearance.

"Meryth!" Verity called.

The shop assistant stared at her. Verity flushed as she noticed the gaze and looked back at the salesgirl.

"Are you OK?" the assistant asked.

Verity nodded and swung round to confront her sister.

She was gone.

The second time she saw her, she was on her way to work.

Meryth was driving.

That's not right. She's not only not old enough to drive, but she's never had any lessons, passed a test, or owned a car. It must just be someone who looks like her. Verity followed the car with her eyes to identify the make and registration.

That was easy. She was very familiar with the dark red Ford Focus. It was their old car. Despite the accident it looked brand new.

Verity shook her head. The image passed. She stared down the road.

The Focus had completely disappeared, and Meryth with it.

Unsettled by the incident, Verity quickened her pace. The bus stop was straight ahead. She sighed with relief. At work she'd confided in her friend Jayne, who had suggested her imagination had showed her Meryth because she wanted to see her again. That seemed a reasonable supposition.

At home after work that night, Verity heard singing and a thumping on the stairs. *Meryth always sounded like a herd of elephants when she ran upstairs,* she thought. She left her cup of tea untouched on the kitchen worktop and went to see if her imagination was playing tricks on her again.

There was no sign of Meryth, either on the stairs or in her bedroom.

The melody hung around in her mind for hours, repeating over and over, but the words eluded her. The song was familiar. Yet she failed to identify it.

The next night, Verity was first home again. Her father had been arrested and awaited his court case in prison. Her mother didn't drive, so the loss of the family car made her journey to and from work longer.

When the song came again, she was waiting on the stairs. This time she heard the words.

It was a song her sister Meryth had loved as a child: *Do You Hear What I Hear?* Made famous by Bing Crosby, who had a massive Christmas hit with it in the early 'sixties, it had been written by Noël Regney and Gloria Shane Baker. Sylvie had bought a pile of old records at a jumble sale, and the nine-year-old Meryth had insisted on playing them on the old gramophone they'd relegated to the garage when Lorcan had bought his CD player. She'd learned all of them off by heart. That had started her interest in music, and before long she'd joined a choir. Even as a small child Meryth had always sung around the house. *Dad always said she had a voice like an angel.*

But how could it be Meryth? She's dead. My mind's definitely playing tricks on me.

Just to be sure, she tiptoed up the stairs and crept along the landing to her sister's bedroom. She opened the door slowly, so it made no sound, then pushed it open and peered into the room.

There was the bed, left unmade since the accident. The window was closed. A stack of books lay on the carpet, beside the bed. Verity picked one of them up and leafed through it. It was one of Meryth's school books: *A History of Medicine through the Ages*. She put it down again and stood up. *Meryth isn't here.* She couldn't help a feeling of disappointment. Perhaps she'd imagined the singing. She turned to go.

A thought struck her. She sang the first line of the song.

The second line came back, in a sweet soprano that was powerful for the owner's age, just fourteen.

Five years younger than me. Five years and a universe younger, and she ends up dead. "Meryth?"

"Verity?" Meryth shimmered into view beside her for a second or two, then disappeared again.

Verity wasn't afraid. *Incredible! Here I am, talking to a ghost.* "I can't quite believe this. I should be scared of you."

"But I'm your sister," the ghost said, "so why *would* you be afraid of me? That's the advantage. Besides, it's not you I've come for."

"What do you mean, advantage?"

"I'm talking to you now *because* you won't be afraid of me."

"So…who *have* you come for?" Verity felt the blood drain from her face, and for the first time a frisson of fear tickled her spine.

"Lorcan Williams. My dad." Meryth shimmered back into being again. "My murderer."

Then she was gone.

Verity had looked up the words of the song on the internet the previous evening, but she had to sing the whole song the next day before Meryth appeared beside her.

"What did you mean yesterday, when you said Dad was your murderer?"

"He was texting. If he hadn't been, he'd have seen the other car and avoided it. *He* killed me."

"It was an accident."

"One that shouldn't have happened." Meryth paused for a moment. "I hope you haven't told them you've seen me."

Verity made a throwaway gesture. "Why would they believe me? They don't believe in ghosts."

Meryth faded for a moment, but Verity could still hear her ask, "And what about you?"

Verity shook her head. "Not until yesterday."

"But you do now?"

"I don't have a lot of choice, do I? You're here – and it's good to talk to you again."

Meryth's image twinkled back into view. She shuddered. "I don't like that disappearing thing. I guess I haven't got full control of myself yet. It feels like I'm dissolving. Horrible!"

"So…can you walk through walls and things?"

"I guess. I haven't tried."

"Why not?"

"No call for it."

"Are you really here to take revenge on Dad?"

"Yes."

"Why? He's miserable enough already. He's not even here – he's in prison. The Police arrested him. His case is pending your inquest."

"Huh! He knows it was his fault," Meryth jeered.

"Don't be so quick to condemn him. He told us what happened. He knew Aunty Alice would be worried, but when he asked you to text her, you were asleep. We all were. So *he* texted her himself. Don't forget, we were hours late after that other accident."

"See, that's just like you, Verity. So forgiving, and so willing to see the good in everyone."

"*You* used to be like that as well. What's changed?"

"Dad," Meryth insisted. Her expression changed to a scowl.

"I don't believe you, Meryth. This isn't you! You and Dad were so close when you were alive."

"He hadn't killed me then!" Meryth pointed out.

"No. Listen to me. Who told you to go after Dad?"

Meryth looked directly into Verity's eyes and scowled. Then she looked away. After a moment she mumbled, "I'm not allowed to say."

"Why ever not?"

"Don't think I don't want to. I just can't, that's all."

"Why not?"

Meryth's ghostly face was screwed up in concentration. "He threatened me."

"Abusers are no different in the afterlife, then…"

"What?"

"Never mind. He hasn't been here since just after the accident. His case comes up next week."

Meryth looked startled. "How long have I been gone?"

"A few weeks."

"I didn't realise – time must pass differently when you're dead. But I still have to do this." She tried to draw a sigh, and failed. "I don't want to go to Hell."

"Listen, Meryth. Dad isn't a bad man. He doesn't deserve your vengeance. He's a man inspired. He's training in prison to campaign against texting while driving – because of losing you. You just can't do this to him! He could do so much good for others because of his own experience. Let him find his own peace – by helping young people avoid what he's gone through. And I'll pray for you, too."

Meryth digested the information for a moment before answering. "That puts a different complexion on things.

You're right. I've been completely wrong-headed." She thought for another moment, then added, "That Lucifer! I can't believe I let him manipulate me."

"Dearly beloved…"

Verity looked around the chapel while the priest recited the service. There were many of Meryth's school friends in the congregation, and even the headmaster, along with the family and friends. She ceased to listen to the priest, except as a background voice. It was easier to deal with the loss of her sister if she blanked everything out, but gratifying that so many people apparently cared about Meryth.

Verity's gaze locked onto the coffin at one side of the room, standing on a daïs, the red curtain behind it – the gateway to the retort. She looked at her mother, weeping openly as she stood beside her. "It's just you and me now, Verity," Sylvie had said as they got into the waiting car. "We have to stick together and look after each other."

At that memory Verity returned her attention to the words of the priest. It was hard to concentrate on anything for long with so many triggers for her grief. She wanted to remain composed.

The priest flicked holy water all around the coffin and said, "Meryth Karen Williams, I command you to go straight to Heaven now, instead of hanging around here on Earth."

Verity felt an intense sadness. *Will Meryth make it to Heaven, or be stuck in Hell for eternity?* She had a fleeting impression of loss, and then the world dissolved into a kaleidoscope of smeared colour as she tumbled to the floor.

"Lucifer" crouched over his scrying-bowl as he watched the scene in the crematorium. *That damned priest! Without his intervention, she'd be mine for sure.* He'd have to do something about this interference. He couldn't let it pass.

He rose and shook himself, and leathery black-red wings burst from his upper back. Then he stepped off the edge of his world and flew to Earth.

In the crematorium garden, he folded his wings so that they disappeared beneath his skin again. Then he sauntered bare-chested through the leafless rose gardens towards his goal. Twilight cloaked the world again. The weight of sin in the chapel was heavy. He smiled to himself. He could draw on the power of sins confessed, and his size and energy would grow at a constant rate. It gave him the advantage.

The last cremation had finished. He sensed the priest in the vestry behind the chapel, preparing to go home. *You can leave by a different door, my friend,* "Lucifer" thought. He opened the door and spied the priest picking up his belongings.

"Before you leave, Father," he said, "a moment of your time." *This is* my *time of day.* And he stepped into the light.

"What is the -?"

Before he had time to ask, "...meaning of this?" the demon lifted his arm and backhanded him across the vestry with a blow to the face.

"You!" The priest struggled upright, reached inside his dog collar, and yanked out a crucifix on a gold chain. He held it up as a weapon against the demon. "Begone, Beelzebub!"

"Lucifer" snatched the crucifix and flung it on the floor. "Lucifer, actually, Father."

The priest backed away, scrabbling for the door-handle. He twisted it open and left in one panicked movement. He pulled the door shut behind him and skidded across the floor to the altar.

"Lucifer" stood with his arms folded across his naked chest. Then he followed the priest. He moved faster and faster until he crashed through the door. He shrugged off the broken shards of wood and masonry.

The priest grabbed the golden cross from the altar and held it up to ward off the demon.

But "Lucifer" seized it. He flung it on the floor and stamped on it. Every footprint daubed dirt on the golden crucifix.

The priest backed away from "Lucifer" and fetched up below a wall-mounted statue of Jesus on the Cross. It was his last possible defence. He was desperate. He clutched the vertical near the base and heaved the whole statue off the wall.

But "Lucifer" had anticipated this move. He was ready. He followed the priest. He wrenched the heavy statue from his hands and dashed it on the floor. It shattered into a thousand fragments. Then he butted the priest with his horns. Finally, he locked his hands around the priest's throat, extended his serpent's tongue into the choking human's open mouth, and slurped up his soul directly as he went limp.

Aaah! The soul of a good man is sweeter than that of an evil one.

The demon's laughter echoed throughout the chapel.

Meryth wandered around the garden where she'd grown up.

There was the apple tree with its swing, and the seat around the trunk, made by her father when she was about five. The patio and barbecue made her think of the hundreds of sausages and beef-burgers she and her family had consumed over the years. As she did so, she imagined she could smell the frying meat. It smelled delicious; but the aroma evaporated with the steam that came off the food. In one corner of the garden was the shed, where she and Verity had played while her dad worked on one of his projects. Meryth turned away, aware of her sympathy for him. The wind fluttered a piece of paper over the wall and blew it around on the lawn. It had writing on it. Meryth bent to pick it up.

She read:

INVITATION FOR INTERVIEW:

Meryth Williams,

with your maker, at a time of your choosing,

regarding entry to Heaven or Hell.

How strange! she thought. *I never realised that you got an actual interview invitation from St Peter!* Her whole experience as a ghost was becoming ever more surreal.

I've made my decision, Meryth told herself firmly. *I've chosen, and I know I've made the right choice, whatever happens to me.* Yet she couldn't help a shiver of apprehension.

As she thought of the coming interview, she found herself at the foot of an enormous escalator that led up into a starry realm. She looked around her at her environs, but there were no roads or streets, and she had no idea how she'd got there. There was just the escalator. Without making a conscious decision she stepped onto it.

It took her up, and up, and up. She tried to see the top of the escalator, but it was hidden in mist, as if it passed through clouds on the way to the heavens. Yet the stars were clear to see above the cloud layer. *Strange.* It seemed like hours since she'd stepped onto the lowermost step, the same one that still carried her.

In one quadrant of the sky a comet flared as it neared its star. She remembered the line about a comet in her favourite Christmas song.

She turned her attention back to the escalator itself. It seemed like a regular escalator, the kind that would take you from one floor to another in a bus station or a department store. In fact, apart from its length, it looked exactly like the one in Debenhams in her own home town. *Even odder...*

As she passed through the mist layer she felt droplets of chill water on her flesh, and realised she was passing through clouds. Her body was wracked by involuntary shivers. Then she was through the layer, and the stars smiled down on her from above. At least, they seemed to smile, and brought a little heat to dispel the cold of the clouds.

Meryth looked upwards again, and saw two beings at the top of the escalator, standing very close together. *Are these my judges?*

The escalator brought her ever nearer to them. The beings had the appearance of men. One she recognised by the curled horns extending from his head; the other wore a crown of thorns. Her vision jumped like a faulty TV input as the escalator approached them. Then she saw, as she glided to the top level, the horned man's beautiful features, and the other man's white robes and ordinary features, his cheeks and chin covered by a beard. *If Mr Horny's Lucifer, he must be Jesus,* Meryth reasoned.

As she stepped off the escalator, Lucifer accosted her. His beautiful features fused into a mask which bore no emotion at all. "Well?" he asked. "Did you complete your mission?"

This is odd, Meryth reflected, *because if these two really are who I think they are, surely they'd know whether I completed it or not? But perhaps they aren't really Lucifer and Jesus, or maybe they don't have the powers we attribute to them.* For a moment her attention was diverted as she stole a look at the man she assumed was Jesus; he smiled at her with absolute serenity.

"Answer me!" Lucifer's face changed, this time to an expression of anger. His brows crenelated. His mouth tightened and turned down at the edges.

Meryth stared up at him as he loomed over her. She felt the chill of the mist enfold her once more, and shivered, but gazed back at him with all the defiance she could muster. Another glance across at Jesus, smiling behind Lucifer, gave her the courage to reply. "No. I did not."

Fury claimed Lucifer's face. "THEN…FEEL…MY…WRATH," he thundered. The serpent's tongue darted out between each word and flicked against his lips. "You failed. You're a FAILURE." The pitch of his voice rose to a scream. Flecks of saliva landed on Meryth's arm, where they stung like acid. *"YOU FAILED IN YOUR MISSION!"*

"I did not fail. I chose not to do it." Even to herself, Meryth's voice sounded insignificant against the storm of Lucifer's howl.

"You FAILED. I do NOT tolerate failures," Lucifer screeched, and his voice was like the swell of an ocean before a storm. "I…WILL…NOT…TOLERATE…YOURS!"

He's hysterical. He's losing control. "I had a choice and I chose," she insisted.

"And you made the right choice, Meryth," Jesus said, from close beside her. To Lucifer he said, "You'll have other chances." Then he handed her something.

It was rolled up like a scroll and tied with a red ribbon. She took it.

"Go on," Jesus said. He was still smiling. "Open it."

Meryth obeyed. It bore calligraphy: red Gothic lettering. "What is it, my…my Lord?"

"It's your certificate. You passed the test. Go on, read it." Meryth read:

Meryth Karen Williams

Graduation

31st October, 2016

You have earned your place here.

Signed , Jesus.

Welcome to Heaven!

In her hands, as she read, the certificate changed. The words on the parchment rearranged themselves until she saw her own face. A feeling of intense euphoria pervaded every part of her body, driving away the anguish she'd felt during her sojourn on Earth: the agony of her fatal injury, the torture of being killed by her own father, and most of all, her emotional response to her family's torment at losing her.

"Walk with me into Heaven," Jesus said. "It's this way." And he gestured for her to follow him.

The parchment certificate dissolved as Meryth stepped past Lucifer, who was hunched over as if in pain or shamed. She hurried after Jesus, trying to catch up with Him. He murmured as if talking to himself.

Within a few steps she couldn't feel her feet. But she carried on, and now she was running to keep up with him. The numbness spread, and soon it struck her that it wasn't numbness at all. She'd felt this sensation on Earth, as a ghost. She was dissolving as she walked. The euphoria lessened as each body part vanished. "Lord Jesus, I don't understand."

"What is it that you don't understand, Meryth?"

"It feels like I'm dissolving, my Lord." The numb feeling was rising all the time.

"Why, yes," he said. "Yes, you are."

"Why is that, Lord?" The numbness was up to her chest now.

"You will become one with the universe. You will return to the stardust you were born from."

She felt her face start to dissolve from the chin up. The last thing she heard was, "You're home, child."

In the sky above, the comet's tail ceased to flare as it fell into its star.

Lorcan got out of the people carrier and went to the boot to collect his equipment, the tag around his ankle rubbing slightly. He picked up the laptop, and shut the boot. Kerry, his mentor and partner in the new campaign, pressed the central locking. The rear lights flashed once and they walked towards the school.

They entered the building and crossed Reception to the open window. "Lorcan Williams and Kerry Barnet, from Accident Avert," Kerry said to the receptionist. "We're here to —"

"Good afternoon, Mrs Barnet, Mr Williams," the receptionist said. "I'll call the head of sixth form for you."

Lorcan looked around the room as they waited. It was bright and spacious, and as the occasional stream of teenagers passed in the adjoining corridors he caught a glimpse of their uniforms – dark crimson blazers and ties, with white shirts and black trousers or skirts and black shoes. He was uncomfortably aware of why he was here, surrounded by young people only slightly older than Meryth.

Later, as the session drew to a close, he realised with excitement that the sixth-formers had engaged with what he'd shared with them, especially when one of the girls came up to him and said, "Thank you for that. I've just passed my driving test, and hadn't realised that I have control over a lethal weapon when I'm behind the wheel. It's brought it home to me."

"I – that's great to hear," he said.

"You did well, Lorcan," Kerry said.

Something about what the girl had said made him think hard. *Control,* he thought. *Do I really have control over my life? I obviously had a choice when I texted Alice, and I failed the test. But I could never have done this job without going through the experience of losing Meryth.*

That prompted another thought. *I'm either fulfilling my destiny or choosing a path which will help me as well as the people I'm helping.*

Kerry's voice cut across his thoughts. "You did say the inquest starts today, didn't you?"

He nodded, and at once, all the hope which had begun to grow in him disappeared.

"Lucifer" toiled up the steps of the building known as "Heaven". It was a tall tower, most beautifully wrought to resemble a jewelled quilt on the outside, with the inside having the appearance of flesh, fresh and living in most places, but here and there rotting – with the stench to go with it. "Lucifer" pictured the conversation he'd have when he found "Jesus": "You have a strange taste in room fragrance, for one of your ilk." He'd never been inside "Heaven" before – "Jesus" had never invited him – and the omission made him wonder if perhaps the Omnipotent had his own flaws.

"Jesus" reclined on a couch before a gigantic monitor, split many times to show multiple tiny thumbnails. He zoomed in and out, changing the number of views several times, before finally settling on one sector of the monitor. As he zoomed in, "Lucifer" saw that he'd selected Meryth's family. Her screen was blank, but the others still held images.

"I've just seen this." "Jesus" pointed to Lorcan's thumbnail, then expanded it.

Lorcan dangled from the upper bars in his cell. His legs twitched once, then again. Then he stilled.

"It was the inquest today," "Jesus" said, with a throwaway gesture.

"Why do you play these games with them? With all of us?" "Lucifer" demanded.

"Think of me as a social scientist." "Jesus" smiled his serenest smile. "I like to discover how they'll react."

"And all of *us*?"

"That too." "Jesus" made a gesture towards Meryth's family. "They're all dead, actually – the accident was more effective than I'd intended – but I thought it would be fun to keep the simulation going and see what happens."

"She was going to be mine. We agreed."

"True, but since she didn't carry out your orders…"

"Lucifer" sighed and spread his hands. "You just can't get the staff these days!"

"…she is innocent, and is entitled to go to Heaven, whilst Lorcan must go straight to your domain. You've laid so many souls to waste recently! I saw you take the priest. If you hurry you can get Lorcan while his body's still warm."

"True." "Lucifer" smirked. *With Lorcan out of the way, there'll be many more opportunities for me.*

"Jesus" locked gaze with "Lucifer". "And with Verity and Sylvie, I decided it was time you got a taste of your own medicine."

"Time I failed, do you mean?"

"If you like. But mostly, Verity passed the test, and Sylvie's done nothing wrong."

"And who are you to dictate who's to get the next soul?"

"Honestly?" "Jesus" smiled again, and this time the smile was full of secrets.

"Honestly."

"I'm *your* maker as much as *we* are *their* makers."

Christmas Shoes - Delphine Quinn

JOE WALKED INTO THE Wal Mart, its vast displays of Christmas decorations screaming at him, assaulting his every sense. Everywhere he looked, lights, mistletoe, trees, tinsel. The smell of pumpkin spice and holiday scented candles permeated the air, so strong it almost instantly gave him a headache. The blaring carols came streaming from the loud speakers overhead, meant to bring joy and festivity, but only making Joe angry. He fucking hated the holidays. He tried to like them. He tried to seem enthusiastic when his wife and kids started decorating after Thanksgiving, when they began rolling out dough and cutting them into shapes of trees and snowmen. But deep down, even his religious upbringing couldn't make him resent the holiday any less.

This would be a quick trip. A string of lights used to adorn the white Christmas tree the Morton family had used for years, had gone out. Amy, Joe's wife, had reacted like the world was ending. He had to get another string *now*. Not tomorrow, not next week. *Now*. She didn't care that it was nearing 9 PM, and Joe had been at work all day, barely home a few hours before she sent him back out, into the snow covered and slush covered streets of their town in Colorado. It couldn't wait. Christmas would be ruined. So it fell to Joe. Tired, overworked, under appreciated Joe, to rush in and save Christmas. Bitter wasn't even the word for how he felt.

Forgoing a cart, he wandered the holiday aisles until he found a box containing a string of mutlicolored lights that matched the ones at home that broke. Snatching them up, Joe walked toward the self checkout aisle, not stopping to look at any of the displays or even to acknowledge other customers. He was on a mission. He wanted the damned lights and he wanted to go home, crack a beer, and relax watching mindless TV. It was Friday, so Joe had the entire weekend to look forward to. Football on both Saturday and Sunday. But he was sure he'd get suckered into more Christmas crap by his wife and kids. Not to mention church on Sunday.

Joe wasn't sure why he bothered anymore with church. He guessed it was because Amy still believed, and wanted their son and daughter raised with Christian values. Joe himself thought you could display good values without praying to a God that either wasn't there, or clearly didn't care much for what was taking place down here on the planet He created. This time of year when Joe was young, used to be filled with fluff pieces on the news about Santa showing up at the local mall with his elves, and tracking Santa's journey on Christmas Eve. Now even the holidays couldn't bring joy to the news, or the world.

Bombings, beheadings, coups and shootings dominated the headlines. The world was going to Hell, and no one seemed to have any idea how to fix it, least of all Joe. It was as if everyone had lost their minds. And mostly, because of religion. That pushed Joe even further from his faith.

Stepping up to the self checkout aisle, Joe approached checkout stand 26, noticing the dirty little boy at check out 27, and wondering if he was there alone. The boy seemed too young to be in a Wal Mart at 9 o'clock without a parent. He looked about Joe's son's age, 10 at most. Even his height and build were the same. But unlike Joe's son, Marcus, who was well provided for, fed, and clothed, this little boy was raggedy and emaciated. The boy's shoes were not just worn, they had holes in them, where the boy's bare toes protruded and showed he didn't wear socks. His shirt, a cheap t shirt, once white, was stained with every color imaginable, from browns to reds to yellows. And his pants were far too small, their lower hems barely touching his ankles.

The boy's dark brown hair was shaggy and covered most of his face, as he was leaning downward toward the coin slots above the scanner, pulling coin after coin from his pockets and feeding them into the eager machine. In the bag beside him, his only purchase sat, wrapped the cheap white plastic bags with a yellow smiling face on them. Joe couldn't help but stare. The little boy was a mess, and it made Joe's heart hurt to see. But even more, he was curious as to what a little boy, no more than 10 years old was doing buying a pair of women's shoes.

Trying not to stare, Joe placed his card number against the scanner and began to ring up his lights. As usual, the self scanner was giving him nothing but shit. Joe couldn't understand why something so simple could be made so fucking difficult? Scan the item, bag it, pay for it, leave. It should be that simple. But it never was.

"UNEXPECTED ITEM IN BAGGING AREA!!!!" the machine screeched at him.

"Oh what the fuck," Joe muttered, moving the box of lights back and forth trying to get the machine to register the weight and let him continue to pay. In his peripheral vision, Joe saw a blue shirted employee approaching his general direction and figured yet again, he was going to spend 5 minutes with some employee barely out of high school who didn't give a shit about his job and wanted out of this Christmas Hell just as much as Joe himself did.

But the employee walked past Joe, and up to the little boy, who was standing, looking at the screen showing the total, perplexed.

"Son, can I help you?" the portly gentleman in the blue shirt asked, in his hand a scanner and a bright white name tag across his wide chest, announcing him as Rob.

"No, sir. I want to buy these shoes. But I don't have enough money, it says." The boy looked down, ashamed. His pockets were turned out, and all that was left was lint and a little boy's seemingly broken heart.

"I see," Rob replied. "Well, are your mom or dad here? Let's find them and figure it out."

"No, my dad's at home. Mom's sick, real sick. Dad says she's going to be with Jesus. I wanted to get her these shoes for an early Christmas gift. I know she'd love them, and I want her to look beautiful when she meets Jesus," a single tear arced down the boy's smudged face, leaving behind a clean line of skin, surrounded by dirt and sweat on the rest of his cheek.

"Oh...I'm sorry," Rob stuttered, clearly not expecting this and it was obvious to Joe that Rob was at a loss. Something came over Joe. Call it the holiday spirit. Call it God's grace. Call it guilt, or altruism. He didn't know. But he felt himself stepping toward the register, and pulling out his wallet.

"How much more do you need for the shoes, son?" Joe asked.

"It says $4.83, sir. But I can't ask you to pay for that. It isn't right. Daddy wouldn't want me to. 'We don't need no charity,' he always says." The boy's face twisted and contorted into a vision of confusion. He obviously was torn. The shoes meant a great deal to him, and his mother was dying. Joe couldn't let this little boy leave without those shoes.

"How about this? I'll put it $5.00, and you can pass it along to someone else in need next time? It is Christmas after all. And we don't have to tell your dad, okay?" Joe pulled the crisp five dollar bill from his wallet and began to insert it into the payment slot.

"Yes, sir. Thank you, sir. Gosh, this is gonna make mama so happy. I saved pennies I found on the ground for ages. Mister, you're a great guy," the little boy replied, a smile finally creeping over his muddied face, revealing teeth just as worn as dirty as his shirt. Everything about the little boy was yellow. It struck Joe as bizarre, but he tried not to judge. A dying mom at home, he couldn't even begin to imagine.

It made Joe think of Amy and what a dick he was to her and his kids during the holidays. He had been selfish. Look at this little boy, just trying to barely scrounge up enough money to get his mom a pair of clearance shoes at a Wal Mart, filthy, unwashed, and frankly, smelly. That could be his son right there. His family going through the unthinkable. Joe decided right then that maybe there was a God. Maybe God had put this child here right in front of Joe to make him see his blessings. Even if not a god, at least something greater than Joe, teaching him a lesson, teaching him to respect and appreciate what he had, because it wouldn't last forever. And when it all came down to it, Joe's petty ideas about how Wal Mart at Christmas was truly Hell on Earth, were pretty fucking whiny and selfish. This boy had nothing. He had less than nothing. And instead of buying himself food or himself a pair of shoes, he was utterly selflessly getting his mother a pair of shoes, to wear when she passed away.

Joe put the five dollar bill into the machine, as it slurped it into its insides and spat out the requisite change and a receipt. Taking the receipt, Joe placed it into the little boy's bag, and held out the coins.

"No, no sir. I couldn't. You've done too much already. Thank you, mister. You know, my mama used to make our Christmases real special. But this year it's different, and daddy says next year she won't be here for Christmas. I'm real happy I get to give her these." The boy smiled, and plucked the plastic bag from its perch, and as quickly as Joe had noticed him, the boy waved at Rob and Joe, and waded into the sea of people herding their way out of the Wal Mart and into the freezing cold.

"That was real cool of you, man," Robert looked at Joe. "You know, that kid has come in here before. At first we thought he might be stealing, but he never did. Just came in with a little change, and bought what he could. Never even seen him in a different outfit. I'm pretty sure you made his night. Have a good one."

Joe turned back to his register, fed the cash for the lights into the machine with a smile on his face. He felt good. For the first time in a long time, he felt *good.* He had done something for someone. He'd changed someone's life. That little boy would probably always remember this Christmas and even if he didn't remember Joe, he'd remember those shoes. And now, it was time for Joe to remember. For Joe to remember how much he loved his wife, and how beautiful she was with flour in her hair, making gingerbread cookies. To remember how blessed he was to have two healthy, well mannered kids. And to create new memories, starting with this string of lights, and this Christmas. It was time to be joyous and grateful, just what Christmas is about.

The little boy smiled to himself, clutching the flimsy bag, feeling the weight of the flats he had picked out for his mother's final outfit. They were simple, black, with a metal flower on the front of each foot. She would love them. Darren remembered his mom once saying that black was an amazing color. "You can wear anything with black, Darren. And, it's slimming. Remember that when you get older, for your wife. Not like your father," she had finished the sentence facing away from Darren, toward her full length mirror, so he hadn't heard the rest. He had just looked on, fascinated by her routine. She picked up glass bottles and sprays and put on shiny jewelry, and covered her face with powders. When she finished, she barely looked like the mom Darren knew. But boy, was she pretty. Darren hoped he'd marry someone just like his mom one day.

The wind picked up, bits of snow caught in Darren's hair, that was so long and unkempt, it hung loose from the back of the $1 beanie he'd bought himself for warmth a few years ago. It stunk, but Darren didn't care. Mom hadn't been able to do laundry for a while, and dad wasn't going to do it any time soon. So Darren wore dirty clothes and didn't care. He turned up the walkway, merely some gravel someone haphazardly dumped along a sort of line that led to their one story, aluminum sided home with the metal roof. It whined with the sound of the wind, metal grinding on metal, the door loose and slamming open, closed, open, closed as it had for years. Darren pulled up the key he kept attached to his belt loop and unlocked the solid door, after moving through the broken screen. He turned the lock and heard it click out of place.

"HELP ME!!!! SOMEBODY, PLEASE!! HELP ME!!" The voice permeated the night the moment Darren opened the door.

"Hurry the fuck up, Darren!" his dad hollered behind him. "Shut the fuckin door before someone hears this bitch."

Darren did what he was told, dutifully shutting the door and locking it from the inside with the same key. He turned back to the living room, which doubled as part of the kitchen and where his parents slept usually. The house had very little space and Darren's mom insisted the single bedroom be Darren's. She was nice like that, he thought.

"Well, boy," his dad yelled, "what'd ya find for her?"

Darren faced Rick, his father, who looked much like himself. White torn up shirt, stained, stinky, and long, messy, dark hair that wriggled around his face, wet with sweat, loose, like eels atop his head. Behind him, was Darren's mom, Lucy. She bore no resemblance to the woman he recalled with fondness getting dolled up and smelling so sweet, like flowers and home. She was held captive by tire chains that spanned her entire torso, wrapped around her and attached to their living room wall. Her legs were held together by plastic ties, and her arms stretched above her, held together by some rope Rick had scrounged up. It surrounded her wrists, wrapped around and around them, making her petite hands invisible. The rope crept toward the ceiling from her upstretched arms, to a hook Rick had screwed into the ceiling. It was supposed to be for tools and ladders, but now it served a different purpose.

Lucy was covered in blood. She wore a red dress, one of the many Darren recalled her going out in those nights she got dressed up. The blood seeped through the cheap fabric, staining it an even deeper red, and her arms showed deep scars where Rick had burned her. Her skin was blistered and angry. Huge yellow bags comprised of skin and pus hung from her arms. Some were the size of Darren's own hand, and he could see the infected areas splitting open, skin torn from skin, revolting white and red liquids dripping steadily to the ground, forming a puddle of orange pus and blood around his mom's weary body. The blowtorch Rick used for work was by his side, with his toolbox. All had similar, deep crimson and orange liquid covering them, where Rick's handprints had gripped or where they'd touched Darren's mom. Terror gripped her face. Her eyes had grown large when Darren walked in, almost hopeful. But as her cries for help elicited no reaction from her only son, her eyes had slowly closed, tears tracing their way down her once pale, soft cheeks, leaving lines across her dirt and blood stained face. She looked completely hopeless and broken. Soft sobs escaped her chapped and peeling lips. Her blonde hair partially obscuring them from Darren's view as she hung her head in exhaustion.

"Well, boy?! I ain't gonna ask twice." Rick yelled at his son, turning away from his tools and wife, his face a map of brutality, wrinkles formed of wickedness and too much alcohol. Eyes black and as cold as the blizzard outside.

"Found her some shoes, Pop. Just the kind she likes. Got sparkles on 'em and everything," Darren held out the bag toward his father. The rustle of plastic cut through the sound of Lucy's crying, and for a moment Darren forgot she was there. In his mind, he pictured her upstairs, waiting for Rick to leave so she could get dressed and go out, leaving Darren alone until the wee hours of the morning when she crept back inside and cleaned up for bed. Rick would arrive home an hour or so later and join her in bed, none the wiser.

"Well now, let's see," Rick opened the bag. "Lookie here!" As he pulled the pair of shoes from the bag, Rick's eyes lit up as much as they ever could have. A twisted smile grew on his lips, as he held the shoes in one hand in front of his wife's face. He tilted them from side to side, waving them back and forth mere inches from his wife's shattered face. "Yer boy's gone and got you some fancy new shoes, Lucy. They look mighty fine, eh? Bet you'd love to try 'em on and strut around like the whore you are for them men you's been fuckin!"

Rick cackled as he set the shoes beside him, avoiding the pool of blood that etched its way from beneath Lucy outward toward Rick's knees on the floor. She looked up at him.

"Rick, I never…"

"Don't even start, whore. I seen you out at the bar when you was sposta be at home like a good woman. Out there paradin' yourself for all the men to see. Did you think I was stupid?" Rick reached his arm back as far as he could and backhanded his wife against her already beaten face. She cried out softly. He hit her again, but this time with his fist. "Boy, you see this? This is what a slut looks like, see? And we men never let a slut get away with steppin' out on us, ya hear? Your ma's committed the ultimate sin, and she has to pay. You understand?"

Darren nodded slowly, and replied, "Yes, Pa."

"Good. Now, c'mere and take this," Rick held out a tire iron from his toolbox. Darren didn't hesitate. His dad was right. How could his mom have done this to them? Dad always said a good woman stays in the home, takes care of the family. He quoted the Bible to his son every day, reciting passage after passage about a woman belonging to her husband, obeying her husband, caring for the home and the children. She should've listened. Instead she'd betrayed the family.

Darren gripped the tire iron in his tiny hand. It was heavy, but it felt good. He'd used it before to brain animals he caught in his traps on their land. Rick had caught him with a dead possum once, its body decimated by Darren's brutal assault with the steel instrument. At first he thought he'd get a whoopin' but his dad just laughed and told him to come in when he was done. Darren had cut open the possum to see its insides and found it was pregnant. He looked at the bodies with awe and wondered what it'd be like to see the insides of a person. When he'd finished with the possum, he went inside like his pa asked and Rick gave him a beer. He said his son was becoming a man. It was the one time Darren remembered his dad being proud of him.

"Hit her," Rick commanded, moving aside to give his son room.

"Baby, please…" Lucy cried out, but was cut short. Darren brought the tire iron down on his mother's head as hard as he could. The sound of her skull cracking and bone shattering echoed through the house. He felt himself smiling and adrenaline poured through him. He could feel the blood rushing from his head to his toes, the pounding of his heart the only thing he could hear. His heart thrummed deep in his chest, and he felt his groin tingling. Darren reached back again, and plunged metal into her skull a second time.

This time he could hear his mother gasping for breath, wheezing, clinging to life like the possum had. Darren didn't like it, so he smashed the steel over and over into his mom's face and head until she stopped breathing, and all he could hear was his deep breaths, sucking in air that reeked of copper and urine. He turned to his father and smiled.

Rick grinned back, and he patted his son on the shoulder. "Good job, boy. Taught that bitch a lesson. Wash up for dinner. At least yer ma got that right. She's left us a holiday feast."

Darren did as he was told. He went to the bathroom, stripped, and showered. When all the blood and sinew and tissue were washed from his body and hair, turning the tub a sickening orange, he got out and inspected himself in the mirror. Wiping the steam off so he could see his reflection, Darren examined himself. His eyes were the same cold, black shade as his father's. He was still a small boy, but he *felt* different. And he thought he *looked* different too. His face was flush, and he felt amazing. Strong. Like a man. And now that he finally knew what it was like to kill a human, he craved to experience it again. There was nothing else like it in the world. The exhilaration was indescribable. He dressed and went downstairs to the table for dinner.

Rick was at his usual place at the head of the table, and Darren took his seat across from his mom's. The table was covered with food, meant to be a holiday meal for the family. It looked delicious, meats, potatoes, biscuits and pies. Darren was ravenous. Rick said grace and began to serve himself.

Darren looked across the table to where his mother would normally be standing, serving Rick and Darren herself. Her body was propped up in the chair, slumped over, still in her favorite dress, the shoes Darren had bought her on her feet.

Darren chuckled to himself as he thought back to bashing in her skull and how it had felt. Rick laughed alongside him.

"Don't worry, boy. We'll give yer ma a proper Christian burial, but we'll have this last meal first, as a family. You made me proud tonight," Rick smiled.

Darren looked at the ruined body of his mother and felt nothing for her. He'd always hated her sneaking out and leaving him alone all night. At first it had made him scared, but eventually it just made him angry. He was glad she was gone.

Cackling to himself in much the same way his father had earlier, Darren looked at his mom's crimson colored body, what was left of her black and blue face, and said, "Don't look so glum, Ma. You look great. After all, black goes with anything, right?"

Joe sat down to watch Christmas movies with his family. The smell of popcorn permeated the air, and the crackling of wood burning in the fireplace warmed his body and soul. He glanced around the room at his family and counted his blessings. They were so lucky to have money and security and each other. He thought back to the little boy with the sick mother. *That poor kid,* he thought. But then he smiled inwardly, recalling how happy he was to have those shoes for his mother. He closed his eyes and said a prayer for the boy and his family, asking God to send His blessings to them. Joe knew his prayers would be answered, and he leaned back into the couch with his arms around his family, content and thankful. *God really does work in mysterious ways*, he thought.

Last Christmas I Gave You My Heart - Duncan P. Bradshaw

SHIRLIE PRESSED HER LIPS together, before pouting at her reflection in the mirror, making sure her lipstick application was even, "Are you sure you don't mind?" A balled up tissue hit her in the face, she turned to Kathy and burst out laughing, "Hey! That's mean."

Kathy smirked, "Of course I don't, it was only a short term thing, I'm sure any feelings he had are gone by now. Anyway, George is with you now, you both seem really happy together."

Shoving the array of makeup back into her purse, which defied the laws of physics with its ability to contain so much crap, Shirlie smiled and checked her hair one last time, "We are, it's going really well actually. I think I know what he's planning for Christmas too…"

"Ooohhh, do tell," Kathy said.

Checking behind her, Shirlie moved in closer, "Do you remember the skiing lodge we went to last year? At Saas-Fee? Well…I checked his phone the other day-"

"You what? You checked his phone?"

"Well…yeah, he's been acting a bit funny recently, and ya know…wanted to make sure it wasn't anything I should worry about."

"And?"

Shirlie shook her head, "Nope, nothing, he had loads of pictures from that trip last year, and the internet was on that site where we booked that little lodge."

"Creepy," Kathy shuddered, "it is a bit weird that he wants to go back there, I mean, that's where we…ya know, last year."

"Maybe, but this year, it'll just be me and him. It'll be nice and cosy. So what are you and Andrew doing?"

Kathy smoothed down her dress, "Not sure yet, though I have picked his present out, you wanna see?"

Clapping her hands together, Shirlie said, "Definitely, what is it? What is it?"

Rooting around in her bag, Kathy pulled out a velvet coloured box, wrapped lightly with a baby blue bow, "Here, have a look, I can tie it up again later."

Taking the box carefully, Shirlie plucked one end of the ribbon, letting it slip the knot and hang in her fingers. She opened the box and frowned, "You're giving Andrew this?" Shirlie held up a diamante brooch, in the shape of a flower.

Kathy snatched it back, "Yeah? What's wrong with it?"

Shirlie started to snigger, "It's a bit…feminine isn't it? Is he going to like it?"

"Of course he will, he loves all this sort of thing, you know he used to have an earring, don't you?"

This set Shirlie off even more, "Oh. My. God. I think I've heard it all now, you ditched George, with his lovely hair and manliness, for a man who loves wearing jewellery?"

"Well I think it's endearing. Anyway, come on, we best get back, don't want the boys to think we're having a poo or anything."

"Urrgghh, you're so gross."

George placed the beer bottle back on the table, and fixed Andrew a stare, "He came after me then, shooting at me, I managed to duck the first salvo, but he must've caught me with at least one bullet, as I started moving slower, and my vision went blurry."

"Shit the bed," Andrew said, dumbfounded, "what did you do then?"

"I ducked into this abandoned house, luckily the door was wide open, I ran up this staircase and limped down the landing. There was this kids bedroom at the end, I hid behind the bunk bed and waited. I could hear him though…coming up the stairs. Why the hell had I gone up them? I should've just headed to the back of the house, try to find a way out through there."

"Yeah man, boxed in huh?"

"You betcha, I knew he had killed the others, as I couldn't hear any of them. For a moment I thought I heard Sticky singing *Crazy Frog* but it must've just been my imagination. After a couple of thuds of his boots on the stairs, there was silence. Like those Western films, just before the big shootout at the end."

Andrew picked up his glass absentmindedly and took a gulp, dribbling some rum and coke down his chin, "Go on, what happened? How did you get out?"

George smiled, "I still had one grenade left didn't I? I pressed R2, it bounced off the wall by the stairs and disappeared downstairs. There was a huge BOOM, and then 'YOU WIN' popped up on screen, couldn't believe it, thought we were gonna lose that one."

"Well played man, we should get on it together some time, would be cool to do summat. Kathy doesn't really like me playing it though…you know what she's like," Andrew replied.

George gulped and wrapped his fingers round the beer bottle, his digits squeaked against the condensation which ran down the glass. "I wouldn't know...we were only together for a few days." He took a big swig of beer, before realising it was empty. George looked around for service, snapping his fingers in irritation. Shirlie and Kathy appeared behind him, Shirlie wrapped her arms around him, "Hey, don't worry sweetie, I'll get you another beer, you boys playing nice?"

Andrew nodded, "Yeah."

Kathy sat down, "So what were you two talking about?"

The pair looked at each other, "Video games. What were you two talking about?"

As one, the ladies replied, "Christmas."

With fresh beverages ordered, and the rigmarole of food selection complete, the group sat back, beginning the pre-eating ritual of small talk. Kathy looked over to George, who was gazing at her from across the table, "So...Shirlie says you two are going back to the cabin this year?"

George went red, before sitting up straight in his chair, "No. We're not. Why would she say that? Why?"

"Oh...sorry, must've got the wrong end of the stick, ignore me."

Shifting awkwardly in his chair, George asked, "So what are you and *Andrew* doing?"

Kathy shrugged, "Not too sure really, thinking we might just have the day to ourselves, you know, see some family on Boxing Day."

"That's what we were going to do."

"Sorry?"

George took a quick sip of his beer, "Last year. That's what we were going to do. You know. Before you ditched me."

Kathy sighed, "I thought you'd be okay by now…it was a whole year ago, I was hoping that it would be water under the bridge. We were only together for a few weeks, it was nothing serious. Was it?"

"Dunno what you mean," George said, wiping his mouth with his sleeve, "I'm fine. Totally fine. No idea what you're on about."

The pair looked at each other, before a tinkling of metal striking glass broke the tension. Andrew placed the cutlery down, and shoved his hand in his pocket, "Sorry, just wanted to give this to Kathy…you know, before the meal starts." He pulled out a folded envelope and passed it across the table to her.

"What is it?"

Andrew smiled, "Why don't you open it and see? That's what presents tend to be, surprises."

Picking it up, Kathy bit her lip, before carefully pulling on the end and opening the envelope up. As she pulled the paper apart, a smile birthed on her face, "No way, you didn't!"

"I sure did."

"Mi ma ma," George mimicked blithely.

Shirlie craned her neck, trying to see what it was, before Kathy passed her the tickets, "A week in New York. At Christmas, can you imagine it? Central Park, all that snow, the lights on Time Square twinkling at night, mmm. Wow, thank you Andrew, this is amazing."

"You're most welcome, It has been a busy year, be nice to have some time together away from all of this," Andrew replied, he held Kathy's hand, and kissed it.

"Well, that's just peachy isn't it?" George drawled. "Just peachy. Don't mind me!"

Shirlie shot him a look, "Don't be like that George. Besides, don't you have something for me?"

George picked up his beer bottle, and took a swig, before burping loudly, "No. Not for you."

Kathy put the tickets back in the envelope and turned on her chair, "Well, if we're doing the whole present giving thing, then you better have this." She took the box from her bag and held it out to Andrew.

"Ooohhh, looks fancy, what is it?" He shook the box theatrically, before tugging on the end of the bow, letting it flutter to the pristine tablecloth. Andrew opened it up, his little face lit up with delight, "Wow, it's beautiful. Where did you get this from?" He turned the box over in his hand, but couldn't see any markings.

"I got it from an antique shop. In town."

Andrew pulled the brooch from the box and turned it over in his fingers, the light danced off the square cut gemstones. He undid the clasp and pinned it, upside down on his lapel. "Do you like it?" Kathy asked.

"I absolutely love it, it's amazing, thank you," Andrew replied.

With a knowing look, Kathy looked across to Shirlie, mouthing, "I told you so."

There was a clatter of glasses being knocked over against cutlery, "What the fuck?"

Everyone looked across at George, who was leaning across the table, peering at the brooch. Shirlie, utterly embarrassed, looked around the restaurant which had gone deathly quiet at the sudden outburst, "Sit down George," she whispered.

Ignoring her, George held the brooch, "That's mine! That's what I gave you last year."

Kathy twirled her hair, "No it's not…I don't know what you're on about."

George ripped the brooch free, tearing Andrew's jacket, "It bloody well is, look, the stamp on the bottom, has a line through the G." He held it up to Kathy, though his body movements were jerky from the booze.

The table fell silent, before a gentle cough made George turn his head. A waiter stood to one side, holding a plate in each hand, "Sir…" he began.

"George, sit down, you're making a scene," Shirlie muttered, trying to hide behind her hand.

With a hearty thump, George plopped back in his seat and sunk his beer in one. The waiter placed the steak in front of him, and did likewise for Andrew, who was still frozen in time.

"Bllllleeeeuuuurrrrggghhh," George bellowed. He picked up a boiled potato and threw it at Andrew, which did at least wake the man from his catatonia and sit back in his chair. In silence, the waiter brought the rest of the food out, as the table descended into stolen glances and nervous drinking.

Kathy avoided the piercing gaze from Shirlie, who was tucking into her winter green risotto. The others, cautiously at first, placed napkins on laps, and picked at their food.

All bar one.

George pushed himself back from the table, clutching the fork and steak knife in his hands. "Hey…Kathy…I had a present for you too. Was meant to give it to you later on, but I don't think you're worth it anymore."

"Please George, just leave it, okay? Let it go," Kathy replied.

"No, I bloody won't. You broke my heart, you know that?"

"I'm sorry. Okay? Is that what you want me to say? I'm sorry. There. Now can we please just eat the meal and then we'll all go our separate ways. Okay?"

George half-burped, half-vomited, wiping his drool and sick covered chin with the corner of the tablecloth. "No. Not good enough. You know…last Christmas Eve, I gave you my heart, and what did you do? Just the very next day? Huh? Yeah, you took it in your perfectly manicured talons, and threw it in the bin. With all the rest of the crap that no one wants, you know, the jumpers and collections of deodorant. Well…this year, to save me from blubbing into my overcooked turkey, I'm gonna give it to someone who's more special."

Dropping the fork onto the floor, George pulled apart his shirt, buttons pinged off and struck the other patrons as they looked on with equal measures of mirth and bewilderment. Clutching the steak knife tightly, George pressed the blade through his ribs and into his chest. This sent a jet of blood over Shirlie, who began to shriek.

Despite hitting a rib, George, in his addled state, continued to slice through the skin, making a crude, but relatively large circular wound around his left nipple. Discarding the knife, he clawed his fingers and grabbed hold of the skin, which formed an island surrounded by a moat of blood. With an ungodly howl, he wrenched the circle of skin off and threw it at Andrew. It landed against his cream jacket and slid down like an obese slug.

Not done, George grinned, and pushed his fist through the mass of muscle and sinew, into his chest. His eyes bulged as his fingernails dug into the side of his heart. He tugged, pulling himself closer through the exertion. Gasping, he pulled again, there was another squirt of blood, which showered the tablecloth, giving it a pinky hue.

"Third time's a charm," George stuttered, a runnel of blood ran down from the side of his lips. With one final herculean effort, George twisted his gore covered hand and ripped his heart free from its aortic moorings.

He slumped to his knees, managing to turn his head to Kathy. Holding the pulsing organ in his blood soaked hands, he waved it under her nose, "This could've been yours…you know…but you're not worth it."

He slapped his still beating heart onto the middle of Shirlie's dinner, "There you go Shirl… Merry…Christmas…"

His present delivery complete, he slumped forward, face planted the table and fell onto the floor.

12 DAYS: STOCKING FILLERS — MATTHEW CASH

Gifts From A Star - Jonathan Butcher

EVERY YEAR, ON YULETIDE eve, after we've put Bethany to bed and our tummies are full of brandy-spiced mince pies and our heads pleasantly muzzy from ginger wine, my husband Steve and I are visited by a ghost.

Not a real one of course – just a reminder of someone special. I never notice the moment that Steve lays the year's special parcel beside the star-topped Xmas tree, but it always stands in jolly contrast with the rest of the presents' gold ribbons and red bows, resembling how our son Nathan himself might have dressed it, were he still here with us.

As with every previous package my husband has prepared, the taping on this year's gift is clumsy, the paper vibrant with pinks and oranges, and the gift inside partially visible through apparently careless gaps in the wrapping. This has become my husband Steve's unspoken tradition made just for us, and every year for a few magical moments it's almost as if our darling boy is with us again.

In many ways, these tender gifts helped save our marriage. I've read that couples can easily fall apart in the face of tragedy but now, 13 years after, Steve and I remain devoted.

When our 8-year-old Bethany, who is three years older than Nathan ever was, performs in her school's Xmas show it's always a relief that it isn't a traditional nativity; that may have been too much to bear. Xmas plays at Bethany's primary school are exciting and fresh: a contemporary take on a fairy tale, or a festive-themed pastiche of a famous film or musical. Nathan would have been 18 this year, and when he was still with us local school performances always told the traditional Xmas tale of little Jesus, his parents, the wise men and the celestial body lighting the heavens above the Messiah's humble barn.

In Nathan's first and final role, he had portrayed that very star. Some kids as confident as our son might have hated the part, which had no lines and required a hideous gold-paper-and-tinsel costume, but not Nathan. Ever-creative and ever-excited, he had relished his time on stage, directing two flashlights up and across his shimmering outfit to create the illusion of illumination. When the two straps around Nathan's arms and midriff had raised him high above the stage, that beaming grin which I still dream about had transformed his face, revealing the absence of two lower front teeth that had recently dropped from his gums.

Steve and I had never been fretful parents, so it hadn't been until Nathan had started to fidget that I had felt the first hint of concern. Even now I refuse to envision his fall, the subsequent rush of bodies, the anguished sirens or the catastrophic aftermath.

The first time that my husband had left a gift beneath our tree, under the guise of having come from Nathan, had taken place the very next year following 12 bleak, agonised months. I hadn't immediately grasped who the package was meant for and who it was supposed to have come from, so I had shredded the amateurish wrapping without care.

That first gift had been six garish blue homemade cookies, much like a set of biscuits that Nathan had made in a cooking class shortly before his death. Initially, I hadn't known how to respond and had debated tossing the biscuits into Steve's face – but when my husband had looked at me, his expression had carried nothing but love. I saw in that moment that he and I were here to stay, and although it would take many, many years, there would come a day when we would find our strength again.

Every Xmas since, Steve has left a similar gift beneath the tree to impersonate a present that our little Nathan might have made for us. Each time I open one my world brightens, as if lit by a star. Those festive offerings have included a scrawled picture of a flower, a Play-Doh racing car, a typed poem riddled with spelling errors, a sugar-paper collage of a smiling family of four, and many others. Without ever commenting upon Steve's ritual, as if careless words might break the spell, I open the gift and imagine that it had truly been made by the hands of our boy, who I'm certain would have grown into a caring, inspired man, but who in my mind will always remain a five year old boy.

So this year, with Bethany safely asleep in her bed upstairs, when I notice the new box-shaped gift beneath the tree, a familiar and almost-mystical glow bathes me. I crouch down and stroke the fluorescent paper, imagining a link between our son's spirit and this house.

I am poised to tear it open when Steve touches my shoulder. "Do you mind…" he begins, his voice faltering. "Do you mind if *I* open it, this year?"

When I look up at him I see that expression of pure, simple love once again. The edges of the gift feel soft and fragile against my fingers.

Steve adds, "I know that this is something that you love to do, but where's the mystery if *you're* always the one who opens it? After all, *you* wrapped it."

I absorb the innocence of my husband's face and hand him the gift. He holds it against his chest, almost as if he is hugging our boy. Nathan suddenly feels closer to me than he had only a few moments ago – perhaps watching over us, perhaps even close enough to touch.

As Steve opens the parcel, revealing a mystery present that neither of us has seen until now, the gold star at the summit of our Xmas tree twinkles on, helping to sweep away the winter dark

12 DAYS: STOCKING FILLERS

MATTHEW CASH

Here We Come A-wassailing - Em Dehaney

ON A MOONSHADOW WINTERY night,

When the sky is a lake of black ink

Afloat with the bloom of the dying light,

The Wassailers will come to drink.

They may bang on your gate or your gantry,

They may tippity-tap at your wall,

They may ring on the bell in your pantry

But upon you they will come to call.

And sing.

Sing of the forest a-withering,

Sing of the dark days ahead,

Of their prayers for a bountiful springtime,

Of their hunger for mead and for bread.

You may say, 'Come in and be warmed

By my yule log and sup on my beer.'

They will lay upon you a blessing

For a happy and healthy New Year.

You may tell them, 'Begone!

My family are poor,

My children are hungry and cry.'

The Wassailers will leave you be.

But beware,

If they find you are telling a lie.

If they see your table a-groan

With the fats of the summer and gin

And your pockets a-bursting with silver and gold,

The Wassailers will let themselves in.

They don't want your money or mutton

They eat meat of a different kind.

A game they will play

If you turn them away,

So keep what I tell you in mind.

Here they come a-wassailing
Among the leaves so green
Here they come a-wand'ring
The fairest to be seen.

The Wassailers are four

And what games do they play?

First is Old Mother Tiptree, Broad of the May.

No virgin she, in her dress of red

With a crown of holly and bay leaves round her head.

Master of the house, are you not entranced

By the way her rounded end sways?

Her bosom is swollen, her lips are plump,

Full setting your loins ablaze.

You picture your manhood buried

In the fleshy wet mound of her cunt,

She tips you a wink,

To pour her a drink

And she laughs in your face with a grunt.

She will hold up her cup for you

To fill with your best barley beer.

When the goblet is drained

Does she let fly a belch,

And powder and rouge disappear.

Her chin now bristles with stubble.

That firm arse, so fulsome and thick,

Has become just a sack of grain tied round her waist,

Teeming with weevils and ticks.

12 DAYS: STOCKING FILLERS — MATTHEW CASH

O Master, she lifts up her skirts,

Presenting her monstrous snake.

The Mother gives life in the death of the Winter.

And, O man of the house, you will take.

Here they come a-wassailing
To take what you won't give
Here they come a-wand'ring
So pray that you might live.

Do you like their game yet, Master?

The Wassailers have barely begun.

After The Mother has left you a ruin,

She beckons forth The Son.

This Wren-boy, this Knave,

Little Johnny Jack

Covers up his face with an old cloth-sack.

He is not a beggar or a singer or a thief

A sick and silent dumb-child

Hiding underneath.

What is in that box, boy?

What is in his box, indeed.

A tiny makeshift coffin

Dragging through the weeds.

You could guess it as a wren bird,

So small and cold and dead,

With its beak pointing upwards and maggots in its head.

You could guess it as a robin,

With its feathers ruby red.

You could guess it as a swan, a goose, a partridge or a hen.

You can guess it as you like, you will ever guess it wrong,

For Little Johnny Jack sings only one song.

O Master of the house, listen to him crow

As he opens up the coffin lid.

His bloody tongue on satin,

Red roses in the snow.

New shoots devouring corpses of leaves,

A foundling child raised by whores and grub-thieves.

You must pay the price for turning him away

As his tongue was cut out when Johnny was a babe.

A penny or a tuppence would have done you no harm,

Now Little Boy Johnny takes your firstborn for his charm.

Here they come a-wassailing
You will not hear them come

Here they come a-wand'ring
Too fast for you to run.

Who will step forward as number three?

O Master! O Mistress!

Just wait 'til you see.

The Slicker, The Cutter, The Butcher, The Flayer,

The Skinner, The Tanner, The Stitcher, The Slayer.

Only one man but the size of two,

His great-helm is hewn of white maple and yew.

A vacant blank space where the visage should be,

He is faceless and dreamless

With no eyes to see.

No eyes to see that which he cuts

No ears to hear the ripping of guts

No nose to smell the piss and the lime

Only a mouth for singing in time.

His bastard-sword slays your kin in their beds

One stroke is all, to split bodies from heads.

His two-handed knife with its handle of stone

Slices and dices, strips gristle from bone.

Skins them like rabbits, hangs them up high,

Keeping their umbles for his Christmas pie.

Hearts and ears,

Livers and lights,

Feet, lungs, brains and other delights.

Here they come a-wassailing
So tell them your sins and don't lie
Here they come a-belsnickling
Winter's a good time to die.

And now for the last

The Apple Tree Man.

A nightmare creation,

Not part of God's plan.

His face is painted sable,

Horns grow from his brow,

He reeks of sweaty stable,

Of asses, ram and cow.

His feet are filthy hooves,

A string of teeth hang round his throat,

Breath like rotten fruit,

A matted winter coat.

He has a little purse,

Made of stretching leather skin.

Golden coins come out of it,

But ne'er a coin goes in.

His game; a simple wager,

He lays down a single bet.

Winner takes all,

The loser must die,

And he hasn't lost a game yet.

All you must do, O Master,

Guess the true name of your foe,

But I'll tell you a secret,

Now listen in close;

There isn't a true name to know.

The Apple Tree Man is older than names

As old as the soil and the seeds,

He cares not for flesh or for coin,

It is on fear that he feeds.

A suffering soul is the sweetest of treats,

And now Apple Tree Man has plenty to eat.

He stripes you with his switch,

You cry out for God, your saviour,

But the time for mercy sat with you,

When you turned away a Wassailer.

So good Master and good Mistress,

While you're sitting by the fire,

Pray think of those poor children who are wandering in the mire.

And if you hear a knocking on a cruel black Christmas night,

Give well to the Wassailers

To stay warm and safe and light.

12 DAYS: STOCKING FILLERS   MATTHEW CASH

I Saw Mummy Kissing Santa Claus - Betty Breen

ALICE WAS EIGHT YEARS old. Well if you asked her she would say eight years, five months and two days. Alice liked being eight. At this age everything was still magical and mysterious. She would play for hours, creating stories that were full of wizards and fairies. This is what she loved to do, day in, day out. To her reality was boring, and to reinforce that belief was her older brother, Thomas. Thomas was fifteen and unlike his sister would sit and watch television or play computer games for hours. This was usually accompanied by the scoffing of a sugary snack. Alice knew they were unalike so she would avoid Thomas as much as she could.

Although Alice loved being eight, it did also bring its heart aches, with many of her imaginary friends being crudely obliterated by Thomas' moody teenage tantrums.

'Oh my god,' Thomas said. 'I can't believe you're still writing to Santa.'

A piece of chocolate fell from his mouth as he spoke.

'If I don't write to him how will he know what I want?' Alice asked. There was only one week left until Christmas so Alice was worried it wouldn't get to the north pole in time.

'You're such a loser. Santa isn't real,' Thomas said as he punched Alice in the arm, making her pen fly across the table. 'God you are so lame.'

'I am not,' Alice said, rubbing her dead arm.

'Uh yeah you are,' Thomas said. He was clearly on a mission to destroy his sister's happy mood. 'Santa ain't real, neither are his elves and there are no such things as reindeer.'

'MUM. THOMAS IS BEING MEAN!' Alice said.

Alice had never fully understood her mother. She was short, round and was always glued to her mobile.

'What are you bloody screaming about now child?'

Alice's mother walked through the dining room, phone in hand, tapping away on it.

'Thomas said Santa wasn't real and that I was lame,' Alice said, as her eyes began to fill with tears.

'What?' her mother said, snapping her head up and scowling at Alice. 'Thomas don't call your sister names and Alice dear,' she placed a chubby hand on the dining table, leaning towards Alice's face. 'Santa isn't real. You can't still believe a fat man comes down people's chimneys and leaves presents?'

Her mother stood up letting out a little giggle.

'See lamo,' Thomas said, punching Alice's arm again.

Alice tried to hold back her tears. 'It's not true. It's not true!"

She ran to her room before she could hear any more.

'I hate them Crunk, I really hate them.'

Alice laid face down on her pillow sobbing uncontrollably, holding her closest companion Crunk. A monkey teddy her father had given her when she was born. There was a knock at the door.

'Hello? Is my little girl there?'

'Daddy!' Alice said, jumping from her bed.

'Hello princess. Oh no, why so sad?' Alice's father asked,

standing at the foot of her bed.

Alice's father was her hero. Always there to take away her worries.

'Oh daddy, Thomas and mummy are so mean.'

Alice sank into her father's embrace, instantly feeling better.

'Let's go make some hot chocolate so you can tell me all about it.'

He gently pecked the top of Alice's head and took hold of her hand as they left the room. By the time they had finished their drinks and Alice had told him all about what had happened, it was way past her bedtime.

'Well I think you shouldn't always listen to what others say,' he said. 'And don't let anyone make you doubt yourself.'

'But why did they say it Daddy?' Alice asked into a yawn.

'I don't know princess. I think tomorrow we should go out and see Santa,' he said, carrying her into her room. Tucking Alice into bed he gave her a warm kiss before she closed her eyes, finally succumbing to her dreams.

Alice awoke to the smell of bacon and eggs. She jumped out of bed, and grabbed Crunk by his frayed tail.

'We're going to see Santa today,' she said, giving Crunk a huge squeeze of excitement. 'Daddy said he's in town with his elves.'

Crunk stared blankly.

As Alice walked towards the kitchen she heard raised voices coming from her parents' room. Alice hid behind the door so she could hear what they were saying.

'I saw the messages,' her father said, 'don't lie.'

'What the hell were you doing looking at my phone?' her mother replied in a high pitched defensive tone.

'What do you think's going on Crunk?' Alice whispered.

'What? Does that really matter? I just did!' her father snapped.

'Well it serves you right for being so bloody nosey all the time.'

'MUM! WHERE'S MY BLOODY BREAKFAST?' Thomas bellowed from downstairs. Alice scurried away, creeping into the dining room and sliding onto one of the chairs.

'Lamo,' Thomas said.

He leaned forward and punched his sister in the arm. Alice rubbed her shoulder without reacting to his name calling. She wasn't going to let anyone ruin her day. Especially her fat stupid brother.

Breakfast was eaten in silence, apart from the sounds of chewing on the crispy bacon, and the slurping up hot tea. Alice's Father smiled at her across the table, her mother raised her eyebrows with contempt before getting up and excusing herself.

An hour later Alice and her family were on their way into town. Her father drove whilst her mother sat, face down staring at her phone. Alice could see her father's face screw up in anger, but he continued to drive in silence. Alice had put on her favourite dress, bringing with her Crunk and her letter to give to Santa.

'Can we go and see Santa first daddy?' Alice asked.

'Of course princess. Thomas, you can go with your mother, and we'll decide on a meeting point.'

'I wanna go to Game,' Thomas said

'I need to get my eyebrows done first,' Alice's mother said.

They pulled into the car park and spiralled all the way to the top floor before they found a parking space. The butterflies in Alice's tummy began to flutter furiously around. She sat patiently in the car as everyone got out. Her parents exchanged a few unheard words before her father came and opened the door.

'I wonder if Rudolph is here?' Alice said to Crunk. 'No, you're right, he needs to rest before Christmas eve.'

Crunk stared back blankly.

The shopping centre was brimming with activity. Families were everywhere carrying countless bags that were bulging from all their contents. Children ran around, some screaming, some laughing as their parents tried to keep them under control. Alice looked in wonder at all the decorations. Miles of tinsel sparkled, as millions of fairy lights twinkled, lighting up the enormous Christmas tree that towered over the sugar fuelled children.

'Right let's meet here in 2 hours,' Alice's father said.

Her mother and brother nodded then disappeared into the crowds. Alice and her father found a long line of excited children, and slipped in behind a family that had four. Two were dressed up as reindeer, while the other two had simply decorated themselves with tinsel and baubles. The queue moved quickly. Some children were being dragged away crying, too tired to go on, whilst others were being quietened with chocolaty treats. Alice's butterflies swirled around again, bringing back the doubt her brother had created into her thoughts.

'Right Alice, we're next.'

Alice's father squeezed her hand as they walked over the marvellously snow covered path.

'Welcome to Santa's grotto, he's been expecting you,' a young woman said smiling down at Alice. She was dressed as an elf, wearing pointy green shoes, and a skirt that didn't cover much, if any, of her thighs. Her top forced her breasts together and up in such a way Alice's father blushed and looked away.

'HO HO HO,' a warm voice sounded from behind a curtain.

Alice and her father walked into a tiny room filled with more festive decorations and a mass of presents. A large exuberant man was sat on a big chair with open arms.

'HO HO HO, come in little girl,' Santa said with a big, rosy cheeked smile. 'And what is your name?'

He gently patted his knee, inviting Alice up.

'A....A.....Alice.'

Alice sat on Santa's lap and took out her letter. She read him her list and Santa sat listening, smiling and nodding at her. When she got to the end she wrapped her tiny arms around his large soft belly, breathing in his sweet scent of cinnamon and orange.

'Well that's certainly a lovely list Alice, I'll speak to my elves right away. For now, here is a little gift to put under your tree.'

Santa handed over a small wrapped box, with a shiny pink bow.

'Thank you Santa.'

Alice jumped down and walked over to her father. They left holding hands and Alice finally felt her fear and doubt melt away.

They all decided to stay for lunch and for once agreed the *'Xmas pizza special'* sounded perfect. Alice couldn't stop talking. Even when her mouth was full of pizza, that was topped with turkey, bacon wrapped sausage, mashed potato, Brussels sprouts and cranberry sauce. Telling her mother all about Santa, she sprayed the table with half chewed chunks of food.

'I need the loo,' Alice's mother said after looking at her buzzing mobile.

'Oh, I do too.'

Alice jumped down, swallowing her mouthful, she skipped after her mum.

'Look Alice, I'll meet you back at the table,' her mother said not taking her eyes off her mobile and walking off into the crowd.

Alice didn't have time to respond. Sometimes she wished her mother would just disappear for ever. She sighed as she walked into the toilets. They had been transformed. They looked how Alice could imagine Santa's would be at the north pole. She closed the cubicle door when the letter she had written for Santa dropped to the floor.

'Oh no Crunk, I forgot to give this to Santa,' Alice said.

Crunk stared blankly.

Alice finished up, making sure her dress was crease free in the full length mirror and left. Alice could see Santa's grotto. It wouldn't take a second, she thought, and figured no one would question her absence a moment or two longer. She skipped across and noticed a sign on the door:

'Gone to feed my reindeer. Be back soon.

Santa'

'Damn it!' Alice said.

She turned to leave and saw the elf from before slipping out of a door. Alice hurried over and thought giving it to her would ensure Santa would get it. She reached the fire exit and pushed hard to open the heavy door.

The next few days had been pretty quiet in Alice's house. Her parents had taken to not talking to one another, unless it was absolutely necessary. Thomas sat, engrossed in his computer games, and Alice enjoyed the alone time to play with her new instant camera.

When Alice had pushed open the heavy door, she had bumped into her mother, who had looked all red in the face and was frantically trying to fix her hair. Behind her was Santa, looking similarly dishevelled. Alice gave her letter to Santa, who patted her on the head before swiftly moving back inside. Her mother then took her and brought her a camera. With extra films. Alice's mother said that whatever she had seen needed to be kept their little secret. Bemused, Alice felt pleased that her mother seemed nervous, and for once was paying Alice some attention. Thinking to herself she would never lie to her father, she accepted the gift.

'Well it's Christmas eve Alice. You excited?' her father said. He sat in his usual spot at the end of her bed.

'Yes Daddy, I'm not sure I'll be able to sleep,' Alice said.

'Well remember Santa will only come when everyone is fast asleep.'

'I know Daddy.'

Alice's father tucked her in tightly and planted a big kiss on her forehead.

'Night night Princess,' he said.

'Night night Daddy.'

Alice rolled over and squeezed Crunk.

When she heard her father had left she sat up and grinned. For what no one knew was, she had a plan. Tonight she was going to take a picture of Santa. No more would she have to sit and listen to her bully big brother or her mother. She would get the proof she needed and make fools of them both. Hopefully making them vanish with shame, leaving her and her father forever.

Alice woke abruptly. She was still in a seated position on top her duvet. She rubbed her eyes and tried to stretch out her sleepiness. There was movement from down stairs, she grabbed her camera and slipped out of bed, placing her feet into her new fluffy snowman slippers. Alice carefully opened her door, avoiding the creek and on tip toes crept across the landing. Getting to the top of the stairs Alice crouched down to look through the banister, where there was a clear view into the front room.

She froze.

In the front room was her mother, dressed in a nightgown, reaching into a big bag, taking out presents and placing them under the Christmas tree. Alice didn't understand what was happening. A rage built up inside her, she must have known my plan and wanted to hurt me again, she thought. Pure hatred consumed her mind.

There was a noise on the roof, the sound of footsteps

crossed over head, making their way to the chimney. The living room filled with thick black smoke which engulfed everything in sight. As the smoke cleared Alice could see her mother again. Now standing deathly still, she stared forward absently. Suddenly the tips of two big black boots appeared.

'Well well, you wanted to see Santa did you?'

A tall, thin man appeared. He reached out with a hand that looked like it had been stripped of its muscle and flesh. He stroked the frozen woman's face.

'Let me have a little look.'

Santa pulled out a piece of paper from a pocket in his trousers, which looked like they were far too big for him. This man didn't look like the Santa Alice had met a few days before. He was dirty and unfriendly. His face looked gaunt, with cheek bones that stuck out; it was covered with pale skin, almost translucent. The hair on his head and face was more a harsh, straw like texture, matted together with thick sticky-looking black bits.

'Ah yes here you are. Oh dear, it looks like you've been a very naughty girl this year.'

Santa circled Alice's mother slowly, running his dirty fingernails through her bright yellow hair. She still hadn't moved. Appearing lifeless, her eyes were wide with fear. Alice gripped hard onto the bannister, turning her knuckles white. Her camera long forgotten.

'Yes yes, a naughty girl indeed. Well I've been waiting for a naughty girl like you. Santa's very tired and you're just what he needs.'

Santa stood with his face only inches away from Alice's mother. He leaned in and placed his mouth onto hers. He started to groan and Alice saw his lips begin to move. They parted as he moved his head back. His tongue remained inside.

It was thick and black, and almost like it was alive, it began to pulsate. Santa arched his head back, as his tongue grew larger. She gagged and her body started to convulse. Santa groaned and grinned with pleasure. Slurping and sucking, his tongue grew fatter. With her convulsions turning into small twitches, Alice's mum went pale.

Suddenly Santa ripped open her night dress and ran a finger nail down between her sunken breasts. Alice heard tearing as she saw the skin of her mother's chest peel open. Santa pulled his hand back and slammed it through her breast bone, making a sound like snapping twigs. He pulled back his arm and in his clasp was the still beating heart of Alice's mother.

Santa's tongue retreated and slithered around its prey, searching for fresh meat. The end of it opened like a snake's jaw, showing rows of needle like teeth. It tore the heart from Santa's hands, devouring it in seconds. The snake-like monster then found the opening where the heart had come from and slithered inside. Alice could hear the munching and tearing of muscle and fatty flesh. Santa's eyes rolled up to the top of his head, showing only the brightening whites. Alice's mother sank to the floor, she looked flat, as lumps of her travelled through the beastly tongue. It resurfaced from the gaping cavity, blood dripped from its jaws as it crunched down on a tough bit of gristle.

Alice snapped her attention to the commotion that was stirring above her. For a second she regained herself and felt her body tremble with fear. Could this really be happening? She had to do something, call for help, shout down at this man to stop. As all these thoughts raced through her mind, all the anger and hatred she felt for her mother took over. She could shout out, but there was a little voice whispering, telling her to stay quiet and watch. Is this what they call karma, she thought?

One by one, small, rodent like creatures appeared in the fireplace. Their faces were long and they scurried on all fours across the room to the lifeless body.

'Enjoy boys,' Santa said rubbing his now distended belly, which was now perfectly filling his trousers.

His eyes were bright, and his cheeks had a rosy glow. He wiped his lips with the back of his full chubby hands.

The creatures sniffed Alice's mother, finding flesh to gnaw upon with their razor like teeth. One chewed on the neck before effortlessly twisting the head off with both hands. It sucked out an eyeball, before spitting it out across the room. The creature then sucked out the other one, and Alice heard a popping sound as clear juices seeped down its chin. Another creature found the discarded eyeball. Using a piece of yellowy fat, the creature beamed as it dunked the flesh into the eye, reminding Alice of how she enjoys her eggs and soldiers.

Chunks of meat lay scattered on the ground, the creatures snapped the larger limbs with incredible ease. Muscle was stripped from bone, making a sickly tearing noise. One creature had climbed onto the, just recognisable, torso. It pulled on the ribs, snapping them one by one. The creature's long snout seemed to smile before plunging inside. It writhed around like a dog tearing up a newspaper, snarling. There was a loud snap. Emerging, it pulled out the spine. Each of the vertebrae gleamed white as the creature licked off the juices with its lizard like tongue.

What was left of the once full voluptuous woman, lay carelessly on the floor, unrecognisable as human, just a pile of unwanted scraps of meat and bone. Alice could see some of her mother's peroxide blonde hair, which was now matted with bits of the brain it had once covered. It laid amongst what could have been a foot or knee; there were no digits to help distinguish its official role.

'The reindeer are hungry and we've got plenty more naughty boys and girls to meet tonight,' Santa said, his complexion now young and healthy.

He picked up his sack and as the room once again cleared of that sickly smoke, they had all left.

'HO HO HO.' was all Alice heard as she finally released her grip on the banister.

The newspapers had reported the crime as *'The nightmare before Christmas'*. They told of how a little girl was found sleeping in the front room, covered in her mother's blood. Several of the woman's body parts were missing. Others lay scattered around the child and in the fireplace. Pieces of flesh and organs splattered the walls, changing the family home from warm and festive to a cold cannibalistic display. The young girl told the police Santa had killed her mother with his *'snake-like tongue,'* before goblin like creatures *'tore her apart with their teeth'*.

Police and other emergency service personnel found either story hard to stomach. Of course everyone knows that Santa isn't real, but then who would want to believe an eight year old girl could commit such an awful crime.

Alice sat in her windowless cell, staring blankly at the white padding that surrounded her. No one had believed her. Her father, brother, judge and jury. *'Delusional'* and *'psychotic'* is what they had said. Testimonies telling of Alice's wild imagination, and defiant nature towards her mother were heard in court. She'd been sentenced to Life in a mental institution, with no chance of parole.

As Alice stared, she thought of how long life is. Her twenty years there so far had been slow. Each day she would be heard screaming, lashing out at others, protesting her innocence.

This was the first year she was allowed to join her fellow inmates for the Christmas festivities. This was a privilege only allowed for good behaviour.

A key turned in the door of her cell.

'Daddy?' Alice said.

'No m'dear,' a nurse said. 'I've come to see if you want to join us.'

Without waiting for a reply the nurse slowly began untying the restraints that kept Alice secured to her hard, bare bed. The nurse was new. Alice didn't recognise her. She wore snowman earrings and a green and red woolly jumper. Lifting Alice up they walked out of the cell and down the endless hall. The nurse started humming.

'What?' Alice said.

'Oh sorry, I've got that song on repeat. It's my favourite, "I saw mummy kissing Santa Claus".'

Alice froze, she started to snarl and she pushed the nurse down to the floor. Using her teeth Alice tore chunks of flesh from the nurse's face, before finally ripping out her tongue. Alice screamed as she pushed her thumbs down, bursting through the nurse's eye sockets.

'HO HO HO'.

I'll Be Home For Christmas - Michael Noe

Fantasy

YOU NEVER FORGET YOUR first love. You can try but they're always there, like background noise. No matter where you are, no matter what you do they always come back. Could be a warm spring day, or maybe you see someone from behind and your heart quickens because for just a moment, that's the woman or man you loved first. I can't tell you what love is. It's different for everyone. For me it was like walking on air, it was the sound of a baby's laughter, the feel of the sun on your face in the summer. You hear a song and you instantly think about them. There's no escaping it either. You can try and hide from it, but it always filters through, leaving you weak and unable to do anything but wish they were there with you. Brian is the man I'm going to marry. We love each other and that's what matters. I think of us as a modern day Romeo and Juliet. So many people want to keep us apart, but you can't stop two people from loving each other. It's like trying to stop the rain from falling.

We were neighbors which is how we met. I wish I could tell you that we were best friends but that would be too perfect. The important thing to remember is we were destined to be together. I never believed in destiny until I met him. Because of him all things were possible.

Reality

Brian was running late that morning. It wasn't the first time, but it set in motion the events that would change his life, but not for the better. It's one of those moments that begin with a simple word. *If.* Such a simple word, but the truth is if he hadn't been running late he wouldn't have met her. Her. The woman that always comes back to him in nightmares. *She's* the reason that he can't trust anyone, and she's the woman that made him hate Christmas. Impossible how one moment could make alter your life and make you hate the happiest season of the year.

It was in fact, the season where most people aren't their happiest, or even charitable. He worked in a bookstore and witnessed people at their worst. It seemed as if the entire mall was full of assholes and, and Brian could have sworn he saw their Santa snorting coke off an elf's tits. It was amazing how he could remain so cheerful when people were at their absolute worst. Greed was all the rage during the holiday season, but he was unaffected by it.

She was coming out of her house at the exact same moment and slipped on some ice that had formed right below her porch steps. It was valiant effort on her part to stay balanced but her pinwheeling arms couldn't save her from falling into a small pile of snow. Brian had seen it all and winced. It was a hard fall that could easily have broken bones. He jogged over to her and offered a hand. "You okay?"

"I think so. Thanks, I'm Grace." She allowed him to help her up and even flashed him an embarrassed smile. She was pretty in a plain sort of way. Her face was devoid of makeup and her hair was hidden by a black beanie emblazoned with the logo of *Iron Maiden.* He wondered if she were a fan of the band or just another trendy asshole who thought it looked cool to wear the logo of a famous band.

The one thing that struck him were her eyes. They were a dark gray that reminded him of summer storm clouds. Her lips were full and pouty which he found sexy. "Nice to meet you. I'm Brian." He extended his glove covered hand which she shook lightly.

"Just wish it'd been under different circumstances." She laughed and began walking toward her driveway. That was the moment that he wished he could have avoided. That one fall created an avalanche of shit. When he looked back on it he often wondered if she had fallen on purpose just to get his attention. They had been neighbors for maybe a year or two, but he was never the neighborly type. He stayed close to home and avoided them as much as possible. Made life simpler if you weren't friendly.

Brian had forgotten the incident entirely by the time he got to the bookstore. Despite the popularity of E readers people still bought books. He expected a drop in business, but as a manager he had had found the perfect way to combat the rising tide of digital. Selling used and new books kept the store in the red and made them quite a bit of money. Not an easy feat given the state of online bookstores, and the flood of digital media. There were people that still loved the comforting weight of a book in their hands and Brian loved them back.

It wasn't a hard job, and at times it took a great deal of patience but he was lucky to be doing something he loved. He had been an avid reader all of his life and even tried his hand at writing but wasn't having much success. There wasn't a lot of money to be made in horror and it seemed as if the market was flooded with zombie fiction. It wasn't something he was all that interested especially when Romero had already defined the genre.

Soon there was influx of customers that drove his encounter with Grace further from his mind. He mentioned it to his co-worker in mild amusement. Winters in Ohio were unpredictable as it was, and this one seemed to settle in for a long frigid stay. Grace was lucky that she didn't break anything. Had she been older she could have broken a hip, or a shoulder. All Grace seemed to hurt was her pride. The moment was unmemorable, but it could have been something more had he not been so focused on running late.

Fantasy

You could say that I fell for Brian. I mean it. The way we met was rather embarrassing, but cute in a Julia Roberts film kind of way. I fell on a patch of ice as he was coming out of his house, and there he was. The first thing I noticed was his smile, and then I noticed that he had a strong grip that made me swoon a little. I had never been attracted to men like Brian, they always seemed weak and too intelligent. They made me feel as if I were stupid, or didn't have anything important to say. There I was walking off my porch and then I was falling. When you fall there's no grace involved at all. You can't look hot and fall. It's impossible.

We had been neighbors for two years and I don't think I'd ever spoken to him before my tumble. I would see him mowing the grass or sitting in his porch swing reading, but I never approached him. Brian was the kind of guy who was so absorbed in what he was doing that he didn't notice anything going on around him. He didn't talk to anyone on our street, but he wasn't branded a weirdo. You see that a lot in neighborhoods like ours. You have that one guy that sits alone and you wonder what's wrong with him. Is he a pedo, or maybe he's a serial killer. You can never tell these days.

I could tell that he was just shy. In school he was probably the guy that feared giving speeches or being called upon in class. I didn't know anything about him, but I was intrigued and felt a spark between us. I wanted to crawl inside his head and absorb his thoughts. It sounds a little creepy, I know it does even as I write it down. People like us exist just outside the fringes of understanding. We're voices crying out in the wilderness just dying to be heard.

Once I got myself situated I headed into work and immediately wanted to Google him. I wanted to see what kind of things he posted on Facebook, but all I had was a first name. If he didn't have a picture of himself posted there was no way I could tell if it was really him. I wondered if he had a girlfriend. No, the way we looked at each other was too intense.

Reality

There are some people who arrive home from work to a nagging wife or girlfriend, plus a few screaming kids. When Brian opened the door the welcoming silence greeted him. After a long day dealing with annoying customers it was nice to come home and relax without distractions. His cat Milo looked at him indifferently before going back to sleep on the couch. There were some people that hated the silence and preferred people to be around them, but not him. He had lived with a woman once and he liked the silence and best of all he liked that no one was around to tell him what to do.

If he wanted to sit and each nachos in his underwear he could, or he could forget the pants all together and just eat them naked. He dropped his mail on the coffee table and turned on the television. He switched over to the news and was greeted with the smiling face of the weather lady. Why she looked so happy telling them that a storm was heading their way was beyond him, but it looked like they would have a white Christmas after all. It was Ohio so there was a fifty-fifty shot either way.

He grabbed a beer from the fridge and went over his dinner options. He debated on cooking but decided on Chinese take-out. It had been a long day and all he wanted to do was sit on the couch and do nothing. The customers had been far too needy and nothing he said or did seemed to placate them. It was getting closer to the end of the shopping season and people were on edge. He saw it everywhere and it only seemed to get worse with each passing year. Even the bookstore wasn't immune to the Christmas insanity. The only day worse was Black Friday and he had convinced his boss that it was one day they didn't need to be open.

The pinging of the doorbell roused his from his thoughts. The food had arrived early, but when he opened the door he was surprised by what he saw.

Fantasy

When I decided to go over to Brian's to thank him, I was nervous. Usually, only desperate girls make the first move, but I wanted to thank him for helping me that morning. Most guys would have laughed at me, but he didn't. He seemed concerned, and the way he looked at me made me feel less like an idiot. I know that we connected and I wanted to see him. I had been thinking about him all day and counted down the hours until I could get out of work. I know it sounds silly that I was thinking about a guy that I had just met, but is it really that abnormal?

I'm not one of those girls that expect to be saved by their version of Prince Charming. I have never read a romance novel and saw possibilities. The things you see in the movies just don't happen. Have I ever been in love? Of course but it wasn't as romantic or as whole as the writers and your friends make it out to be. Romance was dead, and I truly believe that those who spent their entire lives searching for true love were never going to find it because they were too busy looking for it.

When I got home I was nervous. I remember staring at his house as if it had suddenly come alive. The front window was a gaping mouth with gnashing teeth and blood spurting out of its mouth. He wasn't home yet and I didn't even know what time he would arrive, or even where he worked. I tried to imagine what kind of work he did, but I couldn't do it. We had been neighbors, yet never spoke to each other. Sometime I would see Alice, or Bob who lived on the other side of me and we would talk about our day, or the weather, but Brian was an enigma.

What if he was a ghost? As absurd as it sounds, it was at the forefront of my mind. If not a ghost maybe I had hit my head and just imagined that I saw him. The brain was a tricky thing and sent all sorts of messages and visions that didn't really exist. The only way I would know for sure was by going over there. It would prove I hadn't imagined seeing him, or feeling the connection we had. I couldn't have imagined it could I? I didn't want to believe that. I wouldn't. Brian was real and I was going to go over and thank him for helping me. This would prove he wasn't a figment of my imagination.

I sipped tea and watched for his car and felt foolish. I've never acted like this before, but I knew there was a connection. I knew it, but I needed proof. *What's the worst that could happen,* I thought. He could tell me to go to hell for one, or he could welcome me in and something real and defining could happen. This could be mine. *What if he has a girlfriend?* I would soon find out wouldn't I? It would be embarrassing, but I would deal with it.

As I waited I thought of what I would say to him. I have never met a guy and then later thought of what I would ask him or what we would talk about. I didn't want to even try and think about rejection. I saw his living room light turn on and I felt queasy all of a sudden. A million butterflies took flight in my stomach. I was frozen to the chair in fear. This was unusual for me. I was always calm cool and collected, but now? I was scared to death.

It took a great deal of willpower to take the short steps to his house. I waited at least twenty minutes because I know when I get home the last thing I want to deal with is a visitor. They suck the life right out of you. I waited and felt the hours tick by. Everything slowed down and then I made my move. The air was frigid as I made my trek next door. Before I knew it I was on his porch and I was knocking on the door. No time to turn back now, it was too late.

Reality

Grace stood there blinking at him. Her breath hovered around her like smoke. For just a moment he failed to recognize her without the beanie or the pile of snow around her. Brian looked confused then ushered her in. No sense in talking to her in the cold. "Hi," He responded lamely. It had been at least a month since he had talked to a woman, and he couldn't remember a time when one just showed up on his doorstep.

"Hi, look, I'm sorry if I'm bothering you, but I just wanted to come over and thank you." She smiled nervously as she looked around the room. She was eyeing the bookshelves as if she were trying to get a sense of who he was. It made him feel as if he were being examined for something.

"It's fine. You okay? That was a pretty nasty fall." He wanted to add that she fell with style, but he didn't want her to think she was insulting her. The last thing he wanted to do was offend her. They hadn't known each other long enough.

"Yes, no bruises, not concussion. Just a girl with broken pride. Will your girlfriend be upset if I'm here?" The question came out of nowhere, but Brian liked how she broached the subject. It was done honestly and he liked that.

"You're safe. There's no wife, and no girlfriend. Any visits from a jealous boyfriend in my future?"

The dance had now begun, and Brian found her charming, but they had very little in common, but she was easy to talk to. He failed to see the spark that she did, but when his food arrived he hated to see her go. He wanted to see her again, and asked her out. It was one date just to see if they would hit it off. If they didn't maybe they could still remain friends. There didn't have to be a romantic interest did there? Brian didn't think so. Things happened, it was just the way world worked.

The dance was interesting because it allowed you see one side of someone. The other side stayed hidden. It was like Dr.

Jekyll and Mr. Hyde without the potion to turn you evil. Once one person felt comfortable then everything changed. The ugly habits and behaviors came out, but by then it was too late to run. You were stuck, and the odds of leaving lessened every day. All of those annoying habits become sort of cute. It doesn't matter that your other half is a monster, or there's just one number away from being a full set of sixes.

No one ever thinks that anything bad could happen to them. The world is a dangerous place full of traps and pitfalls. People aren't as they appear, but there's no way of knowing all that. Even a guy like Jeffrey Dahmer can appear to be the nicest neighbor you've ever had. As he watched Grace leave he didn't think anything was off or that he should be careful. How do you do you know that someone is dangerous? You don't until it's too late.

Fantasy

I felt as if I were floating home. I never believed in love at first sight, hell I didn't even believed in love at all, but Brian showed me something, He wasn't like the guys I dated, or was even interested in. He was smart which was a little intimidating, wait that makes me sound like I'm stupid which I'm not. I just see the world differently than he does. I see a clear cut black and white while he sees all of these shades of gray. It was invigorating to be with someone that challenges you and makes you see things that you had never seen before.

Brian was an easy going guy that I instantly fell for. There was never any doubt that he was the one. When we went out he treated me like a woman. He opened the door, and pulled my chair out for me. What I loved was that he was interested in *me*. He was wanted to know everything and that was scary because I was afraid of revealing too much, or saying the wrong thing. I would look at him and feel myself smiling for no reason at all. I have never felt that way before, and I never wanted it to end.

I was crazy about him and he was crazy about me. He would send me texts just to say hi, and to see how my day was going. In the evening we would watch a movie and I would go home euphoric that he wanted to see me again. If I could describe him as a building he would be my church. His words were the confessional that I visited as often as I could. He was the altar that I would kneel in front of when I needed absolution. Love to me was my new religion and I hungered for it, and worshipped it like an eager child. I can tell you that I was in love, and being with him were some of the greatest moments of my life.

Why is it when you're in love time seems to slow to a crawl? You spend every minute alone wishing you were with that person and then when you are, there's the fear that this could be the last time you'll ever be together. I didn't want to think about what if, or what I might do if he didn't really love me. Once you start thinking like that things begin to unravel, and you question everything that they do. Nothing is the truth and everything is a lie. That's not how you have healthy relationships.

I wanted us to be like those people in all those sappy love songs. You know the ones by those pop stars that can't really relate to normal people. Hell, half the time I couldn't relate to normal people. I resent people that appear to have all their shit together. It was even harder to maintain an even keel due to the festive holiday season. The last thing I wanted to deal with was a breakup during Christmas. It adds a sinister edge to the season. No one wants to hate Christmas due to a bad love affair.

Let me back up for a moment if I can. I have never been in a relationship and instantly heard a song that stopped me in my tracks and made me think of the person I was with until Brian. Of all the songs it had to be Katy fucking Perry. How girlie right? It's a sad world when a smart educated woman hears a Katy Perry song and gets twitterpated. It's clichéd and not like me at all. I sometimes felt as if I should've been scrawling his name on my walls. I have always been practical, but Brian *affected* me. I just wanted to be with him and I thought that he wanted to be with me too.

Reality

Maybe it's time I take up my own narrative just so I can clear things up. In order for this to have any resonance at all, I need to tell this my way. No more running to a third party and telling them this is how I felt, this is what I said. It has more impact if I just tell it myself. This way you get the raw untapped emotion, and a direct line to my brain. Sounds rather intimate doesn't it? We can have a cigarette afterwards if you want. The thing I want to stress is that no matter what you hear, or read the truth is always out there. The question is, just how open are you to it?

At first I didn't realize how badly things had progressed with Grace. We were neighbors, and then we went out a couple of times, but I never told her that we were together. I liked her, but not in a romantic way. She's a smart, funny, woman but, I don't know, there was something about her that made me realize that there was no real hope of being anything other than friends. How she came to the conclusion that we were a couple is way beyond me. I told her where I stood, but she must not have heard me.

Things weren't always bad between us. We would hang out and she would fall asleep on my couch and I would find my way into my room. Despite what she tells you, there was never any romance. There was a kiss, but she kissed me and I told her that this wasn't going to work. That was the moment I realized that we were not on the same page. She began looking at me differently and it was awkward. How do you tell someone that you aren't feeling the same way they are? What if they don't believe you? It's easy to misread people. I do it all the time but when they tell me they aren't interested I back away and move onto other things. It sucks, but what else can you do?

I can still remember that night we were sitting on the couch together and she told me that she loved me. I was taken aback by it, but I admired her courage for saying it. People often don't say it due to the reality of someone not loving you back. There's nothing worse than that. The world feels like it's being reduced to a pin hole, and you wish a hole would appear so it could swallow you. Once you say it, there's no taking it back. It's always going to be there. This person just bared their innermost feelings to you and now you have to figure out a way to work around it.

I just let the words sink in. I wish I could have said it back, but I didn't feel the same way. You ever notice that it's usually just women who have this problem? A guy will tell a girl that he's crazy about her, and she'll just be brutal in her rejection. I didn't want to hurt her feelings or make her ashamed that she had revealed her feelings for me. What had even given her the impression that I felt the same way? I was pretty clear the entire time we were together. Things were now going to change, and it saddened me. Jesus, I sound like a woman.

"Grace, you know I don't feel the same way. I'm sorry." Is there a way to tell someone that they aren't good enough for you? Once it's out there, there's no taking it back either.

"Oh, wow. I'm sorry. I should go." She stood up and looked at me for a moment. I hoped that she wouldn't start crying in front of me. I don't know how to deal with that. All I can do is stand there awkwardly wondering what I should do.

"No, it's okay. I'm sorry." It was a lame reply, but I don't think she even heard me. She grabbed her coat and headed out into the cold night air. I wondered if I'd see her again. I know she was embarrassed and I was too because I could have handled it better. I stared at the door thinking if it had been a movie the scene would've ended a lot better. A bit more dramatically, and I wouldn't have felt like an asshole.

I eventually went to bed feeling less like an asshole and was glad that I got to spend time with her. She was easy to talk to and I liked our evenings together. She would call me and invite me over for dinner or if she were going out with friends she would invite me along. Grace said that I spent too much alone and needed to interact with people more. I dealt with people all day so the last thing I wanted was to deal with more people. She would eventually pout and out I would go. I should've seen that she was seeing things a little differently that I was. Did she see us as a couple?

Guys are pretty clueless when it comes to women. Some of them are more direct than others, but Grace wasn't like that. What you saw is what you got. Grace made me laugh and was exactly what I needed at the time. I took my life a little seriously, and she enabled me to loosen up a bit. We spent a lot of time together, but I missed something. Were there signs? There had to be, and I had missed them. It's easy to do if you aren't looking for them.

I fell asleep and woke up the next morning the same way I did every morning. I stumbled to the coffee pot and stared out of the window. It was hard to believe that Christmas was a week away. I thought about Grace and wondered how she was. I almost called but I didn't. If she wanted to talk to me she would. We could somehow work through the night before and maybe over time I would feel something. It wasn't impossible, or even something I had considered.

With every woman I've dated there's always been some initial attraction. Something that immediately told me that could lead to something. I even had a Van Halen moment with a girl once and *Why Can't This Be love* was out song. We lasted a solid year before we imploded. That's the weird thing about love, it's not guaranteed to last forever. You can't also can't have feelings for someone just because they have them for you. It doesn't work that way.

I poured my coffee and headed into the living room to clear my head a little. I avoided the television and was soon immersed in the beautiful music of *Orchid*. I didn't want to think about Grace anymore, or what might have been. As far as I was concerned it was over. Last night changed the whole dynamic of who we were. There was no going back now. She must've known that right? I sipped my coffee and watched the snow fall outside. The music and the view of the snow covered sidewalk relaxed me. This was how I wanted to spend my day off. Just sitting on the couch not doing a damn thing.

I got a text an hour later. Here's what I want to clarify. I had no way to know what would happen after Grace told me she loved me. People assume that I must have known, but there's no way I could have. There's no way to gauge how people are going to act. I don't want to say women because men are just as capable of acting irrational and seeing things the way they want them to be not how they truly are. We expect people to act a certain way, but sometimes they surprise you. It's sad and it happens all the time.

I didn't respond right away. I wasn't ignoring the phone; I just didn't hear it over the music. When I finally picked it up Grace was looking at me. I had taken the picture one night while we were watching a marathon of horror films. She had been so immersed in the film she hadn't even noticed that I had taken it. It was shot that showed her in a moment of vulnerability. I loved how it captured her exactly the way I saw her and even thought about her. It made me a little sad to think that I might not see her again.

The text was just like her, simple and direct. *Can we start over?* That was a hard question. The more I thought about it the harder it became. Could it be that simple? Instead being rational and saying no, I said we could try. Why not? Looking back, I can say I made a mistake, but I was supposed to know things would get so crazy? Everyone makes mistakes at some point in their life. It's that pesky thing called being human. Name one person who hasn't made a mistake.

I invited her over and things were normal. We avoided what had happened but deep down it was all I was thinking about. I wondered what she was thinking and later I would know exactly what was on her mind, but I'm getting ahead of myself. After that afternoon I did notice something different about her. She would look at me when she thought I wasn't looking, or come over even when she wasn't invited. It was almost as if she was seeing us as something we weren't.

"You okay?" This was maybe two weeks after we had resumed the friendship. For the last two days she had been quiet and a little withdrawn. I would text her to see how she was doing, but she was avoiding me. I began to think that there was something there that I wasn't seeing.

"I'm fine. Just thinking." She sighed and I saw something in her eyes that scared me a little. It was just a darkness that passed over face like storm clouds. It passed quickly and she was back to normal. Did I imagine it? There was no denying that things had changed. Only an idiot would fail to see it, but I was in denial. We began talking about Christmas and what we planned on doing. I had made plans to visit my parents and she had plans to do the same. We made plans to meet up on New Year's Eve, and again it felt as if she wanted to tell me something and was holding back.

One night I had gotten up to get a drink and I saw her looking at my car. I wanted to call out to her, but instead I just watched as she placed her hands on the hood as if she were Jesus preparing for a healing. I had been seeing a woman at work and finding less and less time for Grace. She had seen us together one night when we came home from a date and there was no way to brace her or Candice for the introductions or icy stares that would shoot from Grace's eyes. She looked sad and defeated as we walked into the house.

She was checking the hood to see if it was warm. Grace was checking to see if I had gone out. Things were progressing nicely with Candice and I thought that maybe Grace felt threatened. A new woman could endanger our friendship, but it was Grace who was pulling away, not me. I had made it clear that there was nothing between us, yet there she was checking my car. It was a little creepy and I wanted to turn away but I was frozen to my spot as if my feet were cement bricks.

Finally, she went into the house and I turned away from the window, but I couldn't sleep. *What the hell was she doing?* It was odd behavior to say the least and not something you expect to see in the middle of the night. *What else is she doing when I'm not looking?* That scared the hell out of me. There was a lot she could be doing when I wasn't looking. I wondered what she would've done if she had seen me watching her. The silence I could handle, but this was some creepy shit.

The only thing I could do was keep an eye an on her. If things got any weirder I would call the police and have them deal with it. I wasn't sure what the laws were, but they could do something. Until then I would watch. It was all I could do. Grace hadn't threatened me, and as far as I knew she hadn't said anything to Candice. I would talk to her in the morning and let her know that something was going on with Grace. I couldn't leave her in the dark. She had to know about Grace and her feelings for me. *What if it's nothing?* It was better to be safe than sorry. If she said I was acting paranoid then so be it, but then again, she hadn't seen what I saw.

For the next two days I only saw Grace once. I didn't mention the car and our conversation was pleasant if not general. "How've you been?" My voice was full of forced cheer. I was nervous and not sure what to say, but I couldn't avoid her. I could've, but she would sense that something was wrong.

"Busy, with Christmas coming up I've been shopping and trying to get caught up. Where's your new friend," She asked. The word friend was said with dripping sarcasm. I could see her smile slide just a little.

"Working. We may meet up after though." As soon as the words were out of my mouth I regretted them. It was as if I were pouring salt on a wound that just refuses to heal.

"Good. Sorry I've been kind of distant lately. Got a lot on my mind."

"I'm glad you're okay." *Why were you touching the hood of my car?* I wanted to add this but didn't. There was no reason to. I wondered what else she had done while I wasn't looking and shoved the thought away. We climbed into our cars and headed away. It wasn't as awkward as I thought it would be and I wished things were like they had once been, but Candice was a part of the equation now, and I didn't want Grace to feel threatened.

Fast forwarding a bit I have to tell you about the cd that Grace had dropped off. I had been busy at work and hadn't had any time for anything else. Candice would stop by and we'd have lunch together but that was about it. I hadn't heard or seen from Grace since that morning we were both leaving for work. The disc didn't have a label on it. As she handed it to me she seemed nervous, like she was thinking about running before she could hand it to me. I had a sinking feeling as I reached out for it. *Don't take it! Once you take it you have to listen to it.* That wasn't entirely true. I could just throw it in a drawer and forget about it. It was a great idea, but I knew I would listen to it.

I didn't even get a chance to say anything. She was already gone into her house leaving me alone staring at the space where she once stood. Deep down I knew that things had taken a turn Problem was that I had no idea just how far left they had gone. I walked inside and stared at the disc as if it had just grown teeth and was threatening to bite me. In a way it did. Whatever she had put on it was going to be bad. I can't tell you how I knew it, I just did.

I placed the disc in my stereo and reluctantly closed the disc tray. *You don't have to do this,* I pleaded with myself to listen to reason, but I did anyway. Logic was gone at this point. Maybe it would explain Grace's behavior. Her sudden withdrawal was troublesome, but the music on that disc scared me. It wasn't the fact that it was shitty pop music. That was fine, but the songs and their meaning troubled me. It began with *Lady Gaga's Perfect Illusion* and just went downhill from there. *Kelly Clarkson's Behind These Hazel Eyes* mixed in with *I Miss You* from *Adele.*

There was theme that hit me immediately. Desperation, and the loss of something that only she felt. As I sat through *Dark Horse* I felt cold and a little frightened. Just when I thought it couldn't get any worse she had put in *I'll Be Home for Christmas, All I Want for Christmas Is You,* and another Kelly Clarkson gem that talked about being in love with someone and it was a drug that they just couldn't shake. How in the hell had I missed this? *You weren't looking for it.* Did I have to really look for it?

I then saw the disappearance for what it was. It wasn't Grace giving me space with Candice, she felt threatened and now? It had to end. She needed to know that there was no chance of us being together. From the pattern of the songs in her head we were already a couple. What the fuck had I gotten into? What the hell did she mean by placing the Christmas Carol at the end? No, that wasn't possible was it? Did she really think that this was her home and I would just let Candice step aside so she could move in? It had to end. I pulled the disc out and headed into the frigid evening air. My thoughts were scattered as I climbed up porch steps.

I felt like a condemned man being led to his death. The door was flung wide as Grace wrapped her arms around me. I could smell her perfume and feel her hot breath on my cheek. I shoved her away with a little too much force. The look of hurt and confusion made me happy.

"Baby what's wrong?" She walked toward me again, but I stopped her.

"This," I waved the disc in front of her face, "What are you trying to tell me? Do you really think we're a couple?"

"We are. You love me Brian. Just admit it. No one loves you like I do."

She made another step toward me, but I backed away. "No, I don't. I already told you this once. Didn't you hear me?"

"Is this about Candice? What? Do you think she's better than me? She's not. I know you better than she does."

"Just stay the fuck away from me Grace." I tossed the disc onto the snow covered ground and headed back home. Once inside I started shaking and called Candice and told her that she needed to stay away for a while.

"You need to call the police Brian. You don't know what she's capable of." She was right but I was too stubborn to listen.

"There's nothing they can do. If she doesn't stop then I will. I'll file a restraining order."

"If you want you can stay with me."

"If things get bad I will I promise. Right now she's just hurt and she's angry. Maybe I overreacted." I looked out the window thinking that she'd be staring in my window. The yard was clear though and I breathed a sigh of relief.

"She's dangerous," Candice sighed loudly as she stumbled over her words, "You may not think she is, but women like that are crazy."

We talked a little longer and I felt my phone vibrate. I looked at the text icon and sighed. *We need to talk.* I tossed the phone onto the couch and rubbed my hands over my face. As I sat there more texts came in each one more desperate than the last. *Why are you ignoring me? Are we okay?* There was nothing that I could say to help her understand that there was no us, and never would be. The phone rang startling me. Grace was now calling. I hesitated for a moment before answering it. I couldn't keep ignoring her.

"What?" I tried to keep the anger out of my voice but failed miserably.

"Why are you doing this? Why won't you talk to me?" Grace had been crying. I could hear it in her voice. There was also a pleading tone that I didn't like.

"I'm talking to you. What do you want?"

"Can I come over?" I could hear rustling in the background and I wondered what she was doing.

"I'm getting ready to leave. I have some things to think about." It was only half true. I wanted to be with Candice not here dealing with Grace. This was the last thing I needed and running away seemed like the best possible option.

"You going to see that bitch? Why would you do that me Brian? What she does have that I don't. I'd die for you. Is that what you want? Say the word baby and I'll carve your name into my wrists. Is that what you want?"

I groaned silently as I envisioned this woman bleeding out with my name etched onto her wrists. It was a sad image, and I wondered if she would really do it. "Who I see isn't any of your business. Look, you can kill yourself, but is it really going to get me to come see you? Do you really want to die all alone?"

"My blood would be on your hands my love. Do you want that? Can you live with that guilt?"

"Jesus, are you fucking listening to yourself? You're fucked in the head you know that?"

I hung up and headed to my car and heard Grace's door open. "Don't leave me! She was on the hood of my car before I could back out. I was both horrified and saddened for her, but it didn't stop me from calling the police.

Fantasy

We were in love. That is true, and Candice stole him from me. She poisoned his head with lies and he believed them. True love always finds a way doesn't it? Yes, I did jump on the hood of his car to stop him from leaving, but he was making a mistake. He's just a dumb boy, he doesn't understand that I was trying to help him. I wanted him to stay with me. I thought by trying to stop him he would see just how much I loved him. I would do anything to prove just how much I loved him. Everyone wanted to keep us apart. Why? Were they jealous? I think that's what it was. What Brian and I had was special and they couldn't deal with it.

We were Romeo and Juliet. We were meant to be together. I would watch him when he wasn't looking. He always looked so sad and alone. I planned to fall that day just so I could meet him. I had watched him for so long and I swear that there was a time when our eyes met. That connection was there. It was real. You can't fake something like that. Brian and I were soulmates. That doesn't happen twice.

He had said some things about me that aren't true. He's told people that I'm deluded and crazy, but he's not thinking clearly. I still love him despite all of the things he's said and done. I heard a song by *INXS* the other day and the lyrics hit home for me. They spoke volumes and no matter what people say they will never tear us apart.

Reality

It was clear that the restraining order wasn't working so I decided to move. I have to give Candice credit for putting up with my foul moods throughout the ordeal. When the phone calls and texts became too much I was forced to change my number, but she would still show up banging on my door and then the cops would come. It was exhausting. You read stories like this, but you never think it's going to happen to you. Was I scared? I was more annoyed than anything.

Candice and I had been packing for about a week, and I found a house close to her. If things worked out between us we would move in together. I was trying to live as normally as possible, but Grace was making it difficult. I was moving out after Christmas which was only three days away. I was exhausted by this point. I took a week off from work which was hard, but once they knew my situation they gave me what I asked for.

"You need to take a break." Candice came into the living room carrying another box that I assumed came from my bedroom. I had been packing nonstop and the house felt cold and barren. She wrapped her arms around and kissed me.

"Okay, I don't think there's anything left. Not even the tree." I laughed despite my sudden anger. This was not how I wanted to spend the holidays with her, but I didn't have a choice.

"It's okay. You and I will have a nice normal Christmas at my place. You'll even get to meet my family. You thought Grace was crazy? Just wait."

"Thanks for putting up with all of this. Most women wouldn't. They would have been gone a long time ago. I love you."

"I love you too. We should go out. There's no reason why we should stay here. We can be a normal couple." I nodded and agreed with her. We were living like prisoners, and I was getting tired of it. Candice went into the bathroom and I went into the kitchen and almost screamed. Grace was sitting at the kitchen table reading a magazine as if she belonged there.

"I told you I'd be home for Christmas." She smiled at me and stood up. There was a gleam in her as she presented a box wrapped in paper that adorned with kittens.

"I don't even want to know how you got in here, but I want you to leave before I call the cops."

She smirked at me and wrapped her arms around my neck. I thought of Candice and prayed that she wouldn't come out now. That was all I needed. "With what? You're phone's on the coffee table sweetheart. You and I are going to spend some time together. Yeah, I know Candice is here, but that's okay. I'll take care of her."

"No, you don't need to do anything. I'll tell her to leave. Just don't hurt her." My voice was heavy with emotion as I tried to think of a way out of this. This was something she must have been planning. I was trapped and now I put Candice in danger.

"How sweet. What have you told her? Did you know you left your back door open? I have been here while you slept, I watched you when you thought you were all alone. You made it so easy baby. You have no idea how I much I love you. As for Candice, I don't know. I heard you! I want to make you suffer. When I kill her I want you to watch."

Knots of gooseflesh rippled over my flesh as the reality of the situation set in. "You know if you kill her you'll go to prison. You won't be able to see me again. Just let her go and I promise you I'll never see her again."

She flashed a smile that sent chills up my spine. It was a look that you see in people that are slowly losing their minds. Grace was calm as she gestured toward the kitchen chair and urged me to sit down. "It's cute that you want her to live. What if I went back there now and pulled her out of the bathroom by her pretty auburn hair? I should kick the shit out of her just for trying to take you away from me."

"If you want me gone, fine. You want me to tell you that you're the better woman?" Candice walked into the kitchen slowly as if she were approaching a rabid dog. Grace walked toward her and slapped her. Candice's eyes widened not in pain but in anger.

"This is all your fault," She screamed. "We were just fine and you had to ruin everything!"

"It must suck knowing that no matter what you do, Brian'll never love you. That has to eat at you. You're pathetic! You come in while he's sleeping and watch him like some kind of pervert."

"You bitch!" Grace lunged for Candice screaming. I grabbed the kitchen chair and swung it at her back not caring that I could really hurt her. She fell to the ground and writhed in agony. As she lay there I felt sad for her, but she had asked for it, and now as far as I was concerned it was over.

Fantasy

This was all Candice's fault. Will I ever see Brian again? I hope so. I haven't stopped looking for him, and I know that I'll find him. It's just a matter of time. We're soulmates and were meant to be together. You can't stop true love. He did love me. I know he did, but he listened to what everyone said and they turned him against me. Am I sad? Not at all. I know something that you don't.

I know exactly where he is and when he least expects it I'm going to pay him a visit. He thinks he got away from me, but he didn't. He should've known that there's no way he could escape. I love him and we'll be together forever.

12 DAYS: STOCKING FILLERS

MATTHEW CASH

O Christmas Tree, O Christmas Tree - Dani Brown

FATHER CUT DOWN THE tree with a chainsaw instead of an axe. Chainsaws classified as cheating. With playful cheer, we teased him about it. Our cheeks were rose-coloured from the cold. Snot dripped from my nose. It wasn't cold enough to freeze.

Father forgot the twine to secure the tree to the roof of the car. There was a lot of swearing when he shoved it into the backseat. Mother sighed. The needles would be in there until July at least. She was certain she'd be hoovering them out next Christmas. Both parents insisted on a real Christmas tree for their family. It didn't matter that we were growing up and couldn't have cared less. It was like their refusal to buy instant hot chocolate – the neighbours didn't even get to see that.

Whilst our parents drove home, we had to stick our thumbs out for a ride and walk two miles up our road because the trucker who picked us up in exchange for a blow job wouldn't leave the motorway. Freezing, with stomachs literally filled to the point of extreme bloating and discomfort with trucker cum, myself and siblings arrived home to mother and father arguing about dragging the tree into the house. My brother had to wipe cum from his chin lest our parents find out.

The tree was normal by all standards. Just a normal tree for a normal family Christmas. I was only in my first year at college but my mother already could feel the clock ticking towards the time when I wouldn't be coming home for Christmas. A husband and family of my own would follow graduation in her secret fantasies. I had my own plans but they didn't fit into the life she wanted for me. The tree had to be perfect. Every tree had to be perfect. No one knew when my last Christmas as a single woman, my parents' child, would be.

It wasn't until they shoved it in the stand that my brother's stomach decided it was not very appreciative of trucker cum. He threw up. I would have noticed the ashen look if it weren't for the cold. Living with roommates in halls, I knew the signs of when someone was experiencing stomach turning.

Mother didn't care that it landed on the tree – it was decoration as far as she was concerned. She had some pretty powerful air freshener that would hide the odour. Bad smells were what concerned her. I swear she bought her air fresheners and candles from the black market. Lucky none of us were born with any breathing problems.

Father appeared rather infuriated. His temper had been slowly rising all day. It's what happens when there's too much pressure to be perfect. I learned how to swallow my feelings long ago. The drugs, abundant in places of learning, hid the stomach cramps and my anxiety I dragged behind me like a balloon wherever I went.

The vein running through Father's forehead stuck out and throbbed with his angry heartbeat. Tears of rage shone from his red face. But he swallowed them with what must have been about one pint of whisky. Mother started on the mulled wine.

Father's vomit also landed on the Christmas tree. Mother was too drunk to notice by then. Father wouldn't realise until his hangover cleared in the morning. Then he would have a new reason to be angry unless Mother cleared it before he woke. His vomit lacked trucker spunk as far as anyone knew.

Having to explain to my parents that in order for us to get home while they were preoccupied with a perfect family Christmas we had had to provide oral sex to the trucker who picked us up made them both angry and disappointed at the same time. I wonder what exactly they were expecting. It was too long of a walk. People who pick up hitchhikers always demand something in exchange.

The jiz took a good few hours before it rumbled in my stomach. I was used to sucking dicks, unlike my little brother – not sure about Big Sis. She was at her final year at university but my parents had lost hope of her meeting a nice man and settling down.

Mother and Father didn't know about my extra-curricular activities. The toilet did. It received the full force of the trucker cumshot, plus some stomach acid and everything I'd had to eat. It wasn't the first time; it wouldn't be the last.

There must have still been some cum in my mouth, stuck between my teeth and the fur of my tongue. The sink received a small dose when I rinsed my mouth out. Antiseptic mouthwash didn't kill it. It was another of my mother's black market purchases, meant for people with an extreme case of halitosis, which was no one in my family.

I went to bed with Father passed out drunk beneath the tree and my brother groaning and clutching his stomach on the sofa. First to bed is first to wake. With school finished until January, there would have been no reason to get out of bed if it weren't for the call of my bladder.

I wiped the crust away from my eyes in the morning and went to the bathroom. Small lizards in bright colours and the odd armadillo walked out in single file and down the stairs. Sometimes my dreams haunted me until after that first morning piss so I thought nothing of it. Another hallucination brought on by the pressures to be perfect.

The lizards came from the toilet. I sat down and had my arse bit. Never before had I hallucinated pain. I didn't have time to process what had just happened, my bladder needed to release. That first morning piss was always the most painful.

The sink wasn't an option. Spiders riding on the backs of turtles flowed out of the drain. My mind said they'd disappear once I'd emptied my bladder, but best not to risk letting a stream of urine touch them. Hallucinations might get angry too.

I ended up pissing in the bath. Relieving myself while standing was another party trick sure to embarrass my parents. Not even Big Sis could do that. They wouldn't care none landed on my thighs. Neither would Big Sis, although she'd seen it.

I debated getting back into bed and reading for a few hours – college allowed no time for pleasure reading - but rainbow lizards, armadillos and spiders hitching a lift on the back of turtles lit a spark wherever my curiosity was stored. No one was awake so I didn't need to swallow it down. They should have disappeared with my empty bladder but didn't. That I may have finally gone insane was my initial thought. Being buried away in the closet with the other skeletons would've been a welcome relief from the perfection my parents demanded.

There was no way I'd be able to concentrate with that smouldering spark of imagination. Curiosity and imagination was the undoing of Big Sis. When my parents were forced to talk about her in the presence of others, their faces went beet red. Not even my mother's thick makeup could hide it. Big Sis wasn't even a liberal arts student – she was studying astrophysics.

The house was quiet to the point of being unnerving. It should have been filled with joy and laughter. And Big Sis seeking my parent's approval. They didn't even want her back here for Christmas. They wanted to write her out of the family tree.

It was Christmas – the family together for the first time since August. Even Big Sis was here with her science books. She'd join us in church for the midnight service if my parents allowed it. She was happy to be home, even if she wasn't loved as much as me and my brother.

The lizards, armadillos and spiders riding on the backs of turtles paid no attention to me. I didn't even get a glance in my general direction. One died beneath my bare foot, ruining my pedicure. Not even that was important to them.

Goo shot between my toes – it wasn't fat and blood but reminded me of cum. Inspection beneath the December morning sunlight shining in through the window revealed the colour to be the same. I thought I would be free of cumshots while I was home for the holidays. Apparently not.

I wiped my foot on the cum-coloured carpet. I doubt my mother had made the connection between the colour and the body substance when she'd picked it. Perfect white for a family that was never dirty. The fuzz of the wool stuck between my toes as lizards, armadillos and spiders hitching rides on turtles streamed past. Only natural fibres for this family.

I went back to the bathroom and grabbed a towel. I wiped and threw it to the floor, taking a clean one with me for any more unfortunate accidents. Mother would pick up the towel without a word. I didn't understand her comprehensive laundry sorting – one small act of rebellion meant the world to me.

I wanted to follow the lizards, armadillos and most of all, the spiders riding the turtles but avoid stepping on them. I figured I could pick up their trail downstairs if I took the other staircase. I ran downstairs, cutting through the house. Nothing unusual, except the silence.

Except it wasn't completely silent.

A low level groaning came from the direction of the main staircase, barely audible. The tree may have been singing its death rattle, pissed off at its being chosen to be adorned with ornaments and cheap tinsel.

The sound was very different to the house shifting and settling. Despite the December chill, I started to sweat. With years of swallowed anxiety, sweat was common. I destroyed many clothes and made sure to purchase multiple garments of the exact same size, cut and colour so my mother and father would never find out. Girls didn't sweat unless they were on the field, the star of whatever sports team they belonged to.

Each drop of sweat danced to the groans. My heart thumped in my chest. I didn't believe anyone was home but I didn't think I was alone either. The cold sweat reached out and grabbed my nightgown. If someone was home, they'd see the sweat drenching the back

The main staircase was in the next room over. Mother kept the doors shut at night but open in the day. They were shut, which would imply that she was still asleep. But I doubted this; snores would have echoed in the hallway – they were the reason my parents slept in separate rooms despite falling in love with each other a bit more every day. She might have gone to the supermarket to pick up extra of everything in case someone unexpected dropped by.

The doorknob was hot. In less than an instant, I pulled my hand away and closed it in a fist. There might be a blister there. I would have to pop it without anyone finding out. Secrecy was common in the perfect family. Big Sis had kept her degree hidden for eighteen months before it was discovered she had no intention of becoming a legal secretary and bagging herself a hotshot lawyer for a husband.

I raised my thick winter nightgown, feeling the chill creep over my piss-free thighs. The groaning was louder behind the door. I didn't think my family would jump out and surprise me with my underwear exposed. I sweated through the thin cotton as well.

The nightgown came to my ankles and allowed me to fold it a few times without taking it off. I wrapped my hand in it to open the door. My lungs were as hot as the doorknob, although I couldn't feel the doorknob anymore through layers of fabric.

It seemed to take forever until I heard the clicking mechanism. The door itself didn't feel hot. I pulled it slowly, breathing my hot breaths, not sure what to expect.

I must have shut my eyes but I only remember the scene when I opened them into the room beyond. I dropped my nightgown. The heat from the doorknob felt nice against my cold sweat.

I could only stare, convinced I was stumbling around in some evil nightmare – the puddle of urine cooling around my body. My mother still kept rubber sheets on my bed in case of any unfortunate accidents.

My thighs didn't feel sticky. If I'd pissed my bed, they would've felt clammy. They didn't even have a coating of cold sweat. The warm air dried all of that away. I forgot for a moment to be perfect. The sight beyond took up too much of my attention to allow space for anything else.

I rubbed my eyes. The action changed nothing except the branches were swaying in different directions to where they were a few seconds before. They didn't exactly look like Christmas tree branches anymore.

Something dripped from the ceiling. Something in the back of my mind reminded me of trucker spunk. It was meant to look like snowflakes from crusty dried semen, but it hadn't dried yet.

The tree moved – or rather the branches did. The trunk stayed still. Each branch went a different direction. I stood mesmerised. Mother would not approve of my gaping jaw but I couldn't shut it.

The tree called to me. Before I could stop my feet, they were halfway across the room. When I became aware of what I was doing, I stopped and backed up being sure to close my mouth.

Without warning, my neck was thrown back and my eyes cast at the ceiling. Covered in what appeared to be a cocoon, I saw the shape of what might have been my little brother. What looked like snakes were wrapped around it. One greeted me with a hiss. Tinsel from the Christmas tree, slithering all over it like snakes.

Something white and creamy dripped onto my forehead landing with a splash. Venom would have been the likely conclusion but I knew it was something else. I closed my eyes against it.

When I opened them again, my head was facing the tree. I was closer. My feet were above the floor. It made me dizzy but, then again, so did everything else in the room.

Rainbow lizards glistened from the tree's tentacles, using their tails as hooks. The tree wasn't special. I believe it was my brother's vomit which had activated it. Whatever it had landed on seemed to have come alive.

The lizards danced when the tentacles moved. Spiders held the legs of other spiders forming into a fancy spider-chain as the snakes were occupied on the ceiling. I don't know where they came from, but it wasn't from my vomit. Big Sis, maybe? She Hadn't choked on as much trucker cock as my brother and me.

A few dangly bits ensured the illusion of cheapness for someone glancing into the window. Every year, no matter how hard my mother and father tried to impress the neighbours, the tree looked tacky. This year was no exception.

Armadillos and turtles weighed more than lizards and spiders. They claimed the lower, fatter tentacles and glistened in the sunlight coming in from the windows.

The tree was pulling me in. I resisted. A battle of wills. Somewhere inside I was hoping this was an hallucination. But I knew it wasn't.

I had to get help. I couldn't run out of the door and to the neighbours. My parents would banish me. I wouldn't even be allowed to sit next to the other skeletons in the closet. I was getting ahead of myself. I couldn't even move, let alone summon help.

More splatter from the ceiling landed in my hair. It was slow to drip – a special sort of non-drying spunk. Wet snow to build an indoor snowman and have that perfect family Christmas my parents insisted upon.

Tentacles reached for my ankles. If my nightgown wasn't so long, they might have reached for my knees or thighs. They missed me by less than an inch. They could grow. I couldn't back away.

Movement was difficult. My pinky was first to break the paralysis. Each part of my body took extra concentration in order to move. Each step back felt like grandma's description of arthritis.

The tree shot white at me – a cumshot to pull me in. It sat heavy on my nightgown but didn't soak through the fabric.

Another painful step back and my foot collided with something. I maintained my balance. It didn't occur to me to take a step to the side. I was too busy concentrating all my thoughts on just moving. I had nowhere to go.

The tentacles grew longer, leaking a white substance and groaning. I tried to step back again but the object was still there. Tentacles reached.

One brushed against my nightgown. The next brushed against my jaw. Without a second thought, I clamped my teeth down. Something worse than even the saltiest of cum rushed into my mouth. It was the largest cumshot I'd ever had. I knew to automatically swallow. That was what the pornstars did and the only way I would ever bag a husband (according to my mother).

Whether it was a defence mechanism of some sort or the thing's actual blood, I didn't care. I swallowed it down like a good girl. I would deal with the repercussions later. I sucked more of the tentacle into my mouth. The tree either didn't notice or didn't know what to do. I was only doing what I had been taught to do.

I couldn't move back but I could move forward and bite and scratch and suck. Instinct prevented me from biting at first. Men hated the biting. If they forced their cocks into my mouth, it was best to close my eyes, suck and get it over with. The few times I'd bit, I'd had my hair pulled out.

The tentacles were defenceless. I leapt without warning and landed in the tree. It would never be my husband but sex was my best weapon.

I felt suction from the tentacles on the back of my neck. It was onto my game. It could play too. Given what had activated it, I was not surprised. I was taking everything in, which would surely haunt my nightmares for years to come but that wasn't my concern at that very moment.

I bit and scratched. The tree withered. The tentacles wept salty tears of white. There was a loud bang behind me. Time slowed down but not enough for me to take in everything that was happening around me.

I heard human screaming. The tree howled, although whether out of fear or a desire to mask the scream I wasn't sure.

I clamped my jaw shut. I would need to practice giving a decent blow job again on a banana before I went back to college. Post tentacle cum-shot, the thing deflated and became rubbery between my teeth.

A struggle came from behind but I was more interested in my own. The tree didn't like biting and scratching. It didn't like being sucked off either but that was not what I wanted to do. Years of forced blow jobs reared their ugly heads. I was angry. A little ball of anxiety and infuriation wrapped in a too-large nightgown.

The tentacle I chomped down on remained as rubber. It oozed clear liquid. The last little drops of ejaculation. I needed to milk that fucker dry.

I dug my nails into another. Any scratch would release an explosive display of jiz. I could feel a pop beneath my fingers. Christmas photos this year would feature me looking less than perfect. Mother would be sure to drop her camera. She wouldn't want reminders of this year.

A tentacle wrapped around my neck, being mindful to stay in the back. Suction pulled at my skin. An injection of something went right through. I couldn't move. It had me.

I could see. I could hear. It was all the more traumatising that way.

Tentacles wrapped around me. When they released, a creamy white substance coated me. Extra-thick cum. It was moist, warm and more than a bit salty.

I could still hear, but the struggle behind me was more than a bit muffled. I had to engage in my own struggle. Biting the substance did no good. I went back to sucking, bring the salt inside me. It was going to take a lot of sucking to escape.

There was movement and a moment later I was hanging upside down. The ceiling was high but not too high. I had a feeling that's where I went, next to the cocoon that was my brother. I could feel the snakes surround me. We were decorative ceiling eggs, hung with tinsel that moved and hissed.

The struggle below was muffled. I wondered who else was battling the tree. I couldn't picture either of my parents with a mouthful of tentacles. If my mother knew how to suck a dick, my siblings and I wouldn't have been here.

I gasped for air as the battle below faded in and out with the movements of what I assumed to be snakes. I couldn't move my arms or legs. Suspended upside down, I could only sway the entire concoction. It seemed like the best way to make it fall from the ceiling. I could only hope I wouldn't break my neck on landing.

It wasn't enough to escape. I set my jaw in determination. Unless the snakes were topping up the cum, I must have thinned it at least a little. I swayed. There was no set order to it. Without being able to move my arms and legs, I couldn't make that sway graceful.

Inhuman hissing rocked me further. A high pitch squeal was the last thing I heard before I lost consciousness. I didn't know what made the noise. I couldn't even guess. There was too much going on.

I was still covered in sticky white cream when I woke up but at least my arms and legs were free. I was propped on the sofa. Nothing broken. Not even in any pain apart from the buried anxiety.

I wiped my eyes. I'm not sure if that made my vision worse or not. Everything was a blur of shapes and bright lights. Steam rose from the floor but that could have been all the cum in my eyes. There were voices but I couldn't make them out.

My mother screamed. It was a short lived sound, lest the neighbours hear.

Someone came with a wet sponge and wiped away the cum. I doubt it was my mother. She would have been too disgusted. I still felt gross. I needed a shower more than anything – a very long and hot one.

My mother's screams cleared the build-up in my ears. I guess she couldn't help it. Maybe she hoped the neighbours were at the supermarket or off to the airport for a bit of winter sun.

"Shut up. I have a headache."

That was my father in a foul mood.

My eyes were cleared. Big Sis was mopping up the mess on my face. My brother was next. He shivered once all the cum was removed. He looked half-frozen. His ordeal in the cocoon had been much longer than mine.

The tree was dead. Red needles carpeted the floor. Bullet holes pierced right through the wall to the outside. Dried spunk snowed on all of us in big flakes. Outside was clear and bright; it was the only snow that Christmas.

The first sirens sounded at the top of the street. My mother started to sob. She wasn't grateful that we'd lived through the ordeal. She was worried the neighbours would see the emergency services at the house. It must have been one of them who'd phoned the police when Big Sis had done the only reasonable thing and shot the tree.

12 DAYS: STOCKING FILLERS   MATTHEW CASH

Pigs In Blankets - Craig Saunders

*'The boar's head in hand bring I,
Bedeck'd with bays and rosemary.
And I pray you, my masters, be merry,
As many as are in the feast...'*

Boar's Head Carol

FLAYED. THAT'S WHAT a sausage looks like without its skin. Roll bacon round it, looks like a shroud, or like it ran a marathon. Burn it, it curls up, like a human might when you set it on fire. Its arms curl in when the muscles contract. The sort of thing you see on the television news, or in Time magazine. Some war-torn country, photo by some lady, correspondent some man, one of them wins an award and there's still a dead, charred corpse someplace.

Christmas isn't about death, or flayed things, or burnt things. It's about birth, too.

Marvin Gregson was born on Christmas. He watched his mother die on Christmas day. Her head turned fat like a sausage as Marvin's father squeezed her neck just as hard as he could. She looked at Marvin the whole time. Marvin chewed, and swallowed, and took another fork full of roast potato, then another. She died, he thought, after around one minute because she didn't seem to see him then. His father kept choking her, though, then he sat down at the head of the table, looked over the carcass of the turkey in the centre, on a dark red piece of cloth which ran the length of a cheap table.

'More gravy, Marvin?'

'Yes please daddy that would be very nice.'

He was ten years old. His mother didn't get any older and when his dad went away Marvin did not look up from his drawing, because his father wasn't making eye contact with him and Marvin knew it was impolite to stare, and that he should say thank you when people gave him things and smile sometimes. He smiled, but Marvin never knew happiness. Not because his mother died when he was ten years old. It was just the way he was built – some part of him left out in the making. His mother told him he was special and he didn't believe or disbelieve her. He had no feelings, no preferences. She spoke words and he understood the meaning of words. They simply weren't important to him, and the way people cried sometimes was a mere curiosity.

The lady from the social services asked if he wanted to maintain contact with his murderer father. Marvin did not. Father, postman, psychiatrist. It didn't matter to Marvin who a man was or wasn't. He didn't wish to see anyone, or not wish to see anyone.

For the next five years, Marvin spent Christmas at three different houses, with three different families. Every one of those people smiled gently. Marvin likened it to being tickled. Half good-natured, half bad-natured. Like pranks, or jokes, or ribbing and the mocking tones children and teachers used with him at school. He knew these things were rude, and he smiled because you smiled when people spoke with you and made eye contact when they looked at you. Not an idiot at all – Marvin was simple stunted. He couldn't remember if he'd been that way when he'd been nine, or seven. At ten...maybe.

Since then he imagined people as nothing more than pigs in blankets. Each time he looked at a person, he saw their throats swollen. Goitre'd, sausage-necked people everywhere he looked.

A not-so nice lady came to one foster home, talked to the older couple with whom he stayed at the time. The older couple had three dogs, one cat, and a bird which could speak. She spoke about taking Marvin to see a 'specialist'.

Autistic Marvin. Marvin's Asperger's. Marvin is unusual. The psychiatrist had a French name and a Swiss accent. His jacket was worn at the sleeves and cuff and collar. He seemed to have just as much trouble looking Marvin in the eye as Marvin once had and the doctor said the names for the way minds work while people nodded and Marvin stared at the pen in a slanted pot on the man's desk. The pen jutted at 88 degrees on the acute side, 92 on the obtuse side. Light came in slanted through slanted blinds. At that moment, Marvin found something he liked. He was fifteen. Something he found a comfort. Not the bulbous, curved and untidy sausage-faced, sausage-people all around, saying words that couldn't be measured because they were curved and turned in on themselves when they got hot. Angles soothed him where words were emotions he could not grasp.

'Marvin is a spectrum, like light, like a rainbow. You're like a rainbow, Marvin,' said another psychiatrist, later, when Marvin was sixteen years old. *'A special, beautiful young man.'*

'Yes sir my mother told me I was special when she died her face looked like a sausage.'

The man smiled but Marvin thought nobody had explained to the man when you should smile and when you should not.

At seventeen Marvin sat seven A-levels in one year, got a huge grant because the Government felt sorry for him, and then went on to Oxford where he learned about mathematics and placed his pencils and pens, his papers, his bed, his clothes, his sheets and cutlery and washing and plates and books and a laptop at angles. A pattern and design haphazard to an outside observer - not to him. Angles became something he could *feel*, and like people who develop or are born with something mis-wired this became a kind of synesthesia, until he began to understand nuance in people's speech once more, translated to him through the language of angles.

Christmases passed.

Twenty-three years old Marvin received his Masters degree. He had never worked. Academia was for Marvin. A man who could understand the outside world but only as an intellectual exercise, and one for which he felt no joy, interest, or need to understand. His twenty-third Christmas he sat with the Dean of Queen's College, Oxford, looking at one of several large tables full of Christmas cheer – the largest Christmas dinner Marvin ever saw, or would. A cloth runner dyed dark red ran along the centre.

'And I pray you, my masters, be merry, as many as are in the feast,' sang a choir.

Chefs, three of them. Marvin knew they were chefs because they wore chef clothing. They carried a boar's head between them. One man sung, his voice obtuse, rotund, even. Behind him, in procession, walked a choir. While Marvin understood the words, the ceremony, the history, he only felt sadness for the boar. Marvin's understanding was crisp and definable – there were no questions, only answers, and each moment, everything which happened every waking second was cosines and tangents and sines, everything definable by three points and distilled to no more than the relationships between those three points. Simplicity. Nothing in life, the world, was more complex than this. Philosophy and sociology and psychiatry. Astronomy, astrology, psychics.

Everything before him – now, the things visible, then, history and emotion – terrene, secular, and as such no more important than dust. In the boar he felt something, at last. Kinship. Spirit.

Speech came in angles from all sides. Everything, each hidden meaning, large and small, cutting into the air like fine lines drawn only for Marvin.

Hello, Marvin.

He stared, instead, at the pigs in blankets. Though they were piled high, he knew there were thirty-six sausages in there, none of uniform shape, or weight, or even composition. He knew there were forty-three slices of streaky bacon, because this was a wealthy table and some were wrapped carelessly like rich people might who didn't care about bacon or money. Skinless sausages. Flayed.

Marvin.

He blinked, turned his eyes from feast to the boar. The boar's eyes, the first Marvin had met in honest curiosity in many years, watched.

The choir which heralded the feast fell silent. Blustering words from ruddy-faced drunk men blew around. The boar's voice was different. More powerful, more beguiling, than those underpinning existence. Not magnetic, nor gravitic. Inside and outside, a thing of the void. The voice of oblivion. Warm. Inviting. The womb of the universe herself.

See my children.

Marvin didn't nod, nor did he have to speak. *The pigs in blankets. Little children. Like babies, almost.* The boar understood him, as he understood it. Very well indeed.

They kill, then wrap them to keep them warm.

The sausages seemed blue. Suffocated. Strangled from their mother. Orphaned flesh, cut away.

A blanket on us to salve the touch of heat on our flayed skins.

Not coddled, these little, dead, pig-parts. Not cuddled or comforted, but dead and burned.

You. Killed by man and wrapped in man.

Dead and broken things merely covered over with blankets like a body in a morgue. The slightest nod to the dead and departed. Decorum but perverse; a body in a morgue lain out under the skin of another.

The choir left when their sick, abase ceremony done. *Here lie the dead.* This is what Marvin heard. *Pull back the sheet, the veil, and see the truth of it...or leave it high so you can sleep at night.*

The boar's eyes drew Marvin back, away from people and their false reality, closer, to the truth he understood - and he *did* understand. Some truths cannot be defined by facts, and pencils, nor angles and mathematics. Truth does not need science.

You are one of the children flayed thus, said the boar.

Am I a trophy?

Marvin felt the orange plucked from his mouth, himself upon a platter and the people cawing around him. Him; charity. They; eaters of carrion.

Truth. Never perfectly spherical, not ellipsoid, not calculable in degrees to the ordinary mind.

You, Marvin, feel nothing but the cold hard geometry of the mind. Would you know more?

Marvin nodded. Such an offer seemed worth a movement, something more than a response of mere thought.

Here is your Christmas, Marvin.

Feast.

Hosannah to the old Gods. Hosannah to the Lords and Ladies.

The walls, the long tables and gowns and the meat stuffed inside flowed away and stone fell aside and trees and grass and bushes grew up all around. Marvin stood in a cold, moonlit night with a great boar beside him and breathed in air crisp and fresh and quiet. A world full of trees and the small sounds of quiet night creatures.

Hunt with me.

The boar moved into the woods and Marvin followed. He saw and smelled that which the boar could, but more. He *felt* it.

I feel.

It was the first time he recognised a thought as his own, or felt the brotherhood of heart and mind. He brought himself low to the ground so the dirt, the sweet stench of it, filled his nostrils, and he ran with the night and the boar underneath the moon and the trees.

The White Hart ran beside him. Above, fairies and Elven kings and the aes sídhe Lords and their Ladies free from their mounds beneath the earth cavorted like of old, across skies new to Marvin.

This is the wild hunt, he thought, and he knew it to be true. He roared, and laughed, and his heart was full of pure joy.

Things of majesty, or those low to the ground and those within the ground, Marvin felt them in him.

You are that child flayed and these blankets they tuck around you while they feast on carrion. Man is not crow or stoat.

Marvin roared, or barked, or howled and ran and tore.

This festival, their houses, their wrappings...they are not truth.

Tooth and nail or claw or hoof.

Worlds and lives are not shapes, are not numbers on Calendars. Mankind is still a beast of seasons, of moons, of chill and warmth, and birth and death.

Blood-warm, bruised jaw and knees and hocks.

Let man bow to his geometry. Join us here. The void is life. The void is death. All is chaos within the turning of a world.

Panting, grinning or just with his tongue lolling from the side of his mouth, his snout.

The void is death and death is truth. Embrace, and know peace.

Marvin kissed the boar on the mouth, the lingering taste of orange bright against his bloodied teeth. Something screamed in fear, something roared in rage, and those sounds were not sharp, or angular. They flowed like seasons and water through long lost groves, grown before men knew of blankets, when boar were kings.

'*The Boar's head I offer,*' he said, holding the Dean's head high before the boar. '*Praise to the Lords and Ladies. Hosannah!*'

Flesh and hide slid down from the boar's head, forming a neck, then haunches, then more.

Marvin's face was covered in gore and blood. Chunks of men hung in tatters from his maw, and flesh clung to the clawed hands. He turned around and round, his trophy in his fist. Grown men screamed and cried and scrabbled over corpses to run, but slipped in blood splashed on century-old flagstones that were hewn from the earth. But they were trappings, too – blankets for children.

The dirt was the earth.

The boar grew, and grew, until it was taller than a man. Bones jutted at the ribs, and the hind legs, where bone grew before flesh. A rank, bestial stench flowed out from it. Marvin held onto the boar-thing's haunch, to steady it, or himself.

Learned men ran, then, and the blood-drench Marvin and his Lord, the flesh-beast, the great Boar, walked over ripped bodies and through the swirled chaos of human-voices.

Outside, the moon shone.

My moon was newer.

It is our moon, thought Marvin. *Yours is gone, Lord.*

The Boar rubbed one heavy shoulder against Marvin.

Yes. The moon. The seasons. Life and death, and always...the hunt. These things belong to us.

The boar's hide thickened beneath the moon. Marvin walked beside it. Sirens screamed like the banshee, heralding the death of men and the return of the earth to the old things.

12 DAYS: STOCKING FILLERS MATTHEW CASH

Driving Home For Christmas - James Josiah

IT WASN'T EVEN CHRISTMAS Eve, that was the day after AND on a Saturday so I didn't have to let them go early at all. I did it out of the kindness of my heart, well that and having them sat around clock watching was annoying me. They hadn't done a stitch of work all day. If you ask me it's bad enough they had Monday and Tuesday off as it was. No one thinks about us poor business owners at all.

Two days, TWO DAYS, the factory was closed because none of the lazy toerags would work. I even offered them double time. But no, they all wanted to be with their families or some nonsense. But I bet you they were all at the sales come Boxing day, spending my money on more crap they don't need. And then they like clockwork, the same as every year, they would have come wanting a raise. The greedy bastards.

AND I took them out for drinks after work. I didn't want to but Stevens said it was the decent thing to do. It's alright for Stevens though isn't it? It wasn't his money he put behind the bar is it? No. It was my mine. My profits they were pissing up the wall.

And of course they were suddenly all comedians, offering to get me drinks.

"This one's on me boss!"
"Let me get this one Mr. R!"
The bastards.

If I had my way I wouldn't make eye contact with, let alone speak to, the staff. If I could replace them with robots I would. That's my dream actually, a work force who doesn't get pregnant, or needs time off. One that doesn't believe in bank holidays, sick pay, time in lieu, or think that fag breaks are a human right. Robots don't need to piss, they don't have "women problems" and they don't cry or threaten legal action. They are utterly perfect unlike that bunch of ungrateful bastards.

I only stayed for a few drinks, four, maybe five, might have been more it wasn't like I was counting. I made sure to stick to the double brandies to get the most out of the tab. I'm not really that much of a drinker but it was the most expensive drink they had and I'd much rather spend my money on me than that shower.

Yes, in this do goody goody politically correct world I was probably over the limit, what ever that means. This country is going to hell. I remember when we ruled the world, we're a bloody laughing stock now. The sooner we take control back from the krauts and frogs the better.

I was top to toe in tailbacks all the way to the motorway. Every idiot in the county in my way trying do some last minute shopping. Because even though the shops have had Christmas crap in since the day after Halloween they had still managed to be caught unawares. I tried to distract myself from the morons and the ever growing urge to piss by putting the radio on. Every single station was playing the same shit songs they do every year. A toothless alcoholic wailing about being a feckless drunk.That Welsh twat wishing everyone a merry Christmas. Everyone! As if that's possible, these superstars live on a different planet. Rich arseholes who have obvioulsy never heard about Kilimanjaro claiming there won't be snow in Africa. There won't be snow in Croydon either but you don't see anyone singing about that.

I turned the radio off and tried to focus on the road. I think I must have been coming down with a cold or something. I was clammy and couldn't really focus properly. Probably caught it off one of the inconsiderate bastards I employ. Why they don't stay at home when they are ill is beyond me.

The motorway was as busy as ever, so much for my tax money being spent on measures to ease congestion. Some little brat waved at me as we sat stationary under signs that told us the speed limit had been reduced to fifty miles an hour. It pulled a face at me, I don't know if he was trying to make me laugh or smile or just amusing himself. Regardless of what it thought it was doing I wasn't playing so I mouthed as clearly as I possibly could that santa isn't real and called him a cunt. Why anyone would want kids is lost on me.

    I got off the road to hell a junction early and decided to try go cross country. For the first time all day something actually went my way. The roads were empty so I put my foot down. Yeah there was signs saying to slow down in the villages. To drive carefully and to think of the children. The way I see it is if your kid is out playing in the road after dark on their own and don't have the sense to understand that getting run over will hurt. Then they deserve whatever happens to them.

    I sped past houses, no doubt council ones, with lights strewn all over them. Each one tackier and more over the top than their neighbour. How these benefit claiming layabouts can afford to put on these tasteless displays every year is criminal if you ask me. It's just further proof how soft this country is. It's not even really their fault, why should they work if we throw money at them just for opening their legs and having as many kids as they can. Most of them don't even know who the dad is half the time. We should bring back national service and only pay out benefits to people who have paid in.

    I'd made up most of the time I'd lost and even though was only a few miles from home I couldn't hold it anymore so I stopped in the Cricketers for a sneaky piss and a nightcap. It used to be a nice little pub did the Cricketers. Was always quiet in there, they did a good roast on a Sunday, there was no TV's on the walls, it was perfect. But then a chain took it over and now it's all pie and a pint for a fiver, quizzes and theme nights. They even got rid of the lounge and put a play area in for the kids. Kids don't belong in pubs, they should be left in the car like dogs with a packet of crisps and a bottle of coke.

    It was full of pissed up arseholes. All singing along to the same crap that was on the radio. It's as if you're only allowed to listen to a dozen songs come December. I swear it's the only way some of the old codgers who haven't been outed as nonces yet make any money. I only stayed for one as the temptation to smash my glass in someone's face was starting to overwhelm me.

As I was getting in the car some busybody asked me if I thought I should be driving. I told them to piss off and mind their own business. They said they were going to report me, I said if they didn't fuck off I was going to run them over. They got out of the way so I chalked it up as a win. It was no doubt them that grassed on me. You can't trust anyone these days.

It had been a long day and I wanted my bed so I floored it out of the car park and headed home. I could see the house, that's how close I was and there she was. Just stood in the road waving her arms like some type of idiot. Now I'm nobody's fool, I've read all about these types of things. How they get some young girl to flag people down and then they carjack you. Or how she gives you some sob story and asks for a lift into town and then tells you she'll say you raped her if you don't give her money. The world is full of bastards, all out for themselves, you need to be careful.

If we're being honest, I wanted to give her a bit of a scare so I left it right until the last minute before I tried to swerve around her. I only clipped her. The stupid bitch knocked my wing mirror off. Brand new Jag, I'd only had it a few months as well. I put it through the books at work and wrote it off as an expense. The Police said her name as Anya or Aneta or some other assault on the tongue. She probably shouldn't even have been in the country. I didn't even see her car in the hedge, so how I was meant to know her were kids in there? Who takes their kids out and about at that time of night anyway. Honestly some people are unbelievable.

The Food Chain - Andrew Bell

I DIDN'T KNOW ANYTHING about Dan Stephens even though we had worked for the same firm for almost ten years. Maybe it was better that way? My name is Jake Campbell, but Dan just knew me as a shirt who answered the phones and dealt with irate customers when they didn't get their orders on time. So when he gave me the envelope of cash I immediately agreed to the job. When he promised that more would come my way once the job was done I almost soiled myself.

As I said, we had worked for Wade and sons Ltd, a meat and farming-produce company, for almost a decade. Not once had we exchanged a civil word; not as much as a good morning, an acknowledging nod of the head, or even a wink of an eye in the hallway.

It was December 20th, not long to the big day. The girls in the office were humming old Christmas classics, hanging baubles from the small tree we erected year after year; to put it mildly no work got done.

Dan was up there with the management, looking down from his ivory tower. To him I was worth less than chicken grain; which is why he probably chose me. If anything happened to me then, I guess, I wouldn't cost anybody a night's sleep. Stephens didn't like me; I gathered that from the outset. He sort of looked me up and down that day when we met at the cafeteria two streets away from the office. It was like he was appraising a new pet dog in a pet shop window; as If he had just noticed me after so many years of sharing the same air. He was just checking me out, I could understand that. He didn't have to make me feel so small and naked, I thought. Was any amount of money worth feeling so insignificant for? When you're talking twenty grand the answer is fuckin' A!

Late-night shoppers huddled together and negotiated the slippery paths, passing the cafeteria window, stepping through icy puddles and muddy doorways to get to the bright, neon-lit interiors of the shops. Old Christmas songs came from overhead speakers. The old tunes you just couldn't escape from. Their voices were high pitched, and the laughter filled the air. It had been snowing for almost three weeks now, and it was set to fill the skies for a further month or so. I sat waiting for Dan to turn up. I had the envelope of cash in front of me, and I couldn't stop fanning through the wedge of lovely money; wondering about all of the things I could do with it. I yawned, feeling a small tear trickle down my cheek. It was getting late and I just wanted to get away from the human traffic, switch on the television, and fall asleep. You see? You grabbed the opportunity when it came by, it was as rare as gold dust. God worked in mysterious ways, and so did we.

In London we don't sleep. I'm not a cosmopolitan person at all, but I know enough to know that when it comes to busy, then it never lets up. When your head hits the pillow, the guy in the next flat is getting ready for work. And around and around it goes. I wasn't really looking forward to Christmas Day. I didn't even have enough cash to treat Beverley to a dinner at the Tavern, our local pub, that was, until Stephens wanted me to kill somebody. I hadn't as far as pulled the wings off of a fly before. How on Earth did he expect me to pull this off without having a complete nervous breakdown?

'Everything you need to know is in here,' he said, treading quickly, breathlessly, into the cafeteria, putting a second envelope next to the one containing the cash. I was shocked at his sudden intrusion. He looked flustered and uncomfortable as though his very presence here could jeopardise his reputation. Then he pushed it towards me. I was about to open it when he pressed it to the table, his eyes wild and sparkling. 'Are you fucking crazy?' Before I could do a thing he grabbed the envelope of money, it disappeared in his jacket pocket. 'I want you to *think* about this first. No half-arsed decisions, understand?'

I felt like a child that had just been deprived of its favourite sweet. I picked up the remaining envelope and put it in my pocket.

'She's killing *me*. You will never understand how that feels. I just…can't trust her anymore. What I can't control, I don't trust. Understand?'

Stephens took a long look at me before turning to leave. When I heard the bell above the door I relaxed a little, and finished my coffee. This could really change my life, I thought, staring at the shadows as they passed the window. I'd never hurt somebody, but I needed the money. For that I don't think anyone would see me in a bad light.

'Why did you pick me?' I remember asking him, as I sat beside him in the work's canteen. 'You don't so much as acknowledge my existence, then you spring this kind of thing on me? Why not one of your shit-for-brains friends?'

'Because, Jake? Is that your name?' he replied, lowering his voice, 'you have nothing to lose. I don't know you and you don't know me. It's the way I like it. One of my buds gets caught, it's game over for him. You on the other hand-'

'I get it, I get it, and merry fucking Christmas to you too,' I said, sipping from a bottle of fizzy orange.

'Just do this for me, and you won't see me again.'

'Sounds good to me.'

'Best of all, I won't have to look at your ugly face ever again either. And remember, you don't know me and I don't know you. Understand?'

No half-arsed decisions. As if I even needed to think twice about the whole thing? My mind was already made up. I thought about what he wanted from me, and what I stood to gain, what Bev and I would gain.

When I got home I locked the door behind me and pulled off my coat. On the coffee table I poured out the contents of the envelope, then went to the kitchen and switched on the kettle. As I was waiting for it to boil I checked my mobile phone. There was a message there. I smiled when I read it.

Looking 4wd to my lil' tigr 2mro night

Xxx   Bev

The kettle came to the boil and I made myself a coffee. Carrying it through to the lounge I sat down to look amongst the scattered pieces of paper, to find what I was really looking for: a photograph, anything that would help. There were telephone numbers, and places she might hang out. Nothing that could really help me. He didn't even give me a name. Hell, for all I knew, she might not even be female!

'She's killing *me*...' I remembered his words, the sudden look of pain and longing in his eyes. This woman was indeed hurting him, I just couldn't understand how. I mean, he must be around six feet tall, built like a brick shit house door. If it was his heart she was hurting…hell, he fooled me because I didn't even know he had one. I've never known someone so highly opinionated as him. I even remember a member of staff running from the meeting room in tears after he had shot one of her ideas down.

I gathered the pieces of paper and put them back in the envelope. I felt the coffee warm my empty stomach, heard it growl.

I had to think this through, I decided; needed to clear my head. Sitting in front of a computer screen day in and day out was frying my brains.

'Fuck it, lil' tiger's going out,' I said, grabbing my coat and closing the door behind me.

Beverley knew how to ease my aches and pains, I thought, grinning. Although we don't get to spend so much time together, when we grab *some* time, it's what I would call quality; with a capital Q. You know what I do, but she works evenings at a local call centre. We had planned to start our Christmas shopping. I had spied a small necklace in a shop window. It was a small sapphire surrounded by sparkling diamonds. I knew it was the one. Dan's money would help, I thought, my smile getting smaller. But...murder?

All kinds of crazy thoughts went through my mind. What if everything went wrong and I get caught. Dan said I had nothing to lose. Maybe he was right- but I do have something to lose: Bev. What if we never saw each other again? What if Dan's money *changes* me? I heard that cash can do that. Lottery winners sometimes regretted their fortunes, wishing they were back at square one; penniless and dreaming. They missed wanting things they knew were just beyond their grasp. This could change all of that. But I knew that soon Dan would pick somebody else from the office cess pool. I had to calm down.

Then...

'You have to cool down, sweets,' I told her as she breathlessly sat down in the chair beside me. I already had the drinks and the packets of crisps.

She wriggled out of her coat and opened her snacks, looking round the bar. 'Quiet, isn't it?'

'Just the way I like it,' I said, sipping my beer. The cold, evening air radiated from her, and I shivered. I had to tell her about Dan, I couldn't reveal his name but I knew that it was clawing down my back. This would be a Christmas like no other.

'Okay, I've got something to tell you,' I said, taking a gulp of my beer. I needed it. 'It's pretty big, and it could change everything. You might run away when I tell you, you might wish that you had never laid eyes on me. You might even regret us. I just want you to know that I love you, and I want us to do this together.'

'Sounds really heavy,' she said, smiling radiantly. 'I like it already,' she added, giving my shoulder a gentle nudge.

'You won't when I tell you,' I said quietly, looking sheepishly around the room.

'I promise,' she whispered, drawing in closer before kissing me gently on the lips, before I felt her tongue lick mine. 'I will be there for you.'

I smiled, kissing her, tasting the wax of her lipstick.

'One condition,' she said, suddenly breaking the kiss.

I nodded.

'Everything you just said?' she asked. 'You have to return the promise.'

'What about it? What part-'

'The whole part-'

'Bev, what are you saying?'

'I don't think beer will be on the menu for a while,' she said, pushing the glass away. 'About, let's say...nine months.'

Always being slow on the uptake, I just nodded and sipped my drink. After a few seconds the penny finally dropped. 'Are you fucking kidding me? We're having a baby? Really?'

She searched my face for uncertainty, but there was none. I jumped up, knocking the table over. Beer and crisps spilled everywhere. The locals turned about in their seats, some frowned and others just shook their heads and carried on with their conversations.

'We're having a baby!' I shouted, picking Beverley up in my arms and spinning her around and around. Bar staff and the other drinkers now understood our jubilation and started to applaud us. 'I love you,' I whispered to her, kissing her like it was for the first time.

That's when we heard the voices. In seconds we stood at the door of the Tavern, Beverley leaning back in my chest, enfolded in my arms. She looked up at me as we listened to the carollers sing 'silent night, holy night.' Her eyes were so brown they looked almost black. Snowflakes gently drifted through the cold winter air, and I couldn't remember a time I had felt so happy.

The next day I knocked on Dan's office door, opening it without invitation.

'Come in-' said a voice.

I went in and came straight to the point. 'This is no joke? You want me to kill somebody?'

Dan put down his phone without another word, got up off his chair and grabbed me by the elbow, lowering his voice.

'What the fuck are you saying?' He looked through a chink in the office curtain. Satisfied that nobody could eavesdrop he looked straight at me.

'This little job you want doing,' I said, 'the price has just gone up.' Blood was pounding in my head now. I can't remember the last time I felt this kind of rush.

'You're not in a position to negotiate-'

'You'll *never* be able to understand just how much I need the money,' I said, trying to lower my voice, but it wasn't working. 'You have money and you know the price of everything but don't know the value-'

'Did you think up this little speech on the bus here this morning?'

'It's two hundred grand or no deal,' I said flatly, before approaching the door. 'Remember, you can ask someone else to do your dirty job,' I added, my heart beating harder than ever, 'but when a body mysteriously turns up somewhere, then a little certain story will turn up for the police.'

'I guess that leaves me no choice, does it?' he said after a long, painful time. Then he smiled at my audacity. 'Don't even think about mentioning names.'

'We don't exist to one another, I understand.'

With that I left the office. With the panel at my back I found that I could breathe again, his last words going over and over in my mind with disbelief.

On my way home, the wind and rain rocking my car, I wondered how I would tell Beverley. We were going to start a family, we had to be totally transparent with each other; no secrets.

'Look, I'm going to kill someone,' I said, my hands grabbing the steering wheel. 'Are you okay with that?' There were many ways that the conversation could go. There could be tears, slammed doors; even one of us running away into the street. 'Whatever you do, don't tell another soul,' I tried. No, that wouldn't work, I thought, steering the car into my street. How about I tell her that we have the best opportunity *ever* and that this chance won't come by a second time? Perfect. I smiled, getting out of the car. I couldn't be plainer than that. Hell, it just might work. That night I would tell her.

I got take out, our favourite pizza: pepperoni. It would be here soon, just in time for her shift to end. The beers were for me, Coke for her. As they chilled in the fridge I went over and over my speech, but I decided to just come out with it.

Bev's shift at the call centre ended in twenty minutes, I thought, the wall clock reading nine forty. Okay, everything will be fine, I tried to convince myself.

I watched the first snowflake fall. In minutes the whole street was a white, untouched blanket. I looked at the car and thought how easy it would be to pick her up from work, but like always, she said she would make her own way here. The wind was starting to pick up too. Maybe heading out would be a bad idea, I thought. Then there was a knock at the door as the grub had arrived. I opened the box and immediately started to salivate.

Finally she arrived. I felt the cold night wind breathe through the flat as she opened the door. I helped her take off her coat, and I knew that tonight our whole lives were about to change forever.

'This is nice,' she said, turning around to give me a hug.

She was referring to the small spread I had prepared. The Tartan blanket was a little ragged around the edges but it served as a cosy picnic surface. A bottle of beer and Coke were chilling in a small ice bucket, and a box containing our pizza was open, steaming, and waiting for us. In no time we tucked in.

We talked about the weather, how awful our day had been, even hinting about possible gifts we were hoping Father Christmas would drop down our chimney this year. The radio played all the golden hits, and we enjoyed each-other's' company like it was back in the earlier days when we first met.

Although my heart was beating dangerously fast, blotches appearing before my eyes, I decided to ask her.

'I need to ask something of you,' I said quietly, one hand holding a half wedge of pizza, the other was resting on her stomach, where a future was growing. 'I wanted to tell you that night at the pub, but that kind of went out of the window.' We both giggled and kissed each other slowly. I wanted her so badly, but I had to get this out there. First business then pleasure. 'But seeing as though we are having a little dumpling I wanted to be completely open with you–'

'Ahhh, the news that would send me running away, regretting we ever met? That news?' she said, sipping from her Coke.

I nodded.

'You know I love you, right? *We* love you,' she whispered, placing a hand over mine, over our baby. 'I want us to be together forever.'

'Okay, I'm going to get this out there,' I said. 'How would you like to make two hundred grand?'

'Are you fucking kidding me?' she said, her eyes lighting up. She hugged me even tighter. Then she slowly loosened her grip, and looked me in the eye. 'Hold on, is this…you know, legal?'

I shook my head, then told her about the manager at work, remembering his last command. Hell, I wouldn't mention his name to the devil himself. I told her everything. What he wanted me to do, she already knew how much we stood to gain; the *three* of us stood to gain. Yet we could lose everything too, if it all went awry.

'I'm scared,' I told her.

'Why?' she took my hand and placed it on her stomach again. 'Think of what we could buy for the baby, what a great start this could be for all of us. I know it's fucking extreme, Jesus, it's murder for crying out loud, but think about the money…just think.'

'We can do it,' I said.

'I know you're scared, so am I, but we can do it,' she said. 'But we do it as a team, okay? We do it properly. Who do we, *you know*?'

I shrugged.

'What's this?' she said, mimicking my motion. 'Well, hadn't you better find out?'

I don't think I've felt so scared. My blood ran cold and my hands shook as I sent Dan a text message. It read:

Dan, I've given this a lot of thought, and I want the opportunity. I was a little aggressive regarding the fee. Believe me I have my reasons. The envelope does not contain a picture. A face, a place, that's all I need. I swear nobody will know about this. J.

Almost an hour passed as we waited for his reply. It was the longest, most uncomfortable hour we had known. The radio was just an irritable distraction now, and I motioned for Bev to turn it off. The pizza and the drinks were gone, and I almost had a heart attack at the trident bleep of my phone. We looked at each other, eyes wide, our heads throbbing as if they were about to explode. I slowly crossed the room and picked up my phone. The message icon was flashing; a little friendly envelope that any other time would have been a welcoming alert. Now it looked so callous and solemn.

'Well?' said Bev, putting her arms around me. I felt her lips against my neck, the hairs rising at her touch.

I pressed the icon.

Download this then destroy your SIM card. You don't need a name. Meet me tomorrow night AFTER it's done. Midnight. Bring her body to the Docklands and you get what you want. D

There was a long collection of numbers and letters, but it was in fact something I could work with. All I needed to do was download it. We looked at each other, our hands touching her stomach as if for encouragement.

'Almost a quarter of a million,' she whispered, then kissed me once more.

It didn't take me long to hook up my laptop. I typed in the numbers, then my finger hovered above the RETURN button.

Beverley nodded, I felt her arm get tighter around my shoulders.

So I closed my eyes and pressed RETURN.

That's when I felt the coldness of the room as she quickly backed away from me. When I opened my eyes once more there was an image on the screen, a face. Beverley's face.

'No,' she whispered, her eyes wide, tears already trickling down her cheeks. 'This can't...this can't be... real.' She had backed up against the wall and had slowly started to curl into a ball on the floor.

I slowly turned around in my seat, eyes unbelieving, head throbbing with shock and fear. Although my chest was tightening like the onset of a heart attack, I felt the air in my lungs. 'Why has he sent me...a picture of you?'

'Think of the baby-'

I sprung from my chair and grabbed her up from the floor, but she was heavy and loose in my grip. 'Don't give me that think about the baby, shit!' I shouted. I wanted to hit her, believe me how much I wanted to. Instead I let her alone, and backed away. The sweat was pouring down my back, sticking my shirt to my skin. I needed a drink and quick, so I walked through to the kitchen. I knew I had a bottle of Vodka somewhere. After what seemed like an eternity I found one. It was cheap and nasty and there was about an inch left in the bottom, but as I poured it into a glass and devoured the fiery liquid, it felt really good.

'Better start talking, Bev!' I shouted over my shoulder, closing my eyes as I felt her scrutiny, eyes burning like lasers on the back of my neck.

'I...didn't... know that Daniel was your boss,' she said. 'Of all the years I have been married to him-'

'Married?' My eyes shut tightly at the mention of the word.

She didn't reply but I knew she had nodded. I felt every moment we had spent together had been one long fucking joke.

'You think this is funny, do you? Making fun of the little guy. No wonder you never let me pick you up at work...you were wiping him off you, not letting me know your love for him-'

'What? You're insane- I love you, Jake. Me and Dan, we-'

'The baby could even be his,' I said, turning to look at her.

She shook her head, tears falling. 'No, this is ours, I swear-'

'YOU SWEAR? Why the hell should I believe you?' I said, spittle flying from my mouth. I crossed the room in two strides and grabbed her by her throat. 'You know what he once said to me, huh?'

She shook her head, grasping my hands, trying to loosen my finger's grip.

'He once said that she was killing him. I suppose he was talking about you. He couldn't trust you.'

'Please, Jake,' she managed to say, gasping for air. 'We are-'

'A family? Convince me I'm doing the wrong thing. Tell me that offing you isn't the best thing that I could do. You and the bastard-'

I felt the slap against my face, and saw the flash.

I let her go, and she stood in front of me.

'I love you,' she said breathlessly. 'I was biding my time, waiting for the moment to end it all with Dan- YOU DON'T HAVE TO BELIEVE ME! Remember a couple weeks ago when I had the bruise on my leg? I told you that I slipped on some ice. I lied; he kicked me! Now I'm walking out of here and we won't ever have to see each other again.'

'Beverley,' I said, grinning. 'If you go, then I have nothing left to lose.'

She backed away from me, but I grabbed her by the scruff of the neck.

His car was right where he said it would be, and the midnight hour was approaching. The exhaust fumes wafted at the cold December air. The Docklands was deserted, except for the occasional seagull pecking at some morsel on the ground. Lights blinked on the horizon, I think it could be ships communicating. I could be wrong; I saw this through tears. My heart beat slowly and I felt as though it would be torn from my soul at any given moment. I wanted to drive my car into the sea. That's how low I felt. Money *does* change a person. It grabs you with its dirty fingers and it plays around with your mind, your very being. Makes monsters of men. I was no exception.

I jumped as I heard the tap on my window.

'You don't have a fucking clue, do you?' I said, not even giving him the chance to say a word. I guess it was another little speech I had prepared but I needed to get the pain out of my chest. 'You don't know how far…a person…like me is…willing to go…' I was choking with sobs.

'Show me-'

'JUST GIVE ME THE MONEY!' I shouted, eyes forward, fingers gripping the steering wheel. 'Are you scared, eh? Do you even *know* how that feels? Well I'm terrified. I'm absolutely terrified. Throw me the cash and you'll have the body,' I said, almost choking on the words.

He wasn't used to being spoken to this way, I knew that. He was used to making demands and getting exactly what he wanted. I had kept the end of the bargain, I wondered just how much of a big guy he was to hold his end up. I felt the envelope hit the passenger seat.

'Count it, it's all there-'

I opened my door and swung out of the seat, brushing past him as I made my way around the back of the car. As I opened the door, I turned to him, and he almost jumped back with the look upon my face. We were nose to nose, almost touching.

'You and your kind are dead to me,' I spat. 'Dead, understand?'

I lifted the bundle from the car. It was heavy, falling to the floor with a dull thud.

'There you go…as agreed,' I gasped.

He looked down at the body.

I stepped over the shape and went back to my car, but before I got inside, I grabbed a small package from the glove compartment and passed it to him. He caught it and looked at me questioningly.

'Congratulations, you're a father,' then I got behind the wheel and sped away, my eyes filling with tears again.

Dan finally understood what I meant and dropped the package, a look of disgust on his face. Blood began to pool about the packages. He felt the first needles of rain tap his cheek when he reached for his dead wife.

I can't even describe the pain of the tears. It was like my head was going to implode. My jaw tightened, I felt the hair on my scalp, its skin shift. And through those tears I started to smile. I wiped them away with my sleeve, thinking of the money and how it would change everything. My sobs became a different sort of noise, like laughter. Before I knew it I could barely breathe.

'Shhh,' came a familiar voice from beneath a blanket in the back seat. Beverley poked her head free, smiling brightly, eyes twinkling in the darkness. 'You'll wake the baby.'

Dan's fingers were shaking, but not from the cold. He was excited but also remorseful as he tore at the bloody package on the pavement. He stopped for a second to compose himself, to breathe. Blotches appeared before his eyes for a second as he calmed down. Then he realised something. The package.

'No,' he ripped through its edges. 'This can't be happening- NO!'

The package was just plain old meat, and it had a very familiar label. He looked over at the baby, and tore at the package. But it too was just bloody meat. As he looked at the card he didn't know whether to laugh or cry. It said:

With compliments from WADE AND SONS LTD, your best choice for the best meat!

12 DAYS: STOCKING FILLERS   MATTHEW CASH

Silent Night - Fiona Dodwell

Christmas Eve, Present Day

OUTSIDE, BEYOND THE WARMTH *of the place he called home, the air was crisp with a sharp, uninviting chill. Snow fell in light drifts, dancing and twinkling as the street lamps shone against their tiny surfaces. It made them look, to him, like distant stars across the darkening night.*

Toby Arnold peered out, eyes squinting at the view beyond his bedroom window, and took in a deep breath. Anticipation. Anxiety. He always felt this way at Christmas time. It brought back memories, like a coffin being pulled from the ground. All earth and ashes, wiped away, ready to bring the dread back home. And that's what it truly was – it was dread.

Toby withdrew his hand, letting the curtains fall back into place, sealing the night outside and heading back over to the bed. That vast, empty space that should be shared with his wife.

His ex-wife, who had taken his daughter and moved to the other side of the world.

Yes, that was another thing that was destroyed because of what happened all those years ago, on that one Christmas he would never forget, that time he would never be allowed *to forget.*

Toby slipped beneath the covers and pulled the thick, red duvet up to his chin. Enjoying the warmth, he slid further down and then closed over his eyes, trying to find the tug of much needed sleep. The memories, though, they stirred beneath the surface, like sharks rising from the depths of still water. That irresistible pull toward what happened then, bringing a heaviness that not only kept him awake, but kept him playing the memories over and over in his mind, like repeated scenes from an old horror movie. A penny dreadful, but one grounded in cold, hard reality.

Christmas Eve 1955

Toby Arnold was seven years old the first time he saw Santa Claus, and it was the *real* Santa Claus, not the over-dressed, fake-bearded staff members that store chains hired over the Christmas season. This was the real thing, so horribly, vividly different from any of the depictions he had seen in any book, film or poster in his entire, short life on earth. The expectation existed then, that when your childhood hero presented himself, he would be red and cheerful with cold-kissed cheeks and a wide grin, the ho-ho-ho of a million childhood dreams abundant and enticing.

The reality, when it actually came, was something different altogether.

His mother and father, full from their evening meal, were waiting for the approach of twelve, to drive over to St Peter's Church on the corner of Thymes Street for midnight mass. Not Catholic, not in any way religious at all, Toby's parents reserved their visits to church for the holiday seasons, when to keep a polite and respectable face amongst their peers meant to attend church when it apparently mattered: Easter, Christmas, the occasional baptism and wedding.

They were good people, though; Toby knew and understood at least this much, even at the age of seven. He had asked them to take him to church, and despite the occasion, they decided to leave without him, instead paying Casey Chalmers the double-rate babysitting fee for the next two hours of their absence.

According to them, midnight mass was too late for a young boy. And besides, they had said with sly smiles, it would be a risk if Santa was to fly by early. Would he not think the family gone, away on holiday, if he was to come and find the place empty of all life? Would he leave, without dropping off the promised gifts Toby was eagerly waiting for?

That had been enough for the young boy's pleas to die down. He couldn't risk that. He agreed to stay home, and listen out for the bells of Santa's sleighs as they travelled across town and to each and every home.

His bedroom was dressed in shadows, the curtains parted ever so slightly, allowing in the moon's illumination. Toby had brushed his teeth, pulled on his blue and green dinosaur pyjamas and switched off the bedside lamp, before climbing into bed.

The door was closed, but from downstairs he could hear Casey Chalmers on the phone, talking animatedly to her boyfriend. Running up his mother's bill – that much he was sure of. He knew it had to be her boyfriend on the line, because her words would not fit a relationship of any other kind. She giggled, she spoke about a night out together, she muttered words about missing him. Beyond that, Christmas carols swam into the night from the stereo his mother had left on, the volume low but not so low that he couldn't catch the words as they drifted towards him...*Silent night, holy night, all is calm, all is bright.*

He wondered how late his parents would be, and then his thoughts turned to Santa Claus himself. Father Christmas. The one person he considered to be his hero, his inspiration. And how could he *not* be? The man who lived forever, who made toys all year around, who could fly through the night sky and know the thoughts and wishes of every person the world over. That was somebody who mattered. Every kid's dream.

He closed over his eyes. If he could just sleep right now, then morning would come quicker, wasn't that what his mum said at night, if he was excited about something? "Fall asleep as quick as you can, then tomorrow will come in the blink of an eye!"

Sleep would not come, though. Not now.

He was too excited.

He was looking forward to the robot building kit he was sure Santa would bring. He was unbearably desperate to see the bundle of board games he was expecting to receive. Would he get the ones he asked for? Would his friends at school get what they asked for?

Toby pursed his lips, his chubby hands clasped together, as if in prayer.

Please Santa, hurry up!

He heard a loud bang from downstairs, the stereo abruptly falling silent. The scratch of the record player as it swung from the vinyl. Then, a noise like falling, like tumbling. A thud.

Casey's voice, producing words that were so wild and panicked that he couldn't even make them out. What was she shouting? What was happening down there?

Toby felt the flesh on his arms and back crawl with goosebumps and he whimpered as the house fell silent. He clutched at his duvet and hunkered down, listening, his ears straining. Had Casey had an accident? Something very bad had happened, he felt certain of it. The air had turned colder, the shadows of his room suddenly appeared sinister to him, as if they were cloaking a thousand watchful eyes.

The house was filled with a deadly, irrevocable silence.

Toby released the breath he realised he'd been holding and then lifted his head. He looked around the room: everything was still. Then, he heard it. Soft footfalls on the hallway stairs, creeping closer, moving slowly.

Toby shuddered, his hands clutching at the edge of the duvet tightly and he squirmed, his mouth turned down, his eyes wide.

Who was it? His parents hadn't returned yet - he hadn't heard their car arrive back. Was it Casey, after all, coming up to say sorry for making a noise? Was she playing a mean trick on him? It wouldn't be the first time. He remembered a few months back, she'd hidden in his wardrobe and jumped out when he returned to his room from the bath. Back then, he wasn't used to her playful ways – he sulked all night, unhappily pouting and not answering any of her questions.

The footsteps became louder as they ascended the stairs and he winced, frightened, suddenly wishing he'd dashed for the wardrobe himself, to hide in, or pushed himself under the bed. Whoever it was, they were coming. They were close.

Peering toward the door, his eyes found the gap between the floor and the edge of the door – he could see two thick, wide shadows beneath. The outline of feet.

Somebody was standing right outside his bedroom.

Toby let out an involuntary yelp and then lifted one hand across his mouth, to stop himself.

There came three, loud raps on the door. Slowly, steadily.

Knock. Knock. Knock.

Toby shuddered and then, seeking out every inch of bravery he could muster, he cleared his throat and then called out. "Who is there?" He ducked back under the cover, like a tortoise wincing into his shell, only his eyes visible beneath the blanket.

"Ho, ho, ho, Toby Arnold! It's Santa Claus. I've come to see you!"

Toby smiled momentarily, but his joy flickered and faded fast. This was not the jolly, sing-song voice of the Santa on television. The voice was thick and low, it almost rippled, as if whoever was speaking was beneath water. The voice sounded *wet*.

Toby saw the feet beneath the doorway shift slightly, and then the voice returned. That grovel of a voice that crumbled and wheezed. "I'm a-coming-in-to-seeeeeee-you, my Toby," the voice rang out, and then a laugh.

Toby immediately thought of his Aunt Meetall, who had smoked a pack of cigarettes a day since she was 15. Her voice always sounded crackly and damaged. Toby smiled. It was probably just his dad, playing a trick on him. It had to be. Maybe they just parked the car up the road, so he wouldn't hear them return after midnight mass -

Knock. Knock. Knock. "TOBY!" The voice boomed. The whole room seemed to shudder and vibrate, the voice seemed unnaturally loud.

Toby knew then, more than anything he understood in the world, that this was no joke. This was real.

He pulled the blanket away from him and sat up onto the edge of his bed. He looked over at the chest of drawers to the right of the door and decided the only thing to do was pull the drawers across the doorway, to stop whoever it was getting inside, stop him getting to *him*.

Toby climbed out of bed, the cold night air hitting with a bite. He stepped over as quietly as he could. He was almost in reach of the drawers when the bedroom door swung open with a loud creak.

He screamed, gasping, his hands covering his mouth, and ran towards the other side of his room, his back to the wall, staring at the Santa *thing* that was now stepping inside the bedroom.

His profile filled the room, the hallway light flooding in and allowing Toby glimpses of his physique. He was tall, impossibly tall, and wide, so that he almost filled the door frame. His beard looked dark, his eyes round and black, with no colour in them at all. He was dressed in shadows cast from the furniture, but Toby could see his baggy trousers and jumper were green - bright green. There was something else, though: it was covered in red, thick blotches.

Blood?

Toby groaned, finally letting his hands fall away.

"Ho, ho, ho, Toby! I'm Santa Claus! I've come to claim my gift!" He laughed, his belly rising and falling, and he placed a gloved hand across his rotund stomach.

"Wh-who are you?" Toby finally stuttered, finding his voice. His back was still against the wall, his hands now clenched at his sides. His ears strained, listening out for the approach of his dad's car, but all was silent around him. Where was Casey? *Where was she?*

The man laughed again and then shook his head. He pouted, almost playfully. "Aren't you listening, young Toby? Silly, silly Toby! I'm Santa. And I'm here to receive my very own special present..." his voice trailed off, and he took a step further into the room, nearer to the child.

Toby groaned again, shook his head. "Please go. Where is Casey?" The room was filled with an acrid scent, like rotting meat, of something decaying and dying. Toby couldn't articulate it, but it smelled awful, of something evil.

It was emanating from the intruder.

The man reached a hand out and slapped the light on, whacking the switch with his gloved fist.

Light reached the room and Toby's eyes settled onto the

details of the one who stood before him.

The red stains across his green outfit were splattered across him in wide, thick splodges, in certain places there were fine mists of red. He looked him up and down, noticing the big, black boots and the large black belt across his waist. Then, his eyes landed on the man's face. The eyes. *Those eyes.* Black holes of nothingness. They looked like black marbles, there was no iris, no white, only round discs of black. If eyes were the window to the soul, as his dad had once said, then this being before him was nothing but skin and bone, no soul at all within.

Toby yelped, felt tears springing to his own eyes.

The man chuckled, taking another step forward.

"If you come downstairs, I'll show you your present, Toby," he said, his lips curled into a snarl.

Toby shook his head no.

"Come downstairs.... *NOW* TOBY!" the man shrieked. As his voice bellowed across the room, books and papers rattled on shelves, the chair in the corner of the room rocked slightly, papers flew from his art desk and landed across the floor.

The room turned icy cold. Those black eyes narrowed sharply on him.

Reluctantly, scared and uncertain about what the man might do – the man, who surely couldn't be Santa, but who also couldn't be a normal human – was like no one he had encountered. He was evil. He was like a man made of the darkest shadows, Toby thought, remembering a demon figure from one of his comic books. Men like this, they were never good. You could never trust them. What choice did he have?

Toby nodded. "Okay. I'll come down with you," he said,

his voice trembling.

Mum and dad – where are you? His mind raced, his heart thudded wildly in his chest. He felt sick then, his stomach churning.

The man turned, ducking out of the room slowly, and began descending the stairs, two at a time. He was big – no, massive – a terrible, unusual size.

Toby blinked back his tears and followed the man down, his small hand clutching at the bannister. He peered towards the hallway as they reached the lower half of the stairs: no sign of Casey. The front door was closed over, the latch in place. How had the man gotten in? Had Casey let him in? Toby was sure nobody had knocked at the front door.

Maybe he climbed down the chimney, a little voice inside his mind suggested, and Toby shivered, goosebumps slithering across his skin.

They reached the bottom of the steps. The nearer he got to the man, the stronger the rotten smell was - thick and suffocating. Toby retched, raising a hand to his mouth. They arrived at the mouth of the lounge, the archway an open space into the living area, his mum's favourite room.

He screamed, and felt pee dribbling warmly between his legs and soaking into his pants as he took in the scene before him. Casey was tied to the rocking chair that was usually positioned to the right of their fireplace. She was bound with rope, and her arms, legs and stomach area were covered in thick, red stains of blood. Her eyes were wide, and she was trying to speak, trying to say something, but a huge wad of tape was across her mouth and stifling her words.

Santa stepped in, closer to the young teenage girl. He bent low and sniffed, like an animal taking in the scent of prey.

Toby looked around the room. What could he do? Should

he throw something? Try to run away? The room was as it always was, except for Casey and her imprisonment to the chair. The fireplace was not lit, mostly his parents used it for show, and only lit up when guests were over for dinner. They'd probably fire it up for Christmas lunch tomorrow, he thought meekly. His eyes scanned the room. The sofa, the bookshelf, the windows that were hidden behind the closed velvet curtains.

Then, he saw it.

The large, ornate mirror which hung on the wall.

It reflected everyone and everything in the room in it – except the man. Except Santa Claus. He was not reflected in the mirror at all, it was as if he didn't even exist.

Toby gasped, recoiling.

As if he was oblivious to the boy, Santa sniffed at Casey's hair, her face, then licked her cheek, which was sodden with blood and the stains of her tears. He stood up straight, then, and turned to Toby. "For Christmas this year," he said, his voice oozing and wheezing, his disc of black eyes fixed to the boy, "you get to make a choice. Who do I get?"

Toby looked at Santa, took a small step back, considered running to the front door when Santa hissed, "Don't even think about running!"

Toby felt the blood drain from his face, his skin paling. He felt the whack, whack, whack of his heart against his rib cage. *Can he read my mind too?*

Finally he spoke. "I get to choose what?" he asked.

Besides Santa, Casey grunted and tried to communicate, but it was no good – he couldn't make a word out with whatever was stuffed across the poor girl's mouth. The wounds beneath her clothes must have been bad, though, Toby estimated, because blood continued to seep through the fabric in several places.

"You, little Toby, get to choose who *my* present is this year. Is it you, is it your mum, or is it your dad? You decide." The man chuckled, and his lips, that looked blue and cracked, turned wide into an ugly grin. He licked them, and then pointed towards Casey. "If you give me Casey, I will leave you and your parents alone. If you let her go, then it'll be you, or your mum and dad. But mark my words, I will be taking one of you," he rasped. He cackled, threw his head back, and Toby watched as his neck stretched and twisted at an impossible angle.

This thing was not human. This Santa Claus was not the man of magic and stuffed toys.

From outside, Toby heard the noise of a car engine approaching.

Mum and dad. Back from church.

Santa's head snapped back into normal position, and his dark eyes rested on Toby. "You, your mum, or your dad. Or her. The girl. Which one is mine? What shall it be?"

Santa lifted his hands in the air, and pulled off his thick, dark gloves.

Toby shrieked.

His hands were mottled, grey, and split open in places. Puss oozed across cracked skin, and his nails were long, like claws. The smell emanating from him seemed stronger now, and Toby, repulsed, coughed, covering his mouth and nose with his hand.

The girl, still tied, struggled, her eyes wide and pleading. She shook her head from side to side, her panic visible even despite the restraints holding her back.

From outside, the sound of an approaching car died down and the engine slowed to a stop. Car doors opening, then closing. Voices.

His mum and dad.

Toby looked at Casey and whimpered. "Sorry," he said, shaking his head.

He turned to Santa and, through eyes filled with tears, nodded. "Yes, take Casey. Leave me and my parents alone!"

The front door opened, and Toby turned towards it.

His mum and dad, coats dusted in flickers of snow, stepped in. Rosey cheeks and broad smiles. "Hey kiddo, why you up so late? What's wrong?"

Toby felt his heart stall, the rush of panic filling his body. What had he done? He turned back, pointing to the lounge. Stunned, he fell back, dizziness overtaking him: the room was as it should be, as if nothing had taken place there at all.

The chair was back in its rightful position; the vinyl stereo suddenly blared to life. *Silent night, holy night.* The lights stopped flickering and settled. The smell had gone.

And so had Casey, along with Santa.

Toby, now on the floor, the smell of his own urine filling his nose, began to sob and wail.

By the time he had changed into fresh clothes, the police had been called and the missing persons report had been filed.

She was never seen again – and neither was the Santa Claus in green.

Christmas Eve, Present Day

And that was why the following years were spent in self-

imposed isolation. Toby opened his eyes, the memories of that Christmas all those years ago burning into him, like blisters upon skin. He lifted a hand, running it through his dark hair and swallowed, the lump in his throat heavy.

He had spent so long, so much time, trying to tell his family about the Santa Claus that had stolen Casey – poor, sweet Casey – that they'd eventually started taking him to a counsellor. They thought he had imagined much of what he'd seen, what he'd heard. That impossible, invisible-to-the-mirror alien that had worn the skin and name of his childhood idol.

Of course, he couldn't blame them. They wouldn't have found this man he had described; he wasn't human. He had vanished, like smoke melting into air. Just like that, gone.

Toby chewed at his bottom lip, still lying back in his bed. A wind was whipping up outside, beyond the house, and he could see through the small slitted gap of his curtains that snow still fell in quick flurries. Many Christmas's had past, there was once a time he thought he could be normal, experience the Christmas season like any other, yet in 1978, when he was 23 years old, he had been visited again.

He had been staying at his parents for Christmas, during university break. On Christmas eve, he had awoken to the two dark smudges beneath his door; the shadows of feet beyond in the hallway.

Knock. Knock. Knock.

The demand then had been the same as before: I'm back for a present, Toby. Who is it to be – your parents, or you? The choice had been made, in a moment of fear sparked by what he was sure would be his own death: he had chosen them. The two people who had raised him, who had loved him. When he checked their room, moments later, they had simply vanished.

Never to be seen again. That horrific truth smeared itself across his soul like dirt. His guilt, the realisation of what he had done, slowly ate away at his soul each day, until really, there was nothing left of him except an empty shell of ugly memories.

Marrying and having a child, the wife and daughter he mentioned earlier? They were long gone. For every person he met that he cared about, they posed a risk. Another present for Santa Claus to come and claim? He could return at any time, demanding another of those he loved. Toby felt tears stinging at his eyes and he allowed them to fall freely, the drops of water sliding across his cheeks and onto the pillows. He had separated from his wife and child, demanding never to see them again. He had been truly stupid to think it was ever a possibility to have someone in his life. He had no one left.

The guilt sliced into him like a knife into butter. An easy, open wound.

He had chosen others above himself, and what did he have left to show for it? The only real gift in life, he thought solemnly, was to have others in it. To love, to care for, to share with. Yet he now had no one, and it had been his choosing. And maybe, Toby thought, the idea suddenly dawning on him with a vivid clarity, that was what it was all about. Didn't Santa know the truth of people's hearts? What was it, that his teacher Sylvia Marlow used to say when he was in 7th grade at school? "Santa only rewards the good children, the bad ones, well, you don't want to take the risk."

Had he chosen differently, would they have been spared? Had Santa seen something in his soul, one that marked him firmly and permanently onto the black list? Had his choosing of those around him as an offering to save himself been a test? Maybe. Did Santa only appear as the red, friendly, chuckling figure to the souls who deserved to see him that way?

The idea was pointless, the answer unknowable.

He was alone now, unsafe to be with any other. Left alone to rot in his prison called a home, dreading each year the chiming of church bells, the Christmas hymns and the season's first snowfall.

Knock. Knock. Knock.

Toby's head jerked up, his heart hammering, his mind frozen. His eyes lowered, drawn to that gap between floor and door. There it was, the two outlines of large feet.

"Ho, ho, ho," the voice said, crisp and cheerful.

Toby threw back the covers and, not caring now, about what would happen, ran over to the bedroom door. He grabbed the cold door handle and twisted it, throwing the door wide open.

Santa. With the black, soulless discs for eyes.

"I'm ready," Toby said flatly, his hands by his sides, lips trembling. He waited, knowing that he was the last and only gift he could offer, on that Christmas that would now be his last.

12 DAYS: STOCKING FILLERS   MATTHEW CASH

Sleigh Of Bones - Holly Ice

MOM AND DAD LAUGHED with my auntie and uncle. They all wore boggly glasses, huge plastic eyes dancing from the frames. I pulled my legs onto the cushion of my chair and smiled at their funny faces. They'd got loud and silly after the 'adult drinks', but they'd let me stay up later than my cousins to watch movies and eat my toffee apple.

I licked my sticky lips and laid on a dusty cushion. My eyes ached to shut, but I didn't want to miss any trick-or-treaters, or the sparklers and fireworks. By morning, all the candles and spider webs would be tidied away for next year like today never happened. The magic, as Mawmaw called it, would be gone.

Uncle Steve raised his glass, as if to prove I might miss something. A huge grin on his face, and with a wobble, he said, 'To another year of family!' He slapped my dad's back and they all finished their drinks, but after that the spooky music faded in and out and my neck fell into the cushion.

'You tired, Cleo?'

I jolted up and pinched my mouth against a yawn. 'No, Mawmaw.'

Mawmaw June's joints clicked and creaked as she pulled herself out of the low sofa, waving off Auntie Shannon. 'Come now, Cleo. Make do-do.' She limped my way, leaning on her Halloween cane, carved and painted to look like a leg bone.

Clutching the frilly hem of my Dorothy costume, I shook my head. 'Please, Mawmaw. I like watching.'

Mawmaw tugged one of my plaits with a huff, her long dress sleeves tickling my nose and chin. 'You're falling asleep on the chair.'

'Can't I have a little longer?'

Her red lips pursed, deepening her wrinkles. 'None of that. I didn't get up to exercise, and I got a story for you. Come now.'

Mawmaw held out her hand and didn't move till I took it. 'What kind of story?'

She winked and tugged, taking me past our carved pumpkins, bowls of sweets and crisps and mini sausages, and up the stairs. I only looked over my shoulder once. Mom waved good night and blew me a kiss.

In the dark upstairs, the music was softer, a low thrum. I couldn't hear talking any longer, but I could hear my cousin's snores. He was as bad as Pawpaw had been.

Mawmaw laughed. 'I tell you, you're lucky you don't share a room with that.'

She pulled a hall chair to my bed and her cane tapped the covers. 'In you get.'

I slipped under the sheets and crossed my arms over the top. 'Is it a good story?'

'Aren't all my stories good, child?' She took her seat and stretched her legs with a little sigh.

I scrunched my nose. 'So far, yes.'

Mawmaw prodded my arms until I slid them under the covers. Only then did she smile. 'There, snug as a bug.' Her hair had fallen out of her tie. Some was dyed purple to match her eyeshadow. She tried a different colour every Halloween.

'I love purple.'

Mawmaw tapped her nose and tucked the covers under my side. 'Why you think I chose it? Now, snuggle down good, and I'll get to thinking.'

I did as Mawmaw said but felt more awake than I had downstairs, even as I rubbed my cheek on the pillow. I wasn't going to miss one of Mawmaw's stories. Mom had told me how scary they were, and this was the night for it.

'I never told anyone this story,' Mawmaw said, eying me, 'but you're old enough.' Her eyes twinkled like my starry nightlight and her joints creaked as she sat back in the chair, stroking her cane's paint. 'I suppose the story begins with the wedding of Esther and Michael Wright…'

On the evening of her wedding, long after little ones like you had gone home, Esther put her hand in Michael's suit pocket and tilted her head so as to peer up at him. 'Are you sure you want to walk?'

Michael ducked to kiss her on the forehead. 'Of course! There's fresh snow to break.' He paused to check the toggles on her coat and pulled her fur hood up, covering her hair. 'All set.'

Esther went on tiptoe and kissed him thanks. He, of course, pulled her to him, until hollers and clapping from the restaurant made him pull away with a laugh. Smoke swirled with his breath, it was so cold.

'How much wine did you buy them?' Esther asked.

Michael chuckled, a night of wine on his own breath. 'Does it matter? Let them enjoy it.' He winked and faced the long trail ahead. It snaked through the woods. Through trees so laden with snow, they looked like sentries, frozen in place and dressed in sparkling ice.

The breeze cut hard too, but Michael was right. The trail was fresh and inviting, all untouched. The air held no hint of the usual wood smoke. You and I know that meant the breeze came from beyond town, over the mountain and down the hills, the wild with it.

'A good night to walk,' Michael said.

He took Esther's hand and laced their gloved fingers together before resting them both in his pocket. And they left their drunk and red-cheeked party behind. The more sober relatives waved from the windows then, not bothering to dress against the cold for a proper goodbye. The loud beats of the live bass drummer followed them into the woods, something like the music below us.

After only a few steps in her too big snow boots, Esther huffed. 'Not quite wedding shoes!'

Michael nudged her side. 'No, but much more sensible.'

'You didn't complain when I walked the aisle!'

'No, never.' Michael pulled Esther to his side and guided her through the thick powdered snow toward their home, a small two-bedroom house on the edge of town, just visible through the trees. It was only a start, but it was more than they would need till they started the big family she'd always talked about. 'Not long now and I'll carry you in.' Michael gestured to the porch.

Esther smiled, eyes glazed as her thoughts took over.

Michael knew she was only tired from hours of hosting. His cousins had made it a promise of their attendance to make a party happen, and Esther was never one for drinks and small talk.

A sharp wind skittered through the trees with a keen whistle, startling Esther.

She jumped, bashing her head on Michael's chin. He righted her and rubbed his jaw, eying a clump of snow which had fallen from a tree. The freed branches sprang higher, in a more exposed seat, bony and dark from their long slumber beneath white sheets.

'Looks like a storm is driving in,' he said.

The couple crunched on, twisting back on the path. Thick trees hid the cabin then, but a half mile and they would be home. The house windows would be dark but small and welcoming, a shelter from the winter cold.

Michael chivvied Esther and they walked a little faster, their knees tiring even as their footprints grew shallower. The wind now roared at their backs. Of course, we know that's nothing new for Keremeos. They don't call the town 'the meeting of the winds' for nothing, hmm?

Mawmaw rubbed her arms, like always when she thought on her old home in New Orleans.

'Go on, Mawmaw.'

She shook herself and continued.

Esther's ears were lipstick red around the tips.

'Not long now, my love,' Michael said.

'Being out in the cold is not as romantic as it looks!'

Esther's mouth was as pinched as it would go and half blue, but Michael laughed, throwing his whole belly into it. 'I'll soon warm you up.'

Esther stopped and tapped his nose. 'I'll hold you to it!'

Rolling his eyes, Michael pulled her forward, but soon turned back the way they'd come. He thought he'd heard something. Was it a bell? Or many tiny bells, crashing together? *Ding ding ding, ding ding ding. Ding ding ding ding, ding ding ding ding.*

The wind raked at their backs, gathering speed. Michael's knees had numbed, sodden with the bone-cold snow. Still, he pushed Esther, his instincts telling him to hurry. Whatever that sound was, it was not one he wanted to explore on his wedding night.

So, they half jogged along the trail. The house was within running distance by the time the bells were a constant ringing, and a panting horse and galloping hoof falls could be heard over it, coming louder and louder.

Michael shoved Esther sideways and faced the sound. He caught a glimpse of a white horse before he fell beneath its hooves. It roared and reared to a halt.

Esther ran to her husband's side, on her knees beside him before she thought to check the horse was still. She saw then that it pulled an open sleigh and, though its hide was white as the snow, its eyes were bulging and red, framed with flecks of white caught in its lashes. Its ears were pinned back to its skull and it snorted smoke into the air with the heat of its wild gallop.

Powdered snow blanketed its bare back but it carried no rider, and nobody rode in the sleigh behind it, though it had reigns covered in rows of bells which jangled in the wind.

'Hello? We need help here!' Esther called to the trees as she checked Michael's heartbeat with her fingers, close to his neck. She felt nothing. 'Please!' she screamed. 'We need help!'

She glared up at the huffing horse. 'Who did this?'

Then she heard an eerie whistle from all sides, and the quiet, clicking trudge of shoes dragging through deep snow.

She pricked her ears to listen and shuddered as she realised the tune of the whistle, the lines it repeated: *Dashing through the snow, on a one-horse open sleigh, o'er the fields we go, laughing all the way... jingle bells, jingle bells, jingle all the way. O what fun it is to ride in a one-horse open sleigh.* A childlike choir of snickers reached her before the song began again, buffeting in and out of focus in the wind. *Dashing through the snow...*

Faceless voices on either side competed, whistling different lines as they swelled through the trees, increasing in pitch all the time until the music stopped dead, and Esther saw dozens of green-hooded figures emerge, their faces shadowed and their bodies no taller than a child's.

She was penned in, and they approached as one green wall. The lead figure chuckled, a shrill sound in the night, and pointed to Michael, unmoving on the ground. 'The horse got one. Good job, Flake!' His voice was as deep as a man's.

Flake whinnied and backed up a step, away from Michael's body.

It was then Esther understood this was not a rescue party. But she had nowhere to go, so she grabbed the house keys from her husband's pocket and brandished them, the points between her fingers like a weapon.

The lead figure laughed. 'You can't take us all.' He nudged the figure to his left. 'Good idea about the wedding. We got us two bodies here, one of each, like she asked. No need for another hunt.'

The second figure bobbed his head and drew a thin knife from his pocket. His eyes couldn't be seen beneath the hood, and he didn't say a word as he balanced, pulled his arm back, and threw, swishing the knife through the air, and into Esther's swallowing throat.

Hot blood slithered down her skin and into the cold white ground, turning it pink, more slush than powder. Her husband didn't even twitch as he cooled, no hint of breath over his lips.

My heart pounded my ribs and I huffed through my nose like that evil horse. 'So they both died? Why?'

Mawmaw shrugged, gathering her dark skirts to untangle her feet. 'The authorities never found their bones, you know. They searched the wood with hundreds of men but only found flesh, left for the animals in a scrappy heap.'

I swallowed sick, sure Mom would not have wanted Mawmaw to tell me such a horrid story. No doubt I would have nightmares filled with red snow and gaping throats.

Mawmaw pushed against her thighs and strained to standing with a sigh and many creaks of her bones, including the painted wooden cane. Was she leaving?

'It's time I rejoin the party. Get some rest, if you can.' Mawmaw winked and left the room, and it was only as the door clicked shut behind her that I remembered the last Halloween at her sister's big house, when Pawpaw was still alive.

She had taken me and my cousins into the hallway, where she kept all the best Halloween decorations to scare the smaller children, and she had pointed out the two skeletons, holding each other's hands, dressed in spiders and cobwebs.

I pulled the covers over my head and shuddered, wishing I could brave the floor to turn on the big light. My hands gripped my knees, but I remembered it clear as Pawpaw's funeral. A hoof-shaped mark had dented the tallest of Mawmaw's skeletons, an inch above the eyes.

12 DAYS: STOCKING FILLERS　　　MATTHEW CASH

The Christmas Story - Matthew Cash

I RECALL NOW, AS I sit in my eleventh century chair by the open fire in my living room, a tale about this season of winter. As I watch the flames devour the logs like some ravenous beast I remember a night like this many, many, years ago. Seventy years ago to this date in fact.

Tears well in my eyes. Tears, not of sadness, not of some happy
recollection, but tears of fear. For tonight, this snow covered evening may very well be my last night on earth!

It was seventy years ago. Seven decades that have passed as if seven days. The story is as fresh in my head as it ever was....

It was Christmas time 1941 and apparently the coldest winter for six years. I had been concerned about air raids as some houses five miles away had been bombed only three weeks previous. Mother said that there wouldn't be any air raids over Christmas but I knew she was trying to keep me from worrying. I knew that the Gerries wouldn't rest just because it was Christmas. Father was not serving in the army due to him having his left leg amputated ten years previous after a horrific car accident. He had told me not to worry about such things as we were always given a warning siren if a German plane was seen. So he put my mind at ease and we were determined not to let Adolf Hitler keep us from enjoying our Christmas.

I had been sitting by the fire reading as was normal for me on dark winter's nights. I remember putting my book down, too excited by the following day's festivities to concentrate on the words before me. I gazed around the candlelit room. It wouldn't be long before we would put them out as it was suggested to use minimal light at night during these years. Mother sat by my side doing her needlework by the light of the orange and yellow flames. Father was sprawled, mouth wide open, tongue lolling out and fast asleep.

I could see mother was overjoyed as soon as I heard the noise coming from outside.

The sound was of children singing. Their voices reminded me of the church choir.

Excitedly I pleaded with mother if I could go down to the main door and listen to them. She smiled and nodded.

I quickly raced into the hallway, not considering that I may wake the servants or my father. Down the staircase to the large oak doors. I could hear them more clearly now.

I could hear the beautiful, yet haunting, words of the Christmas carol, *"O come, o come, Emmanuel"*.

I reached up for the iron bolt and slid it with difficulty across. The door groaned as I pulled it with all my strength. When I finally had it fully open I trod cautiously on the fresh fallen snow.

With all my concentration being on getting the door open I did not realise that the singing had stopped. Taking a few steps away from the house I pondered on the whereabouts of my joyous carol singers. When I felt the bitterness of the strong winter wind I thought that the singers must have moved on.

But then suddenly the main door, which I had left open, slammed shut sending thunderous echoes throughout the house. I ran back to the house with endless thoughts running through my mind. If I had woken Father or the servants I would be severely punished.

I turned the freezing cold door handle and pushed with all my weight. It didn't move an inch. Worried about having to wake up one of the servants or making mother or father come down to let me in made me temporarily forget about the carol singers.

Then I heard it.

When I pushed against the door for the second time I heard *"O come, o come, Emmanuel"*.

The singing came as if it were across the threshold and inside the house!

I realised that they must be playing some sort of joke on me. I had visions of Mother and Father standing at the foot of the stairs chuckling. Cook would probably be waiting with some hot milk and a bowl of roast chestnuts. I giggled and called for them to let me as it was so cold I could positively freeze. All I got in reply was another verse of the same Christmas carol. However this time along with the sound of children's voices was a lady and a gentleman's. Of course I recognised these to be my parents. Playing along with their elaborate jest I requested a verse or two of *"The Sussex Carol"* as it was my favourite. This time I heard even more voices, more ladies and more gentlemen. *The servants too! My*, I thought, *this was a treat*. I would have preferred to listen to them in the warmth of my home however. Also I wished that they would start to sing a different carol.

As you can imagine I was extremely cold, my young body trembling. I reached out and grasped the brass door handle. The pain! The agony!

I recoiled in horror and fell to my knees. I shoved my hand into the snow. The door handle of my house had felt as hot as a furnace! I slowly eased my hand from snow. The smell of my own burnt flesh made my stomach churn. I looked over to the house, tears on my face. The door was ajar.

I stood up, my head full of uncertainty. At the back of my mind I put it down to some freak accident. The five inch gap between the door and post gave nothing away only blackness. It was only for the love and trust in my parents that I returned to that door.
An accident, I thought. With my left shoulder I forced the door open a few more inches. Carefully avoiding the handles I squeezed myself into the house.
Then suddenly to put my utmost fears into reality I heard the solemn eerie wailing of the air raid siren in the village. *Oh no,* I thought. I did not know what to do, go further into the house or make for the air raid shelter in the garden.

My instinct told me to find my parents first so I continued.

I could make out the staircase and hallway ahead of me in the darkness. There was no one I could see or hear anywhere. Firstly I called for Mother, then Father. When I got no reply I hollered at the top of my lungs for the servants. Nothing. Slowly I started to climb the stairs. I was on the third step when something happened that made my blood run cold. My right hand had been holding the banister and my injured left had been swinging loosely by my side. I felt someone's cold hand touch my naked wrist. This hand which I only caught a glimpse of was deathly pale and felt as though it were carved from ice.

A sensation of dread came over me as I turned uneasily to see the owner of that pale hand.

My heart thudded so hard in my chest I thought it might burst. All thoughts of the air raid siren had been vanquished. My breathing became irregular as I gazed at the sight before me.

A white faced boy of about eight years of age smiled up at me. He had neatly combed shiny golden hair. Bright blue eyes sparkled unnaturally from his cherub--like face. He was dressed all in white, just like the choirboys at church. You may think that there was nothing unusual about this happy choirboy standing on my staircase. But when I tell you the following you will understand the sheer horror of my ordeal. This cherub--like boy in front of me faded out below the knees, it was as though he was floating in mid air!

This apparition, this manifestation, this ghost or whatever it was, opened his angelic mouth and began to sing that oh so familiar Christmas carol. He sounded and looked like an angel, surely I should have felt peaceful, but I felt cold, so cold.

I've heard of people who believe to have experienced the supernatural and most of them admit to being frightened at first but after the initial shock have an overwhelming sense of serenity come over them. The singing was the most beautiful I had heard and have since. Yet I sensed something devilishly sinister, like he was a demonic impostor.
Any minute I thought little red horns would cruelly push their way through his small skull, break through his scalp and beautiful blonde hair.

I wasn't far wrong.
It didn't occur to me until I took in the detail of this visitation, that when I walked up the stairs I was in virtual darkness, but now I was able to see the choirboy.

Where was the light coming from? From behind me at the top of the stairs?

I spun round on my heels and stared in unbridled terror at five more cherub-like apparitions. Behind them were my parents and our servants. Each of them held a lit candle. Each one faintly transparent.

I looked at my parents for a sign of love, or at least recognition, but they just smiled, emotionless, down at the solitary singing choirboy behind me. As the ghost to my back finished his verse of *"O come, o come Emmanuel"*, the rest of them joined in. I was horror-struck. I was so scared I could not move. I was beyond scared, I felt numb with fear. So petrified was I, that I could not scream!

The group at the top of the stairs moved downwards as one, towards me over the steps. The first apparition spoke my name softly. Somehow I managed to break from my statue--like state to look upon my caller.
The last thing I remember seeing before I fainted out of sheer fright was the beautiful cherub faced choirboy. His once bright blue eyes burning like red hot coals! The sound of the air raid siren coming out of his little mouth.
And then the buzzing of an aeroplane was the one of the last things I heard before a bright light engulfed everything, a thunderous roar. Then total darkness…..

I was found around midday in the cellar of our house. Our house had been bombed, completely flattened. Luckily the cellar remained intact throughout the blast.

Apparently I was trapped beneath a thick beam that miraculously did no permanent damage.

I was unconscious when I was found and was to remain that way for several days. My parents and servants bodies were found.

As for the spirits of the choir boys I can only guess that maybe they were a sign, a portent of the death and destruction that was about to befall my house. Maybe I was not turned into an apparition like my parents and servants because I was destined to survive the blast?

I have mulled this over for many a year and for seventy years thought of every possibility and still not come to any satisfactory conclusion.

After staying with my aunt and studying through years of university and becoming a doctor I never mentioned this to anyone.

And so I have lived through fifty years as a general practitioner. Now that I sit in my own house remembering the story that happened so many years ago, I am writing this down, so it can be found and hopefully believed. Maybe someone will research my story and find my answers. The last piece of information I discovered was that one of the houses that had been bombed three weeks before mine had been the vicarage. Apparently the vicar had been tutoring the local church's choir. The house
was wrecked but he somehow survived. All the choir boys died.

I don't have much time left, I am in poor health. For the last thirty minutes I have heard the singing of so many familiar voices that have haunted my dreams endlessly. It is time I got this withered old body of mine out of this chair. I am feeling weaker by the hour and it is almost a welcome sight to see the ghostly white angelic face smiling through my window. I must go now: I have some long awaited visitors to greet. I must go downstairs and join the choir.

Farewell my dear reader and Merry Christmas.
Reginald Carleton.

12 DAYS: STOCKING FILLERS   MATTHEW CASH

The Merry Gentleman - Christopher Law

"I'LL ADMIT IT. I'VE got a sick mind. I always have, since I was little. It's the way you've got be if you're like me, if you want to be a success. I did all the things you probably think I did, when I was a kid. Tied fireworks to cats – which is hard to do on your own. Bloody hard. Kicked a couple of stray dogs to death, that kind of thing. Maybe set fire to a tramp or two. It's been a long time since then but the delights of my kind always start out the same. They haven't changed since the first cave-child, the first psycho rugrat, stamped a puppy to death. "

The basement was large, the ceiling low. Four bare brick pillars supported the floors above, creating a central square and surrounding rim. The modified dental chair the skinny man was tied to sat between two of the pillars, spotlit by a tall anglepoise lamp. The bulb was high-wattage and he could see nothing of his surroundings except the bed and the pillars; a section of brick wall with an empty shelf when he craned his neck. Even when the beam was blocked, The Merry Man stood in front it sometimes, for effect, all he could see were suggestions of the room beyond.

The other chairs.

"I was lucky. I never got caught. Do you have any idea how much getting caught effects people like me? All that meddling? The nosing around in things only the special few can understand? Appreciate to the full? It really screws us up. Thwarts our potential. I dodged that, all the concerned teachers and child psychologists. They didn't have them in my time. I got lucky; I am a legend in my own lifetime because I got lucky. I didn't get screwed, forced to think that what I am is wrong. That's what it boils down to. I got lucky. It is why I am pure, why I was chosen for this."

The ball-gag in the skinny man's mouth had a rough texture and an acidic taste – the concrete it was made from contaminated. The bonds holding it in place were barbed-wire; a short strip embedded in the ball's centre, fastened at the back with constricting elastic. Every time his face stretched or moved the elastic dragged the wire closer, the barbs tearing at the corners of his mouth, digging and stretching across his cheeks, under his ears and around his scalp. He could hear it slicing through his brain.

"I am so lucky. I know that. It makes me grateful."

Blood pooled in the skinny man's mouth, forcing him to swallow or choke. When he choked he saw it spray from his nose, squirting through the holes in his cheeks, oozing around the ball. Mixed with the dust from the ball and the bile rising from his stomach his blood burned and stung, churned his stomach more when he had to swallow. The convulsions and suffocated retching made his bowels spasm, toilet-training forcing the wave of filth to rebound after a few squirts, his body automatically clenching and creating a violent backlog. His stomach lurched, pure bile squirting into his sinuses. The exertion made his eyes bulge. He'd heard more than a pint of blood makes you vomit, couldn't guess how much he'd swallowed.

He didn't want to vomit. There was nowhere for it to go but his lungs. The rising bile was enough, burning trails as it dribbled back down into his innards. His eyes ran with tears, the acid residue at the top of his nose eating towards his eyes – following the course that allows some people to cry milk.

"There is, of course, more to it than that. I've put in a lot of work to get to where I am today; into this, and every other part of my life. I don't do it for praise. I'm not one of those show-boaters who wants to get caught, see myself on TV, in magazines. Trending. I do it for the craft. This part of my life at least. My other life, my regular life, is a little more high-profile, for those high enough in society to be allowed to see me, and dreaming children. In a world of self-proclaimed VIPs, I'm one of the genuine articles. Presidents and royalty have fought to be the one standing next to me. They don't get a picture, the unwashed masses will never see me. I give them a copy of the list they're on. A section of it, heavily edited. Their name and a few others, enough to make them feel powerful. They never ask which list they were on; the extract is enough to fuel their egomania. Make them mine. You are all mine, no matter how naughty or nice. They never understand that part – the ego is a terrible cause of blindness."

There was a moment of silence as The Merry Man disappeared behind the light. The skinny man squirmed on his chair - a gynae-dental hybrid – and tried to peer into the gloom, beyond the bulb. All he could see was the suggestion of a shape, standing with its back to him. Razorwire had been used to fasten his ankles and wrists to the chair; he could only move a little without grinding the blades farther in. The pain was sickening, he wanted to sob and scream. The gag prevented him.

"You are moving around far too much," The Merry Man came back from the gloom, holding another strip of freshly cut barbed-wire. He wore thick rubber gloves, could grasp the wire like string. The rest of his body was hidden in a white forensic suit, his gas mask the same colour. "You will ruin it all."

The new strip of barbed wire was wrapped tightly around the man's throat, enough to dig it in, and secured under the chair with another strong elastic tie. Terrified, the skinny man struggled to keep his breathing regular and shallow.

Anything more encouraged the wire to work deeper in.

"Wakey-wakey. You've slept long enough. Everyone is waiting for you."

Her head throbbed, hooked needles thrust through her skull,

slowly turning in erratic circles. She wanted to go back to the darkness, where her thoughts and nerves were quiet. As she opened her eyes she already knew she was hanging from the ceiling. Her arms were stretched above her head, the rope digging painfully into her wrists. The slaps that brought her round were enough to set her swaying, squeezing the rope deeper into the soft flesh. Below her was a shallow pit, only a few feet wide. The bottom was too far for her feet to reach, the margin scanty. Her ankles were tied together, a long way down at the end of her bare legs.

With the masked man holding her face, peering at her through the clear plastic visor, she didn't dare swing for the edges. The relief that she wasn't naked, her upper body covered by a red t-shirt three sizes too large, made her want to whimper.

She held it in.

"Glad you could join us," The Merry Man mocked, pressing his mask close to her face. His eyes were pale blue, his lower face hidden. His cheeks and forehead were wrinkled, bushy eyebrows snowy white. He knocked on her forehead, three sharp taps. "I was afraid I gave you too much. Are you all intact in there, child?"

"Where am I?" her lips and tongue were heavy, semi-numb, the words lisping. In their wake she realised how dry her mouth was. "Who are you?"

"A connoisseur," he replied, the smile reaching his jolly eyes, and backed away. "I hope you are flattered. It's not everyone gets a chance like this. To be centre stage. The lists are long, getting longer every year. I can only ever choose a handful. Precious ones, like you."

She had gone home. She knew she had. Her last memories were of getting into bed, happy enough with the world, ready for tomorrow.

She had to work tomorrow; her last day this year. She didn't go to the sorts of places women got drugged and taken from. Would remember if someone had come round, a stranger at the door.

She was sure she would.

"Where am I?" she asked again.

"Where you belong," his voice was cheerful, booming up from his barrel chest. "Can't you tell?"

There was only a single light, directly above her, strong as a stage-light. She could feel the heat of it on her fingers and forearms, fighting the otherwise foetid, cold atmosphere. Beyond the beam she could see nothing; the world ended a few inches from the pit she hung above.

The Merry Man stood at the edge of the light, disposable white overall catching the light. He was large, several pounds and at least six inches on her. The way he walked was stiffened with age but powerful. In his dotage he was still formidable, knew it as well as the people he met. If she was free, he'd be just as confident.

It would be his mistake.

"Don't you like it?"

"No. It stinks."

"That's your fault, really. For being so late."

"Late for what, dickhead?" she couldn't help coughing, the dryness in her mouth spreading down her throat. The last word was a croak, the defiant profanity lost in a painful cough. The air tasted vile, rancid, like her spit.

"I suspect you are thirsty. Yes?"

She tried to glare at him. She knew she looked terrified; the self-defence classes useless until she was freed.

He laughed and, by an act of will, changed the lighting. The spotlight faded and she was hanging below a circle of smaller lights, soft bulbs illuminating her surroundings, pointing outwards. Four black curtains hung between the bare brick pillars, set in a square. The floor was dirt, the hard-packed and stained kind found around industrial areas, hopelessly contaminated.

"So, thirsty or not?"

He retrieved a hose from behind the curtains; a regular garden hose. The bright green coils were hideous against the gloom.

"Open wide."

"I've always been an artist. I tried using the usual methods. Painting, sculpture. That sort of thing. I was okay at it, but it was never a passion. Not the way my real work, projects like this, not the way they are. This is, the way this is, what we're doing now – this is my passion. I love my work, my calling. I've responded like any decent artist should. I've practised and prepared. Once I was done with being lucky, I decided to be good instead. Not just good. Excellent. Excellent at what I do. It isn't boasting to say that. The few who know about this side of my life are in awe at what I do. They are law-enforcement types. I meet them at fundraisers, help them when I can. They call me The Merry Gentleman. Or, to be more precise, The Merry Man. I prefer Merry Gentleman, don't you? It fits me better, I think. They don't know it's me, of course. Most of them. The others, the ones who know who I am? I have dirt on them."

He chortled, a healthy, happy sound.

"I'm sorry to gabble, overload you with information. I don't often get a chance to talk like this; it tends to all come bubbling out, like laughter. Holding it in is bad for your health. Laughter and words. Both of them. You have to let it out."

The man tied to the second chair was obese, rolls of fat hanging over the edges of his customised chair – his open-air coffin. Oversized zip-ties secured his ankles and wrists to the arms and leg struts, pulled so tight his hands and feet were swelling purple, starting to bleed where the plastic dug in. The ball-gag in his mouth was steel, roughly worked so there were sharp ridges and peaks across the surface, cutting and scraping his lips and tongue.

"All my work is carefully planned. I have a dozen places like this around the world, at different stages of development. Three dozen others like you. Ones who don't know they have been chosen. A gathering of the precious best, the ones I love most. You should be proud, only a very few make it all the way through the selection process. The few I want to sit with, to have as my friends. I hope you are proud. Tell me? Are you?"

The fat man whimpered in reply, drawing another jolly, Dickensian laugh from The Merry Man, so loud it wasn't muffled by the mask. Whimpers escaped as the fat man watched his captor approach, unravelling a coil of barbed wire.

Shrieks followed as the wire was slowly wrapped around his limbs and torso, mummifying him. Blood ran freely, long tears opening in the soft blubber, his own futile attempts to escape digging the barbs ever deeper. Before long they started to reach the larger arteries and veins, blood escaping in geysers and gulps.

If his eyes had been less blurred by pain and fear he would have seen that The Merry Man moved slowly, bending and rising cautiously every time he fed the wire beneath the chair, as if he were old, frail. There was no questioning the strength pulling the wire tight, the deep channels that started in his ample gut, guided in spirals down his thighs by the folds of flesh and angles of the chair spilling blood. The fat man squealed, trying to beg through the savage ball as tears flowed into his stubble. He didn't notice much more than the agony, could barely remember his own name. It didn't matter, not now he was here.

"Sounds expensive, doesn't it? For a hobby? It is, but I can afford it. You don't know who I am. If I told you my name, my real name, it would mean nothing to you. I could tell you one of my other names, or some of the companies I run, you'd know some of those. You wouldn't believe me though. You probably don't even believe that some of the names I could give are real, not now you are grown. That's okay, my ego is robust enough to take it – if anything it makes moments like this better, knowing that people like you cannot accept the truth, can't even start to. Besides, it doesn't matter – right here, right now – that I am the one the people you think run the world turn to. All that matters is that I am in control and you know it. I am your universe. You understand that, don't you?"

The coil of wire ran out, the fat man criss-crossed with bleeding welts. His face was unmarked – after the first experiment The Merry Man had abandoned the constricting barbed-wire feature of the gag. It had been harder than expected to sew up the damage and leave the first of the gentlemen fit for company.

To compensate for the forced gesture of mercy he gathered some ants from the dirt floor and scattered them around the holes and gouges he had opened – the new ball-gag of roughened steel wasn't enough. The ants set to work, mining and dragging the sacrifice away scrap by scrap. Each scrap was ten times the size of the burdened slave. The carnivorous queen's underground kingdom was vast; she helped keep the squatters out. Her soldiers and slaves were fed with the sugar and roadkill strewn across the upper floors, fighting for it with the flies and other crawling things.

When he wasn't here The Merry Man liked to think about the insect colonies, waging war against each other, becoming sentient in the universe he had given them, recognising him as the primal source. It was one of his lesser dreams of domination; one for tired nights and long flights.

Here, in the glorious moment, The Merry Man watched the ants set to work, nipping and tearing at the exposed flesh of the fat man's wounds. The scent trails they laid back to their nest, encased in the poisoned soil, were dotted with scarlet, becoming more vivid as Fatman's skin turned white with blood loss. It was only a moment before the first scouts followed the trail back, the hive-mind always sceptical; cautious, but greedy.

"I imagine you are hoping someone will come release you," The Merry Man said when the wire-wrap was done. He stood above the fat man, gently touching his face, creased eyes almost benevolent. "You think this is just a nightmare. That you are going to survive. You are wrong. You are my friend now. Here until I tire of you."

The Merry Man stood abruptly.

"The people who know you are missing, the handful who might care, will never think to look for you here. You are thousands of miles from everything you know. Mine completely. For which I am grateful. I didn't choose you by chance. But, please, fight against it. As much as you like. A filly is only good while she's being broken. Applies to stallions and geldings too. I'll give you some time to think. Let you settle a bit. Realise that I am your eternity."

Left alone the fat man grasped at straws, looking for a miracle in the noxious darkness. His hands were useless, throbbing with the blood trapped there. The zip-ties were too strong for him to break, flexing his arms only drawing them tighter. The wire across his arms and chest contracted, dug deeper with every movement. There was no escape without assistance, nothing to do but lie still.

Somehow he fell asleep, numbed by agony.

She was alone, hair and t-shirt still damp from the hose. She felt cold, degraded, her soul crushed under the weight of knowing it had only just begun. He had laughed when she realised her bra was gone, told her to be grateful her knickers were still on; they wouldn't be later.

Despite herself she had gulped at the spray of water, chasing it when he took the aim from her mouth. By the end her lips were numb and sore, frozen, her thirst only partly assuaged.

It hurt to make herself swing, the rope used to tie her wrists thin nylon, the knots worked to make them tighten. Stretching her fingers to grasp the rope above only found the coil of barbs worked into the fibre. Her fingers were shredded to the bone before she got them free, hanging uselessly afterwards. Blood trickled down her arms, pooled in the ridges of rope to drip onto her face, rivulets running down her back.

She made herself swing again, wrapping her ruined fingers around the barbs and stretching for the dirt with her bound feet.

For a second she made contact, held it with all her toes. The soil was moist and soft; it crumbled away and left her swinging again. The jolt was enough to tighten the rope around her wrists, finally restricting all the blood flow. She howled with frustration and tried again, with no more success. More blood began to flow from her wrists as the rope burst her skin. She screamed, the pain as much from her impotence as her wounds.

"Warming up, I hear," The Merry Man stepped from behind one of the curtains, his clean forensic suit dark green, the same shade as a plastic holly wreath. "I knew, as soon as I saw you that you would do well. You want to perform for us. It is in your soul. I've always had you on the right list. Are you excited? I hope you are. You should be. This is an honour for your soul as much as it is a delight for mine."

"What do you want? Please let me go," she couldn't help the tears.

"My dear, do I look like the kind of man who will just let you go? After all my investment? Do I look like I would give something for nothing? Because you've asked nicely? Because you begged?"

"What do you want? I'll do anything. Please don't kill me."

"Don't kill me?" he laughed, a hearty, rolling sound. "You will do well. You will sing beautifully."

There was a sharp sting in her neck and a second later she was hanging again, aware that time had passed but with no memory of sleep or fainting.

The rope was gentler now; wide strips of soft nylon, the kind used for climbing harnesses. It scraped against the welts and wounds of before, preventing them scabbing over. It felt better. She didn't even feel the gobbets of pus and half-formed scabs running down her arms, the slow trails of blood reaching the base of her spine.

Her clothes had been changed. She was in a dress now, tatty and tight; her size on a night she wanted to take someone home. It might have been white once but now it was blotched with rusty brown, cold and slimy against her bare skin.

"Ah, the second awakening," he appeared from behind a curtain a second after her eyes opened; long enough for her to find and lose the hope that this wasn't real. "You're fighting it less this time, aren't you?"

"Please, what do you want? Tell me what you want. I'll do anything. Please..."

"I have. I want you to perform, for my friends and I," he gestured at the curtains, heavy black velvet. "Help us in our merriment. Sing for us."

"Will you let me go? Please, I'll do anything you want...please..."

"We already went over this. I'm not that kind of man. I'm really not. All that changes is how long you perform," he grabbed her face and leaned close. "I think you want to take a long time."

Behind the mask his eyes were wide, brighter than before. He was panting, it came through in rasps and sucks. The tops of his cheeks had turned rosy with the exertion, his wrinkles rabid and homeless.

"Tell me you don't want that. Tell me you don't want to stay. Tell me you're too nice to have fun with me. Please, tell me those things – I know you want this. You are just scared, afraid of being greedy. It's okay, I can hear all your wishes. I know what your heart desires. I am your dream."

"I've tried this scene before, more times than I can remember, and it has never worked. There's no reason why. It isn't a grandiose piece. A snip to make it have never happened. Your body won't ever be found, for example. I know professionals. Government agencies. You can believe me or not but, given your history, I think you've worked out way more than I'd ever really want you to. Who I am, for starters – who I really am. You think that will give you an edge. It won't. I'm not taking you for revenge, or self-preservation. You didn't suspect before now, did you? I had no reason, other than I knew you would fit in. With the rest of us. You are perfect for our circle. My circle. My chosen children."

The man in the third chair was well built, still trim a decade after the army. He was the only one of the three to avoid gouging himself by trying to rise before realising he was bound. For the first minute or two he lay still, eyes darting around, returning constantly to The Merry Man, the forensic suit stretching over the rotund gut.

The room was nondescript, the light in the military man's eyes stopping him seeing much detail. He could see the multiple coils of barbed wire around his wrists, strapping him to the plastic covered arms, but not much more. His feet were bound the same way, at the end of the individual leg rests, slightly raised. More wire was wrapped around his body, crisscrossing his chest to loop between his groin and shoulders. All his clothes were gone, the barbs catching on his genitals as they withered, drawing blood. More were stuck in his midriff, scratching as they dug and slid with his breathing.

"I wouldn't even describe it as a particularly hard endeavour. I've worked on projects that have been far harder to get just right. Ones with many more moving parts. Remember that shooting a few years ago? The one that made all the headlines? That was one of mine. Took eighteen months to get that kid ready – after at least as many years of failed attempts. Remember all that fuss about who he was sending pictures to during the attack? That was me. I'm the only one who has ever seen them. Most of them are blurred, but there are three or four I like. There's one, of this girl...twelve years old...very erotic. I sold it. Last week. Got a lot of money. Got a good price. I guess I lied – I'm not the only one who has seen them. But only that one, all the others are mine. I've had the best of the rest blown up and laminated, my excitement tends to leave stains. The pictures aren't as good when they are stained crusty white. Plastic is a wonderful thing, don't you think? I keep the pictures in my den, where only I can go. I do the cleaning in there myself."

The military man tried easing his right wrist from the wire, clenching and flexing in the hope he could wriggle his hand to freedom. It was his weaker side, didn't matter so much if he tore the tendons. He only needed to endure long enough to free his good arm. Give himself a fighting chance.

He screamed into the steel ball, still stained by the fat man's blood, as the modified wire snagged and dug deeper into his wrist. At the tip of every barb there was a hook, designed to catch and drag in the skin like an anchor. The pain was magnified by the resin coating the steel, saturated with a chemical that felt like molten metal against exposed nerve endings. Like the abandoned concrete ball-gag, the wire around his wrist was bound at either end by elastic, quickly stopping his freedom bid. The hooks dug deeper, more nerves starting to scream. He abandoned the attempt, desperately glad he hadn't tried to free his stronger hand – held by the same constricting bind.

"Anyway, enough about the past. I've been trying to get this one right for a really long time. Ever since I was a kid, really - from when I realised this is my calling in life. From the day I knew who I was, what my vocation is."

The Merry Man removed the gag as the captive started to choke on his own saliva and gorge, the pain so bad he was almost fitting. There was white showing around the pupils of his bulging eyes and his face was purple – as the gag popped free his teeth clenched and bit clean through his lower lip and the tip of his tongue.

It made The Merry Man laugh, chuckling as he continued his commentary.

"I used to try getting what I wanted like everyone else, if you can believe it. I tried to be mainstream, for a while. I had friends. We'd hang out. Stuff like that. It was never quite right. I could tell they wouldn't like spending an evening the way I wanted to. They only wanted the gifts I bring."

Pulling a stool from the shadows The Merry Man sat down in the space between the leg struts. Still fighting to overcome the pain, to find the centre of himself, the military man only saw a blurred shape. All his training, the martial arts that had become his life after the army, told him there was a way to overcome this, to overcome anything. All he had to do was find the centre, the place where his mind and spirit were in total mastery of his body. He knew it was close, he'd been searching for it for a long time.

This situation, this agony, was an opportunity; a test he knew he could pass.

"You might want to brace yourself," The Merry Man said. "This bit is going to hurt a lot. I cannot lie."

The man didn't feel the wire cutting deeper into his ankles and wrists as he tried to thrash, the screams tearing his throat. In quick succession his testicles had been pierced onto the barbs around his thighs and placed in a sharpened nutcracker. They split with the squeeze and became the centre of everything, a single nexus of torment, every other sensation, every thought and feeling, subsumed.

"It's Christmas," The Merry Man said to the howling man, the pain too great for him to find oblivion, his mind farther from the calm centre than it had ever been. "Thought I'd use what came to hand. I'll leave you to sleep for a while. I imagine you need it. It won't be long until the party. You'll like it."

The lights went out and the military man sobbed in the cold and dark, involuntary attempts to escape the pain digging the wires in deeper, shedding more blood. Pain shot from his groin, along molten nerves, reaching the roots of his teeth and the tips of his toes.

Eventually he passed out, waking later when The Merry Man returned with drugs that stopped him finding oblivion again. The torments that followed were worse than before, his mind broken long before the perverse brutality reached the final crescendo.

"You see?"

All she could see was his face, the little revealed by the visor of his mask. Just his eyes and half his nose, the hint of a beard on his rosy cheeks, a finger or two of wrinkled forehead above the shaggy eyebrows. The eyes were brighter than she had ever seen, wide with a sanctified killer's conviction. His suit was red, gas-mask green, boots and gloves translucent white.

"All of this is for you. You are the star attraction."

He gestured at the drawn curtains, span her gently so she could see them all.

"It is all for you, my special child."

The space between the pillars was only a few feet wide, just large enough to accommodate a single, specialised chair. No sound, no sign of movement, came from behind the curtains. There were people waiting behind – she could feel their eyes. She wanted to say something but the thoughts jammed in her head and her tongue cleaved to the roof of her mouth, all the moisture gone. A whimper escaped and she tried to escape the feel of his hands.

"Well not all for you," he steadied her swing until she was still. If he was interested in feeling her, he resisted the temptation. His touch still felt like rape.

"A lot of it is for me. You see...even I get lonely over the holidays. I want people to be merry with. I want to see a show with my friends. I have gathered them here, and you are our entertainment – the treat my gentlemen and I have earned. I am, I suppose, doing all of this for myself, but that is no problem. No obstacle to this being a good thing. I could have taken any one of your rivals. Some of them are prettier, and some of them are cleverer. None of them find the balance as well as you. Your daughter might, one day. I have her on the list – she is so small, utterly delightful, so very nice and never naughty. For now, I have you and that is enough."

He left her side and went to one of the pillars, hands reaching behind for the draw-rope.

Terrified of what she would see she looked that way all the same, eyes drawn to the danger. She thought of her daughter. She thought of a dozen others – her mother and younger brother, the older one under the ground, her broken father and her friends. All of them were too far away.

Her daughter was ten, already halfway orphaned. She wanted to be at her side, in the safe place they made when they hugged. She prayed, screaming inside for any listening deity.

"I tried to find people like me," The Merry Man continued, his voice gurgling with merriment. "People who like the same things as me. I wanted people to sit with. People I could laugh with. Same as everybody else, I wanted people I like. I still want that. Never had it; but I still want it. Nostalgic for something that was never mine; never my destiny. Can you tell me that's wrong?"

"No," she whimpered. "Please...I'm sorry...Please..."

"Thing is - like I was saying before, not to you but someone else – I am an artist. I have a vision I have to be true to,"

He stood bolt upright, quivering. "If I'm not, I'll never be capable of being true to anything,"

He clutched his heart, struck a pose.

"I've done a lot of good because of moments like this, not despite of them. I give more to my foundations and charities than some countries make in a year. I have given enough to deserve a few times like this in my life, when the company and entertainment is just how I choose, just what I want. Don't you think? One of you for my own, in exchange for my work? Haven't I earned that, with everything I do? The promises I keep – the dreams I make come true – all of it. Don't I deserve my own moments of pleasure? A time to be my purest self?"

"Yes. I guess," she tried to speak, her hitching sobs and dripping snot reducing her words to hiccoughs and moaning sobs. "Please...my girl...Please, let me go...I'll tell no-one...Let her go...please...do whatever...not her...please..."

"Did you know the dead talk more than the living?"

"No...they talk? I don't know...Please...I'm sorry...Let her go...Please..."

"They do. The dead. They tell better jokes; listen better when you're talking to them. All of my best decisions have been made after I talk to the dead. Which makes it sound like I do it all the time. I don't. Only for special occasions. I would; I will when the world is handed over to me. For now I have to be cautious. It is difficult finding the right company, almost as hard as finding the perfect performer. There are only a few companions who pass every test, almost as few as are gifted with what you have, with a moment like this. To do it all the time would leave too wide a trail. Too many failed attempts to hide what I shouldn't need to."

He drew back the curtain and she squeezed her eyes shut, flinching away with enough force to start swaying again. She heard him laugh and then his hands were steadying her again, her flesh shrivelling from his touch through the thick rubber gloves and rancid dress. He pressed his mask against her cheek, whispered in her ear.

"It is the ones like you that are hardest to find. So many false leads, dead-ends. You hid yourself well, even for one of your kind, but you've always known your fate. I can feel you trembling, eager to embrace it now that it is here. Don't deny yourself. Open your eyes. Your audience awaits."

He grabbed her shoulders and span her quickly, like they were playing Blind Man's Buff. When she was wound as tightly as he wanted, the nylon straps bunched and twisted around her hands, no barbs now, he held her still for a second. Then he told her again to open her eyes and span her back the other way; unable to stop herself she fell into a dizzying circle.

He moved quickly to open the three remaining curtains and clamber into the fourth – empty - chair, sprightly now despite his years. He was still settling as she came to a gradual halt, fussing with the video camera he held pointed at her.

"She's going to put on a good show lads," he called as she realised he was sitting behind her. Twisting, she couldn't see his face. His mask. "Just wait and see. You'll love her. My Best Beauty! For this year at least."

The men in the other three chairs, the ones she had to look at when she couldn't keep her eyes closed any longer, might or might not have shouted and cheered their appreciation. It was hard to tell.

The Merry Man reacted like his friends were happy. All she heard were her own screams, high and shrill like the girls she mocked in horror films, tearing her throat, dripping tears into her open mouth. They tasted metallic, rusty.

Her performance had begun; her childhood dreams of the stage twisted, made wrong but still perfect. Her moment in the spotlight.

In the bay in front of her, the curtain drawn back, the military man had been released from his bonds. The back of his chair was raised and he could have been reclining on a sun-lounger, legs splayed apart. He was still naked, what was left of his skin waxy and grey. Where his crotch and midriff had been there was now a single gaping wound, the exposed viscera the colour of bad meat. Maggots writhed and tumbled inside, hollowing out the rib cage, digging down to split the thighs.

She noticed the number of flies in the room – breeding on the warmth of her breath, camouflaged until now. The stench, now that she couldn't pretend it was something else, grew stronger. Bile rose into her nose and she retched, the acid halting her sobs, making her gasp, suffocated by the vile atmosphere. Flies landed on her face, pausing to vomit and feed on the dirt they found there, their delicate feet drilling into her nerves, dragging her mind from the safety of vulgar delirium.

She screamed and the flies fled, returning seconds later with their friends. One flew into her mouth, bounced around a little until it was drowned in thin hydrochloric acid, swallowed accidentally. It made her retch several times, the last few convulsions accompanied by tears and fresh, whimpering sobs. Bloodied snot dangled from her nose, the strands of spit hanging from her lips as thick as maggots.

She wished she were dead, certain Hell was a happier place.

"See? She's started already. What an aria!" The Merry Man cried. "Show the others. Let them see you - face forward - as you sing. My Beauty! Your audience loves you!"

Leaning forward in his chair, the only one without split legs, more like a luxury lazy-boy, The Merry Man used a long pole to manoeuvre her to look at the other grisly celebrants, the military man staying silent if he felt snubbed at being denied her face.

The tip of the pole was bent into a sharp hook; she tried to swing with it so it didn't dig in so deeply, crying out each time it broke through the dress and her skin. Every time she managed to escape he thrust it back with more force, more precision, snagging and teasing her nerves, working between her thighs. She wanted to stop crying, wanted the pain to create insanity and oblivion, take her away from it all – an eternity in flames seemed better than this reality.

"Isn't she grand?" The Merry Man boomed. "A perfect little starlet! Hear her sing!"

There wasn't much difference now between the fat man and his skinny friend. Both were little more than skeletons, the strands of sinew and skin left hard to distinguish from the thick cobwebs. Undisturbed for years, rats had made a nest inside the fat man's ribcage, abandoned now the master had returned. Spiders and beetles, longer, wriggling things, clambered and fought over the bones, the choicest spots inside the burst padding of the chairs. Her screams echoed in the cavernous ribcages.

The heads of the dead men were the last bastions of individuality. Long enough ago for the hair to have turned grey with dust and a patina of flyspeck and spider's silk to form on the faces, the heads had been removed and preserved, stuffed and mounted like hunting trophies. A taxidermist's oddities – a demon's companions, faces fixed in wide, manic smiles.

The skinny man's smile was lopsided and malformed, the lower half of his face torn away and reattached with thick thread. His lips were thin and his teeth large and yellow, irregularly set.

The fat man's teeth looked fake, too straight and white. The scars of his smile ran to the corners of his eyes. Some of his lower incisors were loose, leaning forward like the loser of a bare-knuckle boxing match. He looked forlorn, dusted with the certainty of damnation.

The military man's smile looked normal, apart from the lost maggot trying to find a way into the plush lower lip, tricked by the feel of skin and stench of death, finding nothing but stuffing.

All three heads glistened, leering and horrid in the stark light. Unlit cigarettes and empty glasses were fastened to their hands. They were having a whale of a time, staring out through cracked marble eyes.

The dangling girl – the entertainment - could almost see them smile as the darkness rose to claim her. They were delighted with her sacrifice, her defeat better than honey.

She tried to scream one more time, only heard her dying rattle.

"So that's it," The Merry Man said as dawn arrived. "All done for another year."

His companions were silent, immobile. Rotten and boring – terrible friends.

The dead were better company than the living; he hadn't lied. It was just only true for as long as they were dying. After that they tended to bloat, fall apart and smell bad.

"I'm glad you all came. It is a shame that you must go, but all things are fleeting."

Some people went quickly, others could linger for years if handled correctly. It was one of the hardest things about arranging a get-together - making sure everyone had the stamina.

"I did love you all, in my way. You enjoyed what I gave. Nothing is free."

In the end they all fell silent.

The girl went first, an hour or so after he was certain her heart stopped. She sang until the end, her spirit taking over when her body failed. Hanging from the ceiling, the last shreds of flesh and skin holding her together succumbed. She split just above her waist, spine severed a moment before her first death, life kept longer than nature could ever care for. Her legs and pelvis fell into the pit with a thud. A splatter of innards followed and she stopped singing, the last note echoing in his ears.

After that it was only a question of time before the others, his friends, followed. The weak little bastards went at the same time, leaving him alone in the foetid basement of an abandoned house. He hated them for it, snapped their thigh bones before dumping them in the charnel pit.

Like always he was exhausted, sad that it had to end. Glad he came.

"I must be getting home," he said, gesturing at the torn corpses, the gangrenous pits lining the perimeter of the basement. "Don't worry about the mess, someone will come by. God's rest, 'til the Devil takes his due, my Merry Men!"

Upstairs he removed the mask and silk forensic overall, sighing as it left his naked, bloated body. He took care dressing in his street clothes, casual for the holidays. Every year the performance was better but he was getting old. He didn't want to ruin everything with a fall putting his socks on too fast. One hip was already replaced and eternity was waiting, sniffing around with pronouncements and opinions, judging his immortality.

He didn't care to hear what eternity had to say, not today.

Outside his car was waiting, summoned as he dressed. The driver, a man who knew he no longer owned himself, held the door open. Three hours and a short private flight later The Merry Man arrived home. The sprawling house was overrun with children, grandchildren, great-grandchildren, nephews and nieces, cousins and friends, estranged aunts and uncles, new acquaintances, every relation possible. Thick snow lay outside as they all joked and smiled, pleased to see his bulk.

It was Christmas Day tomorrow.

He let them think that was why he was so happy, pleasant and delightful, not objecting when the children sat in his lap, played with his beard – long, curling, snowy – and asked for more than they knew.

Last Christmas - Theresa Derwin

CHRISTMAS FOR ME IS all about the three Fs; family, friends and food. I got hooked on the whole concept of a traditional Christmas when I first met Alice. She was a big fan of Christmas, the whole nine yards; a tree decorated to high hell, balloons and trimmings plastered all of the ceiling, which was a pain in the arse taking down by 6th January each year, I can tell you.

We'd only been together a year when she suggested the 'Sad Single Rejects' Christmas dinner. Of course, we never let those who were invited know what it was called, or what we were up to. We just had so many friends and family members who hadn't met the right person yet. They were destined to spend Christmas day alone or stuck with relatives they couldn't stand, so about four years ago we started a new tradition. We invited our best friends who were single and Alice's cousin Paul along to share an early Christmas dinner with us, the last Friday before Christmas.

It began as a small affair; me, Alice and four or five others, but pretty soon it expanded until we numbered ten. A nice even number.

Alice was an angel really. She secretly hoped some of those singletons would hook up and find true love; the kind of relationship we had. And like the romantic she was, she played that George Michael song again and again, but I guess I didn't mind so much.

Yeah, she was special, and what we had was special.

Until last Christmas.

Paul had hooked up with Graham the year before, but had a straight, single friend Dave, who he wanted to invite that year.

I was the chef pretty much. I'd get out Prue Leith's Cooking Bible, The Hairy Biker's Christmas Countdown, and even resorted to Jamie Oliver; though his roasties were pukka.

Normally I'd do duck, gammon and turkey with all the trimmings to add a bit of variety, but last year was our fifth anniversary and I wanted to do something unique. So, I read Dickens' 'A Christmas Carol'. I got hold of Mrs Beeton's 'Book of Household Management' and a guide to the Bronte's Christmas. I decided to do a real Victorian feast; the whole shebang.

It had to be goose. Goose was pretty expensive nowadays, but apparently it was one of the cheapest birds back in the day.

I got the goose from Sainsbury's, laid it all out, cooked it overnight letting all the juices run onto the spuds. Did brussel sprouts, chestnuts, the lot.

We were all tucking in, sharing a glass of plonk, when I noticed Alice had been gone for ages. And so had this Dave.

I didn't know what to expect. I thought maybe she'd gone to wash up the dishes to keep on top of it or something. But she wasn't in the kitchen.

So I tried the bathroom.

She wasn't there.

Next, I tried the bedroom.

She was there alright, in flagrante, with the new bloke Dave. In *our* bedroom. On *our bed.*

Writhing, pumping flesh.

"What the fuck are you doing?" I screamed.

"Brett!"

"Alice – What – the – fuck – are – you – doing?"

Dave stopped rutting and spun round off Alice, pulling the duvet over himself.

Alice was crying as I walked out of the bedroom, staggered down the stairs, grabbed the goose off the table and threw it across the room.

So, the next Christmas came around pretty quick, though every time I heard that song I shuddered. Alice had moved out of mine and straight in with Dave. I saw them together sometimes at the pub, or the cinema, until it got stupidly awkward so I broke the ice and said hi to them. Eventually we got to chatting and a couple times I met Dave for a drink at the local, where we'd watch the footie and he'd moan about 'the Mrs'; my Alice.

So when it came to last night, I thought fuck it, why not? I invited Dave round for dinner and a couple of beers. I didn't bother invite the rest of the sad single rejects.

Dave and I had gone out a couple of times by now so he was cool coming over.

"Come in, mate," I said, opening the door.

"Brett, how goes it?" he asked, lugging in a crate of beer.

"Not so bad, still cooking up a storm in the kitchen."

"Nice one."

Dave sat down, I cracked open the beer. He'd brought some pale ales to go with the food. I'd suggested it. I'd got into Saturday Kitchen where they told you what drinks went with what meat. A couple beers in, I asked about Alice.

Whenever I did, at first, Dave would always tense a little before answering. Think he was surprised still that we were mates.

"Yeah, she's okay," he said, "still nagging. Thank God she's away."

"Away?"

"Yeah, parents or a friend's I think."

Chat moved onto the footie then I said "Food's ready. Done us a starter. Homemade liver pate."

"Sounds good."

We sat at the table. It was a bit gay, mind, but I wanted to show off the main course when it was time.

Dave dived in with the pate and brown toast I'd done. He even slathered on some of the onion marmalade I'd got from M & S.

I wanted to outdo myself this year.

We sat and chilled a bit before the main.

Then I asked him again.

"Where did you say Alice was?"

"Her parents I think, mate," he answered looking flustered, 'cause it was the second time I'd asked.

"Right," I said, and smiled, "I'll get the main. The piece de resistance."

I carried in the veg first and laid all the dishes and spoons out. Then I brought in my infamous Jamie Oliver roasties, the gravy jug, cranberry sauce – though come to think of it, not sure cranberry sauce would go with the meat.

Then I brought in two meat platters and laid it in front of him.

"TA DA!"

Dave was quiet for a second, then, "Er – mate?"

"Yep Dave?"

I sat down and started to sharpen the carving knife, the sound reverberating in the silence.

"Is that?"

"Yep, Dave. Tuck in."

When I'd hacked Alice to bits in the kitchen the day before, she wouldn't stop bloody screaming. In fact, I'd brought the head in on the first platter after shaving her hair off, and her mouth was still open in a rictus grin, her tongue lolling out. The stubble on her head was blackened, her skin was crispy and pink, and there was a good bit of crackling on her cheeks, though her eyes had burst out and hung like glutinous blobs from the sockets.

"Well done or pink?"

Dave just stared at me for a moment open mouthed. I'd figured he was in shock.

"Could've swore she said she was going to her Mum's."

I laughed, then took the lid off the second, larger platter.

"Breast or leg?" I asked, and laughed again at my own joke.

Dave looked up at me then, and I understood things a little clearer.

"I've always been a breast man," he said, grabbing his knife and fork.

I nodded.

Me too.

Wood For The Fire - Michael R. Brush

HUNTER AND I OCCUPIED a small hunting lodge on the outskirts of the estate. A mutual friend had allowed us the liberty to use this place for some time of quiet to get over the hectic term. We were, and are, quiet chaps so we relished the retreat to the country despite that, in deep winter, there was no game to be hunted and away from the house there was a lack of festive camaraderie.

Termed 'Scrooges' from the recent story by Dickens we were at home and content. You could say that we were happy there. We would drink our sherry and bitters, smoke our pipes and relax in our respective books. The one drawback from being so far away from the main house was that the service was erratic. We were sympathetic even when we ran short of comestibles, like game pie, or the bare necessities like bitters or sherry and one night, not too far off Christmas Eve, inside we ran short of wood for the fire.

As there was no reason for us both to freeze outside in the snow, Hunter and I drew lots to see who would have to brave the cold dark night for the log store, stacked against one side or other of the lodge. As I saw his face on realising he had the short straw, I relented. 'Look, old chap, there's no point in being frozen half to death as you might, and, from your expression, also being half shocked to death by the boggies, I'll go and shall return only half dead. Now how's that?' I asked.

'Morris, you're a lifesaver, you won't tell anyone when we get back, will you, that I was an awful coward?' he asked.

'Absolutely not, old chum,' I lied. Believing the wood stack to be just around the corner from the back door, I merely tugged on my greatcoat and set off.

Round the corner I found a small fellow collecting the very last of the logs before making his way off, into the woods, 'I say, good man,' I thought I'd best be on good behaviour considering the season, despite the names the staff had given us, 'we've use for that wood you've got there.'

With that he turned around and looked up at me, the night being well lit with the moon's gentle rays being reflected by the deep snow, and said, 'There's them that 'as greater need then yurselves.'

I looked at this misshapen figure, he was small with long arms and short legs and a face awfully wrinkled by age and he wore the merest of clothing, despite the temperature. Having been taken aback by his odd appearance, I challenged him, 'Let me walk with you and if I agree, then they may keep the wood.'

'Very well, master,' says he folding the meagre supply under one arm, 'best ye take my hand or you'll never manage to follow where I go.'

By this time it was too late save to follow his lead and thinking that if worst came to the worst, I'd be able to deal with the impudent fellow, I took his hand. We plunged direct into the forest, following an old track, barely more than an animal's trail. I kept being caught by branches whereas he was so short as to be able to walk unimpeded by obstacle.

Sometime after losing sight of the hunting lodge I spied a ramshackle cottage. Plainly made from mud and sticks, it almost blended into the background, even when I was on the doorstep.

'My job's done 'ere,' said my companion, 'Ye can take the wood in yourself and decide the justice o' the case.'

With that he dumped what was left of the wood stack and made his way further into the forest. I had barely picked up his load and then knocked on the door when, on sudden impulse, I looked around for the small fellow. Slightly discomforted at his disappearance, I had no time to look round properly as the door was promptly answered by an elderly figure who virtually pulled me inside.

'Not a night to be outside, no sir,' said my new companion once we were both inside and then, 'thank you very much for this, not that it'll do much good now, I reckon,' he said in a mournful tone.

Drawn by his gaze, I looked beyond him to see a slight figure beneath the inadequate blankets, atop the pallet of straw that was leaking out onto the floor around it. As he was taking the wood from me, I was lost in speculation. I could remember no mention of anybody who still resided in the woods hereabouts I was so moved that I asked, 'Is there anything else I can do for you?'

'Why no sir, thank ye but, well,' he carried on, hesitatingly, 'if ye could but mention us in prayers come Christmas mornin', we'd be awful grateful. I just 'ope, sir, tis not too late.'

Well, I argued about sending the doctor or bringing the pair of them back to the hunting lodge there and then all to no avail and so, promising to do as asked of me, I turned around on the doorstep and asked, 'And just how should I know you when I ask for prayers to be said on your behalf?'

'Oh, they'll know us, sir, at the Big 'Ouse, just say tis for the auld couple by the well and that'll do nicely sir and now you'd best be off back to your warmth,' said the man, ushering me out.

Once outside, I could only see the set of footprints made by my heavy feet and when I asked my host about this, he replied, 'Oh, that'll ov been the Gruagach who brought ye', good sir. Now mind ye follow your own prints or ye might not find yer own way 'ome.' With that he shut the door as best he could and left me all alone.

When I returned to Hunter and discussed the night's weirdness, we concluded that if we only told the priest who came for the Christmas service to say a few words, I would have discharged my duty.

All seemed to go well on Christmas morn until we got to the prayers of intercession. When, however, the priest mentioned my two new acquaintances the old lady of the house fainted straight off and there was much excitement. It was only later that I found that the old couple by the well had passed away one winter, many years ago.

Yet To Come - Lex H. Jones

Christmas Eve 1977

THE SNOW ON THE rooftops was close to three inches thick now. Just like the forecast had predicted, it was really starting to come down, the flakes getting thicker with every few minutes that passed. The temperature had probably dropped too, but James hadn't noticed. He'd been shaking since he left work, so an extra shiver from the cold would easily escape his notice. Not even up here, on the ledge of the highest rooftop he could get to.

James had hoped, and naively assumed, that the redundancies wouldn't hit him. Sure they'd been getting closer and closer to his section of the company, but he always assumed that he'd be safe. That his job wasn't one that could be done cheaper by the Chinese. He was so secure in that belief, in fact, that he'd happily missed last month's Mortgage payment to buy presents for the family. The bank had been in touch already, of course, but he'd managed to convince them that his Christmas bonus would clear the back payment, like it did every year. Except now there wasn't going to be a Christmas bonus. Or even another pay-cheque. He got his wages a month in advance, like everyone else, and he'd already been paid for December. The Unions had raised Hell about it, of course, but James wasn't a member. He couldn't afford the monthly subs anymore along with the alimony and child support.

Of course, it wasn't just money that had brought James to the roof of the old mill this evening. Money issues had dogged him his entire life, before he was even old enough to earn his own. Some people came from money, some came from a lack of it. James Hill was definitely the latter. His family was the kind that just couldn't hold onto money. No matter how hard they worked, how intelligent or industrious, their natural state was one of barely scraping by. James had been no different, and that had led to more fights with Marlene than he could even remember now. Which had, in turn, led to the bar on most nights. And that had inevitably led him into Delilah's arms. Well, arms and other parts.

James had been used to being knocked back by life. Whatever happened, he could always console himself that at least one aspect of his life was still OK. 'It doesn't matter that I lost my wife, I still have Delilah'. 'It doesn't matter that I lost Delilah, I still have my job.' And so on, and so forth. But now James had no second half to those sentences. Nothing to fall back on, nothing to console himself with. He didn't even have enough change in his pocket to go to the bar. Not the bar Delilah worked at, of course. He wasn't welcome there anymore either since she found out he was married with children. Any bar would have done. But none of them served free drinks, so here he was, sat on the ledge of the old mill with his feet dangling over the edge.

Posterus walked through the heavy snow, his hands in the pockets of his floor-length black coat. He wore a hooded black sweatshirt under the coat, the hood of which was pulled up as he walked, shadowing his face. The snow obscured his vision slightly, making it difficult to find what he was looking for, his head craned upwards as he scanned the rooftops left and right. He was walking in the middle of the road so he could angle his vision to better see the rooftops on both sides. The snow was thick enough that there were no cars on the road, but Posterus wasn't exactly concerned about that anyway. Cars would pass through him as though he weren't there, just like the pedestrians did. The more sensitive ones sometimes felt a slight shudder whenever this happened, but most didn't notice anything at all.

"There." Posterus said to himself as he caught sight of a man sat on the ledge of the old mill. Not the tallest building he could have chosen, but high enough to do the job.

Approaching the wall of the old mill at a running pace, Posterus faced it for a second and then became something close to a shadow. A shadow which stretched up to the roof, reforming in the human, black-clad and hooded shape of Posterus as it reached the top.
"James Hill." Posterus called as he walked towards the seated figure.
"Huh? Who are you?? Are you a cop?" asked a startled James.
"No. But I am here to help you. My name is Posterus."
"Kind of name is that?"
"The one I was given." He shrugged. This is why I didn't use to talk to them. "Do you mind if I sit down next to you?"
"Suit yourself. But you're not talking me out of it." James said defiantly.
"You've still got some fire in you. That's good. It means you haven't let yourself be completely defeated." Posterus pointed out, walking over and taking a seat on the ledge.
James watched him approach, and furrowed his brow at the fact that the stranger didn't leave any footfalls in the snow. His coat was bizarre too. Long and black, and thick looking, but it seemed to waft slightly as though underwater. The ends looked ragged and torn into strips, which only added to this effect. James shuddered, and this time he felt it.
"Are you from a charity? The Samaritans or something?" asked James, sitting right the black-clad figure about four feet to his right.
"No, not quite. Although not as far away from them as you might think."
"So you are going to try and talk me out of this." James sighed.
"Is that so terrible? That someone wants to help? To keep you in this world?"
"A stranger. Who's probably being paid to be here. Not someone who knows me."
"I know you, James." Posterus smiled warmly, the lower half of his face visible beneath the hood. James noted how deathly pale the man's skin was, the lips blue like those of a corpse.
"Who sent you, then? Was it the company? Bet they're worried about the bad press, huh? Well they better start

worrying, I doubt I'll be the only one."

"Perhaps not. But you're my concern tonight, nobody else. I chose you."

"Why?"

"Because I was told not to. That it would be too difficult."

"But you came anyway. So you're a stubborn one like me, huh?" James laughed. "Gotta admire that."

"Tell me then, James. What do you think is the best case scenario once your skull cracks open on that concrete there?" asked Posterus, stretching a finger slowly and pointing down at the street below. James stared at the pointing finger, at how pale and almost skeletal it was.

'It's all in the pointing', Posterus thought to himself.

"For me? Nothing. It just ends. For everyone else? They don't care."

"It doesn't just end."

"Oh here we go, going to tell me about God being against suicides now and all that business?" James rolled his eyes.

"No, not at all. Charge the words of men against men themselves. Not God." Posterus remarked, then continued: "But whatever lies have been sold to mankind as truths, I can tell you that it doesn't end with your head cracking open like an eggshell. You'd be lost, wandering forever without knowing where to go. You were a decent enough man, so your chain wouldn't be that heavy, but it would still be there. You broke your marriage vows, after all. That alone earns you a few links."

"What are you blabbing on about?"

"Will you take my hand? I want to show you the consequences of what you're about to do. Not to yourself, but to everyone else."

"Take your hand? Why, I'm not the praying type."

"Just give me this moment's trust. What do you have to lose?" Posterus suggested, offering his hand.

  James sighed and took the pale, slender hand in his own. Instinctively he closed his eyes, expecting to be reluctantly led in prayer. When no such words came from Posterus, James opened his eyes, only to see that he was no longer staring out at the city. He was in the country, surrounded by trees and softly falling snow.

"What the Hell?? Where are we? How did this happen?"

"I'm going to show you something, like I said. Show you the world if you don't change your current path, and how it's affected by your passing."

"Is this a dream? You've drugged me or something, right?" James asked, turning around and around as though expecting his new surroundings to disappear.

"No, I haven't drugged you. When we're finished here you'll be back on the roof of the old mill and barely a moment will have passed."

"Finished with what? I have no idea what's going on."

"Then tell yourself this is a dream, or a hallucination. Whatever it takes to best accept it. In the end it doesn't matter as long as you pay attention and understand what you're seeing." Posterus explained.

"Alright, so I'm dreaming. I fell asleep on that roof." James shrugged. "That's why I don't feel the cold and why the snow isn't settling on my shoulders."

"Fine. Now come with me, I need to show you."

Posterus led James through the woodland and out of it, coming to a large field in which a farmhouse sat. There were stables for horses, safely kept out of the snow. As they walked towards the house, James glanced at the car parked in the large gravel driveway.

"That toy on the dashboard..." he pointed at the stuffed yellow cat in question. "That's Marlene's."

"I believe that is your wife's car."

"She doesn't drive a car, she can't afford it." James looked puzzled.

"Let's look inside." Posterus suggested, starting to feel a growing concern deep in his gut.

Posterus led James to the wall of the large farmhouse, and then guided him as they both stepped through it as though they (or it) were immaterial. James looked stunned, but his attention was taken away from it by the sight of his wife sat in

a luxurious living room, reading by the fireplace whilst his children played. There was a piano in the corner, the furniture was classic yet expensive, the Christmas decorations warm and traditional. There was an aura of simple joy about the place.
"Marlene! It's me!" James cried, running over and standing before. She didn't react.
"She can't hear you. Or see you. These are but the shadows of things that may be."
"The future? Is that what you're showing me?"
"The future if things don't change, yes." Posterus nodded, swallowing the lump that had manifested itself in his throat. Something was wrong here. He'd chosen badly.
"Is she rich? Did she remarry? Someone with money?"
"No, she never remarried. Your loss caused her deep guilt. She never found love again. Her money is from the life insurance you took out, after she'd asked you enough times that you finally arranged it. That, plus she sued your company for its part in pushing you to that roof. The money from both set her and your children up with a much easier situation, financially speaking."
"So she's better with me gone!"
"No, that's not the point. Money is one thing, but…"
"But nothing! Marlene and me, we're not going to fix things! We can't, I went too far. She'll never forgive me for Delilah, never."
"People can forgive much if you give them time. All you've seen is one aspect of the world that, on the surface, could be interpreted as being improved for your absence. But that's a very small part of the picture, there will be more that I can show you."
"You don't even sound sure yourself!" James yelled at his hooded companion, the happy scene around them continuing in blissful oblivion.
"This threw me, I admit that. I neglected to consider how serious money and its related evils were to you, but if you permit me the chance to show you something else…"
"Money was what we fought about more than anything! What led me to drink! To Delilah! To everything! How could you

not think this would matter to me?"
"James, just listen to me…." Posterus pleaded, knowing he was losing this one.
"All I ever wanted to do, was provide for them! Give them a nice life, to be happy, to not feel stress and panic every time an envelope fell through the goddamned door! And look! They have that now. And all it takes is for me to do what I was planning to do before you turned up tonight!"
"I don't think us being here is helping." Posterus took James' hand quickly in his own, and the world around them fell away. It was replaced momentarily with the rooftop of the old mill, the two of them sitting on the ledge as though nothing had happened. James got to his feet and inhaled deeply.
"I guess you did help me after all." He said with a mocking snort.
"No, listen. I can show you more, I chose badly there, I admit, but if you just…"
"Thank you." Said James, and then he took a step forward.

Christmas Eve 1987

The ice on the pond was thick enough that it had become a makeshift skating rink. Against local government advise to the contrary, of course, but that made no difference to the revellers currently dancing, twirling and frequently falling on the ice. The snowfall had slowed from the earlier blizzards, but was still coming strong and thick on the ground.
Posterus sat on the park bench staring at the skaters, but not really seeing them. His hood was raised, shadowing most of his face, his hands in the pockets of his coat. He glanced up slightly as a man in a white coat came to sit beside him, holding a cup of hot cocoa. Pinned to the man's left lapel was a

gold-coloured badge shaped like wings, with the words "A2C, Odbody" emblazoned onto it.

"How are you getting along, Po?" asked the man, taking a seat besides Posterus.

"Hello Clarence."

"Thought I'd come in and check on you. You've had nine sick days in a row now, people are starting to get concerned."

"Nine isn't that many, given what happened."

"No, you're right, it's not. But they're worried, and so am I. So I wanted to come and see how you were doing."

"Kind of you." Posterus forced a smile.

"Have you thought about coming back to work?"

"I think about it all the time, Clarence. But then I also think about what happened."

"You know that wasn't your fault. James Mills was a difficult one. He had a 'No Fly Zone' marker on him for that reason. We can't save everyone, and he was deemed impossible."

"Which was exactly why I wanted to try." Posterus defended.

"I know." Clarence smiled, patting Posterus on the back. "And that's why we love you. You're the best there's ever been in the Y.T.C division, everyone knows that. You just lost one, that's all. It happens. We're none of us perfect. Hell, it took me 200 years to get my promotion! I was going nowhere. You on the other hand, well your first case was a resounding success."

"It wasn't anything big like a suicide, Clarence. That first case I took on was just an old miser who'd lost the spirit of the season, that's all. And I wasn't even alone. I had backup from two other divisions, Past and Present, and also we brought in an outside contractor with personal connections to the soul we wanted to save."

"You did your part, rounded off the case perfectly and achieved the desired result." Clarence said proudly.

"I was so nervous I didn't even speak to the guy. Just stayed silent and pointed at everything."

"It worked" Clarence reminded him, sipping his cocoa. "So much that being silent became 'your thing' for awhile. Until you got promoted, started working alone more often and it became impractical. Then it turned out you were good at the talking too."

"Not good enough, evidently."

"You can't let Mills ruin your career. He was a tough one, the worst kind of tough one. Some call them 'too far gone' or 'lost cause', but I hate that. I don't like to think of anyone that way, and evidently you don't either."

"It should never be too late to do right by them. Not at this time of year."

"You're right. And I wanted to help, you know. I could see right away that Y.T.C Division didn't have the tools for this. I wanted to lend you the Alt Projector but they wouldn't sign it out to me. Said Y.T.C could work with their namesake, visions of things "Yet To Come", and that was it. The projection of alternate timelines was for Angel divisions only."

"They do like their rules."

"I think they're worried about setting a precedent if we start breaking them. It's happened before and it's never usually a good result."

"But you were willing to break them to help me?" Posterus turned to face Clarence, a soft smile on his lips.

"Your work always inspired me. If you believed Mills could be saved, then I wanted to believe it too. I knew that nothing you could show him would get him off that ledge, but thought maybe, just maybe, showing him some alternate worlds with different outcomes might help. I never got the chance, and I feel awful about it."

"You can't take that on your shoulders, Clarence. This one was on me."

"It shouldn't have been on any of us. At least you tried."

"Maybe I should have threatened to jump myself to see if that brought him out of it. Worked for you, right?" Posterus grinned.

"Hey! My methods might be a little unconventional, but results are results! All you have to do is show people that they matter. That their life can touch others, even when they've stopped believing it. Especially then."

"I'm going to come back to work, Clarence." Posterus assured him. "I just don't know when."

"How about tonight?" Clarence smiled and handed him a paper file.

"You son of a...This was your plan all along wasn't it?"

"Nope, I did want to come see you. To check in. But depending how it went, I might have considered handing you this. And I think you're ready."

"I don't know...."

"Po…" Clarence put a hand on Posterus' shoulder. "You're ready. Just remember; talking is good, but be you. Cause you're the best thing that ever happened to Y.T.C Division. The Past and Present guys can be sweet and saccharin and laughing all the time. But you're you. So be you."

"You mean try things the old way?"

"Well a little of the old, little of the new. You're good at the talking, but sometimes people need to be made to listen. And they're much more likely to do that when they're close to pissing their pants, you know? Excuse my language."

Posterus nodded, took the file and read it, then allowed a soft smile to spread across his deathly-blue lips.

"I'm gonna wait here until he arrives. And if you send anyone else in, or I see any snipers outside those windows, one of these poor people is going to have a very bad Christmas." Said the man in the leather bomber-jacket, speaking angrily into the phone.

"I hear you Jerry, but I'm not confident Mr Wethers will be safe if we send him in there with you."

"Well you have about half an hour to get confident, or these folks are going to start paying for it."

The black phone was slammed back onto the receiver, then pushed loudly back along the counter. Jerry Simmons wiped the sweat from his face and turned back to the scene behind him. Seven customers, the only ones desperate enough to be in a bank on Christmas Eve, were laid face down on the floor. The two members of staff who'd evidently drawn the short straw and been forced to work this shift, one male and one female, sat close by. The female teller was desperately

trying to stop the blood flowing from the shoulder wound of her male co-worker. Jerry swallowed the lump in his throat when he saw this, gripping the pistol tightly in his hand. He hadn't wanted to hurt anybody when this started, but the male teller had tried to tackle him and the gun had fired without his fully realising it. Now here he was threatening more of them, although he kept telling himself that this was more of an act to convince the police he was serious.
"Hey you, what's your name?" Jerry asked the female teller.
"Doris." She replied, shaking and crying.
"Do you have a medical kit here? First aid?"
"Yes."
"Go get it, then use whatever you have to help stop that bleeding." Doris nodded but seemed reluctant to leave her co-worker. Jerry pointed at one of the customers and said: "You there, yeah the guy nearest to her. You keep pressure on the wound whilst she gets the kit. Then go back to lying face-down when she comes back. Nobody try anything and you'll all get through this, alright?"

Doris got up and quickly made her way to the bathroom for the medical kit. The bank customer nearest to the bleeding teller did as instructed and put pressure on the wound. Jerry sat down on the nearest stool and rested his arm on the bank counter. He wiped the sweat from his forehead again, stopping it dripping down into his eyes. The windows were covered with the security shutters, but he suspected it wouldn't stop a trained sniper. They probably had infra-red cameras and bullets that would cut through those things, he told himself. His only hope was keeping an eye on these hostages.
The lights from the Christmas tree in the corner were casting a large shadow of the tree itself on the wall, which now caught Jerry's attention. The shadow appeared to be moving, growing, stretching up the wall so that it appeared almost like a hooded figure leaning over him. He felt himself shudder, then almost fell off his stool when the shadow dropped from the ceiling, taking the form of a man in a black coat and hood standing before him, his face shadowed.
"Jesus!" Jerry exclaimed, aiming his gun at the figure, only to

realise that his hand was, in fact, empty.

The hooded figure extended a slow, menacing finger in Jerry's direction, pointing at something behind him. He turned and saw himself, still sat on the counter stool, frozen in the act of wiping the sweat from his brow. Everyone else in the bank was frozen too.

"What the Hell?" Jerry gasped.

The hooded figure swept closer, standing before Jerry about a fall taller than he was.

"Jerry Simmons." Said Posterus.

"Y..yes?"

"I want to show you what will happen if you continue down this road."

"Who are you? How'd you get in here?"

"I am the spirit of...."

"Wait, wait, I'm hallucinating this, I must have passed out on that chair. Which means I don't need to listen to whatever crap you're about to say. I need to focus."

The hooded figure became a shadow again faster than Jerry could actually see it transform, only now it seemed to fill the entire bank, stretching out over the walls, floors and ceiling and staring right down at Jerry with two dark crimson eyes in the centre of the hood. Jerry felt a childlike panic and couldn't stop himself crying, as ungodly fear filled his very being. He dropped to his knees and clasped his hands together as if in prayer.

"Oh god this is real isn't it? This is real." He repeated over and over.

The shadow took its more-human form again and said: "You. Will. Listen."

"Ok. Ok I'll listen." Jerry compiled, the unnatural fear that flowed through him controlling his every action now.

"What brought you to this? Tell me."

"You don't... already know?"

"My domain is that which is yet to come. Not that which has gone before."

"I used to work here. I found out that my boss, Harold Wethers, the manager....he was having an affair with his

secretary. My wife is a friend of his wife, I felt she should know. And then he fired me. And cancelled my pension. I can't afford the lawyers he can, and with the fancy friends he has he's ruined any chance I have of getting work!"
"And you think that doing this will help that?"
"What? No, I just...he has to pay."
"He will. Men like that always do."
"Yeah? When? They own every damn authority figure there is."
"Not all of them." Posterus said firmly. "He will pay, when his time comes. But he isn't my interest tonight. You are. Take my hand."
"What happens if I do?"

Posterus said nothing but extended a pale, almost bone-like hand in Jerry's direction. He took it, reluctantly, and closed his eyes tightly against whatever might come next. When he felt brave enough to open them, he was no longer in the bank. He was stood in a cemetery, directly in front of a fresh headstone. Posterus pointed at it, and Jerry clearly read his name, and the date of death; December 24th 1987.
"I die today?? That's what you're showing me."
"How did you think this would end, Jerry? You're not a killer, not a criminal. You're a man who's desperate and angry. But you're using that to threaten innocent lives. You've been pushed too far, it happens. But this doesn't end well for you."
"Does... does anyone else get hurt?"
"Yes."
"How many?"
"If these shadows remain unchanged, then at least three other lives end today. One of which is a police officer. None of them are Wetherby."
"I don't want to kill Wetherby, I don't want to kill anyone. I just want...I just..."
"To scare him. Because that's the only way he'll listen." Posterus nodded sagely. "I understand that. A friend reminded me of how true that can be quite recently, in fact. But this isn't the right path for you."
"What else could I have done?" Jerry yelled, his rage directed

at the grave as though he was truly asking himself rather than Posterus.

"There's a gulf between having a bad day and being a murderer, Jerry. You just let yourself cross it. And now your wife has to live with the knowledge of what you did, your friends, your family…"

"No! I haven't done anything! No-one's died yet."

"This is what will come to pass." Posterus pointed at the grave again.

"No! Alright, what are you? An angel or spirit or something? Assuming I'm not hallucinating this, or even if I am; why would I see this unless it could be changed? It's a warning, right? Of what might be. Not a guarantee of what will."

Posterus said nothing, but silently nodded.

"Then take me back."

"I won't be responsible for your death, Jerrys."

"I'm not going to die. I'll do the jail time, get help, whatever it takes. It's better than…" He glanced at the grave again. "Whatever happens next, this is worse. Because this way there's not even a chance to put it right."

Posterus allowed himself a smile. It always made him happy when they understood. When they realised that it's never too late to make amends. To put things right. It may not always be easy, it may cost you more than you thought you had to give, but it can be done. And that, to Posterus, was always the true meaning of Christmas. The giving of whatever you can to help those that need it. A gift has no real meaning if it's too easily given.

"Take my hand."

Jerry's eyes opened once more and he found himself wiping the sweat from his forehead. He looked up just in time to see Doris returning with the medical kit. Glancing down at the gun in his hand, he took a deep breath, then placed it down on the counter. With his now-free hand, he reached for the phone and dialled the number of the negotiator he had been speaking to previously.

"Detective? It's Jerry. No, nobody's died. I'm going to open the doors and come out. I've put my gun down. Yes, I'll raise my hands so you can see when I walk out. Please send a medic in for the bank teller."

Jerry hung up the phone, and turned to see the bank customers slowly daring to raise their heads and look at him. "I'm sorry," he said, before slowly approaching the main doors and opening them.

Christmas Eve 1988

"So how are you finding New York?" asked Clarence, approaching through the falling snow that steadily filled the pathways of Central Park.
"Not like I remember it. But it still has the same heart in the ways that really matter." Posterus replied, leaning against a streetlamp.
"I have a special treat for you." Said Clarence, taking a paper file out of his coat. "After the sterling work you did last year, I've managed to get them to give you this case. I said it would have nostalgic value for you."
"What makes you think I appreciate nostalgia?" Posterus smiled, taking the file.
"Everybody does at Christmas!" Clarence beamed. "It's when we think back to happy memories from the past, whilst also enjoying the present and looking forward to everything yet to happen. And on that subject…" he pointed at the file.
"So I'll be part of a team operation again?" Posterus noted as he read through the case details.
"Yes, but this one's tough. He needs the pants scaring off him, which is where you come in. The other divisions will do their bit, but we need you to really hammer it home. We figure you'll be the deciding factor in this one."
"Frank Cross at the I.R.C Broadcasting House. Also known as

"Lumpy", apparently. He makes television shows and treats his employees like crap. Mean old ass, forgotten the true spirit of Christmas. You're right, this is nostalgic."

"You can thank me tomorrow." Clarence smiled, patting Posterus on the back. "Merry Christmas, Po."

Posterus nodded and placed the file inside his coat as Clarence disappeared into the snow. He cracked his fingers and craned his neck from side to side, ready to get to work. "Merry Christmas, Clarence," he spoke into the snowfall, and then made his way to the Broadcasting House.

You Better Not Pout - Kayleigh Marie Edwards

KATIE WAS ALONE IN her room as the last traces of daylight slithered away into the shadows. She sat motionless on her bed, her favourite teddy clutched to her chest. The air in the room was tinged with that particular icy cold that only came with snow, but she didn't notice.

Her closet door lay ajar, allowing a glimpse of what appeared to be a bulky, shadowy figure just standing there in the gloom. Katie didn't notice that either. She. Was In. A Mood. It was only a week until Christmas day, but she was already furious. She didn't know how or why, but for the last three years, she had apparently made the Fat, Beardy Bastard's shit list.

When she was six, she had written the sweetest letter to him and had requested the Barbie Dream Boat. On Christmas day, she tore the paper off the biggest gift to discover rollerblades. She was grateful, of course, but a little disappointed. That was until Poppy, her younger sister, opened a Barbie Dream Boat. True, they had both asked for it, so she always knew she only had a fifty percent chance of being the benefactor of such a brilliant gift (her parents were under the impression they shared their toys with each other). However, she'd been really good that year and Poppy… well, in her opinion, Poppy was a shit.

When she was seven, Katie figured she better try harder with her letter to Santa, and wrote it entirely in jolly, festive rhyme. She asked, enthusiastically, for a Gameboy. Once again, upon Christmas morning, she hurried to the Christmas tree and freed her gift from its glittery wrapping. What she opened was some sort of handheld console, sure, but it wasn't the Gameboy with Tetris that she had been dying for. She figured she'd forgive Santa; perhaps he was like her dad when it came to games and he'd got confused and brought her the wrong device by accident. That was until Poppy opened a Gameboy. And it was pink. Pink! She was especially confused that year because she had been pretty damn excellent in every area of her life; her colouring was all inside the lines, her homework always done early, she tidied her own room. Poppy, on the other hand, had just the week before emptied an entire jar of mustard into the fish tank.

Last year, when she was eight, Katie had thought of nothing else for the run up to the festive period. And by run up, we're not just talking the twelve days of Christmas; we're talking the full twelve months on the calendar. From Boxing Day onwards, Katie was obsessed with being on top of Santa's good list. She got up and made her bed every morning. She joined gymnastics and practiced her routines every single night, and she had become quite the local celebrity for it. There was even talk of her joining a professional junior squad – a fact that her parents were particularly ecstatic over. She never said a swear word. She never answered back, even if her parents were taking Poppy's side when it was *definitely* Poppy's fault. She ate all her vegetables. She went to school and worked really hard (even the day she felt really poorly and her mum said she could have stayed home), and she got gold stars for everything. She had one hundred percent attendance and full marks in everything. Her dad had started to call her his 'little genius'.

When she wrote her letter to Santa that year, she requested, nay, pleaded for, a Roald Dahl book set. She loved Roald Dahl stories, especially *The Twits*. Imagine her dismay, her fury, when Poppy opened that Roald Dahl collection. Her eyes bore into Poppy's skull, thinking that she felt like a twit herself. She also thought that her sister was something that sounded a bit like a giant peach, only the word she was thinking of began with a 'B', and she wasn't allowed to say it.

She just couldn't understand it. She knew that Santa was always watching, even when she was asleep. She hadn't shouted or cried or so much as pouted all year and not only did she not get the present she wanted, but she was clearly being punished for something by having to watch her sister's face light up when she received the books instead of her. It was a fate worse than coal. It was downright cruel.

"What's with the face?" Katie's Mum asked, reaching into the closet and pulling out Katie's big, puffy winter coat. Katie was so engrossed in her broiling hatred that she hadn't even noticed her mum enter the room. She shrugged.

"Well, I know something that will cheer you up," Katie's mum continued, motioning Katie to follow her out of the room.

"Where are we going?" Katie demanded, suddenly noticing her mum had her coat on too. Katie's mum smiled and winked, but didn't reply. Katie already knew anyway; they were going to the Garden Centre. It was a Christmas tradition to go there every year and sit on Santa's knee. Katie normally counted down the days for such an occasion, but she was simply not in the mood today.

Two thoughts crossed Katie's mind as she sat in the car, watching the dark, gloomy world go by. The first was that Santa was the last person she wanted to see, and she ought to slap his face and add a bit more redness to his cheeks. The other was that the Garden Centre was the most stupid place in the world for Santa to hang out. It was full of plants and boring things and weird smells, and she hated it. She just hated everything.

Katie's mum followed her daughter, who was actually *stomping,* into the Garden Centre. She thought it was the weather nipping at her fingertips and toes but now she suspected it was actually dread. When Katie was mad, there were signs. Sometimes her words came out garbled or mixed up, and she got this insane look in her eyes – it was the way they just didn't move. She'd fix her gaze on something and then it was like the rest of her went on a holiday somewhere and just left those staring eyes behind like they were anchored to whatever they were staring at. The fixed, stony expression on Katie's face was reminding her of the tantrum of 2012.

Poppy had apparently found more eggs that Katie during their annual Easter egg hunt, and the next thing anyone knew, Katie was screaming about Poppy always getting more than her and all the eggs were smashed to a melting pulp.

Then there was the considerably severe rage of this year's Halloween. Both Poppy and Katie had expressed that they wanted to be witches, but insisted that both of them couldn't be witches. Mum wasn't sure of the reason, but she knew better than to ignore them and dress them like twins, so she got Poppy the witch costume and dressed Katie as a cat. It seemed only fair, since Katie had been a witch the last two Halloweens.

The fixed look had appeared, and Katie had mumbled something along the lines of 'if you want a cat, I'll give you a cat'. Mum wasn't sure when it had happened, but half of the furniture ended up slashed (as if by tiny claws, naturally). Katie had fiercely denied that she was responsible for that, but there was no denying that she had peed on the rug; her dad caught her running from the room pulling her pants back up.

Those crimes were bad enough, but what really concerned Mum was the twisted 'revenge' that Katie was trying to take out on her sister. She'd gone into Poppy's room to check on her youngest, slumbering child only to find Katie stood over the bed, rubbing her thumb against Poppy's face. To someone who wasn't aware, that might merely seem odd. To Mum, it was demented and bordering on psychotic behaviour. Katie had been having a huge wart on her thumb treated for weeks, and had been lectured over and over to keep her hands clean because warts spread.

When asked, Katie had smiled her sweetest smile and explained that she was just trying to help Poppy look more like a witch.

The only comfort that Mum had, on this festive day at the Garden Centre, was that Katie had never thrown a rage fit in public before. So she hoped for the best.

Katie slammed the glass door open, hoping it would shatter. It clattered against the shelf behind it, but didn't smash. If Katie knew a strong swear word, she would have uttered it. She'd been hoping that all that gymnastic training would turn her into the Hulk for occasions such as this.

Fists balled at her sides, she looked around for the guy in the red suit. The first thing she saw was a large rack of shovels, rakes, and what looked to her like giant forks. Useless.

Next, she laid her eyes on a huge stack of bags of smelly dirt. She rolled her eyes, feeling her face getting hotter. Again, useless. Why anyone would pay for dirt when you can just get it from your own garden was beyond her. People, she thought, were stupid.

She turned to the right, noticing that that was the direction everyone seemed to be going in. She followed the crowd past useless shelves of useless seeds, and useless shears, and useless pesticides.

Katie's Mum caught up with her daughter just in time to see her shoving her way through the queue towards an unsuspecting Santa.

Santa beamed his broadest smile though couldn't help the quizzical furrowing of his brow as he watched the most adorable little girl stomp towards him. He guessed she was about ten or so, and she reminded him of Matilda with her cute little hair ribbon and matching shoes. She looked the image of a pretty little doll, apart from a face that was clearly red with anger and not from the cold.

She reached him and folded her arms across her chest, huffing.

"Santa, I have to talk to you," she declared. Santa tried to hide the smile from his lips; angry children were hilarious but they knew if you were laughing at them and they really hated to be patronised, in his experience. He pressed his hands to his tummy, threw his head back enough to make the white bobble on the end of his hat jiggle, and gave her his most enthusiastic greeting.

"Ho! Ho! Ho-!" he bellowed, cutting himself off on the last 'ho'. The second he had opened his mouth, the little girl's eyes had taken on a terrifying dark and fixed concentration. Her pupils were boring into him so hard he imagined screws slowly twisting into his temples.

"Don't you 'ho ho ho' me," Katie spat. She thrust a pointing finger in his face, and Santa flinched. "For three years I worked really hard to be on your lood gist!"

Now that she was face to face with him, she couldn't contain the anger anymore. She was mildly aware that she was already slurring and mispronouncing things, but she didn't care enough to correct herself.

"I've been good! I've been nice, not naughty! I watched out! I never cried! I didn't pout! I wrote you lice netters!"

Santa looked around, simultaneously wondering where the hell security was, and feeling kind of embarrassed that he needed to be rescued from a child.

"I hate you! I wanted that book set!"

Katie's nostrils flared as she was forced to take a second to breathe in again. Santa tried her with his jolliest smile.

"Uh, little girl, why don't you tell me what you want for Christmas this year?"

"What for?" Katie exclaimed, throwing her arms in the air, but never taking her eyes off his face. It was incredible how they were widening, yet remaining completely still, at the same time. Creepy, Santa thought.

"You'll just pring Boppy what I ask for anyway! You...!" Katie trailed off, mustering enough anger to go through with what she really wanted to say. She was aware that her mother was almost in grabbing distance, but consequences be damned. If she was on the naughty list, she may as well enjoy a cathartic naughty moment.

"You are an asshole!"

The room fell into a stunned silence as Mum grabbed Katie by the arm.

"That is enough, young lady!" she hissed, her cheeks blazing with embarrassment. She apologised to Santa, and continued to mumble apologies to everyone else as she dragged her daughter back through the huge queue.

Anger expelled, Katie was already calming down before they got to the door. That was until she heard him laughing. Santa was laughing. Only a moment later, she heard stifled laughter, and then un-stifled laughter all around her. Everyone was laughing at her. She didn't understand what was so damn funny, or why everyone was joining in with the dickhead on the festive throne over there, but a mist as red as Santa's suit descended.

Katie ripped her arm out of her Mum's grasp, and darted across the room in no particular direction. She looked around, needing to do something, but she wasn't sure what. All she knew was that she was angrier with Santa than she'd ever been with Poppy before, and that was pretty angry.

As she twirled on the spot looking for inspiration, the Garden Centre suddenly didn't look so full of useless things after all. Before she knew what she was doing, she was grabbing a green bottle of some sort of pesticide off the shelf and sprinting back towards the jolly red bloater as she spun the cap off.

He was too alarmed to do much as she flung herself onto his knee, but he foolishly opened his mouth in what would probably have been a scream if she hadn't rammed the top of the bottle in and started pouring.

She dropped the bottle as he pushed her off his lap, but it wasn't enough; she had to do more.

Other kids and parents started to scatter across the centre but their screams were muted to Katie's ears. Instead, there was just a ringing, like that time she'd stood right next to an outdoor speaker while the local orchestra played.

Santa fell off his chair and onto his knees, retching and coughing. Katie jumped to her feet and ran into the crowd before her mum could grab hold of her again.

The next thing she ran into was the huge mound of packaged dirt. Without thinking or stopping for even a moment, Katie slammed her fingernails into the packaging, managing to gouge just a small hole at first, but within seconds she had torn the bag open and was running back towards Santa with two handfuls of manure.

Santa looked up at her, still gasping for air, his mouth hanging open and dribbling animal poison.

"Eat dirt!" Katie screamed, laughing at her clever use of words. She shoved the dirt in his mouth, feeling his teeth graze

309

both her small but freakishly strong hands. She yanked them back as he started choking.

She regarded him for a moment. He was clearly choking and in some sort of pain or unpleasantness. His suit was splashed with insecticide. He now smelled a bit like the Garden Centre.

But it wasn't enough.

She realised that she may have committed a sort of festive faux pas with her actions. Santa, who had for the last three years deemed her behaviour not good enough for the good list, had now seen her face, and she was sure he'd never forget it. Instead of the wrong presents, he probably would never bring her a present again now. Perhaps she had acted too hastily, she thought.

Rage once again cut into the calm that had threatened to bring her back to Earth. Suddenly, the image of her receiving no gift at all, but having to watch Poppy open twice as many, was too much.

The decision was barely a conscious thought, but Katie determined that if she was never to have a present from Santa again, then no one else would either. It wasn't fair.

Katie's mum reached them once again, but instead of seizing Katie and dragging her out of there, she made the mistake of rushing to Santa's aid. It was perfect.

Katie raced back across the centre towards the entrance, knowing exactly what to go for next.

Poor Santa barely saw it coming as the child charged towards him with a rather large weapon that looked almost comical considering such a small person was carrying it.

"Die Satan!" Katie screamed, thrusting the pitchfork into Santa's throat.

Ho. Ho. Ho.

If We Make It Through December - Amanda M. Lyons

I TOLD HER IF we make it through December we could get away from here, take that vacation we were always talking about, let our little girl run and play someplace where the sun was bright and there weren't so many troubles. I keep reminding myself of that as I go, trudging on through the snow; damn stuff is as deep as my knees. I keep trying to remember because the cold is in my bones and I'm feeling more tired as I move, the wind whipping down out of the mountains and straight up my back and then my front, the cold snow blasting at me as it comes. I really want to bring them the world, you know, all the blessings in it wrapped up and ready for their bright faces on Christmas. We just have to make it through December and then we'll be ok. I promised, I swore to it.

I lost my job, damn near six months ago now. That was what started to kill her a little, kill them both if I were honest. Libby, she knew the job going meant that Christmas was a done deal; we weren't going to be able to manage more than a meal to eat most likely and she started preparing for that as best as any wife can. Sammy, our baby, she couldn't really know, how could she at five? She kept asking about her presents and all of that like normal, wanting to know what she might get. We'd explain it, that Santa'd have to make it up to her another year, but it got to be a broken record and I'm ashamed to admit a couple of times she got the rough side of my tongue for asking when it was a bad day. I tried to make it up to her, to Libby too, it's just been hard is all, being without a job and having to make a living off of whatever grub work I can find in these hills where nobody has money to give themselves.

That's how we make do for now, I go around and I take up little jobs for the others, some I do because it helps me feel better, working at something for the old folks even thought they can't afford more than a few apples or a pie in return.

Others they offer some bread or some other little things we've been running low on for the work I do. I grew up here, I know the way it is for everyone, but damn if it don't make me so mad sometimes, can't nobody really survive once winter hits and I had the bad luck to get laid off in the middle of it. I think…I think sometimes it's a good thing the snow hits me so hard, cools off the anger so I don't think so much about that as I do about getting home to them where it's warm and we can be happy in what we do have.

I've been away all night and day working over at the Tompkins' place, helping them get the wood cut and stored away for the rest of the winter. Hard working boys they have, but they're all grown up and moved to their own places so that it took a bit for us all to get together and get the job done for their parents. I swear I still hear the sound of the axes chopping away it went on for so long. Tommy, he missed the wood and whacked his foot real good the one time, damn good thing he had on those steel toed boots, but I'd bet he'll have a bruise underneath all the same. It was hard work but it got me some good for all of it. Mrs. Tompkins baked us a real nice piece of gingerbread, threw in some milk and a little dolly from her collection for Sammy. Means I have a present now, a black haired cloth dolly with big button eyes and a stitched on smile between apple cheeks. A sweet treat and a present for Christmas, can't beat that.

We're gonna make it. I tell myself that every time that I get lost in that fog and forget myself. I think of Sammy and Libby running around at a beach someplace, sand all over and the sound of the ocean, all of it lit up with that sunlight that lasts forever, and I think we just have to make it through December. I almost get warm from the thought of it, can almost feel that sun making all the pain and the cold disappear, but it all comes back in and I swear I almost cry when it does.

Snow swirls in thick walls all around me as I carry my bundles home, it almost takes the air from my lungs with the intensity of the wind and the way that the cold itself takes it right out of me. My lungs hurt in my chest, my legs little better than numb trees where they're under the snow as I move up the mountain to get home. It's not so far now. I just have to manage the last while.

Libby and me have been married for ten years now, we planned real hard for there to be the right kind of place for a little one before we tried. We were so careful to lay everything out so we wouldn't have to face this sort of thing, at least we thought we had it sorted out. I think that was the worst part, running through that four month wall of safety money, the just in case fund not making much difference when push came to shove. I kept promising them I'd get a job to replace the other one, something would kick in and we'd be doing ok, but nothing ever came and we wound up here instead. I know my wife's a strong woman and she'll help me and Sammy get through the holidays with not much to celebrate with, but I wish I had been able to keep her from having to do it. Sometimes I worry I'm just taking her down with me, her and our baby girl. I think maybe I should send them to go live with her family and then just keep trying to do right by her until I get it right. I even told her that once and she couldn't say anything at all, just teared up like I broke her heart.

Maybe I made her think about her daddy, dead before his time in the mines that took so many of us mountain folk over the years. She made me promise never to go there for a job as soon as I lost the other, made me swear it. She and her momma, her little brothers, they were all away at some family thing when the mines caved in on him and the rest of the crew. He stayed to work because they couldn't afford to risk him losing the job and they paid dear all the same. She made me promise her to never leave her a mining widow and I asked her to never stop believing I had it in me to make it right for us. She told me that was fair enough and she knew I would.

I can see the lights on our house coming up on the horizon now, she always does put out those few strings of lights, wraps them around the spouting on the old place, and lights up a sure as they do when she gets them going. Blue, green, red, yellow, and white bulbs standing out against the snow and marking the house out in the dark make for their own sort of warmth in my heart. It costs us a little extra on the light bill but I let it go, knowing that it soothes us all a bit to have them to look at when everything else seems sort of lost. Beautiful as it is, and as much as it's a part of me being from here, the mountains can be a mighty cold place. Desolate and lonely even in summer, the cold and the snow add their own ghosts to the whole affair once it drifts into winter. Those lights seem to chase away the demons now as I carefully work my way up the hill to our house.

    I can see the way those lights color the snow and twinkle in reflections on the glass of the windows as I get closer, in a strange way I can swear I feel them warm me even from several feet away. It has to be some trick of the mind, something I fool myself into thinking to make the slog a little less painful than it is with the way my legs have gone numb and my arms heavy from swinging with their bundles at my sides. All the same, I stop where I stand and I think back to that beach with them dancing around, the sound of the snow becomes the sound of the sea in my ears and my soul, gone cold and dead in the wind and emptiness, bursts alight with the joy of their laughter. I mutter my mantra to myself as I get lost in that moment, "If we make it through December, I promise."

    Then I take one last icy breath in the midst of the winter madness and I start making the biggest strides I can manage to bring them the humble offerings I've carried all this way. I feel good knowing that I have something now, it almost warms me as I step onto our porch and stamp away the snow on my boots and pants.

    It got damned cold the last week or so, bad enough that Libby worried about me every time I went away to work no matter how much I tried to reassure her that I was going to be fine. She was worried enough about it that she even forbade Sammy to go out in the snow, afraid she'd never warm up enough after she got back in with the heater staying on 68 to maintain the fuel bill we could afford even with the government help we got paying for it. Libby herself, who always seemed to struggle to keep the cold out of her bones once they set in, was wearing her thick sweaters on top of two or three layers of long johns and long sleeved shirts that always seemed to dangle down over her hands, the fingers cold and pale blue no matter how she tried to warm them. I could already feel them touching my face to try and warm my own skin, only a little colder than her hands my cheeks a reddish pink in contrast to her blue fingertips. I amuse myself by imagining how she laughs with surprise when I touch my hands to her belly under her clothes, Sammy giggling at our ankles.

I kick off my boots in the mud room, gratefully unzip and remove my heavy winter coat and pull off my wool hat with a crackle of static as my hair sticks to my head in response to all that stored up friction. With a few more moments taken to hang everything up and gently knead a little life back into my legs, I slip in through the entryway and glide into the living room where I find them sitting on the couch, snuggled up in front of the TV. It's one of those shows the little ones are always getting into and then growing out of so quickly, about some dogs rescuing people in brightly colored scenery. I looked down at my hands, the doll free in one hand and the food still stowed away in their closed bag waiting to be revealed. They hadn't even realized I was home yet and I was looking forward to the way they would squeal, perking up after all the grim days when things were a little less bright than I wanted them to be. I had brought them Christmas when it had been denied, small and simple but so much more than I had hoped all the same. It was easy enough to envision it as I looked at their tilted heads over the bright afghans that covered the couch but not so in a moment.

I promised them if we made it through December, got through the Christmas that wasn't, that we could have so many things, a vacation, a dream, a future. But we didn't make it. I come around the couch to look at them and it all comes rushing in like some awful nightmare, the truth about my family tearing away at my heart, their very lives a false front I maintain to get through every day since the night I came home to find them just like this.

It got cold, you know that, but what you don't know is that one of the nights I was away the furnace cut out and all that cold got in here. Having passed out watching Sammy's cartoons they were never even aware of it. They died peacefully in their sleep, frozen in perfect loving peace, Sammy curled tight to her mother, who held her in that same motherly embrace I knew from a thousand other nights. I remember falling to the floor wailing in agony at the sight, my eyes thick with tears as I repeat the gesture again, reliving it in my head every time I come home because it's the only way I know how to cope with not being here to protect them from everything. Through my weeping I struggle to look at the way they are now that the heat has been back on for a few days and time has begun to render them less than pleasant. Their faces sagging and coming apart in places as decay slowly robs me of even the illusion of their happiness.

After a while of this, the weight of their loss thick in my chest, I take out the gingerbread and milk. I place a couple of broken off pieces in each of their hands, press the doll to Sammy's side and gently place her fragile arm down over it in reverence. Then I gobble the rest of the cake with the milk, crumbs dangling from my lips and my clothes as I grieve them. For the hundredth time I wish that I was here, that I could have fixed it long before they came to harm or that I had gone with them. I tell myself that I have to make it through December without them, to keep my promise and take them to the beach. I close my eyes and try to remember my little daydream about it, but I can smell them so thick in my nostrils and I can hear the wind blow outside and I know that I'll be lucky to make another day.

Slay Belles - Ash Hartwell

TOMORROW WAS CHRISTMAS EVE and time was running out for those parents still hunting down those last minute stocking fillers or this year's must have toy. Women hurried from shop to shop with steely determination while men loitered around brightly lit perfume counters and lingerie stores with confused indecision. Carol singers performed on the main concourse adding a festive atmosphere to the bustling crowds and a giant Christmas tree dominated the central hall. Large decorative baubles and long strands of glittering tinsel hung from the giant fir tree's branches while life-sized toy soldiers stood guard over huge gift wrapped presents piled around its base.

A few seasonal stalls selling an enticing mix of festive goodies lined a winding lane of fake snow and twinkling lights. Sweet stalls bedecked with multi-coloured candy canes and bags of chocolate covered nuts stood side-by-side with those selling greetings cards and snow globes featuring Santa Claus or scenes of Victorian children skating. The lane led to a large chalet-style hut inside which sat Santa Claus himself. He perched on a large throne in the dimly lit grotto handing out presents from an oversized sack to excited children. Three elves in cute pointed hats with bells on the end and short green tunics showed the children and their parents through to the inner grotto. They checked two large scrolls to see if the boys and girls were on the naughty or nice list making sister's promise not to tell Santa if they moved a younger brother from one to the other so he could meet Santa. Each child received a toy and had a selfie taken with Santa before another elf ushered them away to continue their shopping trip.

It was in this frantic, festive chaos that Ray and his associates thrived. Ray belonged to a gang of pickpockets and shoplifters although they disliked the term *gang* as it implied they were violent thugs. Ray and his friends viewed themselves as business associates who practised the arts of their profession with skill and finesse. Today had been a good day at the office, the overcrowded shops and busy Yuletide shoppers had proved easy pickings.

"Excuse me?" Ray, wearing a warm smile, approached his target. "I noticed from your bags you've been to Toys R Us. Could you point me in the right direction, I've been looking for it or twenty minutes?" He offered up an exasperated laugh, throwing his arms up in mock surrender. In that instant of movement, David swooped past removing the woman's purse from her open handbag. Ray listened politely as she directed him to the store then, wishing her a merry Christmas, he strode off in the direction she'd indicated. The theft would go unnoticed long enough for both men to disappear into the crowd and even then their mark would think she'd left her purse in the last shop she'd visited.

Ray and his associates had a prearranged meeting point close to the Christmas tree. They'd finished for the day and tomorrow they planned to head home for the holidays so it was time to relax. Their festive spree had taken them to fourteen malls in ten towns over twelve hectic days and tonight they planned to celebrate with what they laughingly termed the office party. A party funded exclusively by their marks careless generosity.

Noel and Jimmy were sitting on a bench when Ray arrived and he saw David and Jon on the other side of the hall weaving their way through the crowd. Noel pointed to where a large man dressed as Santa Clause perched on a ridiculously small chair watching three young women dressed as elves tidying up the entrance to the grotto.

"Look at that lazy bastard! He spends all fuckin' day sat on his fat arse then just watches them, like some pervert, while they clean up." They watched as the women swept up the rubbish and emptied the bin into a black plastic sack while they waited for their friends.

A leering smile spread across Ray's face. "Maybe we should invite those smokin' hot elves to our party, you know, to show our appreciation for all their hard work." He looked at his friends who eagerly nodded their approval as he started walking up the glistening lane between the stalls towards the chalet-style grotto. His friends followed, jostling one another in their high-spirited exuberance as they exchanged lewd, half whispered comments.

As they approached the grotto, Santa stood up. "I'm afraid gentlemen you are too late and, may I venture, too old for the grotto." His eyes twinkled as he laughed at his own observation.

Noel took a menacing step forward but Ray placed a restraining hand on his arm. "We know Santa, we're here to ask your elves to a party and that has nothing to do with you."

"On the contrary, Raymond, it has everything to do with me. I will not allow them to become involved with boys from the Naughty List. I've had my eye on you for the last few days and you're nothing but thieves and scoundrels." Santa stood his ground in the silence that followed while Ray wondered how this fat man in a red suit knew his name.

After an awkward few seconds, David laughed softly, "I think you take this job a little too seriously, man. So while you try to get a grip on reality we'll ask the young ladies what they want to do."

Santa offered up a rueful smile, "Have it your way then." He turned to speak to the three women who'd been watching the exchange from a few yards away. "Goldie, Francesca, Muriel. Would you come here please? These young men would like to ask you a question." The women walk up next to him and eye the group with coy smiles. Jon whistles softly; the women are even prettier close up.

Noel smiles back, feeling unusually nervous, and asks, "We were wondering if you would like to come to a small party we're throwing later this evening?"

The blonde stood on tiptoes to whisper in Santa's ear. He gave a resigned nod then sighed, "If you wish Goldie. Do you feel the same Frankie? The elf with deep burgundy-coloured hair poking out from beneath her pointy hat smiled and nodded. Santa turned to the last woman whose eyes sparkled as she struggled to contain her excitement. "I don't think I need to ask you Muriel. Okay, you may go but I'm not going to be responsible for what happens." As the three young women jumped up and down excitedly, he looked at Ray and added, "Write down the address, they'll be there."

Noel looked at the bearded man with badly concealed contempt. "Are you their father or their pimp?" Santa looked at him with a mixture of confusion and pity before turning away and walking back towards his grotto followed by Goldie and Muriel. Francesca waited patiently for Ray to write the address down then winked at him before hurrying after them without saying a word.

"Well that was fuckin' weird!" Jimmy looked at the others blankly.

The business associates had rented a luxury tourist chalet on the edge of town at the end of a quiet lane. It was an expensive extravagance but Ray had argued the case on two important grounds, first, it was Christmas, if you couldn't indulge at Christmas, then when could you? Ray's second reason was far more practical; it cost them nothing, it was all paid for by petty cash stolen from careless Christmas shoppers.

It was a little after seven when Noel said, "Is that sleigh bells?" He peered out of the window at the snow covered lane outside as the sound grew louder. "Are you guys listening?" The others murmured or nodded in response as they gathered at the window behind Noel, their attention focused on the shimmering chime of a hundred tiny bells.

Then the high-pitched chiming stopped. No sooner had silence descended on the glistening, snow-covered lane beyond the frosted windowpane, their guests arrived. The three women walked up the short driveway, their short, figure hugging dresses were all of an identical style yet each wore a different glittery Christmas colour. Goldie, as her name suggested, wore gold which complemented her fair skin and blonde hair, which she wore pinned up. Francesca's dress was a deep purple and she wore her hair loose, swept away from her face and held in place by a hair grip covered in mistletoe. Her darker complexion and large brown eyes set her and Goldie in stark contrast to each other while Muriel wore emerald green. Her long, coal-black hair fell down her back in soft curls and was interwoven with green ribbons. All three wore brown pixie-style boots with colour coordinated tinsel wrapped around the top and finished with a dainty bow.

As Ray pulled the cottage's door open to welcome their guests, Santa's voice boomed loud through the clear dark evening air, "Be good." Again the sound of tiny bells filled the air before fading away with his distant laughter, "Ho ho ho." Ray flashed a welcoming smile as the others jostled for position behind him. When they partied in a strange town it usually meant beer and pizza and never included girls and they were all aware five into three didn't go.

The three elves smiled politely as they stepped into the room. Ray swung the door shut and turned the key, locking the young women in, before slipping it into his jeans pocket. Muriel watched him with a wry smile before taking him by the hand and leading him towards the patio doors, only pausing briefly to crank up the volume on the television, tuned to show continuous rock music videos.

The other two women began moving to the rhythm of the music gesturing for the remaining lads to dance with them as Muriel pushed the double doors open and lead Ray out onto the snow covered terrace. She nodded for him to shut the doors behind them. Then, once they were alone, Muriel giggled and ran off towards the hut containing the cottage's snow equipment. Ray followed hardly able to believe his luck.

Muriel skipped across the snow and swung the shed's heavy door open with ease before disappearing into its dark interior. Ray reached the door, breathing hard from the effort of running through the deep snow, and fumbled for a light switch. He heard a metallic scraping sound followed by another of Muriel's infectious giggles from somewhere in the darkness.

He smiled and shouted into the black void in front of him. "Come out, come out wherever you are." His hand found the light switch and he flicked it down. All Ray saw as the lights flickered to life was a large metal shovel moments before it crashed into his unprotected face.

The first blow knocked him to the ground, stunned but conscious. The second, delivered to the back of his head, caused Ray's world to spin violently as he slumped motionless on the floor.

Muriel stepped from the darkness to drag his body out into the snow where she left him lying face up while she retrieved the shovel. A trickle of blood ran from the open gash on Ray's head, staining the snow, as Muriel returned to stand over his body, waiting patiently for him to regain consciousness.

After a few minutes, Ray moaned softly and began to open his eyes. Muriel raised the shovel again. Ray's eyes open wide and he tried to scream as Muriel brought the shovel down edge first, severing his head from his body. Leaving the shovel embedded deep in the snow next to the decapitated corpse, Muriel turned the shed's light off before retrieving the key from his pocket.

Muriel's return to the party went largely unnoticed as Goldie and Frankie danced provocatively for the remaining members of Ray's troop of thieves. Goldie had singled Jon out for special treatment, her body pressed against his, her hips gyrating to the music, her lithe body swaying in time with his. As Muriel rejoined the dance, Goldie took Jon by the hand and led him towards one of the bedrooms winking at Muriel as they passed each other.

"Hey! Where's Ray?" Jon called over his shoulder as the blonde guided him to the door. Muriel smiled licking her lips, but did not reply. "Oh man! How fuckin' cool is this." Jon was still laughing excitedly as the bedroom door swung shut.

Goldie guided him across the poorly lit room towards the unmade bed. Turning to face him, she started pulling his T-shirt up over his head. Jon frantically pulled at it, desperately trying to speed things along, while simultaneously kicking his trainers off. Finally pulling his head free from the confines of the tight cotton he looked at Goldie, his arms still wrapped in the shirt. He thought she looked different and when she gently shook her head Jon realised she'd let her hair down. He closed his eyes as the stunning blonde stepped in closer, expecting to feel her soft lips on his.

The first blow felt like a gentle nudge. Bewildered, Jon opened his eyes just as Goldie pulled the thin steel hairpin out of his neck's soft, yielding flesh. For a second bewilderment turned to confusion then he felt something warm trickle down his neck and he realised he was bleeding.

"What the fu…" Jon struggled to free his arms. His words died in his throat as Goldie raised her bloodstained hand. The steel pin glinted in the weak light as she swung it down, plunging it deep into his neck for a second time.

This one hit its target. As Goldie wrenched the pin from his neck a thin arc of glistening, ruby red blood sprayed across the nearby bed. Jon finally freed one arm reaching a shaky hand to his neck in a futile effort to prevent his life simply ebbing away with each beat of his heart. Goldie stepped back allowing him to drop to his knees. He looked towards the door; it was agonisingly close. He reached out his arm, his shirt hanging limply from his wrist, his energy slipping away with each passing second. The blood formed a glistening dark sheen on his bare chest and shoulder as it continued to pour from his open wound. He opened his mouth to call for help but his cry fell silent even before it formed in his throat.

Goldie stepped away as Jon's lifeless body slumped forward the steel pin protruding from the base of his skull. Three minutes later she too returned to the party, all trace of Jon's bloody demise washed from her hands. The three remaining pickpockets cheered as Goldie pulled the bedroom door shut cheekily wiping the back of her hand across her pouting lips. Frankie clapped her hands together barely able to contain her excitement before breaking away from her dance with Jimmy, signalling for him to follow her to the kitchen. She took a bottle of wine from the fridge then began rummaging in the draw looking for a corkscrew. Taking her lead, Jimmy opened the overhead cupboard in search of glasses for their romantic aperitif.

In one swift movement, Frankie removed the largest knife from the draw and with one stride, plunged it deep between Jon's ribs, cutting his heart in two. He stood as still as a statue his eyes wide and staring, his arms still in the air. He was already dead his body just didn't know it. A wineglass fell from his limp hand which Frankie deftly caught and placed on the kitchen side before lovingly wiping a trickle of blood away from the corner of his mouth. Then his body simply folded over and sank, like a slow-motion replay, to the tiled floor.

Straddling Jimmy's still twitching body Frankie pulled the knife free and returned it to the draw, flicking it closed with her hip. In the main reception room, Noel and David danced on with their colleague's killers, unaware of the danger around them. Muriel and Goldie took a few steps sideways turning their partners so their backs were towards Frankie as she returned to the room. The two men stared excitedly at Santa's elves, mesmerised by their writhing gyrations and seductive smiles, David even laughed when, out of the corner of his eye, he saw Noel stumble forward over the low coffee table. Noel had always been clumsy around attractive women.

David's mirth died on his lips as Frankie's second swing cracked across the back of his skull. The darkness engulfed his thoughts and his legs buckled sending him crashing to the floor where he ended slumped across Noel's prostrate form. Frankie hunched over the two men, her arm raised the meat tenderising mallet ready to crash down again should either man show any signs of movement.

Neither did.

After a few moments, Frankie returned her weapon to the kitchen before joining her friends in a silent group hug. They had not uttered a single word since entering the apartment only half-an-hour or so before, there had been no need each knew what had to be done. They waited patiently for Santa to return, his sack bulging with goodies and they still had much to do before sunrise.

The following morning when the contract cleaners arrived to clean the holiday cottage for the next visitors they discovered a seasonal wreath of dark green holly and blood red berries, interwoven with strands of mistletoe, nailed to the cottages door. Fitting snugly inside the ring of holly, its lips thrust forward in a grotesque pucker, was a severed head. Their hysterical scream alerted the inhabitants of several nearby cottages and within ten minutes two local police officers were stepping carefully over around the cleaner's stomach contents splattered on the cottage's steps.

In total they discovered the remains of five male victims. The severed head belonged to a body found two days later buried in the snow just outside the maintenance shed. The layers of discoloured snow lead them to his frozen corpse. Their efforts hampered by the fresh fall of snow overnight which turned the surrounding countryside into a winter wonderland. The local press described entering the cottage as *walking into a winter slaughterland,* a headline that became synonymous with the events of that day.

The second victim stood just inside the door dressed like a wooden toy soldier. Someone had driven a long metal spike into his anus and up into his neck securing the base to a wide plinth making it appear he was standing to attention, guarding the entrance to some bizarre grotto of carnage. The strange red blusher applied to his cheeks in large red circles gave his features an oddly clown-like appearance, his hair matted in the bloody remains of the back of his head.

Police found two more headless bodies lying in the bathtub. Their genitals were also missing, crudely hacked away leaving the body covered in minced up body tissue. The forensic team discovered the heads suspended from the tree like two giant decorative baubles surrounded by the dangling testicles of all the victims. Each head had a hole drilled through both temples and the skull had been partially hollowed out. The faces had a twisted, tortuous look of pain and the eyes were missing, a string of fairy lights threaded through the boreholes so when the lights flashed the empty eye sockets twinkled in the darkened room.

They found the last of the young men who'd occupied the cottage in the week leading up to Christmas suspended by rope entwined with tinsel from the large wooden beams supporting the roof. A longline of loose, uneven stitches ran down his naked torso then across his abdomen stopping just above his pubic area and the open wound where his genitalia had once been. They discovered his internal organs in small boxes, wrapped in Christmas paper and secured with decorative bows, under the tree. When the police tried to lower the body it split open like a piñata, showering the police officers below with an assortment of what turned out to be stolen credit cards and wallets stuffed with cash. This had mixed with a large volume of semi-congealed blood which suggested he'd been alive when his killer removed his organs with imprecision. At least, he'd been alive when the killers (police were sure this was the work of more than one man) started the barbarous process of disembowelling him. Mercifully he would've bled to death quickly from the slashing wounds inflicted as they hacked his body apart.

Meanwhile, in the fake wonderland, three elves got ready to open the grotto at the end of the twinkling, glistening lane in the mall. Santa was yet to arrive and a few early shoppers loitered around the stalls waiting their child's chance to meet him. A young boy took a candy cane from one of the stalls when his mother and stallholder were engrossed in their transaction. Once done, she took the boy's hand and half dragged, half walked him through the little lane to take their position at the front of the queue.

From somewhere high above the mall's clear roof, or was it playing through the public-address speakers, the boy couldn't tell, came the distant sound of approaching sleigh bells. Then there stood Santa, but he didn't have the jovial smile the boy had come to expect, instead he wore an intense frown.

Santa bent down to the child's level and whispered in his ear, "Stealing candy means your name goes on the naughty list." He nodded towards the three elves standing in front of the grotto then added, "My elves don't like naughty boys. They think the punishment should be harsh."

The little boy handed Santa the sticky candy cane he'd been clutching tightly since they left the stall. A jovial grin instantly spread across Santa's face. "Ho! Ho! Ho! And what can Santa get you, little boy?" But the boy didn't answer. He just hid behind his mother's legs staring at the three elves, screaming.

A Bauble And Twelve Drops - J.G. Clay

THE SCREECH SENT A chill down his spine, his hand twitching and almost unleashing the freight of coins stuck to his sweaty palm.

Noddy bastard Holder! Next time, I go to Wolverhampton...

He left the thought unfinished preferring to bask in the dull afterglow of annoyance and anger. A chorus of voices took up the chant. Matty-Bob glanced over the bar furtively at the drunken singers. He knew all of them by face; some of them by name. They were younger than he; clad in the latest designer wear, faces flushed with intoxicant and merriment, spittle flying as they hoarsely grappled with the intricacies of the annual Slade singathon. He knew them well enough to know that Mariah Carey would feature as part of their Christmas karaoke act. Only an hour's worth of social drinking remained. Besides, what self-respecting lad would sing 'All I Want for Christmas Is You?' Biting back a sneer, Matty-Bob waited for the squat leather jacketed man in front to finish paying.

He looked up at the ceiling, desperately trying to avoid eye contact with the gaggle of drinkers still left in the Lion. The traditional Christmas Eve afternoon session had left him bereft of vision and ability to speak without giving the game away. He was drunk, but there was no need to advertise; not when there was only three bottles of beer left at home. More drink was required before the lonely swaying shuffle back to an empty house, avoiding the binoculars of Dear Old Doris, the one woman neighbourhood watch.

That was the norm these days.

Above him, garish tinsel swayed to the tune. He squinted, the glint of the décor tickling his optic nerves. The sparkling decorations were not overly exciting, red and green being the colour scheme of choice. That had puzzled him for the last four years of living in this strange market town. Wherever the eye roamed, the colours remained the same, uniform; red and green. The lights on the mammoth tree squatting forlornly in the market square, the tinsel in the shops and pubs, even the shit paper decorations dragged from dusty attics once a year and displayed proudly through windows – all red, green, vibrant, yet artificial somehow, as if the town was making a show of how much it enjoyed the festive period. As for the people, well. To prove the point, the stocky old gentleman in front cursed loudly, a five pound noted fluttering from his thick fingers. Matty-Bob shuffled backwards, allowing the man space to squat and retrieve his lost currency. Terry the barman – dour, hairless, clad in a Metallica t-shirt that had seen better days and too few many wash cycles looked on at the show impassively.

Retrieving his money with a slur of triumph, the man finally paid. Matty-Bob stepped back a little further, unsure of which direction the tray of drinks was going. The older gentlemen – vaguely recognisable, his eyes rheumy under bushy eyebrows - murmured his thanks.

"Cheers, me old booty."

Matty-Bob put in his best sober smile, silent, willing his tongue to return to normal size so that he could order some drinks. The old man paused, his face sober and serious.

"Don't forget, new 'un. The bauble and twelve drops." All conversation ceased around them, 'Frosty the Snowman' burbling away, blissfully unaware of the undercurrent it rode on. In unison, they all uttered a phrase.

"The bauble and twelve drops."

The liquid jolt of fear carved through Matty-Bob's drunkenness. He had seen this happen many times previously, but had never gotten used to it. It made him think of pod people, hive minds and Midwich Cuckoos. He gulped, his tongue seemingly swelling further.

The moment passed. The old man shuffled away, studying his tray as if it were a new life form. The gaggle of lads over the other side of the bar resumed their conversation, snatches of slurred words floating to the still frozen Matty-Bob.

"Heard that new rapper, PAK1. Pretty funny his name, considering he's a pak-."

"So I said her, how do you like your eggs in the morning. She says-."

"Villa are fuckin' rubbish shite, mate-."
"Whatever happened to Pete The Neat?"
A space cleared for him. He took it gratefully, cautiously glancing at his own reflection. A round brown face stared back, the eyes red-lined and doleful, the lips pressed tight and straight, the hair almost gone.
Terry gave favoured him with a look, blank and uncomprehending.
"What'll you have, squire?"
Matty-Bob ordered.
His tongue had returned to normal size.

A hiss. Matty-Bob's senses, percolating in a stew of gin and real ale, perked up at the sound. He lifted the bottle aloft – his own personal FA Cup Final – studying the runnels of condensation frosting the glass, before lifting it to his lips and tipping.
Houston, we have lift up… fucking lift in…lift…whatever.
He fought back the giggles, not wanting the precious lager to explode from his face. Christmas morning would be better spent sleeping off the inevitable hangover, not scrubbing beer stains from the laminate flooring so considerately supplied by the landlord. With that in mind, he carefully set the bottle down on the wood, sighed and relaxed. The lights on the small artificial tree - red and green of course. It was in the rental agreement – blinked on and off, lazy and sated. Maybe they knew that their rest period was coming. Blearily, he looked around, his head bobbing. The house was nice, for a bachelor pad. And cheap. That had been the main attraction; one of the very few. He wouldn't have signed the odd rental agreement. He wouldn't have moved to this town.
It was a normal market town, on the surface. Nestled comfortably in the Northamptonshire countryside, with more pubs and eateries that it warranted, the town bustled with life. An old church dominated the market square, glowering over its inhabitants in the style of an Old Testament god. The main road sprang to life at the weekends. It looked normal.

But… A strange pall hung in the air, a psychic whiff of things and deeds, long dead but unwilling to be forgotten.

But… People had a habit of disappearing. Little Pete Murphy, 'Pete The Neat' as he was known. The famed horror writer Harvey Dellar, upping and leaving not long after his smash bestseller '*Softly Dreaming, Slowly Dying*'. Others too, not as famous but important to someone. After all, where not all people important to someone?

But… The plastic enjoyment of Christmas. The fake smiles hiding a weary terror that started show through the cracks. The informal curfew on Christmas Eve; everyone home by midnight. The colour scheme of the décor. And, of course.

The Bauble and 12 Drops. An odd custom. One even written into his rental contract. Given the price of his house and the ease of travel to work, Matty-Bob had never questioned. These days, he couldn't afford to. There was nowhere else he could rent a two bed house on his own. Economics made one blind in this day and age.

He had gone along with it. After all, it was one tree bauble, probably fashioned in some Far East sweatshop. And twelve drops of the good stuff, Dracula's favourite tipple. He had litres of the stuff swimming around his body. Twelve drops was a small price to pay.

He checked his watch, more out of habit than necessity. The large clock on the living wall told the time adequately.

23.30.

Relief flooded through him, making his body seem more boneless.

Still enough time to leave the bauble and saucer outside his front door.

Leaning forward awkwardly, he shoved some earphones in and grabbed his bottle. Fifteen minutes and Primal Scream. Then he would complete the offering.

Matty-Bob settled into his armchair, letting the music, booze and the hypnotic lights of the tree take him.

Within seconds, he was asleep.

We Three Kings of Orient Are

One in a taxi, one in a car,
One on a scooter, bibbing his hooter,
Smoking a fat cigar....

He giggled from the deep watches of sleep, the childhood nursery rising unbidden from the soupy fog of memory. Wakefulness nipped at the heels of the laugh, stirred by his emotion. Matty-Bob inhaled deeply, his half asleep face creasing a little. An odour – cinnamon, spice, mulled wine and something meaty yet familiar – saturated the interior of sinuses.

Mum's making mince pies, he thought groggily, grasping at the blanket of sleep now trotting off into the distance. As he increased his efforts, a thought came to him.

Mum's got her own place. His eyes flew open, his body ramrod straight.

The world lurched sickeningly, the early hangover wrenching his brain and shaking it vigorously. His stomach bubbled in a stew of stale gin and ale. Sweat sprang from his forehead as his guts rolled lazily. He clenched his teeth, forcing the soupy alcohol back down to its rightful place. He had paid good money for that.

The room was dark. Not unusual. Sometimes, he turned the light the off before crashing back out of the world into dreams more pleasant than reality.

The room was cold. Again, nothing out of the ordinary. The heating was on a timer, saluting and playing the Last Post, long after he had pulled his duvet over him.

The room was occupied. Matty-Bob frowned, his addled mind trying to make sense of this.

Three shadows stood before him, silent and unmoving.
Burgling smackhead bastards!
Rage, fuelled by the dregs of alcohol, surged through him.
Go for the big one first. The other two'll bottle it.
Gathering his strength, he coiled.
One...two...
"What time is it?"

The query stopped him dead. In the queer silence, he fumbled for ananswer, raising his left arm. The night made it virtually impossible to read the dial.

Cheap shit watch, he cursed.

"I see that you cannot see. Shall we have some light?"

The question, couched in pleasant terms and tones, uncoiled a serpent within Matty-Bob. He recognised it by its greasy slither as it wrapped itself around his organs – terror.

The middle figure raised a hand, clicking its fingers, the sound of bone against bone. Confused, Matty-Bob looked around him as a light began to seep from the walls; dim at first. He gulped theatrically as the luminance took on colour – red and green. The room was now softly illuminated yet his eyes stung. There was a harsh quality to the light, alien and unforgiving. It hooked at his eyeballs in a thousand places, an unpleasant sensation of pins and needles. With a will of their own, his eyes alighted on his watch. He jolted, his insides squeezed to a pulp by the serpent.

3.15am. Christmas Morning.

"Merry Christmas, my friend."

The voice was jovial, deep, that of an old friendly uncle who had not visited in a while. Torn away from his watch, his gaze tracked to the three figures, no longer shadows. The fog of old booze dissipated, chased away by the visitors.

The taller of the three – the speaker – held some semblance of normality. His face was wide, pleasant, a little jowly and careworn; the face of a man who could sell you anything. His black hair, slicked back to form a widow's peak, shone lustrously in the unnatural light. It looked fake wig-like. He was dressed in a tastefully tailored three-piece suit, the portion of his white shirt that was visible, gleaming. The suit's colour was anything but tasteful. The red jacket clashed horribly with the green trousers and tie. Only his red shoes matched the jacket. The man smiled, his eyes remaining unmoved.

"Please do not be put off by my companions. They don't bite."

The hunched figure on the left shifted forward, the sour perfume he had tasted earlier becoming stronger. The lace of the wedding dress it wore had rotted, gaping holes exposing mealy mottled brown flesh. Its hands were encased in leather gloves; one red, one green. A veil obscured its face, a fact for which Matty-Bob was thankful. The hunched thing pointed at him.

"You have been a naughty boy, haven't you?" The thing spoke in honeyed seductive terms. "If Santa existed in this realm, he would have your bones for Christmas breakfast." Matty felt his crotch become warm as his bladder let go. The eye watering stink of ammonia laced the sweet, fraught air.

"Dirty boy!" The laced figure spat. The taller man held up a hand.

"Enough, Tolparethon. You can see the poor boy is terrified."

Another voice piped up from the right. It was mechanical, lilting, sing-song.

"He haaaas good reason toooooo be terrified. Deals aaaaare not maaaade lightly."

The third figure stepped forward. Matty-Bob shrank back in his chair, his voice robbed by fear and near insanity. The creature had no face, just a blank screen. It made him think of an IPad transplanted into someone's face. Webs of skin held the screen in place, tiny screws glittering in the red and green light. The thing with no face. Like its peers, was dressed incongruously; a one piece leather garment, a deep red leather criss-crossed with green. It raised a hand, splaying its two fingers in a 'Spock-like' gesture. The screen of its face flickered, static swirling before resolving itself into a visage he knew all too well. The severe hairstyle, the eyebrows and the pointed ears gave the face identity.

"Liiiive lond aaaaand prosper."

Again, the tall man raised his hand to silence the creature.

"Enough!" He favoured Matty-Bob with an apologetic nod. "Bhabiṣyat has a rarified sense of humour. It remains a mystery, even after millennia of companionship."

Despite his terror, Matty-Bob felt an unwelcome stirring of curiosity. Willing his lips to move, he spoke, his voice croaky.

"And… and you are?"

The man smiled. "Aktuelan is my preferred name." Aktuelan, Tolparethon, Bhabiṣyat."

This is just a dream. Too much booze, too many late nights, maybe some dodgy food. Like in that Dickens novel.

Aktuelan clapped his hands together. Matty-Bob jumped, errant drops of piss squeezing from his bladder. His heart, wild and swollen, now lodged firmly in his throat, blood thumping in his ears.

Blood, blood, why am I thinking about-?

"Please, please forgive me for startling you," Aktuelan said, wiping away tears of mirth. "I love that book. As do we all." He stopped, his face serious. "No. We are not cheese induced nightmares nor friends having a 'jolly jape'. We are your Landlords."

Matty-Bob trembled, his voice a strangled squeak
"My what?"

"Your landlords. Rather, the owners of this little pocket of land. We were here first." A dreamy look came over the tall man's face. "I haven't told this tale in a little while. I've never needed to."

The three drew straight, shuffling together, their arms touching. A sweet chorus of voices bled from the walls, soft and melodious as Aktuelan took up the story.

"We came here when the plague had reduced the land to a charnel house, helping where we could, leaving when the strain became too much, never settling. Something about this area caught our attention, a 'flavour' if you will. You must have sensed it yourself." Matty-Bob nodded. "We are three only. Our power is not great enough for to withstanding the "*Necrotic Fascia*' beneath the earth. But we do what we can. All we ask for is a bauble and twelve drops of blood. That is all that is required."

The background chorus fell silent abruptly, the piss smelling atmosphere thickening. Matty-Bob's bowels churned. The Landlords stared down at him, their postures stiff and hostile.

"You have a cheap house, a pleasant environment to live in. The odd incursion happens, granted, but we keep you all safe.

Everyone benefits, everyone pays. Or at least has done for the last thirty years." Aktualen's skin rippled a little. Was that a trick of the light or his own battered senses playing games? Matty-Bob left the question unanswered.

The screen-faced one jabbed a finger at him, a new face appearing on the dull glass. The strange visage grinned at him, its skin translucent showing a tracery of veins. The eyes were covered with some type of dark goggles. Matty-Bob convulsed with fear at the travesty of humanity. Bhabasiyat spoke, the smile of the creature on screen never wavering or moving.

"You haaave broken the teeeeerms of our agreement. Noooo exceptions can beeee made."

Shit. The one condition on his rental agreement that could not be defaulted. The one thing he had been warned of. And all because-.

"I got drunk and fell asleep."

Aktuelan's face fell in disappointment. The lace clad creature snorted in disgust.

"What a pathetic excuse." Her voice, became a rasp, fury and malice bleeding from behind the veil. Her eyes glowed green. "When Count Raum tried build his nest here, did we fall asleep? When Lucifer -that pathetic bag of offal, May His Name Be Spoken In Scorn -tried to sneak through the *Necrotic Fascia*, did we go and have a few pints and forget our responsibilities? You do not see what we do. Yet you mock us with poor excuses!"

Matty-Bob fell silent, swallowing convulsively.

"But how do you know I didn't do it? Someone could have nicked the offering…"

"Doris. Dear Old Doris from across the road."

The nosey old bat! As terrified as he was, Matty-Bob felt the first stirrings of righteous anger. The old lady hadn't even bothered to wake him.

"Not her responsibility", said Tolparethon. The three stepped forward, raising their right hands in unison. The air around them seemed to twist and warp. The red and green light from the walls became a glare that boiled the sweat from his skin. The air became stifling with the stink of rot.

"Please. Let me off this time. You can have the twelve drops and the bauble."

Aktuelan's face fell, a wistful almost sad expression on his face.

"I'm afraid not. The offerings are carefully calibrated. One missed invites disaster. The agreement is over."

The Landlords drew themselves straight, all humour gone from their strange demeanours. Aktuelan stepped forward.

"In order to retain balance, full payment is required. After all, you've always said that you have plenty of blood. Let's see if that's the case."

Aktuelan smiled, his mouth full to the brim with glinting razors.

Toothy maws opened up on the palms of their hands. A bizarre conglomerate of needles and spines oozed from their hands, dripping with red and green bile.

Matty-Bob gave up the struggle. He only hoped it wouldn't hurt for too long.

"Of course it won't hurt for long. We are not monsters. And it is Christmas after all."

He squeezed his eyes shut as the spiny masses stretched out towards him, penetrating the skin of his face.

Sometime later, he finally screamed.

The Landlords had lied.

It did hurt.

From Whence Alas Came The Flesh - Kitty Kane

AS I SIT AND WAIT for my loyal manservant to appear trudging over the snowy summit of the winter strewn hills, my mind begins to turn, turn back to this time last winter. The time whence I became the man, the king that sits here now, pondering and looking back on just when I became the monster I am today. A knock at the door interrupts my reverie, ah, tis the kindling wood cutter, bringing his tithe unto the castle, as I usher him in I feel the need to share with the old man my thoughts, I like to share.

In years gone by I have been heralded by my loyal subjects and peasants as Good King Wenceslas, alas those days are gone. Admittedly, at first it bothered me that I was not so adored by my subjects anymore, but as Daniel my manservant reminds me often, am the King dammit and the kingdom is mine to do with and within exactly what I wish. On occasion I wish I was still loved, had not become what I am, but I am what I am, I was born from the circumstances that befell me and my Kingdom back in the worst winter in living memory, I shall explain if you are able to tarry a while with me before heading back out into the blizzard? Yes I'm sure you do have many that are in need of your kindling wood good sir, but you would do your king such a service if ye would remain in my company slightly longer.

Please, enjoy this glass of mead, my cellar is well stocked with warming beverages, enjoy the fire, roaring in the grate, enjoy the hospitality of your king and ruler, tis rare given to those not it the upper echelons of society. You will? Oh joy, I shall join you with the mead , I have such a tale to spin unto you sir. What is it they call you again? Noel? My what a perfectly apt name you have sir to sit here and drink with your king at yuletide eve, yes, perfect your name is indeed Noel.

As I am sure you are aware good Noel, I have long strove to be a great and good king to you all, my subjects of my Kingdom, yes how I've loved you all. Twas always my way upon every yuletide to go out into the winter, and gift unto some of my subjects that were maybe suffering hardships born of the winter, alms. Out into the cold I went every year to deliver alms, I believe I may even have visited your cabin one yuletide? Oh I did? Yes my mind tends to keep sharp clarity of times gone by. Apologies for my digressing, I shall attempt to keep my tale on track.

The winter last year was harsh, the harshest as you know, even we here in the castle suffered along in the dark and frozen winter months. Prematurely invoked by heaven knows what freak twist of meter a logical circumstance, even we blessed richer folks suffered much. The cattle froze in their stalls, the castle stock of foul all died from exposure, the pigs were turned as always unto the woodlands to root for acorns and such the like, and to fatten to be enjoyed in the coming months died painfully, with the bite of frost tormenting them upon their skins that so resemble our own. The premature freezing of the land and gardens proper put pay to any vegetable storing to assist with the winter food stocks. As you know good Noel, the harvests all failed, wild and planted alike, we suffered greatly.

The pain brought about by hunger and starvation is a harsh pain indeed, a gnawing eating upon one's insides, and a dire emptiness of sustenance and energy, even the lucidity of the mind begins to vacate the starving man.

The day was bitter, the blizzard howled around the castle proper, and the outlying annexes bore great drifts of snow, some as high as the buildings themselves. From my vantage point I saw the poor widow whom abides in my cottages down yonder bring out a bundle. I wondered briefly what this could be, until I spied what looked like the leg of a piglet jutting out from under the rags. My ire swelled within me then good Noel, it seemed to me that the widow, from whom I had not received a tithe, had been holding back upon her king some bounty of which I, as ruler of these lands of course had a right to.

Driven by rage, and hunger of course but mostly rage I collected as many warming clothing items and swaddling cloths as I could wrap around my once ample personage, and I stormed out into the howling blizzard. I could not tell ye good sir how long my journey took me, my rage was red, driving me onwards, and onwards I continued until my snow and ice covered destination loomed white in front of my tired and frost bitten eyes. Upon that door I hammered Noel, my fists swathed in cloth yet still feeling the burn of frostbite made little noise upon the door of the dwelling, so I brought in my frozen and numb foot to make myself heard.

From within I heard a shuffling gait slowly approaching the door, but I did not stop my hammering Noel, oh no sir my anger was now at the level of blind anger. Unstoppable rage coursed throughout my body, I seethed until the tear stained and skeletally thin visage of the widow appeared through a slit that appeared signifying the doors opening.

Before she could change her mind, I rammed that door with my shoulder. My strength was minimal in comparison to my strength prior to this cursed winter, but hers was no match for mine, even changed as it was. With brute force I pushed into the humble dwelling. The widow, startled to find herself invaded suddenly recognised by her liege and hastened to curtsy as is expected.

I did not acknowledge the gesture as my rage was still coursing throughout my person. I made myself into a position where the widow had no choice but to look at me, roughly grabbing her ice cold chin I forced upwards her face and demanded she look at me. With watery eyes she obeyed my command, and briefly the thought crossed my mind that these were the eyes of a much younger and prettier woman than first appearances allowed. Spurred on by my anger, I backed her further into the cottage, and began my questioning of her.

" Good woman." I began, voice raised in my ire. "Not one hour ago woman, I saw from my castle yonder, you carrying a bundle containing what I suspect is pig meat! The castle has yet to receive tithe from yourself, my workers came to ask and the answer from your abode was you had nothing to tithe. I demand woman that you take me to the place I just witnessed you hiding the pig meat, and give unto your ruler what is due!"

The woman began to shake her head, concocting a likely story I assumed, but as her rheumy eyes met with mine, momentarily I questioned my rage. But rage such as I had about me that day was not for quieting easily, and it surged back as quickly as it had paused.

"Take me woman, immediately to where you concealed your bounty, if you shall not willing give unto your ruler that which would stave his gnawing hunger, then it shall be taken forcibly from thee. Now on your feet woman and lead the way!"

As I propelled her out of the doorway Noel, she gave slight stumble, and turned upon me beseeching eyes, tears threatened once more to fall, but they froze upon her face as the bitter wind did moan. She started shuffling along the snowdrift submerged pathway that gave access to the rear of the property, sliding and slipping in the piled fall. Twice she turned back to look upon me, and twice I m early pointed her onwards. I pondered briefly that perhaps she had something to say unto me, but in my ire I cared not for her words.

As we traversed the semi perilous walkway, when we neared the final few feet of the path she turned unto me and with bowed head and downcast eyes, she hastened to curtsy once more as is required when addressing one's liege, and spoke in a surprisingly melodious voice

" Please sire.. Esther is my name, please sur, tis no pig meat your good self spotted me with, twas nothing for eating, simply I was taking out that which was ruined. I beg of ye sire, thou shalt be disappointed if we continue along, I swear sur no pig meat has graced my kitchen in many a month,"

Once more my anger surged, and I demanded we continue to the snowy destination I had seen her end her earlier walk. I felt that the peasant was being deceitful to her ruler, and was braced to administer discipline as required for insubordination. The woman's gait slowed further and became even more of a shuffle as we neared what was clearly a small ice and snowbound mound. I demanded of the woman, of Esther that she bend and clear the freshly fallen snow from what I was convinced, absolutely convinced I was good Noel, was a hidden supply of pig meat. But oh was I ever mistaken sir? A greater mistake I had never made in my life.

Esther bent and delicately swiped at the fresh snow, slowly and with almost reverence, Puzzled at this i demanded she increase the speed of her labour forthwith, which she did after a fashion. The freezing tears were tumbling down her weathered face far more freely now, creating small icicles that glistened brightly against her browned and wind burnt skin. As her labours began to show fruition, a bundle came into sight.

Approximately the size of a three month old piglet, which of course Noel, I truly had believed it to be, the bundle came into view. Nestled there in the crispest, whitest snow was this package. My desire to know was not being satiated fast enough. I be lived the widow to be stalling for time, and sizing her by her bony shoulders, I briskly tugged her away from the buried bundle, and in my heavy handed haste, the widow she did stumble and fall into snow, where she remained.

For a moment good Noel I pondered if my haste and resulting violence had done for the woman, laid in the snow she cut a tiny bedraggled figure, and one step towards her I took, until I saw she was indeed still breathing, in fact she was sobbing. Sobbing in a most heartrending manner Noel, deep sobs of despair. No care to the woman's plight gave I then, my hunger gnawed inside me, my body was using quickly it's small supply of energy, and I bent unto the bundle myself.

The cloths were greying but clean, and as I peeled back the layers, the widows sobbing increased in volume and intensity. She began to rock, having pulled herself from her prone snowy hollow that her fall had created around her. She set up a high pitched keening sound that grated upon me Noel, oh how it grated. Simply wishing the noise to stop, I backhanded the widow across her tear tainted face, sending her spinning to the frosty, unforgiving ground. She cried out quietly, beseeching me to cease my exploration. Of course I would hear of no such thing.

As I peeled back the final layer from that cold and stiff bundle Noel, I suffered such a shock. Far from being the suspected stash of pig meat, revealed among the cloths was a perfectly formed, child's face. Oh what a cherub lay on that cold, hard ground Noel, the shock of what I saw sent me reeling backwards into the drifted snow. Stunned I shook my head, attempting to clear the fog of rage from my mind, but also cope with the shocking discovery I had made.

Shakily I regained my footing and turned to the widow. Seizing her once more by her shoulders I demanded she tell me why this poor child lay here in the cold, blue and with the sweet smell of death about him. However the blessed woman would not answer her liege. Down casting her eyes she shook her head, at first gently and then with more vigour. My rage coursed once again, renewed by this refusal to answer my questioning. I grabbed at her once more but she had the gall, the utter gall Noel to duck from my grasping hands and begin to dash back towards her dwelling.

Momentarily surprised by her renewed hast, I paused a little and, even slipping as she was the woman got a small head start. There was no way good Noel that I could allow this slip of a thing to refuse to answer her king, her ruler dammit. I rushed unsteadily after her, cursing the compressed snow our journey not ten minutes prior had caused. Slipping and sliding I caught up as she attempted to vanish into her home. I thrust my arm into the gap of the closing door, and levered it open once more.

Pushing through again in an action replay of earlier, I once more sized ahold of the infuriating woman. Shaking her hard I demanded again she tell me what fate had befallen the child. At first it looked as if she would refuse, but then the stubborn look upon her face wavered, just a tiny amount, as she resigned herself to telling her lord and ruler what he demanded to know.

"Sor.. Please Sor, I dint kill im Sor, loved that boy greatly. I jus cudnt feed ee proper Sor. I cudnt feed me proper Sor, so I cudnt feed the wee un proper. Ee got ill Sor, an I cudnt fix ee.. So don be standin thur in my umble abode judgin me Sor, I loved that wee un with my ole art. Since my usband never returned from that last useless unt for grub to feed thysel an them other pomps up at yonder castle of thee's, i's ad no food to make the milk to feed my babe. An now ee's dead an all, and it be your damned fault..Sor!"

This last the woman hissed unto me with venom flashing in her tear filled eyes. I went to grab her once more, but she eluded my grasp. What a madam she was that day Noel, no idea how to be in the presence of her liege. Faster this time I lunged once more, this time taking handfuls of her hair. Pretty hair as it happens. Many moons had passed since my hands had felt the softness of a woman in them.

As if sensing my thinking, the widow glared into my own eyes. Who knows what she saw there Noel, they say the eyes are the widows to the soul, but whatever it was, it caused her to make a terrible decision. She spat Noel! Yes I can see by your face that you understand the vile disrespect born of this action. The sputum landed upon the bridge of my nose, and trickled, warm and sticky down my face.

Well I don't mind telling you Noel, that now the red mist descended fully. A veil of unadulterated and uncontrollable rage. Grabbing blindly, I seized her once more. As I did so my fingers brushed her ample bosom, the same bosom that had ceased to feed her child, that now lay cold and dead on the snow covered ground, but I digress again.

This touch stirred within me that most primal of desires, and to my shame, I forced her backwards until she backed into the rickety old table which had pride of place beside a barren fireplace. Pinning her down onto the table I roughly shoved up her skirts, flipping them including the petticoats up and over her stomach. I grabbed with both hands her worn and threadbare upper clothing, and ripped it open to reveal a better view of that which had tempted me so.

As she lay upon that table, knowing my unclean intention, I saw the hatred in her eyes, but that did not halt me, indeed nothing would have right then halted my carnal craving for this disrespectful peasant woman. Unable to curb the urge any longer, pinning her down with one arm across her throat, I used my spare hand to tear away her much darned and re stitched bloomers. Discarding them upon the flagstone floor, like so much rubbish, I am ashamed and mortified good Noel to say I forced upon her myself, with much ardour, took her violently upon that table right there in her kitchen.

She did not scream, she attempted to struggle and bite and scratch, which only caused the pace of my attack to increase. The struggles excited me, and perhaps a blessing for her, the interlude was over rather quickly. Pulling myself off of her I straightened my apparel , and leaving her there with my seed running from within her I hastened once more out into the blizzard. The first stirrings of shame and regret rising within me like a fever.

I was about to set off to my castle, when I don't know what force caused me to think so, but I turned once more to the dwelling, trudged back along the perilous pathway until I came to the now almost snow covered bundle again. I stooped and picked it up, cloths and all as they were frozen to the poor tykes body. He wasn't heavy, and with some reverence I carried him along, all the way to the castle proper, but for why I did this, right then, I did not know, but I know now Noel, oh do I know now.

I placed the child, cloths and all upon the rug by the fire. Of course my good and loyal Daniel had set and lit the fire, and it roared ,welcoming home the master of the castle. Leaving the poor child there, I hastened to my rooms to discard my snow sodden clothing. My labours of the day, added to my depleted energy due to having had little of sustenance in my belly for a long while, combined to cause me a sudden fatigue. My four post bed had never seemed quite so inviting as it did right then Noel. Thinking to rest my aching bones momentarily, I laid myself down atop the eiderdown, and must have fallen into a hugely deep slumber.

When I awoke, the full, moon was riding high in the night sky, and the snow finally seemed to be taking respite from its relentless down pouring tirade it had dumped upon my Kingdom mercilessly for weeks. Encouraged by the sight of a snowless sky, I bounded out of bed, grabbed my robes and opened my bedroom door. As I entered the long east wing hallway that led to the castle proper, I smelled a smell I hadn't smelt in months. The aroma of roasting meat! I hastened to increase my pace along the wing. My mouth watered at the wonderful aroma. Daniel must have done the impossible and found some meat to feed the castle with. Joy and hunger coursed through my weakened body, and I closed the remaining distance quickly.

I pushed open the door to the castle kitchens, and was very surprised to find the incredible aroma weakening as I entered. In fact, no activity was occurring in the kitchens at all. Bare table tops mocked me, and the roasting pit was empty, not even any ashes adorning it's great. Puzzled, I followed the mouth watering aroma and was surprised to find my route ending in the great hall. The fire roared, and comprehension washed over me as I saw the bundle in front of the grate.

I dashed over, seizing hold of the dead child , the searing heat scalded the delicate flesh upon my palms. I cursed and rolled him gingerly towards me, oh such a shock awaited my weary eyes. The poor tyke was cooked, roasted like a Sunday joint, horror washed over me as tears sprang to my eyes. But then something else forced it's way to the fore of my thinking. Hunger, the hunger and aching in my belly was so obscenely very powering, my weakening body craved the protein that had alluded it for such a long time. Saliva filled my mouth, the aroma was all encompassing, something happened ten to my humanity Noel, I lost the ability to hold control over my actions.

Taking from its place upon the wall on one side of the fireplace an ornate dagger, I carved deeply into the roasted thigh of the peasant child. Slicing the meat into a manageable slice, I crammed it into my watering mouth and chewed with wild abandon and much gusto. The taste was sublime Noel. Like a suckling pig slow roasted over a fire pit, tender and running with juice, which I presumed to be the blood of the baby, I lost myself in my feasting.

How long I gorged I know not, but by time I was once more in possession of my senses, turned to see my nan servant standing not three feet away, a grimace upon the weathered face I knew so well. No judgement was present, just a curiosity and a clear sparkle of piqued interest in my meal. Slicing another well roasted chunk, this time from the tiny shoulder of the child, I speared it with the point of my dagger, and held it out to Daniel, who with the merest hesitation took the morsel and nibbled it.

I looked into his eyes as he did so, and saw that he certainly understood what he was eating. We looked upon each other differently in that moment than we ever before had. In less than 24 hours I had become rapist and cannibal, but I'll tell you good Noel, no shame felt I. Carving another serving for Daniel my mind whirred with self questioning, but no guilt for the consumption of the child did I feel, and no disgust crossed the face of my manservant. We sat there, beside the hearth rug, and stripped to the tiny bones the carcass of the poor child, and Noel, I swear upon my life, no sweeter meat had I ever tasted, nothing compares.

Since that time we have of course had greater fortune for some of the year, the land yielded a meagre crop, and some fish was brought by the fisher folk which we salted for preservation, and some of my land dwellers brought me some horse meat, gleaned from ancient old nags. The meat was tough and unpalatable, not like the child meat upon which I had shamefully partaken, a cumulative shame on a day of shame. But did that shame cow me good sir? No, I craved to feel once again upon my lips that meat so tender, and on verbalise g my terrible desire, I was perversely glad to see the same desire in the eyes of my loyal Daniel. Nodding once firmly he span, collected his cloak, trudged to the stable and ten minutes later I saw him galloping off into the darkening distance. No words had he uttered regarding his destination, and no care gave my mind. Simply the overpowering desire to gorge was all encompassing.

As I touchily and impatiently paced my halls, the thoughts of the wonderful tastes weighing strongly on my mind, I was taken back to the day I found the dead child at the home of the widow. I don't mind telling you sir Noel that other feelings stirred within me, caused by my remembrance of that day. A hot desire, an arousal of the carnal kind swelled in my loins. My manhood hardening frustratingly pushing against my clothing, it masked rationality, and I found myself seizing my outdoor cloak and setting off once more to the dwelling of the widow.

I did not knock this time as I arrived, my ardour was strong, the urge for release powerful to the extreme. I found her sat in the kitchen afore the empty fire grate. Her too young for her face, sparkling eyes found mine, and I knew she saw my intention, just as I saw the resignation in hers. I doubt, good Noel, that she would have offered much resistance, but the brute which had been born within me seized a hold of her humble and thread bearing clothes and swung her around and down onto the floor. Tearing at the cloths, I suffered a shock. Such a shock.

Rounded and swelling with child, the widows malnourished belly stood proudly. Hastily, calculations in my brain told me this swelling gravidity was likely born of my very own seed. I felt the colour drain from my face, my ardour immediately dampened by this discovery deflated, once more flaccid against my thigh. Ire rose, irrationally directed at the prone gravid peasant woman afore me. Back handing her about the face I demanded she tell me if this was indeed the fruit of my loins she grew within her. Again and again I slapped her, not a single verbalised cry did she make. Tears leaked from her aquamarine eyes, but not once did she avert them from the uncomfortable hold they had upon mine own.

In reply to my violently demanded question on the siring of the child within her belly, she simply uttered a single "yessor", telling me indeed that my prior raping of this woman had born fruit. The thought of fruit had my mind suddenly spinning, the taste of the prior firepit roasted child , oh what wicked thoughts, my corrupted mind was tainted beyond repair then Noel. All I could think of was that sweet tasting flesh. The widow of course knew nowt of my feasting upon her dead offspring, and I could only imagine the terror and disgust she would have felt if she did. I was already a rapist and server of violence upon the woman, upon Esther.

I felt the features of my face twist into a grimace, and putting my visage a mere quarter inch from her now tearstained and pained face and a primal growl came from my lips as I addressed her.

" Hear this peasant, the child within you bears my blood, in turn the blood of my father and forefathers, you will accompany me this day to my castle yonder where you shall dwell until your loins give unto this world my child. The choice is not yours, you come willingly or unwillingly but you will come, now this very day." Pulling her up roughly, clothing still wide open, belly leading, I propelled her out into the bitter wind. Dragging her along, her footing failing as she struggled to stagger in time with my long legged and fast paced gait. The last few feet to the castle proper, I somehow found the strength to swing her over my shoulder, and hastened in through the servants entrance.

Not quite certain where to secrete the woman , I hurriedly spun her down the spiralling staircase to my wine cellar, the very one in fact Noel that I referred to when telling you of my ample mead stocks. Down among the barrels and Racks, I threw Esther upon the unyielding floor. Nary a sound did she make as she lay exhausted upon the flagstone, creatures of the darkness scuttled away, alarmed at this strange intrusion into their nightly abode.

Shame fills me once more as my temper and ardour mixed again, and once more a satiated myself upon the woman, even as my child kicked in her womb. Oh Noel, how terrible a thing I did then, but not as terrible as that of which I had already partaken, the consumption of flesh of man, surely no greater evil abides in any man than abode in me right then. I hastened away with my face burning my shame.

Time passed painfully slowly, the excitement burning within me as any new parent, but my happy expectations were most foul by nature. Far from longing to hold in my arms the apple of my eye, I was imagining feeling and tasting once more that most divine tasting delicate, tender flesh. The flesh good Noel, of a human child. My, human child.

Oh goodness sir...you look awfully nauseated , my tale is a harsh thing to hear I realise, but my good man, when you have dined upon manna from heaven as I have, you simply must have more. It becomes an insatiable desire, the choice is no longer mine own. I crave that sweet meat over anything. Oh I see the horror in your eyes, but frankly I think I'm so far gone to the dark side I've little humanity left in my blackened soul. Oh look, I see Daniel on the horizon, and it looks as if he has had success Noel. You will of course, stay for dinner. No, where are you going , I can't let you leave without granting you proper hospitality, no I do insist sir, my tale is not quite done. Please stay there sir while I speak momentarily with dear Daniel. No sir, twas not a mere request, I quite insist.. oh my, Noel? Noel, oh bother why did you make me need to hit you, you should have just complied.

Ah sir! Tis indeed good to see you awakening, our meal will soon be with us. Oh I am sorry Noel, you look mystified at the change of surroundings. Yes it is indeed a cage you are resting in. The first man to grace one of my little cells with his presence. All women you see, if you note your neighbouring cages left and right. These are my battery women, whore's and street urchins mainly I'm not fussy, they must be old or indeed young enough to bear the fruit of my loins, to in turn become that beautiful tender food of the gods. Across from you is the bearer of today's fine meal, oh I see the sight of a woman splayed ass under at the belly and womb is causing you distress good Noel, oh I do indeed understand sir, really I do, that takes me nicely back into my tale, how splendid.

Oh I share your chagrin at the exposed innards of the lady fair. Esther was the first for me, oh those entrails steam so as you remove them, and my oh my do they stretch a long way! Daniel doesn't like me to play with the innards to much, but it's fun when I can. Oh yes, back to Esther, she as I said was my first. After secreting her in my wine cellar, I could think of nothing but the magnificent meal she incubated in here belly. I had to partake, I just had to, the urge was primal and encompassing Noel, pray what is more natural for man, than the desire to consume that which he craves.

I went to her, Esther, one last time. I think she thought what urged my visit upon her on this occasion would be once again of the carnal kind, but this time my desire was more primal, I could endure no more waiting. Tedious and tiresome to the extreme, I must have my prize. Crossing the flagstones I reached for her, she flinched, attempted to duck my grasp. Me, her king!! How rude! Anyway, I clasped her thin arm in my vice like grip, reached around behind me, gripping the shaft of my dagger handle firmly, I pulled it from its worn scabbard and put it to use forthwith.

I slit wide open her delicate throat, arterial blood bedecked the cellar, her aquamarine eyes widened as she desperately attempted to draw in life giving breath, but inhaled only blood, drowning in the crimson torrent. Laying her down before even the last spark died, I cut wide open her belly, and curled within was my prize, like a pearl in an oyster. The child lay in its sack of fluid, a girl, I had not tasted girl, would she be sweet? Would she be rich? The fluid in which she lay splashed warm over my feet. I grasped the child by the feet and hastened to make my retreat.

Not far had I reached when it felt as if my bounty had snagged upon something. Looking back I noticed a long, spiralling, bloodied cord tethering the infant to its dame. Seizing once more my dagger, I cut through the surprisingly tough to cut fleshy rope, finally freeing the babe. As I jerked the child once more I hear a sound. Faint, and tinny. It sounded to me as a newborn lamb. I glanced down, down at my own child, and do you know what I did then good Noel? I slit her throat too. Bleeding her out right there on the stairs I took her to the kitchens. I'm not a great cook Noel, in fact before I embarked upon this monstrous part of my life I had never needed cook a thing myself, so new to me was trussing a joint of meat.

Poor Daniel looked a little shocked when he saw my efforts, but he loyally came unto the aid of his liege and friend. We pricked the softest skin with silver forks, rubbed a little

354

salt and pepper in and placed the tiny child in the oven. The smell was wonderful as our macabre meal cooked. Our mouths watered, the waiting was agony, but when at last our meal was roasted to perfection, twas with much gusto that we feasted. We knew then dear Noel, that we were forever changed. Cannibals, monstrosities and animals, but we cared not, our hunger was satiated and led the way to what you see before you this day. My child meat battery farm is likely the only one of its kind, and now you have been honoured to see it Noel.

Well good Noel, I think my tale is done, oh how I have enjoyed our time sir, but now I fear you would be a threat to my orchard of the sweetest fruit, and we can't have that, but as it is yuletide, before I deal your death unto you, I insist you join me in my meal, oh look, here comes Daniel now, oh we are in luck. A boy child, tasty, see how the skin crisps so.. tastes much like bacon fat Noel, from which end of the meat would you wish me to carve your portion, Noel? Noel? Tsk... how rude fainting at the dinner table, oh well, Daniel, the knife please......

Sweet Silver Bells - Tamara Fey Turner

FROM THE FIRST TIME they called, his world changed. That was many Christmases ago. He'd listened to their ringing. He'd let go of all his cares and concentrated on their song. It was joyful, perhaps, in the beginning.

Now the bells not only came with the snow season as a holiday treat, they were his daily feeding. They reverberated in his head continuously. They were his constant companion, always raising their sound as the cool breeze turned frosty, and the day of celebrating the birth of the infamous baby messiah approached.

The bells did not bring good cheer. They were dark, rusty, steely, and relentless. Pounding. When the sound of the bells raised, he heard nothing else. Nothing else existed. He use to wonder how many others o'er hill and dale obeyed them. He wondered nothing now.

The paralysis of his thoughts and loss of control of his actions increased daily. Overpowered by the lovely bells. Beautiful silver bells. Ding Dong. Ding Dong. That was their song.

Their commands were everything. At first he had sung with them. Now, he simply performed their will. The enjoyment of them gone, although their consumption of him was darkly satisfying. He loved the bells. He needed them. And he hated them.

They were the strongest now that they had ever been. He knew soon he would no longer exist. He longed for the release into utter insanity. He no longer resisted the glorious bells. It was no longer an option. He had no free will. His humanity had completely betrayed him last Christmas when he had taken the hearts of his wife and daughter.

"Trevor, what are you doing? Where did that blood come from? Are you hurt?" Angie's shrill voice pierced through him that night, but it did not deter him from his mission. The bells' mission.

After butchering six-year old Sloane with a hacksaw, his bare hand had reached in to take her still-warm heart. The heart that had still be beating when he began to quarter her.

Sometimes he could still feel it in his hand when he closed his eyes. The sweet metallic smell of her blood. The memory of how easily he sawed the head of his daughter from her fragile neck while she was still alive.

He could still recall the terrified look on his wife's face when she began to piece together what was in his hand that winter night. She shook uncontrollably as she tried to get out of bed, as she tried to escape him, and her death.

Insanity set in quickly as he closed the gap between them, as Angie screamed their daughter's name and begged him to stop ... as a smile split his face open farther, as he took the first delicious bite of the tender heart in his hand ... as the blood of his wife commingled with that of his daughter, both coating him like raspberry syrup. Angie had been unable to save their daughter or herself from the will of the bells. The sweet silver bells.

He savored their bodies more than any of the others. He felt proud that they would always be with him in a way most others could never understand. He had thought that would be the end, his grand finale. But the bells weren't yet done with him. They seemed to enjoy his helplessness. He knew they were joyous he had relinquished all power and control to them. The bells were happier than ever. They had left him nothing. Nothing except the dark feelings that caused brief excitement when they demanded blood.

Past the edge of insanity and well into its depths, Trevor had already begun this season's hunting. Three days ago. His freezers already contained two carved and well-wrapped bodies. This had not appeased the bells. Not this year.

In past years, the first season's blood was mild. Or that's the way he remembered it. The brutality had to build within him and be represented in the kills. This season's first was gruesome.

The long, thin blade had slid across the young girl's throat like it was cutting softened butter. Her blood had been warm and delightful as he peeled back her head by a handful of hair and filleted her skin like a banana all the way down to her feet. With her head and feet both at the bottom of her body, he used a freshly sharpened hatchet to whack them away. Only a thin layer of fat lined her beautifully exposed meat. He licked his lips at the sight as he began to quickly section and wrap her. She was so lean. He hoped it would be enough to keep her from drying out in freezer.

He portioned off the back of her calves, his favorite cut. He placed them and as much blood as he could collect in a stainless steel serving bowl. He would eat these first. Raw. He craved more of her, but his appetite wasn't what it used to be. There was no need to debone the rest of her, that would take care of itself later during cooking. Human flesh should be cooked after it's frozen.

People have always loved Christmas time. It's their excuse to be kind and generous and to carol. Everyone loves the bells. And the bells also love Christmas.

Shaking his head hard and pressing the palms of his hands against his eyebrows and forehead, his long, thin fingers curled and began to dig. Pulpy scalp stuck under his nails, but he did not notice. Pain was a distant memory. He was completely desensitized to it in any form. He no longer felt remorse for his countless victims or their families or even his own. He simple existed. For the bells.

Throughout December his apartment always smelled amazing. Soups. Meat pies. Stews. Two freezers filled with human treats. This year was no exception. Normally this satisfied the bells, kept their anger down. This year it was only a slight relief. They remained overwhelming. Demanding.

Trevor had only left his apartment for essentials in the last few years. He'd had no personal relationships since slaughtering his family last Christmas. The bells no longer allowed Trevor sleep. His sleep depravity amused them.

On Christmas night, the last night of the mandatory hunt, as dictated by the carol of the bells, they rang louder than they ever had before. Trevor sat at the dining room table he'd once shared with his family.

The steak knife presented a rare slice of meat to his mouth. Blood fell to the back of Trevor's throat and ran down his chin. His last hunt of the season was complete. Blood also pooled on the floor, his own blood, as he continued to eat his own calf.

He tried to envision his wife and daughter sitting with him, enjoying his flesh as he'd enjoyed theirs. But he could not remember the way they looked now, only the way they tasted. At least they were all together in some way. Their fates determined by the bells. Their flesh digested by the same stomach. Trevor smiled as he licked the knife.

The bells never stopped caroling.

Merry Merry Merry Merry Christmas.

All I Want For Christmas Is Ewe - Matthew Cash

"YOU'RE NOTHING BUT a fat, useless, stinking, fucking fat drunk." Daisy shrieked, her eyes squinting like they had the power to eject the same type of venom as her poisonous, puckered mouth. Her pristine blonde hair extensions fluttered in the breeze from the open doorway.

"Yer said fat twice," Eddie said, fingers laced over his belly and around his beer can. One thing he couldn't abide, lack of vocabulary, "obese, overweight, would 'ave been acceptable substitutes. Or if you wanted to go down the offensive route you could've said, 'you're nothing but a fat, useless, stinking, whale of a drunkard.'" Eddie paused and sipped his ale, "but no, you have to use small words and profanity, don't you?"

Daisy stared at the fat, useless, stinking, whale of a drunkard in disgust. His tattered white vest pulled down barely over his round belly, which was so big he used it as a fucking drinks stand. It was grotesque, the way it ballooned over the band of his tracksuit trousers. She couldn't believe she had married him.

Although fifteen years ago he had been a vibrant doting son, big and strong like only a busy farmhand could be.

But since his harridan of a mother kicked the bucket and the farm downsized, he did less and drank more.

Nothing phased or upset him, all he cared about was his pathetic farm which lost more than it made. She flicked her gaze over her shoulder to the red sports car, engine idling, behind her. Gordon, her lover, was everything he wasn't -good looking, rich, and good-looking, hell that was enough anyway. "I'm leaving you Edward, and you'll hear from my solicitor about divorce."

Eddie drained his can and tossed it over his shoulder before crossing his hands back over his belly, defiant. "I'm not agreeing to a divorce."

Daisy scowled at him maliciously, "I'm leaving you, I am in love with Gordon, I had sex with him in our bed."

"I know all that, I caught you remember?"

Yes, she did. And she expected a bit more of a fucking reaction when he had opened their bedroom door.

They had been in the throes of passion, Daisy straddling the younger, athletic Gordon in the position he referred to as 'the reverse cowgirl,' her back to him, hands resting on his well-toned abdomen, and she was cumming harder than she had ever done in her life. It had been amazing, then Eddie walked in, still in his filthy farm clothes, something she always berated him about, saw them and rolled his eyes. Actually rolled his eyes like she was doing something clichéd and typical.

"Ey," he had said in that horrific common accent of his, "yer could have at least worn some decent socks me old matey."

He had been referring to Gordon's socks, which were still on his feet, his left big toe pointing out towards the artex ceiling.

Eddie had then bent down beside their frozen, coital display, carefully moved their entangled underwear, and grabbed his tartan slippers. Almost like an afterthought he acknowledged her, "Don't forget to change the sheets afterwards, there's a love, not like last time, ey?" He then winked a piggy eye and went downstairs to sit in front of the television.

"Anyway," Eddie continued, drawing her from her flashback, "I ain't giving you a divorce, and I'll not ever sign no papers saying otherwise." All he had left was his mother's farmhouse and the animals, the place was slowly sinking into disrepair, he wouldn't let her have anything.

"Fine, well the solicitor will be in touch."

"Wait," Eddie called.

Finally, Daisy thought, now I'll get some kind of reaction. She looked at her husband quizzically.
"Merry Christmas," Eddie said warmly with a smile.
She span around and went out of the door, seething at her emotionless pig of a husband. Fuck Christmas and fuck him. It always amazed her at how bloody sentimental he was about Christmas time.
Daisy got in the passenger side of the sports car, Gordon grinned awkwardly, but gorgeously, "Alright?"
"Of course I'm not bloody alright." Daisy shrieked at him making him cower behind the steering wheel like a frightened child.
Gordon drove off, the twin beams of the car's headlights cutting swathes through the darkness over the farm that Daisy had paid absolutely no attention to.
"Merry, fucking, Christmas," she muttered scornfully out the window towards the small farmhouse.

Eddie moved his considerable bulk across to the kitchen and upped the temperature on the thermostat, it was a cold one this year. He pulled another can of ale from a crate that sat on the kitchen worktop and slumped back into the chunky, threadbare armchair that sat between kitchen and dining room. The Christmas decorations that hung all over the house were gaudy and ancient but Eddie loved them. They had been his mother's, as had the farm. He sighed, he missed his mother, she has been a good woman, not like Daisy. The inheritance money had nearly dried up, the farm didn't make much money either. Over the five years since she passed he had sold off a few of the animals and most of the land. Some of the animals he couldn't part with though, and the thought of using them for meat was a no go. Eddie had been a strict vegetarian since a child and when he learned where meat came from. He loved animals, they were better than people, more understanding and less judgemental.
The only money that came in was from the goats and dairy

cows, of which he only had two left, Monica and Phoebe. Rachel had gotten ill last winter and never made it to the New Year.

Eddie raised his can in a toast to the empty kitchen and the memory of two lost beloved ladies, "to mother and Rachel."

The chickens brought money in from the free range eggs, and old Chandler the stallion was always popular with the local kids who wanted riding lessons, but the money was a pittance, as his mother used to say.

Daisy had wanted to turn the farm into a bed and breakfast, get rid of the stinking animals, convert the barn into a Swiss chalet. A Swiss bloody chalet. Oh how he had laughed at that. She hadn't cared for the animals anyway, saw them only as money makers. She wanted him to get rid of the pigs if he wasn't prepared to sell them for meat, and the money he got for Jemima's wool wasn't worth the effort.

Jemima was the last survivor of a whole herd of sheep and Eddie loved her. She had been known simply as number 69 to everyone but him, due to the number she had sprayed onto her side. But disease had struck the flock and all but her had perished. She was old, blind in one eye but he loved her.

Any animal that doesn't make money needs to go, Daisy said. Even the duck pond. She wanted that filled in, the 'useless' birds slaughtered and the land to be used for something more bountiful.

Eddie sighed and pulled his jumper on. It hadn't been what he has hope for, marriage. Whilst they nursed his dying mother he planned to turn the farm into one of them family places where the parents could bring the kiddies and show them the animals. Teach them all about the history of farming and agriculture. He would give them the tour, teach them how to care for the animals, lambing season would be popular too. Springtime was great on farms, All that new life, cute baby animals bouncing about the place.

It would have been great.

Eddie wiped a tear from his eyes when he wondered how he was going to pay for the shipment of feed and bedding that he desperately needed to order for the animals. It really was getting colder now, and his bank account would not be sufficient. On the day before Christmas Eve he found out she had withdrawn almost everything from the bank. DAISY had bled him dry. All he had was his animals, what he referred to his furry family.

The days rolled on and whilst Daisy was whisked away somewhere sunny for sand, sea and sixty-nines, Eddie was trying to cope with fast diminishing temperatures and livestock who were almost out of food or hay. He wasn't too bothered about himself, the bills were always paid a few months in advance and he had enough food to last him for ages. But he wondered how he would look after his animals.

Outside was a winterland of Arctic proportions, the ground rock hard with a frost that never lifted, the ducks skidded around on their frozen pond, the cows relied on whatever feed Eddie could give them. The sun had fucked off and done one big time, and the clouds above bulged with the threat of a never-ending blizzard.

Eddie studied the weather and knew that this was going to be the harshest of winters he had ever experienced in his fifty years. As he sat surveying his land, supping at a flagon of his father's moonshine he had dredged up from the cellar, a blazing star twinkled briefly between the swollen bastard snow clouds. Like the star over Bethlehem filled the shepherds of millennia past with awe and wonder this celestial body ignited something within Eddie as he lolled in the Eddie-shaped mould of his armchair. He opened his mouth and lifted his right buttock and simultaneously burped and farted. Then jumped straight up and out of the chair as something extraordinary happened.

A bright, blazing blue beam, as bright as the sun, seemingly shot down from the star parting the snow clouds.

Eddie pressed his face against the cold glass of his window and watched with transfixed with delirious ecstasy as a figure, glowing blue from the light, floated down to the farmyard.

A spectral cow, he could tell it was Rachel by her markings, beautifully washed and preened hovered upright outside his kitchen window. Her forelegs paddled the air in front of her whilst the rear stood still above the frozen ground. She was lit with an ethereal luminescence, her eyes sparkled with blue love and affection. A blinding disc of white hovered like a planetary ring around and above her head, and glowed with the same inner light as the massive white wings that spread around her.

Tears of complete joy fell down Eddie's face, he fumbled with the back door lock and ran out into the yard to greet his angelic cow. All around him in the now lit farmyard he could hear his animals becoming excited, the lowing of Monica and Phoebe the cows, the neighing of Chandler the horse, the snuffles from the pigs, Jemima's distinctive bleat and the various quacks and clucks from the ducks and chickens. They sang out their animal hosanna for the return of their lost friend Rachel.

Eddie fell to his knees on the soft snow and hard mud, gazing up in religious ecstasy at the floating cow who had spun in the air to face him. Her bulging udders pulsated at eye level, the teats waving this way and that like she was under water.

A voice came from her wide mouth, her big thick tongue moving unnaturally to pronounce words and sounds not designed for one of her species. She sounded exactly as Eddie imagined, all animals had a voice in his mind, silken, creamy soft tones that enveloped him like warm chocolate. She told him, praised him, thanked him for all his good work, instructed him of what to do before he and her friends could join her in the pastures of Heaven. Before she left him her udders burst and baptised him with thick, gluttonous cream, sparkling with heavenly gold light.

It took him all night, but he was relentless and unstoppable now he knew his mission in life. Rachel the cow angel had spoken to him, told him the way it would be. At first he wondered whether the ever-fermenting, decades old moonshine of his father's had addled his brains, and that the whole religious visitation had been concocted by whatever poison it had mutated into. But when he awoke, early on Christmas morning, covered in Rachel's thick colostrum, her womb filled with the calves she was unable to bear whilst alive, he knew it had been real.

Everything was white when he peered from his bedroom window, the blackened carcass of the burnt farmyard buildings jutted out of the snow like the spindly twig arms of a overturned snowman.

The barn where Chandler, Phoebe and Monica and the goats had resided had taken the longest to burn, the wood damp and cold with the recent weather. But when the fuel Eddie had doused the remnants of the last haystacks started burning the wood soon dried out and went up.

He left the pigsty and chicken huts, they would be covered by the snowstorm by now anyway. The amount of snow that had fallen since Rachel's departure had been miraculous for one night's fall. Four feet, he estimated, and that had all been after he had destroyed his farm.

"Oh well," Eddie said to no one in particular, "best get ready for Christmas dinner."

Daisy swallowed her pride and got out of the taxi. She couldn't believe the last few weeks she had had. The holiday had been great, Gordon even greater, but he had been so dull. Dullness she could have put up with if it hadn't been for the bloody barmaid at the hotel they stayed in. She had caught them at it on a secluded part of the beach. She had taken ill with a migraine and left Gordon to go out alone. Afterwards, early evening, she took a stroll to clear her head and saw them fucking behind a sand dune.

And now she was back. There was no doubt that Eddie would have her back. Sure, she would have to eat humble pie for a few days, be the dutiful housewife, let have sex with her other than on his birthday, but he would have her back. And she had nowhere else. Yet. She would spend the next few weeks searching for somewhere new to live, she would persuade him somehow to sell up, sell the animals and the farm. Then she would take the money and scarper.

Daisy froze when she walked down the wet lane to the farm entrance, the melted snow had caused floods nearby but the ground was high up here. "What the fuck?" Their huge red barn was devastated, burnt out, laying on the ground like a upturned dead spider.
A fire.
Did they have insurance? She was certain that Eddie would have. A smile lit up her face, insurance would mean a pay out. Money. If somehow Eddie had been caught in the fire she would have his life insurance too. Suddenly her dreams of turning the land and buildings into a bed and breakfast were becoming realistic.
She could use the money to rebuild and set up business.
She passed the pigsty, chicken huts and run and saw that they were deserted.
Her blood ran cold, what if that robbing bastard had sold all the remaining animals and buggered off with all the money? It would surprise her, Eddie wasn't that sort of man.
She left the empty huts and turned to the farmhouse. It too seemed quiet, empty.

The door was locked, curtains drawn. Daisy rooted in her bag for her set of keys and entered the house.
The smell hit her straight away, a strong animal reek. Chickens waddled across the filthy carpet, pecking at morsels amidst the detritus. The kitchen was a mess, the cupboards raided, their doors hanging from busted hinges. The chickens

congregated around a burst sack of economy cornflakes.

Something shifted in the half light, beside her in the lounge. "Jesus fucking Christ." She exclaimed as Chandler the horse snorted at her, lifted his tail and dropped great, big dollops of steaming shit on the rug. He moved casually to a hay bale that filled up the dining table.

Monica and Phoebe lay on the lounge carpet, the three piece suite was ruined, the plasma television covered with a dry translucent film of animal saliva.

A rustling and the scuffling of hooves tore her eyes away from the cows in the lounge, as two goats came trotting down the stairs, her best lingerie wrapped around their horns, half chewed. The black goat that Eddie called Ross gazed at her, his lower jaw going side to side as he chewed on her gusset. All around the walls and furniture had been gouged by horns or nibbled by teeth. Sodden paper Christmas decorations had turned into a soggy mulch on the floor where they soaked up animal urine.

A sudden waft of sweaty shit and rotten food came from the cellar door, the pigs had found the contents of the pantry, sacks of potatoes, dried fruit and pickles.

Quacking came from the downstairs bathroom, their four ducks taking it in turns to dive in and out of the overflowing bathtub.

Daisy whirled around and around, her home was ruined, everything was destroyed. A hollow groan escaped her throat at the madness, Eddie had obviously flipped his lid, her leaving him having a more serious effect than he had made out.

A thud from upstairs, and groans of pleasure. Daisy was struck by an unexpected bout of jealousy. He never made

noises like that when we had sex. Eddie had always been a quiet lover, missionary, a few thrusts and a grab of one tit was generally all she got before his face screwed up like he had constipation and he came. Even when he came it felt as though it just oozed out unenthusiastically, rather than gushing like Old Faithful as Gordon had.
But as she climbed up the stairs, over the contents of her wardrobe, her best dresses ruined, she heard bed springs boinging and the headboard banging. The dirty old bastard was going at it like a demon possessed. But who the hell would he have up there?

Daisy reached out to touch the door handle, waiting for Eddie's panting to reach a crescendo. He had ruined epic sex for her and Gordon that time, she never did feel like she even came close to cumming as hard as she was when he had caught her at it. She would ruin his fun too.
She heard his breathing become more rapid, the headboard smashing against the wall, the bed sounding like it would explode at any point, his voice was raw and rough with lust when he growled out, "oh God yeah Jemima."
Daisy gasped and yanked open the door. But Jemima was what he called the...
Jemima baa'd at her as if to confirm her suspicion. The ewe stood on the bed, Eddie naked behind it, fingers digging deep into her greasy wool. Daisy stood slack-jawed, words failing her at the scene of perverse bestiality before her. She lowered her eyes and saw that Eddie still had his socks on, the heel of the right one was completely missing. After what he had said to Gordon this was the thing that tipped her over the edge. She stared at her sheep-shagging husband and pointed at his holey sock, "you fucking hypocritical cunt."
Eddie sheepishly pulled out of Jemima, the sheep bleated disappointedly and walked across the bed to chew on the pillow.
"You're crazy," Daisy said retching and shielding her eyes from Eddie's erection, "insane. You'll go to jail for this."
Maybe that would work in her favour, he would surely get a

severe prison sentence for this, not only was it animal cruelty, but she was pretty sure having sexual relations with them too was a crime. She could let the bailiffs come and take everything they needed. Hell, they could bulldoze the place for all she cared. Whatever was left she would take and leave him for good. She looked at her emaciated husband, covered in his own, and God knew what else's filth. He'd even lost weight since she had left. Pitiful. With any luck he would miss his animals so much in jail that he would kill himself. Then she would get his life insurance too.

Eddie raised his head and grinned at her, his teeth caked with plaque, old food and what looked like wool. There was a sinister element to his expression, one she had never seen before. He reached out a doughy arm behind him and grabbed what appeared to be a wooden staff. Daisy recognised it as the ancient shepherd's crock that used to hang above the fireplace, his grandfather's.

Eddie pointed the curved end towards her, his voice dripped with an evil she would never think him capable of, "I am the Shepherd and this is my flock."

Daisy turned and bolted for the bedroom door, with Eddie's severe mental deterioration who knew what he was capable of. She made it to the top of the stairs when she felt the hook of the shepherd's crock loop round her ankle and caused her to trip. She bundled down the staircase and landed at the bottom in a heap. At the top of the stairs Eddie appeared, still naked, still erect, and laughed. To her amazement he began to sing as he descended the stairs. "whilst shepherds watched their flocks by night, all seated on the ground."

The fall had hurt her but she didn't think anything was broken, the crap on the stairs would have cushioned part of the fall.

He muttered something inaudible and her ribs were suddenly crushed by the front right hoof of Chandler. The weight of the horse shattered her ribcage and sent splinters of bone through her lungs instantly.

Chandler's other leg hovered above her face, frozen, waiting for the order from Eddie.

"An angel of the Lord came down," Eddie sung, arms spread

out, joyous as he stood over his wife.

Daisy choked on her own blood whilst she fought for air that would not come.

"And glory shone around." Eddie said with a hint of sadness, then nodded to the horse. Chandler stomped his hoof down onto Daisy's head putting her out of her misery.

Author Biographies

GRAHAM MASTERTON:

After 35 years in which he established himself as one of the world's bestselling horror authors, Graham Masterton has turned his hand to crime.

Drawing on the five years in which he and his late wife Wiescka lived in Cork, in southern Ireland, he has created a series of novels featuring Katie Maguire, the first woman detective superintendent in An Garda Siochána, the Irish police force.

Graham was born in Edinburgh in 1946, the grandson of John Masterton, the chief inspector mines for Scotland, and Thomas Thorne Baker, a scientist who was the first man to send news pictures by radio.

After joining his local newspaper at the age of 17 as a junior reporter, he was appointed deputy editor of Mayfair the men's magazine at the age of 21. At 24 he became executive editor of Penthouse.

His career at Penthouse led him to write a series of best-selling sexual advice books, including How To Drive Your Man Wild In Bed, which solid 2 million copies worldwide and 250,000 in Poland alone, where it is has recently been reprinted.

After leaving Penthouse he wrote The Manitou, a horror novel about the vengeful reincarnation of a Native American spirit, which was filmed with Tony Curtis in the lead role, and also starred Susan Strasberg, Burgess Meredith and Stella Stevens. Three of Graham's horror stories were adapted by the late Tony Scott for his TV series The Hunger. Over the years he has published five collections of short stories, several of which have won awards.

Graham has also written historical sagas like Rich, Maiden Voyage and Solitaire, as well as thrillers and disaster novels such as Plague and Famine and the latest -- Drought.

In 1989 Graham's Polish wife Wiescka was instrumental in

his becoming the first Western horror novelist to be published in Poland since World War Two, and his sex books have not only won popular success in Poland but acclaim from the medical profession.

He was a regular contributor of humorous articles to the satire magazine Punch, as well as scores of articles on sexual happiness to American women's magazines.

He has encouraged younger writers in several countries, including France, Germany and the Baltic States. For the past 15 years, he has given his name to the prestigious Prix Masterton, which is awarded annually for best French-language horror novel. He was the only non-French winner of Le Prix Julia Verlanger for best-selling horror novel and he has also been given recognition by Mystery Writers of America, the British Fantasy Society and many others.

He edited an anthology of short stories by leading horror writers, Scare Care, in aid of children's charities, and has been honoured by the Irish Society for the Prevention of Cruelty to Children for his fund-raising. He also supports an orphanage in Gorzec, Poland, and a charity in Wroclaw which gives refuge to young people forced into prostitution.

He currently lives in Surrey, England.

Graham Masterton is mainly recognized for his horror novels but he has also been a prolific writer of thrillers, disaster novels and historical epics, as well as one of the world's most influential series of sex instruction books. He became a newspaper reporter at the age of 17 and was appointed editor of Penthouse magazine at only 24. His first horror novel The Manitou was filmed with Tony Curtis playing the lead, and three of his short horror stories were filmed by Tony Scott for The Hunger TV series. Four years ago Graham turned his hand to crime novels and White Bones, set in Ireland, was a Kindle phenomenon, selling over 100,000 copies in a month. This has been followed by five more bestselling crime novels featuring Detective Superintendent Katie Maguire, the latest of which is Buried. He has also published a grisly 18th-century crime novel Scarlet

Widow. Graham's horror novels were introduced to Poland in 1989 by his late wife Wiescka and he is now one of the country's most celebrated authors, winning numerous awards. He is currently working on new horror and crime novels.

Bekki Pate:
Bekki Pate was born in Nottingham and currently lives in Wolverhampton with her partner and daughter.
She is the author of horror novels The Willow Tree, The Shadow Beneath and The Pale Man, and the short story collection Into the Dark.
She has also recently had a number of short stories accepted into anthologies due to come out in 2016.

Along with spending time with her daughter and partner, Bekki is an avid reader, her favourite authors being Stephen King, Elizabeth Kostova and Richard Laymon.

Her facebook page can be found here:
https://www.facebook.com/BekkiPate1/?ref=hl

Edward Breen:
Edward Breen is a Kent based writer, husband and father to three cats and a human child. He loves horror and fantasy and writes short stories mainly. One of his many manuscripts will, hopefully, become a novel some day, but for now you can catch him at https://dwreadswriting.blogspot.co.uk as well as on Facebook @Edward Breen.

Helen Claire Gould:
Helen has been writing since her teens, having read her first two Science Fiction novels at the age of nine.
Shortly after suffering some miscarriages in 1992 she began writing for therapeutic reasons. She joined a British Science Fiction Association Orbiter, then a Cassandra one, then became administrator for a third. She had joined the Peterborough SF Club, where she met her husband, and contributed to the club fanzine A Change of Zinery. She set up

the Peterborough Science fiction writers' Group, editing two small press collections of short fiction, Shadows on a Broken Wall and Mother Milk, Father Flywheel. She organised a weekend workshop on writing for comics and had book reviews published in the BSFA review magazine, Vector.

In 1995 she returned to full-time education. After graduating from Anglia Ruskin University in Geology and Planetary science in 2000, she taught Geology and Creative Writing evening classes, and edited further collections of short fiction by her Creative Writing students. From 2004 – 2006, she contributed geological articles to Deposits, an amateur magazine with high production values. She organised and ran a series of writers' workshops for the 2013 Peterborough Arts Festival.

Floodtide is her first published novel, but she has several more novels and short stories, most of which are set in her own fictional universe. Find out more at www.Zarduth.com

Her next novel will be The Zarduth Imperative.

Delphine Quinn:

Delphine Quinn is a new horror/extreme horror author who has had early success submitting shorts to various publications. She is currently working on an upcoming collection of stories titled Asylum, as well as a full-length novel, both of which she plans on self-publishing. Delphine lives in the central United States with her husband and her cat, Coco. In her free time from work and writing, she likes to binge watch TV shows and movies, or indulge in her unhealthy obsession with reading about sociopaths and serial killers.

You can find out more about her via her newly created Amazon Author page: http://www.amazon.com/-/e/B01GUKYHV6
Or her Facebook page:
http://www.facebook.com/delphine.quinn.5

Jonathan Butcher:
Jonathan Butcher writes vile and subversive stories for about 75% of the time, and quirky, quaint or cute ones for the rest of the time. While he would love to spend 100% of his writing time focused on fiction, he probably spends less than 10% of it doing so. He does, however, consider himself 236% focused on becoming the best author he can be.
Jonathan lives, laughs, loves, and loafs around in Birmingham, UK. If you introduce him to any good/weird stories, music or films, you will immediately be put into his good books.
Follow him here: www.facebook.com/jonathanbutcherauthor

Em Dehaney:
Em Dehaney is a mother of two, a writer of fantasy and a drinker of tea. Born in Gravesend, England, her writing is inspired by the dark and decadent history of her home town. She is made of tea, cake, blood and urban magic. You can find her at www.emdehaney.com or lurking about on Facebook@emdehaney posting pictures of witches

Betty Breen:
Betty Breen writes because she must and loves doing it. New to the world of writing this is her first publication (of many). A creative a heart, watch this space for more from this new entry into the Horror sphere. Catch her on Twitter @just_betty5

Michael Noe:
Michael Noe is a horror writer from Barberton Ohio. He is the author of Legacy, The Darkness Of The Soul, Legacy 2 and the short story collection Insecure Delusions. When not writing, he reviews books on his website Slaphappy Fun Time and collects vinyl records. You can find him at

https://www.facebook.com/michaelnoeslegacy/ as well as http://slaphappyfuntime.blogspot.com/?zx=9dcec248a7c0b9ba

Dani Brown:
Born in Oxford but raised in Massachusetts, Dani Brown is the author of "My Lovely Wife", "Middle Age Rae of Fucking Sunshine", "Toenails", and "Welcome to New Edge Hilll" out from Morbidbooks. She is also the author of "Dark Roast" and "Reptile" out from JEA. She's the person responsible for the baby blood bath that is "Stara" out from Jaded Books Publishing. She has written various short stories across a range of publications. There's always more coming soon. As of writing this, "Stef and Tucker" haven't been released but they will be soon (if "Dancing With White Walkers" hasn't happened by the time you read this).

When she isn't writing she enjoys knitting, fussing over her cats and contemplating the finer points of raising an army of dingo-mounted chavs. She has an unhealthy obsession with Mayhem's drummer and doesn't trust anyone who claims The Velvet Underground are their favourite band.

She currently lives in Liverpool, England with her son and 3 cats.

You can contact her on facebook at https://www.facebook.com/DaniBrownBooks/.
Amazon https://www.amazon.com/Dani-Brown/e/B00MDGLYAY
Official and sometimes updated website
http://danibrownqueenoffilth.weebly.com/

Craig Saunders:
Craig Saunders is the author of more than thirty novels and novellas, including 'Masters of Blood and Bone', 'RAIN' and 'Deadlift'. He writes across many genres, but horror, humour and fantasy are his favourites.

Craig lives in Norfolk, England, with his wife and children. He likes nice people and good coffee. Find out more on Amazon, or visit:

www.craigrsaunders.blogspot.com
www.facebook.com/craigrsaundersauthor
@Grumblesprout

Fiona Dodwell:
Fiona Dodwell is a published author who has released several paranormal titles including The Banishing, Nails, The Ouija Trials, The Redwood Lodge and Obsessed. She has been passionate about the paranormal since she was a child, and this reflects in her writing. As a child she spent hours engrossed in books about the subject instead of playing with friends outside. She has taken this interest with her into adulthood, and has been part of many notable paranormal investigations. She has studied an Exorcism and Possession course, and also written articles for Paranormal Underground and Supernatural Magazine.

She is currently represented by Media Bitch Literary Agency.

All of her titles are available online.

You can find out more about Fiona and her work at: www.studyparanormal.wordpress.com

You can follow Fiona on Twitter: @Angel_Devil982

Or if you prefer Facebook, you can search for her under Fiona Dodwell Author and find her public page.

Holly Ice:
Holly Ice loves the unknown, the idea that someone or something dark could be just out of reach. If a day came where all the monsters were real, she'd love it (as long as they weren't out to kill her in particular). A number of her works have been published across the horror and spec fic genres. Updates can be found at www.hollyice.co.uk

CHRISTOPHER LAW
Christopher Law is the author of Chaos Tales, Chaos Tales II: Hell TV and the soon to be released Chaos Tales III: Infodump, plus a gaggle of other shorts and a clutch of novels he will get published. You can find him on Facebook as Christopher Law Horror Writer and at evilscribbles.wordpress.com. Other than that he's rather dull and middle-aged, still has a great view of the castle apart from the hill in the way and is thinking about getting some kittens.

Michael R Brush:
Michael R. Brush was born in 1970 and raised in Newcastle-Upon-Tyne. Shortly afterwards he was told off for reading too much, at the detriment of his other school work. Now his love of books has come full circle and apart from writing this story 'Wood for the fire' he is the author of Mycroft and the Necromancer. He also co-edited and contributed to Challenger Unbound, an anthology faithful to the original hero of The Lost World by Conan Doyle.

Michael is currently living in the West Midlands with his wife, Sarah and their rescue dog, Peggy.

Theresa Derwin:
Theresa Derwin has lived in Birmingham since birth and her career has been pretty varied; from Warehouse Packer, then bar work, to being a crap waitress then swiftly into retail, Admin, Professional Student and dosser until finally entering the Civil Service in 1999. She left the Service in 2012 on medical grounds, then decided to pursue a career as a writer.

Theresa writes humorous fiction including SF, Urban Fantasy & Horror. She has about twenty five anthology acceptances behind her. She also writes a number of book reviews and at her site www.terror-tree.co.uk Her first short story collection is Monsters Anonymous from Anarchy Books published 2012, followed by Season's Creepings 2015. Her next collection 'Wolf at The Door' came out March 2016, along with novelette 'Pride, Pistols and Pentagrams' coming 2017 from

Quantum Corsets. She mentors fledgling authors and teaches creative writing. You can follow Theresa on Twitter @BarbarellaFem or find out more about her work at www.theresa-derwin.co.uk.

She has loved horror, fantasy and SF all her life, thanks to her father who raised her on 50s Sci-Fi Universal Monsters, tango and popcorn. Her love of the bizarre, (including her Dad) remains constant, to this day. She also owes a great debt to Rog Peyton from the BSFG who introduced her to alternative fiction at the tender the age of 14.

In 2013 Theresa ran the successful literature convention Andromeda One.

In 2017 she commences research into a three year study of #WomeninHorror literature.

Theresa Derwin – writing genre fiction since – her last cup of coffee.

Lex H. Jones:
Lex H. Jones is a British cross-genre author, horror fan, and rock music enthusiast who lives in Sheffield. He has written articles for The Gingernuts of Horror and Horrifically Horrifying Horror Blog websites on various subjects covering books, film, video games, and music. When not working on his own writing, Lex also contributes to the proofing and editing process for other authors.

Lex's first published book, Nick & Abe, is available for purchase from Amazon, Waterstones, and various other book sellers. The book tells the story of God and the Devil spending a year on Earth as mortal men, to see who has the most to learn about the world they created.

Links:

https://m.facebook.com/LexHJones/

twitter: @LexHJones

https://www.amazon.co.uk/gp/aw/d/190858694X/ref=mp_s_a_1_1?ie=UTF8&qid=1471524844&sr=8-1&pi=AC_SX236_SY340_QL65&keywords=nick+and+abe

https://www.amazon.com/gp/aw/d/190858694X/ref=mp_s_a_1_1?ie=UTF8&qid=1471524868&sr=8-1&pi=SY200_QL40&keywords=nick+and+abe&dpPl=1&dpID=41cevbN9BaL&ref=plSrch

Kayleigh Marie Edwards:
Kayleigh Marie Edwards is a writer based in South Wales who has a hard time taking anything seriously. She's been published in several horror anthologies, has had 4 theatre scripts staged, and regularly writes articles and reviews at www.gingernutsofhorror.com and www.spookyisles.com. She enjoys comedy, and all horror, particularly zombies, and also likes blah blah blah she's not Stephen King or anything so you probably don't care. She can be found on facebook and contacted for story/article/script commissions at ofthedead@hotmail.co.uk

ASH HARTWELL
Ash Hartwell was born in Maine, USA sometime during the hippie sixties. He now lives in Northamptonshire, England where he started writing around 2010. He has had around fifty short stories published in anthologies from Stitched Smile Publications, JEA, Static Movement, Horrified Press and Old Style Press to name a few. In 2015 he published his collection Zombies, Vamps and Fiends through JEA and will shortly see his debut novel - Tip of the Iceberg - which will be published

by Stitched Smile Publications where he is a VIP author. He is still alive and therefore not yet famous.

https://www.facebook.com/ash.hartwell.31
http://www.ashhartwell.co.uk/

J.G Clay:

Born in the leafy peaceful surroundings of Leamington Spa, J.G Clay is the Midlands Master of The Macabre. Now in his early forties and residing in the leafier English county of Northamptonshire, Clay's boyhood dream of bringing his unique combination of cosmic horror, dark fiction and science fiction to the masses is being realised. With the first volume of 'The Tales of Blood And Sulphur' under his belt, he is poised to unleash Gods, Monsters and weird events upon the world. Under Clay's guidance, the Dark will become a little darker and Horror will go One Step Beyond.
When he is not destroying worlds, J.G likes to spend time with his family and friends, exploring the world of bass guitar, adding to his eclectic collection of music and watching as much geek TV and film as his eyes and brain will allow. He is an avid reader and a long suffering but ultimately optimistic fan of Birmingham City FC.
He hates cucumber, extremists of all stripes and colours and reality TV shows.

Links
Website: www.jgclayhorror.com
Facebook: https://www.facebook.com/jgclay1973
Twitter: https://twitter.com/JGClay1

Kitty Kane:

Kitty Kane, AKA Becky Brown is an emerging horror writer that hails from the south of England. Kitty is a lifelong, avid reader of horror fiction. Her influences over the years are wide spread but include James Herbert, Clive Barker, Edgar Allen Poe, Jack Ketchum and the late, great Richard Laymon. Although writing has been a pastime that she has indulged in for most of her life, she is currently lined for her first published works as part of several collections for J.Ellington Ashton Press, as well as interest in a forthcoming novella. Her style ranges from more traditional short horror stories to bizarre fiction and poetry.

Kitty is also one half of writing duo – Matthew Wolf Kane, alongside another emerging talent, Matt Boultby. Their joint venture has already seen them published twice, with subsequent works due for release.

Tamara Fey Turner

Tamara is an American writer living Los Angeles with her tabby cat Gus

Matthew Cash:

Matthew Cash, or Matty-Bob Cash as he is known to most, was born and raised in in Suffolk; which is the setting for his debut novel *Pinprick*. He is compiler and editor of *Death By Chocolate,* a chocoholic horror anthology, and the *12Days Anthology,* and has numerous releases on Kindle and several collections in paperback.

He has always written stories since he first learnt to write and most, although not all, tend to slip into the many layered murky depths of the Horror genre.

His influences ranged from when he first started reading to Present day are, to name but a small select few; Roald Dahl, James Herbert, Clive Barker, Stephen King, Stephen Laws, and more recently he enjoys Adam Nevill, F.R Tallis, Michael Bray, Gary Fry, William Meikle and Iain Rob Wright (who featured Matty-Bob in his famous A-Z of Horror title M is For

Matty-Bob, plus Matthew wrote his own version of events which was included as a bonus).
He is a father of two, a husband of one and a zoo keeper of numerous fur babies.

You can find him here:
www.facebook.com/pinprickbymatthewcash

https://www.amazon.co.uk/-/e/B010MQTWKK

Printed in Great Britain
by Amazon